New York Times bestselling author **Christine Feehan** has had over thirty novels published and has thrilled legions of fans with her seductive Dark Carpathian tales. She has received numerous honours throughout her career, including being a nominee for the Romance Writers of America RITA and receiving a Career Achievement Award from *Romantic Times*, and has been published in multiple languages.

Visit Christine Feehan online:

www.christinefeehan.com
www.facebook.com/christinefeehanauthor
@AuthorCFeehan

***Praise for Christine Feehan*:**

'After Bram Stoker, Anne Rice and Joss Whedon, Feehan
is the person most credited with popularizing the neck gripper'
Time magazine

'The queen of paranormal romance'
USA Today

'Feehan has a knack for bringing vampiric Carpathians to vivid,
virile life in her Dark Carpathian novels'
Publishers Weekly

'The amazingly prolific author's ability to create captivating
and adrenaline-raising worlds is unsurpassed'
Romantic Times

CHRISTINE FEEHAN

DARK TAROT

PIATKUS

PIATKUS

First published in the US in 2021 by Berkley,
An imprint of Penguin Random House LLC
First published in Great Britain in 2021 by Piatkus

1 3 5 7 9 10 8 6 4 2

Copyright © 2021 by Christine Feehan

The moral right of the author has been asserted.

A CIP catalogue record for this book
is available from the British Library.

Hardback ISBN: 978-0-349-42832-1
Trade paperback ISBN: 978-0-349-42833-8

Printed and bound in Great Britain by Clays Ltd, Elcograf S.p.A.

Papers used by Piatkus are from well-managed forests
and other responsible sources.

Piatkus
An imprint of
Little, Brown Book Group
Carmelite House
50 Victoria Embankment
London EC4Y 0DZ

An Hachette UK Company
www.hachette.co.uk

www.littlebrown.co.uk

*For Denise Feehan
and her love of tarot cards*

FOR MY READERS

Be sure to go to ChristineFeehan.com/members/ to sign up for my *private* book announcement list and download the *free* ebook of *Dark Desserts*. Join my community and get firsthand news, enter the book discussions, ask your questions and chat with me. Please feel free to email me at Christine@christinefeehan.com. I would love to hear from you.

ACKNOWLEDGMENTS

As with any book, there are so many people to thank. Mercedes and Melissa Baker, two extremely talented artists, were such an inspiration to me. Thank you so much for working so hard to create a unique tarot deck for me to use in a short period of time. Your talent is inspiring! Brian, thank you for believing in me and pushing me to continue against incredible odds. This was a particularly difficult project! Domini, I have no idea how you continued under the circumstances, but you kept going when no one else would have. You are a modern Liona and a true inspiration. Denise, you know this book would never have been written without you. Thank you for the concept and for your belief that it would turn out to be extraordinary.

THE CARPATHIAN FAMILIES

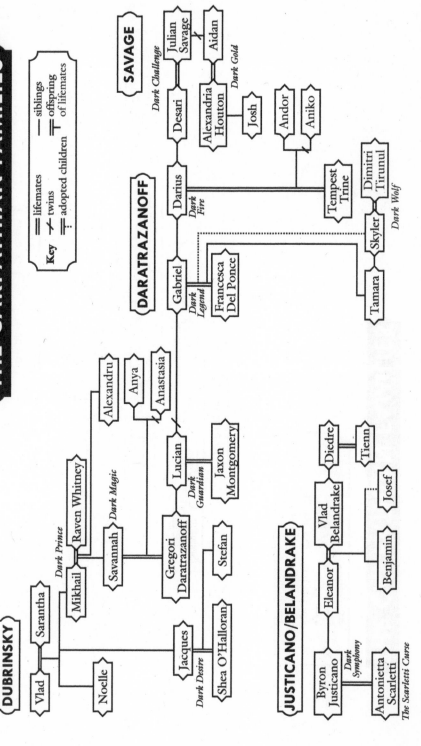

Key
- = lifemates
- ⤙ twins
- = siblings
- ⊤ offspring of lifemates
- ⊤ adopted children

SAVAGE

Julian Savage *Dark Challenge*
Aidan
Alexandria Houton *Dark Gold*
Josh
Desari
Andor
Aniko

DARATRAZANOFF

Darius *Dark Fire*
Tempest Trine
Dimitri Tirumul
Skyler *Dark Wolf*
Tamara
Gabriel *Dark Legend*
Francesca Del Ponce

DUBRINSKY

Vlad
Sarantha
Mikhail *Dark Prince*
Raven Whitney
Noelle
Jacques *Dark Desire*
Shea O'Halloran
Savannah *Dark Magic*
Gregori Daratrazanoff
Stefan
Alexandru
Anya
Anastasia
Lucian *Dark Guardian*
Jaxon Montgomery

JUSTICANO/BELANDRAKE

Diedre
Tienn
Vlad Belandrake
Josef
Eleanor
Benjamin
Byron Justicano *Dark Symphony*
Antonietta Scarletti *The Scarletti Curse*

THE CARPATHIAN FAMILIES

Key
- **=** lifemates
- **Y** cousins
- **⋏** twins
- **V** parents not lifemates
- **ᴔ** triplets
- **⌒** offspring
- **⊤** offspring of lifemates
- **—** siblings
- ***** monastery ancients
- **^** converted male

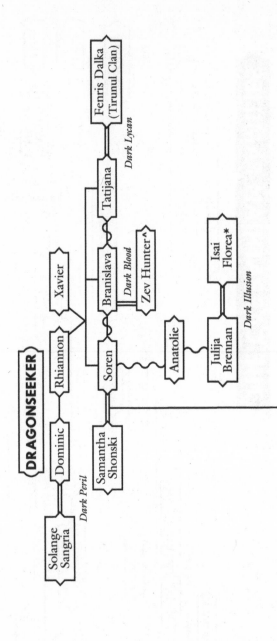

DRAGONSEEKER

Solange Sangria

Dark Peril

Dominic

Rhiannon

Xavier

Samantha Shonski

Soren

Branislava

Dark Blood

Zev Hunter^

Tatijana

Fenris Dalka (Tirunul Clan)

Dark Lycan

Anatolie

Julija Brennan

Isai Florea*

Dark Illusion

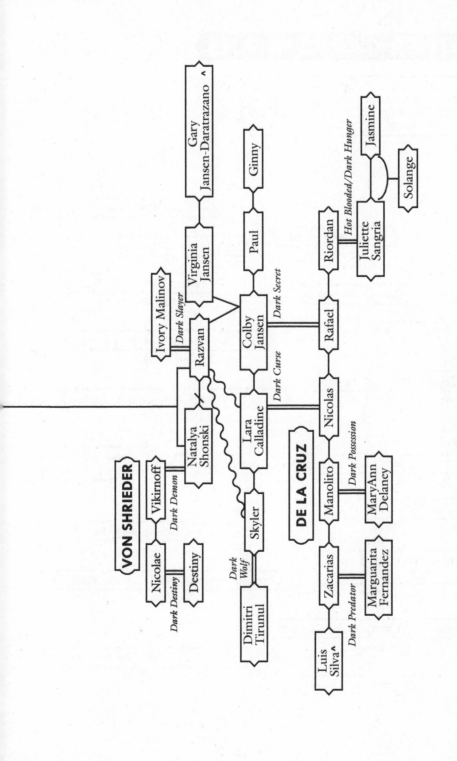

OTHER CARPATHIANS

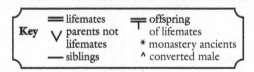

Key
= lifemates
V parents not lifemates
— siblings
⊤ offspring of lifemates
* monastery ancients
^ converted male

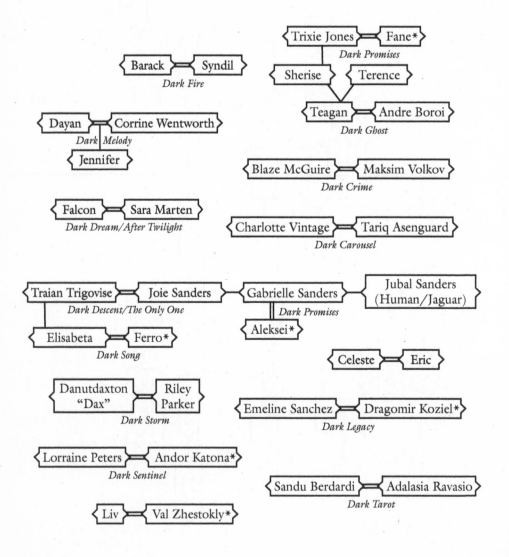

Trixie Jones === Fane*
Dark Promises

Sherise   Terence

Teagan === Andre Boroi
Dark Ghost

Barack === Syndil
Dark Fire

Dayan === Corrine Wentworth
Dark Melody

Jennifer

Blaze McGuire === Maksim Volkov
Dark Crime

Falcon === Sara Marten
Dark Dream/After Twilight

Charlotte Vintage === Tariq Asenguard
Dark Carousel

Traian Trigovise === Joie Sanders   Gabrielle Sanders   Jubal Sanders (Human/Jaguar)
Dark Descent/The Only One

Aleksei*
Dark Promises

Elisabeta === Ferro*
Dark Song

Celeste === Eric

Danutdaxton "Dax" === Riley Parker
Dark Storm

Emeline Sanchez === Dragomir Koziel*
Dark Legacy

Lorraine Peters === Andor Katona*
Dark Sentinel

Sandu Berdardi === Adalasia Ravasio
Dark Tarot

Liv === Val Zhestokly*

dark tarot

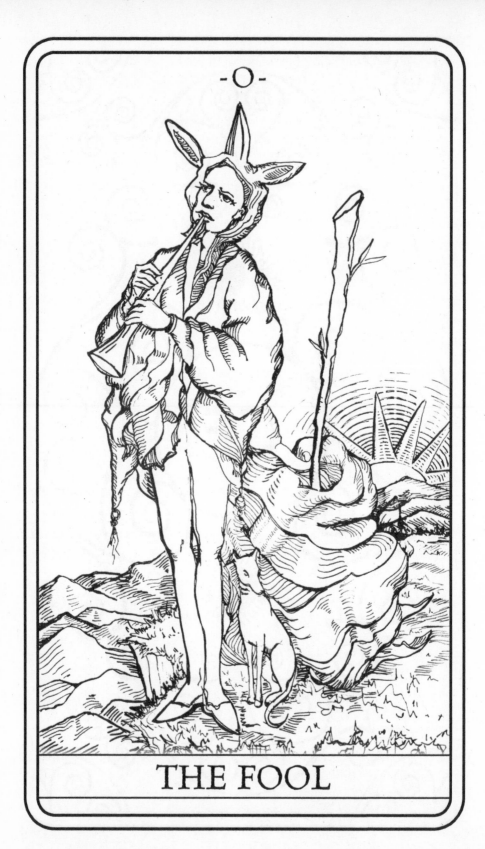

-O-

THE FOOL

Sandu Berdardi had a decision to make. He sat on the roof of a building facing the ocean in the dark of night, watching the waves as they came and went in a never-ending show of power. He was like that sea. He scrubbed one hand down his face, knowing his time had been up centuries earlier. He had hung on far too long. A matter of honor. Always it came back to that. Honor. It was inked on his back.

Olen wäkeva kuntankért. Staying strong for our people.

Olen wäkeva pita belső kulymet. Staying strong to keep the demon inside.

Olen wäkeva—félért ku vigyázak. Staying strong for her.

Hängemért. Only her.

He was an ancient Carpathian. There were few of his kind left in the modern world. They rarely scarred, not unless they had been wounded mortally and somehow managed to survive. He had several scars. Tattoos didn't take on their skin. Those had to be carved into flesh repeatedly and stained with special plant-based ink.

The oaths tatted onto his back were all about honor. His entire life had been dedicated to honor. Here he was, on a rooftop, far from the Carpathian Mountains, in a country he didn't understand, surrounded by people he didn't understand. His time had definitely passed. He knew he needed to go back to the monastery or to choose the dawn.

More and more, he needed to be alone, away from everyone. Hunting alone was a delicate balance that added an extra level of danger. Not because he feared dying, but because he feared what he became when the violence called to him—took control of him. He had learned there were things in the world every bit as monstrous as vampires, and he was one of those things.

He had held on grimly to his honor, held to the code etched into his skin, but he knew time was slipping away from him. His soul had gone from tattered to scarred. There was no removing scars. There was no coming back from some things. His time was over. A Carpathian male had few choices once he lived beyond a certain time, and Sandu had certainly surpassed that time centuries ago.

He didn't have the social skills to be in the company of modern humans for a prolonged period of time. He hadn't wanted to learn those skills, although it was apparent it was necessary if he was going to remain here. He doubted if he would. He no longer belonged in this world, and he hadn't for centuries. He'd recognized that fact many years earlier. He didn't have an anchor to keep him sane. He'd left the monastery with his ancient brethren in the hope of finding his lifemate, the one woman who could save him, but the world was a big place, and time made it even bigger.

He was a renowned vampire hunter, but truthfully, that only added to how dangerous he was. He had gone into the monastery, recognizing that he was no longer safe around humans, or even Carpathians. When Carpathians were born, their souls were split apart, the dark half residing in the male, the light in the female. The male had to find the keeper of his light and bind them together. That had been the way of their people until their ranks had been decimated.

There were few Carpathian women. Recently, the prince of their people had discovered that a few human women with psychic abilities could carry the souls of the Carpathian males and become their lifemate, renewing hope when hope had been lost for so long. With a world so vast, it wasn't like there was a beacon guiding them to the right woman.

Sandu had come to San Diego to help his fellow ancients, but it was time for him to leave—one way or the other. Colors had long since faded from his memory, along with any recollections of his childhood. He had lost all ability to feel emotion after those first two hundred years. The longer he lived, the more the whispers of temptation had grown stronger. If one killed while feeding, they could feel a rush, but they would become the very thing they hunted—the undead. He had kept his honor over the centuries, ignoring those whispers and tracking the vampire to destroy him. Now, even the whispers were gone. He hunted. He fed. He lived in a gray void. He searched in vain for his lifemate.

Each kill of the vampire had brought him closer to the edge of madness. Like so many others, he considered meeting the dawn, which was basically suiciding, but that didn't seem honorable, leaving behind his lifemate to be born over and over with no satisfying love life. When he became too dangerous, he had entered the monastery with the hope of gaining better control before returning to the world and once more searching for his other half.

He had left that retreat, but now, after so many battles, he knew it was time to return, or to leave the world for good. He had that decision to make and he had to make it alone, away from his brethren. They would seek to influence him to stay with them in the compound set up on the outskirts of the more rural part of San Diego.

You are very conflicted.

The voice came out of nowhere, filling his mind in spite of its softness. Feminine. Gentle. A statement but definitely tentative, as if she knew she was intruding and didn't want to but feared he might really be contemplating suicide. He remained silent, studying each note, wondering how she gained access to his mind and why the sliver of moon over the water suddenly appeared a different shade of gray.

I don't wish to disturb you, but sometimes talking things out can help.

That was a clear offer. Her voice. He blinked rapidly because all around him the world was changing. There was white froth on the waves. The few people on the sidewalk were in brightly colored clothing. His stomach lurched, and behind his eyes there was an explosion of agony, which he quickly cut off. He toned down the way he was seeing, fading the hues to almost shadows so his brain could get used to it.

Who are you? He kept his tone strictly neutral. Nonthreatening. He tried to get a direction on her, but it seemed impossible, as if the notes were far off and being dispersed through several filters.

I am Adalasia. I'm sometimes called Lasia.

She didn't hesitate to give him her name, and her soft voice, although muted, rang with truth. In these modern times, few women were called by that name. It was very old Italian, mostly used around the twelfth to fourteenth centuries. There was no way she was that old unless she was Carpathian. Even mages wouldn't be that old. Many times, when someone set him up to be murdered, they feared giving him their true name, yet she hadn't hesitated. He was suspicious of the way she had slid so easily into his mind, and he couldn't quite get a direction on her—yet.

I am Sandu. And yes, there is a decision to be made.

A journey. She made it a statement.

In many ways. It is not a single journey, but in many directions, and it is a dangerous path I will travel. I will have to ask another to embark on that path with me. Deliberately, he tested her. He had been contemplating going on a journey alone, but no longer, not since the moment color had been restored to him.

Time passed while the waves crashed and foamed. He thought Adalasia might have slipped away from him she was so still, but there remained a feminine presence in his mind. He had been alone for endless centuries, a long gray void of nothingness, but even with her being so still, she brought him comfort.

He heard her sudden intake of breath. *What is it?*

This person you speak of embarking on the journey with you? Is this a new relationship? A love interest?

He considered that. A love interest was a way a human would define a relationship. A lifemate was so much more. His other half. He couldn't survive without her. He was speaking with her right at that very moment. Was she as moved as he was? Most likely she was unaware of the significance of their exchange. No other would have been able to penetrate his defenses.

I have yet to meet her, but she is within my reach. That was honest enough.

This journey is not without risks, but it is worth it. You may need to expand your views, be willing to experience new visions that are not your own.

She sounded reluctant to say the least. She also sounded as if she was giving him a bit of a lecture, telling him to expand his views as if he was too narrow-minded to see other people's ideas that weren't his. Did that mean she thought he didn't listen to other people's opinions? That could be true. At least not human opinions. He had been around for centuries and seen countless scenarios. In the grand scheme of things, humans were babies, thinking they were experts.

The journey I must undertake to another land?

Again, there was silence, as if she was mulling something over. *Must you? Go to another land, or do you want to go to another land? You have to decide for yourself if it is a want or a need.*

The reluctance was much more pronounced.

Adalasia, you have an idea you do not wish to share with me. Are you a seer?

I can sometimes be a guide. The admission was hesitant.

For the first time, Sandu heard a discordant note, as if she wasn't telling the exact truth. That displeased him. Lifemates didn't lie to each other. She didn't realize she was his lifemate, but she was the keeper of the other half of his soul. Did she know that? Was she aware? He knew there was no mistake. She had restored color into his world. Color and emotions. As he sat on the roof watching the waves come and go, catching the sheen of the moon, he experienced a variety of unfamiliar feelings he had to sort through in order to identify.

You are sometimes a guide? He echoed her statement.

She sighed. *I can't always see everything. In your case, the way is murky. There is danger everywhere I turn. I can't see a clear path for you.*

He believed she spoke the truth. Her assessment didn't surprise him. Clearly, she was upset on his behalf. She sounded as if she thought she was failing him. He had a much clearer direction now. She was behind him, somewhere away from the ocean. He needed to keep her talking, and she wanted to end their conversation because something she saw frightened her.

Do you believe in monsters? Sandu kept his mind calm and his voice absolutely matter-of-fact so as to sound as if he were merely engaging in discussion. For one terrible moment, it flashed through his mind that she was talking to a monster. He shut that down, not wanting to take a chance on sharing with her any of the battles he'd been in.

He stood, keeping his weight from the rooftop, hiding his presence from anyone who might look up. He was a big man and would draw attention if he wasn't concealing himself. He took to the sky but stayed low, skimming the rooftops, moving slowly in the direction he was certain she was. He didn't want her to know he was on the move. She seemed a little skittish to him, but he wasn't certain why. She didn't seem like a woman who lacked confidence.

As in human monsters? They certainly exist.

He was definitely closer. The farther he got from the roaring of the waves, the more he heard the sounds of laughter and music surrounding her voice. Blending with it.

Yes. Human monsters. Have you ever encountered any monster you thought might not be human?

His question was met with silence. She hadn't withdrawn. He felt her presence. At least a full minute went by. He was guided by the sounds of the music and laughter.

Who are you? Her voice was very low. She sounded frightened.

Never your enemy.

You're a hunter.

What did she mean by that? Did she know what a Carpathian was? Was she a female Carpathian? If so, what was she doing without protection in the city where vampires were known to slaughter prey?

I am merely someone at the crossroads. Wondering which direction to travel on his journey. Searching for my lifemate to travel with me, but I have a need to know if this is a good idea right now. Keeping her talking to him when she wanted to stop was the best of ideas.

There is always calculated risk when starting any new journey, whatever it may be. My next client is here and I have to go. It was nice talking with you, Sandu.

Before he could say another word to her, she was gone and he was alone. He had been used to being alone, and yet after sharing his mind with her and their brief exchange, he felt—bereft.

She'd left him abruptly, as if she was afraid of something. Of him. Of something she saw. He had dark, violent memories, and he had protected them. He knew she couldn't possibly have gotten past his shields. Even if she was Carpathian, and that didn't feel quite right to him, he was too strong. Too old. Too experienced. Too brutal . . . But then . . . she had caught him off guard and entered his mind so smoothly. Very seamlessly, as if she'd been doing it forever.

He kept moving slowly over the rooftops, invisible to the crowds and cars below, following the faint sounds he had picked up in the background. Increasingly, he was deeper into the city. He preferred the outskirts, where he could breathe without the smell of fuel and exhaust. Without the continual scent of bodies crammed into small spaces. Office buildings and malls meant hundreds of people talking, seemingly all at once. He had to sort through those conversations, tone them down, hear what was needed, and discard the rest. Cities were not places Sandu would ever feel comfortable.

Within a matter of a few minutes, he had found the faint note he was looking for. It was blended in the muted voices that were blurred in the background of so many other conversations. He adjusted his line of travel until that blurred conversation became just a little stronger. The fact that those in the buildings he traveled over continued to be so much louder no matter how much he tuned to those other sounds, filtering out the notes he didn't want to hear, meant she wasn't inside those buildings. She was somewhere else. Under them? In the middle of them? Was she surrounded by them?

Was magic involved? He didn't feel the prickle of energy on his skin or in his mind. He was far too old for a mage to fool him for long. No, the notes he sought were below the louder ones, and he was beginning to move away from them. He doubled back and once more sat on a rooftop to scan the area for his greatest enemy—the undead.

This time of night, the malls were closed, but the bars and nightclubs were full as people had gotten off work, eaten and were looking for company and a good time. He knew from his long experience that vampires would welcome the hunt in the crowded, dark taverns, luring their victims outside, where they could take their lives and discard their bodies like so much garbage.

Sandu found no evidence of the undead anywhere nearby. He was uneasy but could find no reason for his alarm to be giving him even a vague warning. Somewhere close, his lifemate could be in danger. The apprehension might be about her. He'd been in her mind, just as she'd been in his. There was now a path forged between them, whether she knew it or not. That meant he would feel any threat to her.

He floated to the sidewalk, keeping away from any of the people coming and going from the various buildings around him. The pull on him was strongest toward the narrow alley between two structures. He walked that way and turned into what appeared to be nothing more than a sparsely grass-and-dirt-covered path between the buildings. There were no lights other than what was spilling from the windows on either side.

There was no doubt that others had come this way. The grass had been trampled, and the dirt had been pressed deep and tight. As he continued down the alley, he came to a fork. He could choose either way to proceed. Both sides seemed to be well traveled, and the strange muffled sounds of laughter and multiple conversations were coming from either direction.

Sandu stayed still, listening, filtering through the various voices and the muted music and sudden flare of laughter only to have it cut off abruptly. He caught that one soft note he'd waited for. *Her* note. She was somewhere behind the buildings in the maze of alleyways. He felt the pull of her and took the very narrow passage to his right. Beneath his feet, the grass and dirt gave way to brick and dirt. He knew others had come this way because he felt the concentration of their cells left behind as they passed. Hair. Skin. Nails. It was all there, unseen by others, but to him, it was glaringly obvious.

Sandu had undertaken many journeys in his life over the far too many years he'd been alive, but none were, perhaps, as foolish as this one. He walked soundlessly along the narrow pathway, following the whisper of the note that had gotten under his skin when nothing ever had—ever could. It was impossible, and yet those whispers called to him in a dark conspiracy he couldn't ignore. There was something here other than the path leading to his lifemate.

He needed to figure out what he was getting himself into. Where was this often-traveled alley taking him to? He wasn't alone. No one was behind him. There were people in front of him. Several. More a good distance in front of him. Over his head, on the rooftops, he felt the presence of others, not that they were necessarily paying him attention—at least not yet. He had cloaked his presence for the moment. There was zero fighting room in the alley, and he was assessing the situation.

His life was an endless, empty void. He woke. He took what he needed to survive, and he hunted prey. He was an excellent hunter, and once a target was acquired, it was rare that he missed. But this . . . this was something that was different. Something new in his very long life, and anything new or different was intriguing and therefore potentially dangerous.

Sandu knew he shouldn't be intrigued—it was an impossibility for his kind. He shouldn't feel anything at all, and yet—he did. There was an odd thrumming, like the beat of a drum in his veins, answering that whisper of a note he followed. It was as if his very heart tuned to that strange note buried among all the voices he heard. His lungs wanted to breathe in tune to that nearly muted sound. His lifemate. There was no mistake, as much as his mind kept telling him it couldn't be true that he'd found her.

It had to be a trap. If it was, it was new. He'd seen many over the centuries. He hunted the undead, and the master vampires were skilled and intelligent. They could never be underestimated for one moment. If, as a hunter, one began to believe they were smarter or faster, one would lose their life every time. There was a reason the undead survived long enough to become master vampires. Masters were rarely alone. They had pawns and they used them ruthlessly. They recruited humans. Sometimes psychic humans.

Colors and emotions could only be returned to him by his true lifemate. There was never a mistake. That didn't mean his lifemate wasn't under siege, kidnapped or part of the conspiracy to trap him knowingly or unknowingly.

Sandu looked carefully around him before uncloaking his presence.

The narrow pathway he was in was very dimly lit. His shoulders barely fit in places. It was the perfect location to ambush the unwary. Above him, anyone could walk along the rooftops and stalk their victims, dropping down quickly to rob them of fat wallets and then hastily disappear back onto the safety of the ridges and gables out of sight.

As he proceeded deeper into the labyrinth of alleyways, beneath his boots, the broken brick and dirt turned to much older cobblestone. He could tell this part of the city had been built over many times. The narrow passageways began to widen, revealing several spacious areas surrounded by small shops.

The sounds. The notes. Perhaps it wasn't *all* the sounds or all the notes. He paused to listen, straining when he had such acute hearing, he could track a human miles away. He held his breath and forced his heart to slow to a crawl so he could better hear. Several voices blended together. He heard them clearly through the sounds of many others speaking as they bargained in the various shops or with the street vendors. It was all coming together in his mind now. The various alleys coming in from between buildings were leading to a central location. This had to be, by the smells and sounds, an outdoor alley market, an underground artists' paradise.

People crowded this odd venue at night, squeezing through the dimly lit and narrow alleys to get to the wider spaces where the street artists displayed their wares. Small shops could be found in the intricate maze, and there were little markets scattered throughout where food and drink could be purchased. This was not a place one found law enforcement, or at least, it was rare to find an officer venturing inside.

Street vendors called out to those crowding around the steps of the shops, trying to entice them to buy from their carts or see their wares. As he came into sight, a small hush fell over the groups of people as they looked up, watching his progress. Anyone in his way quickly moved out of it.

Sandu was used to that reaction to his presence. Not only was he a big man, all flowing muscle, his face carved with angles and planes and harsh lines, but his eyes, so black they were ink, glowed with red flames, especially in the dark, like now. He looked feral. He looked exactly what he was—a predator. He could disguise what he was, but why bother?

He kept walking, not changing his pace, following the soft note buried deep in the sounds of so many others speaking. The closer he got to what he sought, the louder those around it broadcast. He registered everything as he moved along the alleyway that had suddenly opened up into a mini city.

The deeper he immersed himself into that small world, the more there were small shops and back porches and steps, with little markets set up in the wider spaces. It didn't seem to matter that the narrower paths were dimly lit; the backstreets flourished with life. This was a far different world from the one the streets just beyond portrayed.

A few taverns blared live music from behind closed doors, adding to the chaotic sounds of swelling conversation as Sandu approached the very epicenter of the mini city. The round cobblestoned center held plants surrounding a few trees. Dispelling the darkness were colored, strung lights shining behind the trees, silhouetting twisted branches reaching upward toward the sky. The colors at first dazzled his eyes, even though he'd made every effort to fade the effect. It was difficult not to stare at the vivid red, blue and green shining so brightly. Even the silver was so much more beautiful than a dull gray.

The shops and bars were a little larger here, but not by very much. Artists had their paintings or pottery set up under bright canopies to protect them from weather. At first glance, the roundabout looked chaotic, but Sandu could see there was an order to the madness. Each of the street vendors had their own space and were careful to keep within the confines of that space. They didn't block the steps leading to the stores directly behind them, allowing customers access to the taverns or shops in the buildings.

The roundabout held a much larger crowd than any of the wide market spaces had held. The smells of food were stronger. The music seemed loud enough to shake the buildings. Sandu had to tone his hearing down when he was trying to establish where the single note he was tracking was coming from. He ignored the effect he was having on the crowds as he moved in a circle facing the buildings, waiting to catch the soft note among the loud sounds of so many conversations and the cacophony of music pouring from two different bars.

There it was. A low murmur. A woman's voice. *Her* voice. Adalasia. She was real. Not a figment of his imagination. He went completely still, his heart pounding, blood thundering in his ears before he could get control. He immediately swept away that unacceptable reaction. Emotions had no place in the life of an ancient, a hunter of the undead. He had no idea if his woman was being held hostage or if she was his enemy. No matter which it was, she was his lifemate and he would sort it out. To do that, he needed to be in absolute control.

Like all the shops in the buildings, the name was over the door: *The Guide*. That told him next to nothing about what went on inside. There were two windows, one on either side of the door, neither particularly large. They were rectangular in shape and, like the other windows in the strange little mini city, seemed dingy. He could see books on shelves and various items on tables and display cases. The items appeared old, as if perhaps the shop held antiques.

An uneasy feeling had him making the circuit a third time, studying each shop with the same attention he'd shown The Guide. Someone was observing not only him but the antiques store. Had the observation simply been one of idle curiosity, Sandu would have ignored it. Humans were often curious about him. When he didn't bother to tone down his predatory appearance, he drew attention. This attention felt different. It felt threatening—but not toward him, toward those inside that shop.

He didn't feel the presence of the undead. This threat felt more human and yet . . . not. More. He let his gaze shift around the crowded roundabout. People were wary of him and gave him room, but they were back to shopping and talking with their friends. That allowed him to study the crowd and ferret out the one or ones threatening whoever was in that little shop. It didn't take long before he zeroed in on three men and a woman whose wares were set up almost directly across from the shop. They had a green-and-white-striped umbrella-type canopy over their paintings. The woman sat in a chair drawing a portrait of a man with a boy standing next to him with what appeared to be colored pencils.

The four did their best not to stare at the antique shop, but their focus was on that shop. He had no doubt that anyone coming and going into the shop would draw their attention instantly. Deciding to test his theory, he once again approached The Guide. There was a small clock on the door saying a reading was taking place and would be over in another seven minutes, to please not disturb. He thought that was interesting. He wasn't certain what "a reading" entailed, but the fact that someone would lose business while they did a reading had to mean they did fairly well.

He took another slow circuit of the roundabout, listening to the conversations. Three women couldn't wait for a fabric shop to get their latest fabrics in. They cost the earth, but they were the best. Another group of women loved the yarn offered by a shop owner who spun and dyed her own fiber from various animals she kept on her farm. There was a shop specializing in quilts and another in homemade jams. A leather shop made belts, wallets and boots.

These shops and the outside vendors were not only artists but the real deal. They were craftsmen. Experts in their field. This place was unique. They weren't charging small amounts of money for their wares. This was a chance to get jewelry or a vase or artwork by a master before anyone else. The people who came here knew it, and they paid for the privilege. Without the police to enforce the law, who kept them safe? Who patrolled the dimly lit alleys one had to walk before reaching the inner mini city? Were the ones he'd noticed on the rooftops keeping those shopping in the markets safe from thieves?

He'd spent enough time looking at the pottery offered at one of the stands. The work was beautiful. He considered purchasing something for his brethren, Andor's lifemate, Lorraine, or Ferro's lifemate, Elisabeta. Both women would no doubt appreciate the beauty and craftsmanship. He did so, arranging to have the pottery shipped, as he wasn't about to carry it around with him. That added to his authenticity as someone who appreciated the arts. All the while, he kept an eye on the four under the brightly striped canopy. They were definitely watching the antique shop—and him.

The door to The Guide opened, and two men emerged along with a woman. They stood on the steps leading to the shop, talking for a moment.

For the first time, Sandu got a good look at his lifemate. She was stunning. Beautiful. Gorgeous. She took his breath away. Perhaps it was that way with all lifemates. He was certain his brethren thought that way of their women, but he had eyes only for his.

She would be considered tall by human standards. He liked that. He was a big man, and he didn't want to spend eternity bending in half to kiss her. She had curves. He was a man who appreciated curves on a woman. Her hair was thick and glossy black. She had it drawn back from her face in a high ponytail that fell in waves like a waterfall. He expected her eyes to be dark like her hair, brows and lashes, but they were a startling blue. This, then, was the woman he'd spent centuries searching for. She could have died and been reborn countless times. She was the keeper of the other half of his soul, and she was beautiful.

"Thank you, Lasia," one of the men said, holding out his hand. "I appreciate your time."

Adalasia took his hand with a flash of her small, white teeth. The moment her hand was enveloped in both of the stranger's, Sandu could barely contain the need to leap across the space between them and rip his spinal cord from him. The growl threatening to escape was shocking. He'd never had such a visceral reaction in his life.

He took a deep breath to try to breathe away the deep, primitive reaction, a primal rage that was as cold as ice and hot as a raging volcano. Animalistic. The kind of darkness that enfolded him in battle. He couldn't have that happen here. Not with her. He was an ancient, in control at all times, too powerful not to be. He breathed away the need to kill, forcing the power in his body to recede along with the sharp fangs.

"Of course, Adolf, anytime."

Her voice was soft. The notes like music, penetrating right through skin and bone, deeper still, through his heart, to pierce his black, black, very tattered, very scarred soul. He could almost feel the way her amazing voice managed to weave together pieces of that broken travesty. He was at his most vulnerable, unable to see properly—and at his most lethal. An unknown male was touching his lifemate. There were enemies close—humans, but enemies nevertheless.

"We've benefited from your guidance so many times, Lasia. I can't imagine what we would do without you," the other male said as he slung his arm around Adolf's shoulders.

The need to kill receded slowly as Sandu recognized that the two males were obviously a couple. He breathed away the monstrous response that had arisen so strong in him followed by so many other unfamiliar emotions he hadn't ever had to cope with. Jealousy? Was that a true emotion an honorable Carpathian would feel? It was a little humiliating to think that he would experience such a thing. He stood still, breathing, letting the air move through his lungs, waiting for the terrible crash of unwanted feelings to cycle through and leave him so he could think rationally.

Sandu allowed himself the luxury of drinking her in while the two men took their leave and moved down the steps and away. He immediately cut off anyone else from entering her shop simply by standing on the lowest step. There would be no way to get around his large body. He heard her swift intake of breath, and then her eyes met his.

"Adalasia." He said her name with deliberate gentleness. "Sandu Berdardi." He gave her the courtesy of his name.

Her gaze swept the width of his shoulders, his tall, intimidating form, his dark eyes and hard demeanor. Because he was a man who noted every detail, he caught the slight tremor to her voice.

"Adalasia Ravasio. How did you find me?"

He ignored the question and gained a step. That put him nearly to her. One more stair and he'd be on the same one with her. She didn't give way.

"You can't be here. You have to go." She whispered the warning, ducking her head as if she feared someone might overhear or be able to read her lips.

He gestured toward her sign, the one that said she did readings. "I've come for your guidance." He took another step, forcing her to back up to the shallow porch.

"I read your cards. There was danger all around you. You have to go while you can, Sandu. You might think this is all silly and a game because I read cards, but I'm not wrong. You have to leave."

He stepped up onto the porch beside her. She wore a long, dark olive-colored skirt that fell around her ankles in soft ruffles. Her camisole was very modern, much more so than he would have approved, but now that he was close to her, he could see the way the lighter olive-colored material showcased the swell of her breasts. The laces going up the valley between her breasts drew attention, making him want to explore those curves.

He put his hand very gently on her flat belly and exerted pressure to back her through the open door. "Are you concerned about the three men and the woman watching you from across the way?" He reached behind him and closed the door firmly.

Adalasia gave a little sigh and moved around him to open the door and turn the sign around that proclaimed she was giving another reading. "You're a stubborn man."

"It's best that you realize I have no intention of leaving you behind. If I leave this place, you will be traveling with me."

He delivered his statement in his low voice, so he doubted if his words sank in at first because she was settling into a chair in front of a table when her dark lashes suddenly lifted and her cobalt blue eyes narrowed with laser sharp intensity.

"I'm sorry? What did you just say?"

He sat down across from her. "You heard me and don't act surprised. You already read the cards. At least you said you did. I imagine the reason there were all those hesitations was because you didn't like the things you were seeing regarding the two of us."

A soft, very attractive flush spread from her neck to her face. "It's possible I did see things in your cards that I mistook for involving me. I've never connected psychically with anyone like that before, with the exception of my mother, and certainly not with that kind of strength. It was exhilarating. This tremendous rush. Sometimes I feel alone, even surrounded by so many people, and to suddenly have that connection felt like a gift. I lost my mother last year and it's been really difficult." She shrugged, striving to look casual. "That's all it was. I put myself in your reading, which was easy to do since it was a distance reading you weren't even aware of."

Sandu was as adept at reading people as Adalasia was at reading cards. She knew better, and she was lying. There was a slight tremor to her hands as she moved them over the deck, but there was also something else, a kind of loving feel to the way she touched the cards.

"Did your mother read cards?"

Adalasia nodded. "Yes. This deck has been handed down mother to daughter for generations, but according to my mother, some see more than others. That can be both a blessing and a curse."

Sandu immediately had the feeling she saw much more than her mother had when she read the cards. Her fingers were long and slender. A woman's hands. This was no fake diviner. She had a true psychic gift. She'd been born with it, and her talent was exceptionally strong. He felt it when she touched the cards. They felt almost as if they came alive for her.

Almost reluctantly she pushed the cards across the table to him. "Shuffle."

He went to pick them up and immediately felt a sting, much like a thousand needles penetrating his hand, as if the cards themselves were trying to get into his skin. He pulled his hands back and looked at her. He hadn't actually touched the deck, and yet he knew the power there was part of him. Trying to enter him. "You shuffle and lay them out for me."

She frowned at him. "What's wrong?"

"The deck is very powerful. So am I. The two forces feel each other, perhaps as a threat." He watched her face carefully.

Her large eyes went a dark blue. She regarded the deck on the table. "May I?" Without waiting for his consent, she placed her right hand under his left palm and her left palm over the back of his right hand. "Put your hands as close to the deck as possible without me touching it."

Sandu did as she asked. He felt the same wave of needles biting into his flesh, desperate to get to his bones, to his organs. Inside of him. Evidently, she did as well.

Adalasia removed her hands from his and lifted her gaze to his. "I've never had that happen in all the years I've done readings for people. Who are you?"

"You know who I am. The cards told you earlier when you consulted them. You asked about my journey and discovered it was our journey together, didn't you?" He didn't ask why the cards recognized him. And they did. He would ask. Just not yet.

She made a little face. "Well, yes, but I explained that. I most likely inserted myself into the reading accidentally because I had connected with you psychically. I've never done that with anyone else. It would be natural to make a mistake like that." She shuffled the cards and fanned them out, ran her palm over the top of them and then shook her head and shuffled them again.

"It's always going to be the same. Our journey is together."

"It isn't," she denied and laid the cards very decisively out in a pattern.

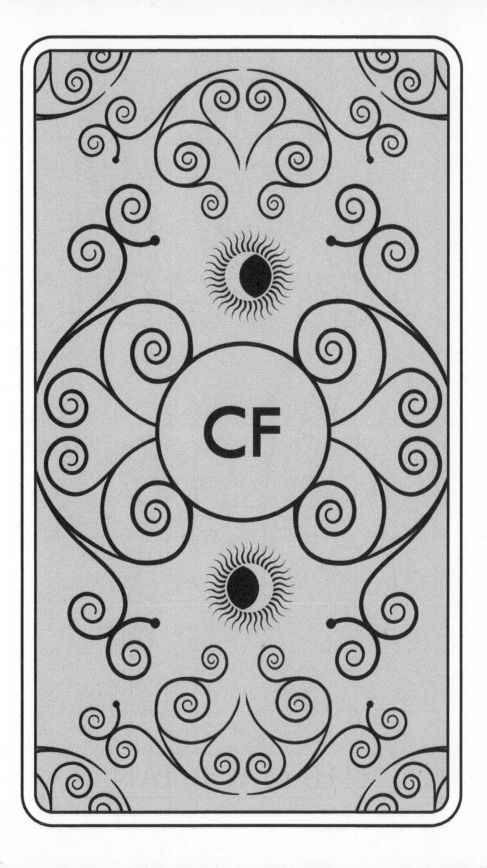

-I-

THE MAGICIAN

D o you know what those people are after? Why they're watching you?" Sandu kept his gaze on her hands as she laid out the cards in a pattern on the table.

"No, I wish I did, but they're definitely watching me. The first one to come here was the older gentleman. He said he wanted a reading." Adalasia glanced at him from under her feathery lashes. "The moment he came into the shop, I knew something was off about him. I'd had a sense of uneasiness all morning, and twice I even laid out cards. Both times I was warned of danger."

Her teeth pressed into her bottom lip as though she was trying to make up her mind whether or not to tell him something else. She'd been in his mind. They shared a formidable connection through that psychic bond, but without her knowing, there was an even much more powerful one. She was his lifemate. They shared the same soul. She didn't want to trust him because there were too many things about him that scared her. He looked like a predator. Even her cards condemned him as dangerous and as something other than wholly human. He already had some kind of proprietary claim on her she didn't understand but felt. But that connection was strong, and she'd been alone with her fears.

"My mother told me of a man coming into the shop for a reading just before her death. She had gotten similar warnings from the cards before he came in. She described the same man and the cards' reactions to him."

"Cards' reactions? The same as mine?"

Adalasia shook her head. "No, nothing like that. When we have someone shuffle the cards and fan them out, or we lay them out to read, the cards tell us certain things for that person. At the same time, we learn things about them. The man called himself Mr. Castello. My mother read the cards for him, but she left certain things out just as I did when he came. When she told me she didn't give him a full reading, she said it was because she was afraid, that the cards warned her he was there to kill her."

She looked as if she was about to gather up the cards that she had laid out on the table between them, but he stopped her by laying his hand gently over hers. She pulled her hand away and put it on her lap.

"You don't like what you're seeing. Do the cards say I'm here to harm you?"

She shook her head.

"Adalasia." He waited. A clock ticked several seconds off loudly. Finally, she looked up at him. "It would be an impossibility for me to harm you. I can protect you. In fact, I *will* protect you from anyone wishing to harm you."

"I'm not looking for a relationship."

"I'm very pleased." He sent her a faint grin. "Since I don't particularly want to have to choose pistols at dawn to fight for you, or something equally as antiquated, we'll just keep it between the two of us."

That got an answering smile from her. "Pistols at dawn?"

"I saw the matching antique dueling pistols you have in the case. They're authentic, aren't they?"

"Most everything in this shop is authentic."

"Including the tarot cards. You said they've been handed down in your family from mother to daughter for a few generations."

Adalasia glanced out the window of her shop as she nodded. "That's correct."

"Has anyone ever tried to get them from you? Has your family ever been robbed?"

"My mother was murdered in a home invasion." Her voice roughened, as if she could barely speak.

Sandu wanted to soothe her, but he resisted using his abilities. She needed to be able to tell him everything in her own way without interference, even if it was difficult for her. The more time spent in her company—and in her mind—the more easily he read her character. She was independent. She thought for herself and made her own decisions. She wouldn't like him suddenly inserting himself into her life and taking over.

"A few things were taken, but not her tarot cards. We have antiques that are worth a great deal of money, such as those pistols, but they were left alone. Cash was taken and two ornate knives. Nothing else. Not even jewelry. The police thought the killers must have been interrupted."

"You don't believe that."

She shook her head. "No, I think it was him. Mr. Castello and his friends. I don't know what he wants, but it has something to do with the cards." She looked directly into Sandu's eyes. "I'm a little worried that it might have something to do with you and this journey we're supposedly on together. I tried to warn you to stay away." She made a little face at him. "You're not a very good listener."

"You didn't tell me everything the cards said. You've picked them up, shuffled and laid them out twice now without reading them aloud to me. You don't like what you see."

Adalasia looked more unsettled than ever. "You come from a very old family, Sandu. Very old. Your lineage is as old as mine. Older."

He didn't tell her that he was an ancient. There was no rebirth. She might see that in her cards and not believe what they were revealing to her. He simply nodded his head. "I have no memories of my family or my childhood."

Her vivid blue eyes softened with compassion. "That must be terrible for you."

He shrugged. "I'm used to it." He studied her expression. "Why are you so afraid of me that you put that same fear into your cards?"

She tapped her finger over the table beside the fanned-out cards. "The needles in your skin? You think that was fear?"

He hesitated, knowing it was more than that. One didn't lie to their lifemate. But he could tell a partial truth. "That was power answering power. The cards are tuned specifically to you, although they recognize me, don't they? I feel the way they would accept me as your partner, but you're afraid of me. Because you fear me, they do as well." Sandu kept his voice very low. Gentle. He didn't like that his back was to the window.

She kept lifting her gaze to it rather anxiously, as if she saw the enemy approaching. His alarm system was going off.

She raised her chin. "I am *not* afraid of you. It's more that I'm afraid of the path we're both bound to now that you've arrived. I have to admit, in spite of the reassurance that I'm supposed to go in that direction with you . . ." She scooped up the deck and placed it carefully in a faded velvet pouch, coming to her feet. "We have to go now. Hurry. With me." She held out her hand to him.

Sandu refrained from smiling. His lifemate really had it in her pretty little head that she could not only give him orders but that she was protecting him. He wrapped his fingers around hers and obediently followed her lead, making certain his much larger body was between hers and the front door of the shop. His woman had a lot to tell him. She didn't want to reveal her secrets, and he was reluctant to take them from her, something that would be easy enough to do if she persisted in refusing to share details with him. He wanted her trust, and trust had to be earned.

Adalasia moved quickly between the heavy cases in the antiques store, opening an ornate door to a back room. There was confidence in her step. The moment Sandu had closed that door, she picked up the pace, rushing now toward the exit leading outside.

"Wait," Sandu caught at her waist, halting her. "Someone is out there. They expected you to make a run for it." He set her to one side to listen, scanning the alley. "One man, standing just to the side of the stairs. You stay behind me, Adalasia."

She bent, drawing her skirt up to reveal soft boots and then the bare skin of a shapely leg. Up higher, on her thigh, she wore a leather harness. She drew a wicked-looking knife from the scabbard and concealed the blade against her inner wrist. "Go," she whispered, glancing back toward the front of the store.

He opened the door and was out, moving with blurring speed, straight at the man waiting for Adalasia to emerge. The watcher held a gun in his hand. He looked to be somewhere between thirty-five and just under forty. Olive-complected, he was a handsome man with dark hair and eyes. Sandu read his intent; it wasn't to murder Adalasia but to kidnap her for some purpose Sandu didn't have the time in that second to pull out of the man's mind.

Sandu hit him hard, at the last moment remembering to use the strength of a human. A strong human. Very strong. At the same time, he reached for the weapon, easily took it from the assailant, turned and caught up with Adalasia as the man crumpled to the ground. She gave a muffled little cry as she sidestepped the body. He groaned and writhed, tried to rise and fell again.

Adalasia took the lead again, nearly running along the back alley, turning a corner and once left and then right, circling back around to the store, Sandu pacing right behind her.

"Where are you going?"

"I have to get home."

She wasn't in the least out of breath, which told him she was in very good shape.

There had been an apartment over the antiques store. Sandu considered that she lived there. When she caught up a ladder and went up it fast and was on the roof, he was certain he was right. He followed her up.

"You realize they'll go looking for you there."

She sent him a quick look over her shoulder as she hurried across the rooftop, running, crouching low as she did. Sandu cloaked them just in case, as well as muffled the sound of their footsteps.

"I'm not going to stay there. I have some things I have to get before I leave."

She was sure-footed. She'd made this run before multiple times. It was very dark. The sliver of moon didn't throw much light, and yet she avoided the two large fans and knew exactly when to leap from one building to the next without even slowing down. Adalasia had clearly practiced for just such an event.

She was at a window, crouched low, peering in. Sandu towered over her. "Let me," he said gently and moved her aside. He wasn't asking, but he thought it was better to keep orders to a minimum and, for the ones he gave, do his best not to make them sound like commands. In his world, he was always obeyed. She didn't look the obedient type.

"You do realize we're still connected. My mind and your mind. I can catch little snippets of your thoughts," she informed him. She sounded amused. "You're definitely the bossy type. I got that right away."

Heat blossomed low and wicked in his belly, like a tight fist. At the same time, a deep well of laughter came out of nowhere. He had forgotten laughter. Real laughter. The kind that could rush through one's body with joy and elation. His lifemate.

Sandu found himself smiling down at her. Her breath hitched. Her eyes went dark. She wrinkled her nose at him. "Just get on with it. Whatever you're about to do."

"I'm about to see if you've got anyone waiting inside for you." He quickly scanned her apartment. It was empty. "We're safe to go inside."

She didn't ask him how he could tell. That would come later. Just as claiming her would come later—just before dawn. He needed his brethren to help him safeguard her through the day. They would be in the ground and she would be vulnerable to attack.

Adalasia hurried to a back entrance and used a code on the heavy metal door. It unlocked and she went in, Sandu right behind her. She didn't waste time. She rushed to her bedroom, pushed the bed aside and yanked a small bag from a compartment in the floorboards.

"I have to change."

Sandu didn't see, nor did he quite understand why she was shooing him out of her bedroom, but he stepped into the wide living area, where there were several comfortable-looking chairs. The room seemed spacious in spite of the fact that there was no definition between it and the kitchen or eating area. It was clean and appeared warm and welcoming. Everything in the apartment seemed older, as if even the furniture was restored antiques modernized to be comfortable.

He reached out to four of his brethren, ancients who had been secreted in the monastery because they had become too dangerous to remain outside of it. Some had remained for centuries; others had come and gone. Like Sandu, they had come to the States to help out one of their own.

Benedek, I have need of you. I've found my lifemate and there is trouble. Sandu used the path of monastery brotherhood, one not known to all

Carpathians. Benedek Kovac was a fierce fighter. Like most of the ancients, he was a big man, brutal and vicious when it was called for, with
midnight black eyes and flowing black hair. For all of his predatory, feral
ways, he was an incredible artist.

Where do we meet?

Sandu told him. He called to his next brother. *Petru, I have need of
you. I have found my lifemate and there is trouble. If possible, would you be
willing to meet us at the caves?*

Petru Cioban was a brother to have at one's side in a battle. His unusual mercury-colored eyes gave the appearance of liquid silver. Sometimes a storm settled there, and that silver turned darker, but it was
always a mercury and so unique there was no looking away when he
wanted to mesmerize. His hair was just as unusual. The same silvery-
white color as his eyes, it covered his scalp and hung thick and long down
his back, held in tight bands to keep it under control.

Petru was an ancient with instincts for strategy, for taking down the
enemy in unusual ways. He could fight with any weapon and was lightning fast with them.

I will be there, he agreed without hesitation.

Sandu was grateful, but not surprised, that his brethren had responded so quickly with affirmations. A lifemate was sacred. The lifemate of an ancient was extremely sacred. Each of them carried that oath
on their backs. They might hide it from the world, but it was there,
carved into their skin, an oath to their lifemate that they would stay
strong for her no matter what it took or how long it took to find her.

*Nicu, I have need. I have found my lifemate and we are in trouble. I do
not know where my quest will take me, but I am looking for brethren willing
to accompany us on our journey. If you can travel with us, meet us at the caves.*

Nicu Dalca was an ancient worn from the centuries of battling master vampires, chasing them across continents and having to kill childhood friends who had turned. Still, he held on to his honor, staying true
to his oath. He had been in and out of the monastery, coming for a respite
when the battles became too much but leaving to look for his lifemate
when the call was strong enough.

He was leaner than some of the other ancients, but all muscle. Grim-faced, gray-eyed, with long black hair, he had a scar that curved from his left temple and eye. He was lightning fast in a fight. There was something in him that animals responded to. All animals. If he was in the vicinity, unlike most animals that ran from Carpathian hunters, recognizing they were predators, they responded to Nicu. They guarded him, spied for him, even the fiercest of them.

I will be there.

Nicu sounded a great distance away. That didn't surprise Sandu. Nicu was restless, just as Sandu had been. More and more, he traveled away from the Carpathian stronghold. Sandu had been fairly certain he would welcome a dangerous journey and protecting a lifemate of one of the ancients.

Afanasiv Belan was a brother who could be unpredictable when it came to fighting vampires. He was a vicious, brutal strategist, well versed in magic, extremely intelligent. He could outsmart most master vampires when he chose. Sometimes, he simply chose to do battle, hand to hand, roaring through the skies as if he had a death wish—and he might well have.

The brethren called him Siv rather than his longer given name. His eyes were mesmerizing, a deep blue-green. His hair was blond, and he was considered by all the ancients to be a very dangerous man. Sandu called him brother and knew he would be a good man to have at his side if this journey was as dangerous as his lifemate's cards seemed to think it was.

Siv, I have found my lifemate and there is trouble. The journey may be long. If you can get away and travel with us, and a few other of the brethren, meet us at the caves.

There is always trouble when one finds a lifemate, I have noted. I will be there.

Sandu found himself smiling. Siv was right. So far, each of his brethren who had found their lifemate had also found trouble. He had a strong foreboding that the beautiful woman in the other room who was taking *far* too long was going to be the greatest trouble so far of all of them. And wouldn't you know, it would have to be *his* lifemate. The others would never let him hear the end of it.

"I am still reading your thoughts," Adalasia said as she came out of the bedroom, her satchel in one hand. The other was up, fingers pushing at her hair as if that would help to tidy the wild, wayward fall. She'd put the mass of silk in a braid, but hair had escaped. "Your opinion of me is awful."

He flashed her a smile. She was breathtaking, even with her hair disheveled. Especially with her hair a wild mess. She wore what appeared to be older jeans, ones she'd owned for a long time. They'd been washed so many times the blue was faded to nearly white. They fit her curves like a glove yet looked as if they gave her room to move. A simple tank top was under a loose jacket. The jacket had loops and zippers inside it. He knew she had weapons in those loops and closed pockets, as well as items she considered valuable to her. She wore the same boots she'd had on with her skirt.

"You ready?"

Adalasia nodded. "You have a place in mind for us to go?"

"Go out the back to the roof. I'll take us from there. You've trusted me so far." Sandu indicated the back door. Even though he'd acted as if she'd taken a lot of time to change and use her bathroom, in reality, it had only been under five minutes.

She moved very quickly through the apartment to the back door and, once again, stepped aside to allow him to scan for intruders. He indicated it was safe and she stepped through, waited for him to step outside, where he cloaked both of them while she locked the door.

"I'm going to pick you up. We're traveling a different way. It might be uncomfortable if you choose to open your eyes. I've got you safe and you'll have to trust that I do." He didn't wait for her agreement. He simply reached down and fitted an arm beneath her knees and one behind her back to lift her, cradling her against his chest. "Put your bag in your lap and your arms around my neck. You can push your face into my chest with your eyes closed."

For the first time, he really felt her trepidation. She'd been nervous, but this was real fear. She had to force herself under control to keep from fighting him. "Tell me what you're going to do. It will help me."

"We're going to move through the air." He spoke matter-of-factly. She stiffened, and the fingers linked at the nape of his neck tightened. "Look at me, Adalasia."

She had courage. Her eyes met his. "What are you?"

"The cards warned you I had certain powers. I do. You aren't as afraid as you should be. Somewhere you've heard of someone like me."

"But you're not real. You were never supposed to be real," she whispered.

"I've got my arms around you. Do I feel real?"

"Yes," she agreed faintly. "But if you can take to the air like . . . If you can do that and you're real, then the other things I read about, the legends, the blood, the ground, are they true?" Her whisper had grown to the softest of threads. She was on the verge of flight. Of fight.

Had someone written about Carpathians? A written record couldn't exist. Not if they were to survive. They had to stay secret. More than once, Carpathians had been hunted along with vampires until so few were left they were nearly extinct. It hadn't helped that other species had waged war to stamp them out.

"We are going to take one crisis at a time. You believe in your tarot cards. We have a journey to take together, *ewal emninumam*." He couldn't keep the caress out of his voice. The last thing he wanted was to frighten his courageous woman. "I believe that is what was revealed to us. I cannot harm you. It is an impossibility, nor can I allow any other to harm you. Think of me as your guardian."

"What does *ewal emninumam* mean?"

He smiled down at her. "Sweet goddess. Now close your eyes."

She turned her head into his chest and closed her eyes tight. Sandu didn't hesitate but took to the night sky. He would share the night sky with her once he got away from the city. The blaze of city lights could easily drown out the beauty of the reality of the stars and moon.

You're a blend of all the elements. Earth. Air. Fire. Water. She whispered into his mind. *The magician wields so much power because he understands the true meaning of above and below. You do, don't you?*

He was Carpathian. He was elemental. He was of the earth. She sang to him, called, healed him when he was wounded. Cared for him when he sought solace in her arms. *Yes.* He answered her.

You can bind with elements.

He felt her struggle to understand. *Did your cards tell you this? I am more than your magician, Adalasia. Much more.*

She moved in his arms. It was subtle. She didn't lift her head from his chest, but she did shift as if she might try to put distance between their bodies.

You didn't say if you can bind me to you. There was real fear in her mind.

You did not ask this question. You stated that I can bind elements. I asked if your cards told you this. You did not answer me. He had distracted her. He felt her frown.

The magician card is always present in my readings for myself or for you, but no, it is there in the history. We are playing word games here, Sandu. Can you bind me to you in some way?

You already know the answer to that question, or you would not be trying to scare yourself, Adalasia. You are the keeper of my soul. Are you aware that you are?

She was silent for so long he wasn't certain she would answer him. He let her be as he moved away from the sprawling city. San Diego was deceptive in that it didn't appear to be as large as it was. He preferred the mountains, and he especially preferred to be as far as possible from cities.

The San Bernardino National Forest was three hours away by car, but far less than that when flying straight and rapidly. Eight hundred thousand acres of forest and cave systems gave Sandu a feeling of being home. He could set up safeguards and protect his lifemate from any trouble—human, vampire or otherwise—while he slept beneath the soil.

I am not sure what you mean.

There was both truth and untruth in Adalasia's carefully guarded words.

Have you heard the term lifemate? *Was that used in this history you refer to that is no more than a legend?*

Again, she fell silent for some time. *I am going to open my eyes. I don't want to continue this conversation right now.*

She was honest enough to avoid something that was upsetting to her. He much preferred that to her lying to him.

We are in the air. Fairly high up and moving quickly, heading for the San Bernardino National Forest. Your enemies will not easily find you there. We can make our plans for our journey and how best to start it. Let me drop lower and slow down so you won't get dizzy. I'll tell you when it is safe to open your eyes.

Her fingers tightened around his neck. *I can't believe we're actually in the air, but I can feel the wind rushing around me. I can hear it. Why don't I feel cold?*

I would never allow you to be cold.

His assurance seemed to buy him more trust with her. The fingers at the nape of his neck began to knead into his skin like a cat, but there was a wholly intimate component to it. Just as there was an intimate factor to speaking mind to mind. Each time she spoke to him, her voice brushed that whisper into lonely places he thought would never be filled. His soul might still be torn in half, the blackened remains tattered and filled with holes, scarred in too many places to count, but already he felt lighter just having her close.

"Try now. If the wind is too much, let me know and I will shield you more."

She shifted just a little bit more, one hand curling tightly around his neck, anchoring her, the other fisting his shirt while she turned her body, careful of her satchel. *Sandu!*

For a moment he was seeing out of her eyes, a dark world streaking below them, passing too fast. She shifted her gaze to the stars above and gasped again.

It's beautiful. Scary but beautiful. She clutched his shirt tighter and dug her fingers deeper into his skin. *Is this real? I feel as if I'm in a dream.*

There are many things I wish to show you, ewal emninumam. The earth is a beautiful and exciting place.

He had forgotten the beauty of the night sky until he saw it through her eyes. He wanted to see the forest and the caves, gemstones and waterfalls, so many places he'd traveled that had all been colorless battlegrounds to him. He would view them so differently with her by his side.

How was Adalasia so easily accepting the things he was showing her—taking her through the air? Most humans would never understand the abilities a Carpathian had, yet she took them in stride. There was trepidation, but she didn't fight him; she came with him. She didn't argue; she followed his lead. She had training, all those weapons she so easily carried on her. The "history" she had in her mind. His lifemate had her own secrets, and their journey together was going to be one very interesting path.

The system of caves Sandu had found was not one that had been explored or used by humans as of yet. The ancients had discovered it the way they often did—by following a tiny bat or listening for the sound of the creatures underground. In this case, the opening was a very small crack no one would ever notice, where an earthquake had shaken the ground enough to cause a shift. A boulder had moved no more than a scant millimeter or so, enough to allow bats to penetrate inside that long, narrow fissure.

The fracture wasn't the only one the ancients had discovered. The system was fairly large, and there were several places of entry, allowing airflow into the caves. They had made certain to conceal the largest of the fissures, placing safeguards around them to keep people and vampires from finding their place of safety. This was an area they could retreat to when they were wounded and needed to find healing grounds.

He dropped down to the floor beside the large boulder, where the slight crack was hidden by moss and debris. Setting Adalasia on her feet, he kept his hands on her waist to steady her. "My brethren will be meeting us here to ensure your safety."

She raised one eyebrow as she looked around. The white knuckles of the hand clutching her satchel were the only indication of tension. "I doubt very much that Mr. Castello and his friends would be able to follow us here. I think we've successfully lost them." There was the tiniest note of amusement in her voice in spite of her nerves.

"Mr. Castello is not our only enemy. I believe we have more than one." He watched her closely.

Adalasia pressed her lips together and then nodded her head slowly as she took a cautious look around. "Are there wild animals out here? I'm not really afraid of too many things, but I don't know that much about defending myself against wild animals. I've mainly learned self-defense against . . . humans."

There had been more than humans in her mind. For one moment, a hellish image had arisen, just a small glimpse that came and went so fast he couldn't catch it. Red, glowing eyes staring at him out of rolling orange, yellow and red flames. The thing of nightmares. The undead? He was well versed in the vampire. Was she? And then there was . . . him. At times, in battle, when he became that brutal, vicious fighter, uncaring of anything destroying his opponent, his eyes took on that same red, glowing with fierce, fiery flames. Had she seen him in her nightmares? He pushed the thought from his mind.

"Bears perhaps. The usual animals one finds in a forest. They won't bother you." He waved his hand, creating a small archway, allowing the opening to be large enough for her to enter. When she tried to step back away from the cold, very dark interior, he was behind her, and she ran into his large frame.

"I am *not* going in there."

He waved his hand again and sconces lined the narrow hallway every ten feet, illuminating the dry floor in spite of the sound of dripping water.

"Now you're really freaking me out. Stop doing things like that."

"I told you, I'm not going to allow anything to happen to you." He took her hand to give her confidence. So far, she'd surprised him by not trying to run from him, but she was on the verge of flight. She just didn't have a way to run.

"You're asking me to put a lot of trust into a total stranger." She continued to eye the interior of the cave warily, still not moving.

Sandu reached down and lifted her, cradling her once more against his chest, ignoring the way she stiffened. "I am not a total stranger. I have not been a stranger since you walked in my mind." He entered the cave and closed the entrance behind him, sealing them inside.

Her breath caught in her throat, and she buried her face in his chest. "I'm going to die in here. Underground. With a really gorgeous insane person."

The urge to laugh came again. "Are you thinking of bashing me over the head with your bag? I see the thought in your mind."

"It occurred to me it's a little late." She lifted her head from his chest and looked up at him as he carried her through the maze of tunnels. She didn't look to see where they were going but kept her eyes on his face. "The time for bashing you one and making a run for it was *before* we came inside. Now I'm stuck with you. I have no way out, and I think you're keeping me warm. It looks like it could be pretty cold in here."

He smiled down at her. "It's good to know I'm safe while we're in the caves."

She nodded. "You are."

"This journey we're taking together," he ventured as he brought her into the chamber he'd chosen to use to keep her safe during the day. "This is about your history, isn't it? The history of your family, perhaps? Is it tied to those men?"

He set her down as he once again waved his hand to install the sconces on the upper walls to illuminate the chamber for her. He did it casually, not really giving it thought. He added things from her home: a rug, comfortable chairs, a bed.

She sucked the side of her lower lip into her mouth and bit down with her small teeth. "Our histories were entwined, Sandu."

"Our futures are entwined," he corrected, turning to face her.

"Perhaps, but our histories were entwined as well."

"I am an ancient. There are few of my kind left in this world, Adalasia. You know I'm not human." He took a step toward her and framed the side of her face in his hand, his thumb moving in a caress over her cheek. "I don't believe you are an ancient."

She was beautiful to him. Her skin like silk. She was courageous. She didn't flinch away from him, her eyes looking straight into his. Long lashes swept down and back up again. His thumb glided along her full lips. Silky there as well.

"I'm not an ancient," she whispered. "It's difficult to take in that you're actually real. I knew of you only as a legend."

He could hear her heartbeat calling to him. The pulse beating so steadily in the side of her neck fascinated him as no other ever had. He swept the pads of his fingers over that pulse point. "Who told you of the legend?" He murmured the question as he dipped his head toward hers. Toward that beckoning drumbeat.

He ached for her now. He felt the slide of his teeth. One arm slid around her back, pulling her into his body, locking her to him. He kissed that steadily beating pulse. Swept his tongue over her soft skin and then sank his teeth deep. She cried out, the bite of pain giving way immediately to something else altogether. He shared her mind, so he knew that shocking painful bite became a dark, erotic heat that swept through her body.

He'd taken blood millions of times over centuries to sustain his life. But this was different. This was an aphrodisiac that poured into his system and flooded every cell in his body with an erotic heat. He drank from her as the ritual binding words rose up like a great storm in his mind. He could no more have held them back than he could have held back the tides. *Te avio päläfertiilam. You are my lifemate. Éntölam kuulua, avio päläfertiilam. I claim you as my lifemate. Ted kuuluak, kacad, kojed. I belong to you. Élidamet andam. I offer my life for you. Pesämet andam. I give you my protection. Uskolfertiilamet andam. I give you my allegiance. Sívamet andam. I give you my heart. Sielamet andam. I give you my soul. Ainamet andam. I give you my body. Sívamet kuuluak kaik että a ted. I take into my keeping the same that is yours.*

Adalasia stirred in his arms. *Wait. What? You're binding us.*

Sandu very reluctantly closed the twin holes over the pulse beating so frantically in her neck and opened his shirt. *You are my lifemate. The ritual has to be complete. Yes, I am binding us together. Soul to soul.* He lengthened his fingernail and opened a line on his chest, pressing her mouth to the crimson drops that were for her alone, distancing her from the act so it wasn't difficult for her, so she would only taste the ambrosia of his blood.

He threw his head back, need and a very different hunger moving through his body as her mouth moved on him and her tongue lapped at his gift to her. It would have been impossible to think, but the ritual binding words were imprinted on him before his birth, and they were forced from his mind and pushed into hers, weaving their torn souls back together.

Ainaak olenszal sívambin. Your life will be cherished by me for all time. *Te élidet ainaak pide minan.* Your life will be placed above mine for all time. *Te avio päläfertiilam.* You are my lifemate. *Ainaak sívamet jutta oleny.* You are bound to me for all eternity. *Ainaak terád vigyázak.* You are always in my care.

He cupped the back of her head, holding her in place, letting the distinctive spice of her blood rush through his veins, the dark needs of his kind celebrating the shocking reality of finding his other half after centuries of waiting for her. It seemed an impossibility, but she was there with him in his arms, drinking from him, taking enough for a true exchange. It took three exchanges for a conversion. Two more and his woman would be fully Carpathian. Fully able to be in his world, sleeping beneath the earth with him, instead of vulnerable above it when he couldn't protect her.

Very gently, he stopped her and allowed her to come out from under the light thrall he had induced in her. It didn't surprise him that she stepped away from him, putting a good portion of the chamber between them.

"What have you done?" she demanded, pressing her fingertips to her lips.

"Only what was necessary."

"You bound us together." It was an accusation.

"You knew it was necessary."

"I most certainly did *not*." Tears shimmered in her eyes.

His heart contracted. He hadn't expected that. "Why are you so upset? All along, you've known what to expect." He kept his voice gentle.

Low. Suppressing his nature. His need to leap across the room and take her in his arms whether she liked it or not.

"We were supposed to talk about it." She backed up more.

Sandu waved his hand, and a chair immediately was behind her. When she felt it against the backs of her knees, she dropped into it and gripped the stuffed arms.

"We were supposed to *discuss* it," she whispered again.

"There is no reason to discuss binding us together," Sandu said. "That had to happen." He felt no remorse, although he didn't like to see his courageous woman truly upset, and she was. "If you know I am ancient, then you know I can't stay with you during the day. You must sleep, and I have to weave safeguards to protect you. I have to be able to monitor you and know where you are if we ever are separated. You have to be able to reach for me. This is a protection for both of us, as it restores my soul to me. I cannot turn."

Her lashes fluttered. "Cannot turn?"

"There are monsters in the world that are very real, Adalasia, as you well know. I am a Carpathian. When we are born, our soul is split in two. A female is given our other half to hold in her keeping until we can find her. She holds all the light. We have only darkness in us. We lose all color and emotion after two hundred years. Eventually, we have nothing but our honor to sustain us while we look for our lifemate. I hunt the undead, but without you, I could go down that path. It is not possible now. You are the keeper of my soul, born over and over until I found you."

He saw knowledge in her expression. In her eyes. There was wariness. And exhaustion. She was at a breaking point, and he didn't want to push her any further. They had accomplished far more in one night than he ever thought possible. He would command she sleep and go to ground. They could start their journey the next evening together.

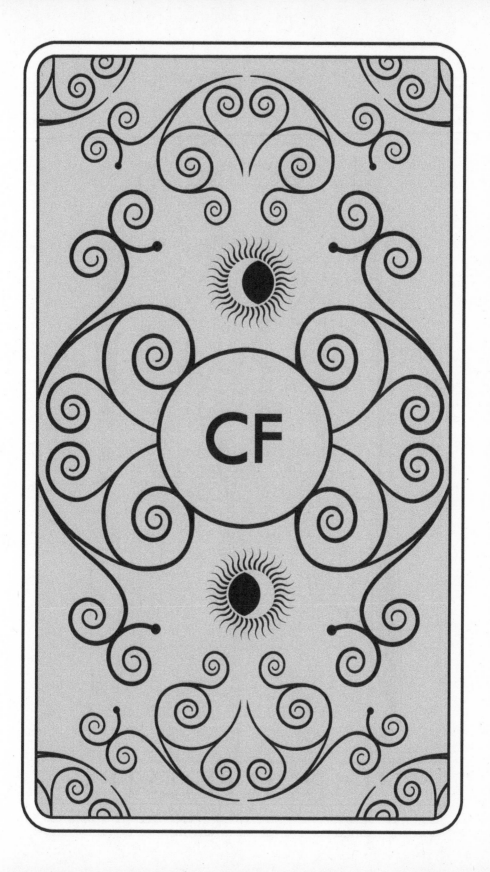

-II-

THE HIGH PRIESTESS

Adalasia realized that being alone in a cave system with five very large, scary-looking men and not feeling intimidated just underscored how far from normal she really was. Okay, maybe she did feel some trepidation. A little. Her mouth was drier than usual. It took some work to control her heartbeat, but there were some good reasons for that.

She was in a labyrinth of caves somewhere in the San Bernardino National Forest, one no one knew existed, with ancients no one knew existed, and she didn't even know how to get out of the caves. She was fairly certain all of the men existed on the blood of humans. She was the only human in that chamber, but they looked well-fed to her. She glared at Sandu.

They fed aboveground, not on you. They are here to protect you, Adalasia.

Of course they were there to protect her. Just as he was there to protect her. She pushed down her resentment. They were all waiting for her to start. To give them answers. Where did one begin? She couldn't help looking at Sandu. He was so gorgeous in a rough-looking way. She tried not to let the tremendous pull he had on her or the fact that physically she was attracted to him persuade her in any way.

He had taken decisions out of her hands by binding them together. Maybe she would have agreed to it once she understood what it meant, but he hadn't asked. He hadn't told her exactly what it entailed. He'd *taken*. He'd compounded that sin by taking her blood without her permission. Again, she most likely would have given it to him freely, but she thought they were entering into a partnership. Now she knew that wasn't so. That meant she had to be very, very careful what she told any of them, Sandu included.

Was this really about him? His past? His family? She moistened her lips and decided to just plunge in, although she wasn't going to tell perfect strangers everything, even if they had fangs and she was the only human and they were underground in a cave system she couldn't hope to find her way out of alone.

"I read the tarot cards not only for others but for myself. My deck is very old and has been in my family for generations. It's been passed down from mother to daughter, the same deck for centuries. Long before credit was given for tarot readings." She had to admit that. There was no getting around it.

The one Sandu had introduced as Siv turned his blue-green eyes on her, studying her intently, as if he thought she might be lying. "How would these cards hold up through the centuries and not disintegrate into dust with time and use?"

It was a fair question. She put the velvet pouch on the table between them. The cards, from being contained in the sack, held concentrated power, and she knew the moment she released them, all of the men would feel it. They were sensitive to energy, just as she was. She opened the bag carefully and shook the deck into her waiting hand, observing the men's reactions.

All of them, including Sandu, sat back slightly as the power radiated outward. It was a distinctly feminine energy. She gathered it easily as she swept up the familiar cards. They nearly leapt into her hands.

"What do you sense?" She asked the question to answer the question.

"Blood," the one introduced as Petru said immediately. "Carpathian blood. Female." Already the energy was pulling back into the cards. "What is this? What kind of trick are you playing?"

Adalasia became aware that Sandu had gone very still. If there was a way for an ancient to go ashen, he had. He stared at the cards in her hands and then slowly lifted his gaze to hers. All traces of tenderness evaporated. A shiver went down her spine, icy cold. He looked what he was, a killer. Top of the food chain. An apex predator.

"That is not just any blood," he said softly. "You had better start talking fast, Adalasia. That is the blood of my family."

The other four Carpathian hunters looked from Sandu to her. There was no friendliness in their expressions, either. She took a deep breath. She hadn't been truly afraid. Now, her heart pounded. She knew they heard. When she had awakened, her hearing had seemed to be much more acute. She knew theirs was, too, just by little signals they gave one another. Before, those signals had made her feel safe—sort of—but now she was just a little terrified.

"Sandu, you had the opportunity to feel the card's energy in my shop. I thought you felt the connection then. Why are you reacting now?" It took great effort to control her heartbeat in the midst of the predators surrounding her.

"The cards hid the source from me. They only showed your fear of our relationship. I knew there was a connection to Carpathians, but not specifically to my bloodline."

His tone was low, so soft it should have been calming, but instead, she felt a distinct threat. A frisson of fear slid down her spine. She stayed silent, afraid if she opened her mouth, her voice would tremble, and she refused to give him—or the others—the satisfaction of knowing they were scaring her.

"Adalasia, how did the blood of my family get on those cards?"

Her gaze jumped to his. The red flames leapt higher. She forced herself to give a casual shrug. "Unfortunately, there are many things I don't have answers for."

"It is possible that because I have your blood in my veins, I was able to discern the origins of the blood on the cards," he mused aloud.

She lifted her chin, determined to distract them. "It is my practice each morning to give a reading to myself to start my day. A few weeks ago, I began to see that danger was drawing close, just as my mother had said it had with her. Then I began to see a man come into my readings, one that was to take a journey with me. It was a very dangerous one, to find the origins of the cards and secure them from those who would twist them for their own purposes. If he was the right man, I would be able to connect with him telepathically. That would be how I would know."

She shuffled the cards and fanned them out without looking at Sandu. "There is a legend in our family. One that seemed absurd until I met you. That legend said this man would come, and he would be my life *partner.*" She bit that last word out between her teeth, forcing her gaze to meet his. Letting him see that perhaps that legend handed down in her family for centuries had gotten it all wrong.

I see that you are very angry with me, Adalasia.

She didn't deign to answer him because it was too late to undo what he'd done. He wasn't sorry. She didn't detect remorse, and if he lied and said he was sorry, that would only make things worse between them.

"Tell us about the cards," Benedek prompted.

Adalasia was more than happy to turn her focus from Sandu, although she had to choose very carefully what she was going to give to these men. "My family was given the task of guardian to the cards. We're the gatekeepers, and supposedly, at one time, we had others who watched over us. Our guardians are gone, vanished over the ages. I believe Castello and the others are part of a group who want the cards."

"Why didn't they take them when they killed your mother?" Sandu asked.

She could tell he wasn't ready to accept everything at face value, not with the blood of his family on her cards. She couldn't blame him. She hadn't looked forward to explaining. She hadn't wanted to get to this point with him. There were things she might be able to tell him when they were alone if she ever came to trust him, but the others? She kept her hands steady with great effort. The familiar feel of the cards helped.

"They can't wield them. Only my family can. Mother to daughter. That's how it works. The cards will only talk to a member of our family." She shuffled again. "The cards are capable of hiding themselves. It is possible they did." She had taken them off her mother's body before the police had arrived.

There was silence throughout the chamber as she laid out the cards on the small table and studied them. Only the steady drip of water could be heard—that and the sound of Adalasia's heartbeat. If she could hear it, they all could. There were gaps in her story, too many, and she knew it. Sandu knew it. He was allowing her to get away with it for now. She knew he wouldn't forever. His black eyes held those fiery red flames. The flames burned low, but she could see they leapt every now and then when he turned his gaze fully on her. A little shiver went through her body. She didn't want to ever get on the wrong side of him.

She let her gaze slide over the other four. They watched her with the same unblinking, very focused eyes of predators, like Sandu, but they didn't have access to her mind in the way he did. He could share with them, even connect her mind with theirs, but there was an intimacy Sandu had created between them when he had bound them together with his ritual words. Just the thought of him doing so without any discussion stirred her temper. She tried to push it down hastily. There was too much at stake to allow him to see too much of her.

She should have known there was no hiding anything from him. Those black, merciless eyes found her, the red flames burning over her skin like a physical touch.

"Why do these people want the cards?" Petru asked.

"My guess would be to open the gates. I don't have those answers. I know only the bare minimum. Four decks that were to be protected. The cards guard the gates, and we're the gatekeepers, mother to daughter for centuries. As I mentioned, at one time, we had others guarding us, but they were killed or corrupted, leaving us on our own."

"You keep talking about the gates," the Carpathian called Nicu said. "What gates are you guarding?"

Adalasia sighed. "Everything I say is going to sound as if I'm making things up."

"Like our ability to fly?" Sandu suggested. "I think if you can believe that of us, we can believe what you tell us."

She had to give them something, so she took a deep breath and let it out. "According to everything I was told as a child, there is a wild creature in hell, which can't be let loose on the world, trapped behind four gates. Each of those gates can only be opened by a specific alignment of the tarot cards. Only one of the ancient decks can make that alignment. I have one of the decks, and these people that were watching me are after the deck."

Sandu looked at her sharply. She was telling the truth, yet she wasn't.

"They had a chance to take the deck along with your mother, but they didn't. They murdered her and left the deck with you," Sandu said. "Why?"

There was no emotion in his voice. She knew if she touched his mind, there would be none there, either. He could close off his feelings when he wanted, but she couldn't. The moment he said "murder," she was thrown back to that evening, opening the door to their home, tired after working but looking forward to seeing her mother. The entire living room was wrecked, furniture overturned and broken, blood pooled on the floor and splattered on one wall and across her mother's favorite antique gold brocade chair. Her mother lay like a broken doll, small in her death when she'd been so vibrant in life.

Adalasia's fingers stroked the cards, needing the comfort of them. Her mother's hands had been on these cards long before she'd ever touched them. Willing herself not to let the burn behind her eyes give way to tears, she lifted her chin at Sandu and his brethren. Men so like him. Men without emotion.

"How could I possibly have the answer to what the murderers were thinking when they killed my mother?"

Sandu's eyes leapt and burned with fiery flames. "You cannot lie to a lifemate. You know the reason. What is it?" he challenged.

It took a few moments while she struggled to keep her emotions under control before she lifted her furious gaze to his. As it was, she knew her voice held both grief and recrimination. There was no way to prevent it.

"Perhaps I didn't want to discuss my mother's *murder* with men who have absolutely no empathy toward me or her. I can assure you, Carpathian, this lifemate bond you thought was so important between us is pure bullshit. Everything you said has no meaning whatsoever. I reject every single word of it. Shall we get on with this?" She said the last through clenched teeth.

There was a long silence. Very long. She realized that all of them were staring at her in a kind of shocked way, if one could be shocked without expression. She didn't care if her declaration of their precious lifemate ritual offended them. It was how she felt. Sandu might look like he was the hottest catch in town, and she'd been conditioned to believe he was her perfect match, her prince coming to claim her, but he wasn't. That didn't negate the fact that she had a job to do.

I hurt you. I am sorry.

Adalasia didn't want to hear the sincerity in his voice or feel it in his mind. She pulled at the messy knot in her hair and continued doggedly on. "I read the cards over and over, and from what I've discerned, it seems this journey we're undertaking starts with Sandu and what he can tell us of his childhood. Now that he's confirmed the blood tied to the cards is from his family, we can get some answers. Obviously, I wasn't alive that long ago. What I do know is unreliable."

Sandu raised an eyebrow. "If you think I can help with that, I have no recollection of my childhood. Not a single memory. I couldn't tell you what my parents looked like or where we actually resided. I would imagine it would have been in the Carpathian Mountains, if that helps."

The dripping of the water seemed louder than ever. Adalasia sank back in her chair, one hand going to her hair again. She'd put it in a messy knot on top of her head and called it good. Sandu hadn't thought to provide her with a mirror. He'd remembered a bathroom—of sorts. The bare minimum. A toilet and sink. Towels. A shower. No mirror. She was certain she looked pretty bad when all of them were seriously good-looking, although she no longer cared about how incredible Sandu looked or the magical things he could do.

"That's just not possible. Everyone remembers their parents. Their childhood. You can't have lost all of your memories." He was the beginning of their journey. He had to remember or they had no starting point. So far, he was pretty useless.

She leaned toward him as if she could see into his mind by looking into his eyes. He still hadn't quite forgiven her for having the blood of his family on her cards. She should have told him before he was with his friends. He almost viewed it as a betrayal. Maybe it was. She still wasn't over him binding them together without discussing it with her first. She wanted in on all decisions, particularly the ones that would change her life forever. She really was upset with him for so callously bringing up the murder of her mother in front of his friends. She wasn't over his betrayals.

They really knew nothing about each other. He could be so emotionless and she was all about feeling. That didn't bode well for their future. She had the beginnings of a headache. Still, she looked down at the cards she'd laid out and heaved a sigh.

Three times in a row. There it was. The High Priestess. That should tell her something right there. This man, Sandu, the one that was *supposed* to be her man, thought he protected and guarded her. The High Priestess card depicted a nighttime scene. Sandu was all about the night. At its most basic, the card meant that she protected and guarded even if she feared what she was getting into. This was an opportunity for self-growth.

Sandu shrugged. "I have lived centuries without emotion or color and no hope of finding you. My memories faded fast, and it is possible I allowed it. Should a vampire manage to overcome my strength in those first few centuries, perhaps I didn't want my family to suffer."

Centuries without feelings, without experiencing emotion, Adalasia, he reminded softly. *I was alone most of that time. Completely alone, until I was in that monastery with these men who were like me, too far gone to be let loose on the outside world.*

Adalasia knew it would be a mistake to look at him. To really see him. *You're a stranger. A complete stranger. I know nothing of you. You don't know me at all. I took you at face value, and I'm not willing to do that again. There aren't excuses to just take from people. I might have given you willingly had you asked or talked with me. Had you bothered to take the time to get to know me and treat me like I was someone special, but you didn't.*

She had to ask herself why his betrayal hurt so much. She shuffled the cards and fanned them out because she needed the familiarity of them in her hands for comfort. Her mother had read her stories at night like most mothers read their children. Hers had been all about demons and the woman and her hunter partner who fought those demons, and together they saved the world. Each story centered around the couple. How he came when she was lonely. How they laughed together, fought the worst of the demons and survived every kind of battle thrown at them. The stories grew more exciting and adventurous as she got older. He was always there, fighting at her side. Her partner, treating her with love and respect.

You are someone special. There was that caressing note again. Sliding into her mind, over her skin, sinking into her bones. *You are my only. I will make many mistakes, but never think I make them because I do not think you are special.*

Adalasia tried to drown him out. She had counted on him. Waited for him. Believed in him. She had been prepared to send him away in order to protect him even though she was so lonely and afraid of those watching her. She had developed a fantasy of her prince. When she saw Sandu and he was so beautiful—a gorgeous, rough and dangerous man— she couldn't help but be thrilled. He had seemed perfect. Scary, but she needed that. Dangerous, but she really needed that in a partner if they were going to battle demons from the stories she'd heard all her life.

Adalasia, you are not capable of holding grudges.

She tilted her chin. She did her best to shore up her defenses in her mind, to give him pure steel. *I can hold a grudge forever. You don't know the first thing about me.*

I have been in your mind, ewal emninumam. You are soft inside, all empathy, while I am all hard edges. You carried my light that was in your soul for far too long, lifetime after lifetime, and having all that light, yours as well as mine, gave you that compassion and understanding.

Compassion, she conceded, *but not understanding. Don't assume I'm a pushover.*

I hurt you and I did not mean to do so.

His voice was a caress. It seemed to stroke the inside of her mind like a whisper of a feather, a sensual brush that swept through her. She made the mistake of looking at him again when she knew better. Those flames were in his eyes, but this time, they ignited a different kind of heat, one that moved through her veins in a slow burn that grew hotter and hotter until it reached her feminine core.

The sudden ache was shocking, especially since they weren't alone or getting along, and it was so strong and compelling. If his tone had simply been sexual, she might have been able to cope, but there was too much sincerity, and she didn't dare trust him. She didn't dare trust anyone. She was trapped underground with the five of them, and he knew it.

She sent him a glare. "We have to sort this out." She said it aloud, more for his benefit than for the others. She had to get back on track. Find a starting point.

She sat in silence, looking to the cards to guide her. Since she was a small child, she had been beside her mother, listening to the stories of her grandmother and great-grandmother guiding others on their journey through life. It was her turn. She needed to have the wisdom handed down to her through her bloodline.

Adalasia knew that wisdom wasn't always about knowledge and conscious mind. Sometimes, she had to listen to her intuition. Her intuition told her that Sandu had called each of these four men to him for a reason other than just to help him guard her. He was a powerful being. Why so many? Sandu might not even understand why he had asked these specific four to make the journey with them, but intuitively, he had invited them, and they had accepted in spite of him warning there would be danger.

"All of you have spent time with Sandu. You must have memories of things he has told you of his past. Things you may think are insignificant. People or places he has mentioned. Something or someone that stands out in your mind." She kept her voice matter-of-fact.

Sandu leaned back in the armchair, his long legs sprawling out in front of him. He gave her a little smile and shook his head slightly. She figured he could melt the panties off a girl with that look. She didn't need the distraction, but then she'd been studiously avoiding every single card that gave her any indication about the journey of her love life—including whatever light the High Priestess card might shine on it. Raging passions. Intense emotions. Her gaze flicked to Sandu again. He certainly could inspire both in a woman—in her—and she wasn't the type of woman to fall for a man just because he was good-looking. She was done with fairytales.

I'm happy you find me attractive. It would not be good if my lifemate was not in any way sexually interested in me.

Adalasia narrowed her eyes at him. *I'm fairly certain I didn't have anything about being sexually attracted to you in my mind.*

You were thinking in terms of raging passions and intense emotions and me inspiring you.

He looked at her with his dark eyes that had that curious red gleam, like warm candlelight, sexy as sin. Why was she thinking that when she should be thinking feral, predatory animal?

"You know Lucian, Sandu," Benedek said. "He and his lifemate have a residence somewhere in the States. He may recall something of your childhood."

"Lucian?" Adalasia echoed. "Who is Lucian?"

Sandu smiled at her. A charming smile. A sexy smile. He was definitely doing his best to win her over. She tried thinking of him as a shark. Unfortunately, that didn't fit him very well. It was all that hair. It should have been dark to match those black eyes of his, but instead, it was light with those impressive streaks of silver and gold. She had to stop looking at him. Or thinking about him. He was already arrogant, and she was far too susceptible. She was predisposed to think of him as her partner, and she couldn't let her guard down for a minute.

"Lucian and Gabriel Daratrazanoff are twins. They are legends in our world. Definitely skilled fighters, few have ever come up against them and lived. Lucian knew Gabriel had a lifemate, and to keep him from turning or suiciding, he deceived his brother into believing he had turned vampire so Gabriel would hunt him until he found her. Lucian is a protective man."

"He resides here in the States?"

"Yes. He chose to stay here. He travels back and forth between here, France, where Gabriel resides, and the Carpathian Mountains, where he consults with the prince," Nicu volunteered.

Sandu raised an eyebrow. "You certainly are aware of Lucian's business."

"I've run into him a time or two in my travels, both in France and in the Carpathian Mountains. Both times, I needed blood to survive, and he gave it to me without hesitation," Nicu admitted.

"Where is his main residence?" Sandu asked.

"I believe he owns an estate in Montana somewhere in the wild. He keeps wolves," Nicu said. "Most people don't go uninvited to his home. It isn't safe."

Adalasia didn't like the sound of that, but when she looked down at the cards, she knew that was exactly where they had to go. She sighed. "You really need a good jolt to the brain, Sandu. That way we wouldn't be taking chances like this."

Sandu laughed, and the sound was mellow and rich, sliding into her body like a fine wine. She gathered the cards. "We have a direction to go. How do we get there? Car?"

"Fly," Sandu said.

She raised an eyebrow. "Really? I'm not flying across the United States like a bat. Or a bird. Or whatever you were."

He laughed. "We do use airplanes, just like everyone else."

"You do?"

"We didn't just emerge from caves."

"Just from the monastery," Benedek pointed out. "We haven't been out that long, but we're learning fast. We just take information out of people's minds."

"You can read anyone's mind?" She carefully placed the cards back inside the velvet pouch. "At any time?"

Adalasia didn't like the sound of that. She thought only Sandu could read her mind. She was going to have to be very, very careful and work on the exercises her mother had insisted she learn as a child that would aid in strengthening the barriers in her mind against demons. She didn't know if that would help in stopping these men from reading her, but she hoped it would.

Adalasia pushed to her feet. Immediately the five men stood as well. "So, how do we get out of here and onto a flight to Montana, or wherever this Lucian might have his home? How do we contact him so he doesn't get upset that we're coming to see him?"

"We have our own plane," Sandu said. "Carpathians rarely take the chance of flying with a full flight of humans. The risk is too great. Our plane is specifically equipped to allow us to sleep during daylight flights."

"Do you have your own pilot, or does one of you fly the plane?"

"We have a human pilot," Sandu said. "Zenon Santos has been with us for a long time now and is very loyal. He comes from a family in South America, studied in England and grew to love flying in service to his country. When he got out, he asked to be employed in some capacity as a pilot. Since we needed pilots, we hired him immediately."

"He knows about you? That you're Carpathian?"

"Yes. He comes from a family that has lived in a symbiotic relationship with one of our families for centuries. They have passed the secrets down from father to son, mother to daughter, and protected our kind just as we have protected them. They have fought by our side when the vampire attacked full force in an attempt to wipe us out."

That was interesting. They had humans as allies, ones they trusted. The humans trusted them. "Are there others like them? Humans that know about your species?"

Sandu lifted her into his arms when she had gathered her things into her satchel. "A few." He nuzzled the top of her head with his chin, causing her hair to get caught in the bristles along his jaw, connecting them together.

A shiver of awareness ran down her spine. Each strand of her hair seemed to deliver information to her, which was an impossibility, right? *Right? That can't be.* It certainly seemed to be as if not only the cells and nerves in her body were aware of him, but now her hair was, every hair on her body tuned to him.

What are whiskers on animals? They are really a guidance system, or radar, with a bundle of nerve endings telegraphing to the animal everything it needs to know. Prey. Distance. Air pressure and currents. If he can fit through an opening. How far away his prey is or if danger is close to him. Whiskers are their tracking systems, guidance and radar. They perform acrobatic stunts and know when and where to strike on prey, all because of those whiskers.

I don't have whiskers. She tried to be indignant.

He bent his head to the nape of her neck and scraped his teeth along the hair there, sending jagged little shocks through her veins, like tiny spears straight to her sex. *You have bundles of nerve endings, and they will continue to grow more sensitive.*

She turned that information over in her mind as they moved with blurring speed through the cave system. The other Carpathian males went before them, moving toward some unknown exit. She didn't even hear the grinding as they widened the crevice so they could emerge, and then closed it as if it had never been tampered with as she tried to puzzle out what he meant. She was missing something important, something he meant by saying her nerve endings would grow even more sensitive. Why would they?

The night breeze was cool on her face, and Adalasia looked around her. Sandu hadn't set her down, so she knew they were going to take to the air. She positioned the satchel on her lap more securely and tightened her arm around his neck.

"You're safe, *ewal emninumam*," he whispered. "I would never allow anything to harm you."

There were times, like now, she could hear the sincerity in his voice, and she would begin to believe him, which was a little frightening in that she'd never trusted anyone outside of her family. Now, suddenly, with no real explanation but her cards, she was supposed to trust this stranger with her life . . . and if the cards were right . . . her heart. The problem was, he was hiding things from her, and even though he'd asked for forgiveness and he'd sincerely apologized for hurting her, she knew he wasn't in the least bit remorseful for binding them together or taking her blood without her permission.

Wrought iron gates, tall and intricate, the iron twisted into beautiful rods of art guarding the estate, opened inward to allow the car entry. Their chauffeur took them up the long drive to the house. Everywhere Adalasia looked were tall ferns, bushes and trees, giving the estate a wild, forestlike appearance. She looked up at the house. The structure was several stories high, with turrets and balconies jutting out in all directions. There were beautiful stained glass windows everywhere, as well as stained glass woven throughout the walls. She'd never seen anything like it. The house appeared to be a mixture of old-fashioned and modern, but very, very beautiful.

Far too close, they heard the hunting cry of a wolf. Another took up the call and then another. The sound sent alarms rushing down her spine.

"Adalasia, stay in the center of us," Sandu ordered softly. "If Lucian feels threatened, he can be extremely dangerous."

She didn't have to be told twice. She *felt* the danger. She looked back toward their chauffeur. Lucian had sent the car for them. It was already leaving them, driving away. She wanted to call it back. Sandu slipped his hand around hers.

"Lucian is a good man, *Sivamet*, just careful when his lifemate is close. It is something all of us must do. That is why you have four of my most trusted brethren surrounding you. Should anything happen to me, they will escort you to Tariq if we are here in the States, or to the prince in the Carpathian Mountains to ensure your protection."

Just him saying the words, putting the idea into her head that something could happen to him, made the air rush from her lungs. She wasn't certain why, but the idea of losing him made her feel instantly desolate. She gripped his arm as they climbed the steps to the front door. The wind rose along with the howling of the wolves. The pack sounded as if they were coming much closer. She swung around to face behind them. The forest and brush were too close, giving wild creatures too many places to hide.

"Let's leave this place. We don't need to be here."

Nicu dropped back to the bottom stair and faced the vast yard calmly. He held his arms out as if greeting old friends. His voice was a soft murmur, the words in another language, and Adalasia vaguely caught phrases she understood but was uncertain how she knew the language. It was old-world, a dialect long gone, she was certain, and one she hadn't heard before. Sandu occasionally uttered a few words, but why should she recognize and understand what Nicu was saying?

"My brethren. Long has it been since I have seen you. Come to me."
Nicu walked into the yard and sat on the ground, his arms still out in
welcome. "I brought friends to see our brother. While he welcomes them,
let us renew our kinship."

Adalasia held her breath as wolves emerged from the trees and brush
from every direction, rushing toward Nicu. One nearly knocked him flat.
She covered her mouth to keep from screaming. *Sandu, you have to help him.*

Nicu needs no help with animals.

The massive front door opened, and a beautiful man stood there, his
dark gaze flicking over the tight group of ancients, to her, and then to
Nicu and the wolves rolling around together in the front yard by the
stairs. Amusement slid into the deep black velvet of his eyes.

"Please do enter of your own free will." He stepped back and gestured to allow them to walk inside. "Nicu, stop playing and come in as
well. The pack has a job to do, and you are not helping them train the
younger ones."

Sandu swept Adalasia into his arms before she could walk through
the doorway. He carried her in and put her on her feet once they were
inside. Lucian turned to look at him, his gaze sweeping the two of them.

"Your lifemate?"

"Adalasia," Sandu answered. "She is bound to me but not yet converted."

Adalasia didn't clench her teeth, but it took effort. He'd used the
word "converted," but she wasn't asking in front of Lucian. He hadn't
liked Sandu carrying her inside, but she wasn't asking about that, either.
There were too many things Sandu hadn't told her that he should have.

She smiled her best professional smile. She was extremely proficient
at putting people at ease. "Thank you so much for seeing us, Lucian, at
such short notice. Your home is truly lovely."

"Thank you." Lucian inclined his head courteously.

Sandu had moved close to her, so close he actually positioned her
under his shoulder, her front to his side. One arm slid around her waist.

Benedek casually moved up to her other side. "It has been long since
I saw you, Lucian."

Petru came up on the other side of Sandu. "You look well, Lucian."

Siv stepped around them and gripped Lucian's arms in the old greeting of warriors. *"Bur tule ekämet kuntamak—*well met brother-kin."

Lucian answered him. *"Eläsz jeläbam ainaak—*long may you live in the light."

Siv stepped back. "I add my appreciation to Sandu and Adalasia's."

Nicu came through the door, looking as immaculate as always. "Have I missed anything important? Greetings, Lucian."

Lucian shook his head. "Now that you've gotten reacquainted with the wolf pack, Nicu, and could find the time to join us, come into the library where it's warmer. Adalasia will not have to have Sandu keep her body temperature up for her. I have a fire going." He led them into a very large room that Adalasia could have spent months in.

The library was massive. Very comfortable-looking chairs had been set out in a semicircle in front of a large stone fireplace. The flames were already dancing, and she was immediately drawn to the warmth. On three walls were floor-to-ceiling bookshelves, a ladder on railings, the only way to get to the top shelves. Adalasia had always loved books. She couldn't help herself; her gaze kept straying to the titles. So many. She could tell many were very old and in different languages. For a moment, she wished the men were gone and she could just spend the entire night right there, going through those books. She would hang off that ladder . . .

Not if you are Carpathian, Sandu pointed out. *Then you can float to the top shelf.*

If I was Carpathian, I'd still use the ladder because it's completely cool and looks fun. She lifted her chin at him. *Human things can be fun, Sandu. Don't be a snob.*

He laughed, that rich, mellow sound that fascinated her. Lucian's dark eyes swept over the two of them and went back to Sandu. "I see your lifemate amuses you, Sandu."

"She reminds me often that I need to be much humbler."

"Ah, yes. In the early days of our relationship, I believe Jaxon did the same." A small smile lit his eyes. He gestured toward the chairs. "Please.

Adalasia, Jaxon will be here shortly. She is assisting a friend with the birth of a horse on a neighboring ranch. There was a problem, apparently. These things happen. She knows you are here and will return as soon as she can."

Sandu frowned. "Lucian, I'm sorry. You must have been with her when you got our message. I would never have taken you away from her side had I known the two of you were busy. We could have waited another day."

"The matter seemed urgent. Jaxon is secure at the moment, and should she have need, she has only to summon me." He looked around the room. "No doubt, we could vanquish any foe daring enough to go after my lifemate. She's a force to be reckoned with."

When they were all seated and comfortable, Adalasia looked to Sandu, not knowing how much she should disclose to Lucian. She hadn't disclosed all that much to Sandu, so she let him do the talking.

"I found Adalasia under strange circumstances. I knew I could no longer stay with Tariq. I had to make the decision to go back to the monastery or meet the dawn. I sat on a rooftop and contemplated which path to take. In doing so, Adalasia reached out to me. She connected telepathically with me."

Lucian held up his hand and looked to her. "You heard him? His thoughts?"

The other Carpathian males stared at her as well. No shock showed on their faces, but she felt it. She didn't like to be under the spotlight, but she nodded. "Yes, I feared for him. I could tell he didn't think he felt emotions, but he did. Very strong emotions. The instant I connected with him, I also knew he was the one the cards had been showing me would come."

She hesitated. He had been in the prophecy, the one handed down from mother to daughter. Her other half, the one she was waiting for. She had been so certain. He'd felt right, but now she wasn't as certain. Sandu unexpectedly slid his thumb over the back of her hand as he pressed her palm into his thigh. She didn't want that intimacy, but she didn't pull away, not with all the others watching them so closely.

"I understood, through the cards, that I was to undertake a very dangerous journey with this man, a stranger." She touched her tongue to her lips to moisten them.

"So, you spoke to him," Lucian persisted.

"I didn't want to," she admitted. "I'll admit I was a little freaked out, but more importantly, my mother had been murdered, and the people I was certain had been responsible were watching me. They seemed to be waiting for someone. I had the feeling they might be waiting for Sandu to show up. I had no real reason to think that, but I rely heavily on intuition, and mine told me he could be in danger if he came near me. Still, I couldn't stop myself from reaching out to him."

Lucian nodded as if it made perfect sense to him when it didn't make sense to her. She didn't know why, when she was such a disciplined person, but she hadn't been able to stop herself from connecting with Sandu and possibly putting him in front of Castello's murderous guns. At the time, she didn't know the first thing about Carpathians.

"We spoke for a short while," Sandu said. "During that time, I became aware she was my lifemate. I could see color again. Emotions were restored, although I have been too long without them, and it is in my nature to act without feelings. Too often, emotions disappear, and if I am not close to Adalasia, colors dim."

Adalasia knew all about his emotions disappearing. She hadn't realized his ability to see in color dimmed. *Perhaps I am not your true lifemate.*

You are my lifemate, ewal emninumam.

Adalasia's chin lifted. She clenched her teeth at the whisper of male amusement she heard in her mind. *Too bad I'm not feeling it.* She gave him her haughtiest voice.

His thumb did another slide over the back of her hand. Slow. Intimate. *Then I will have to make certain I do a better job of making certain you do when we are alone.* There were all kinds of promises in his voice.

She ignored the little shiver that went down her spine and lifted her gaze once more to Lucian's. His eyes saw too much. She knew he was waiting for an explanation. "I broke the connection between us. I'd like to say it was strictly because of Castello and my fears for Sandu, but I read the cards. I'd been reading them. I knew Sandu was . . . *more*. There is a legend in our family, and I feared he was part of that legend from all I was reading in the cards. A stranger would come who was not a stranger but my other half. Soulmates. A passionate, intense relationship would follow, but dangerous. A life-threatening journey. Danger surrounding us every step of the way. A path once on, there would be no turning back. I saw all that and it was terrifying."

Adalasia looked at the floor, determined to be honest in this, when she refused to trust these people, knowing they were risking their lives.

Look at me. It was a command, nothing less.

She was ashamed, but not for the reasons she knew Sandu would think.

I can't. I should have had the courage to tell you about Castello so you could have known what you were walking into. About what the cards said about our journey together. It wasn't just your journey. It was mine. In our family, we knew one of us eventually would have to make it. I thought I was prepared. Trained. But when the time came, I faltered. That much was true, and he would hear that truth in her voice.

You are much too hard on yourself.

"Adalasia," Lucian said. "Any human woman who might have an inkling they are a lifemate to a Carpathian male would want to make a run for it. That just shows you have good sense. Especially if Sandu is that male."

"Did you know him as a child?"

Lucian gave a slow shake of his head. "No, Sandu is from an ancient lineage, very powerful and not from our region. His family guarded not the Carpathian Mountains but another range altogether." He pressed his fingers to his eyes as if going inward, trying to pull up long-forgotten memories. "I am sorry, I know you came here for answers, but as to your childhood, Sandu, I don't have any knowledge to share."

The flames from the fire threw shadows on the wall, where they took odd shapes that danced and stretched across the paneling, reaching toward the ceiling one moment and then toward the walls on either side of the room the next. The crackling seemed overly loud in the silence that followed Lucian's declaration.

"That's not exactly true," Adalasia countered. "Already, we know Sandu isn't from the same region most of you are from. We didn't have that information before. Is his surname correct?"

"We didn't have surnames that long ago," Lucian said. "Our families took them when the world around us began to change and names seemed overly important. We moved from place to place, and usually our names reflected the moves. Because we lived long lives, we didn't want people to associate our name or features with someone they knew in the past. Now, it is even much more difficult because of cameras everywhere. His surname is not going to be of much help."

A wolf howled. Another one took up the cry. Nicu rose just as the fire shadows flickered in a kind of macabre dance, morphing into hooded figures. Lucian and the other Carpathian males stood as Jaxon entered. Lucian's lifemate was small and slender with a cap of wild blond hair. She smiled at them and then flung her arms around Lucian's neck, going up on her toes to kiss him.

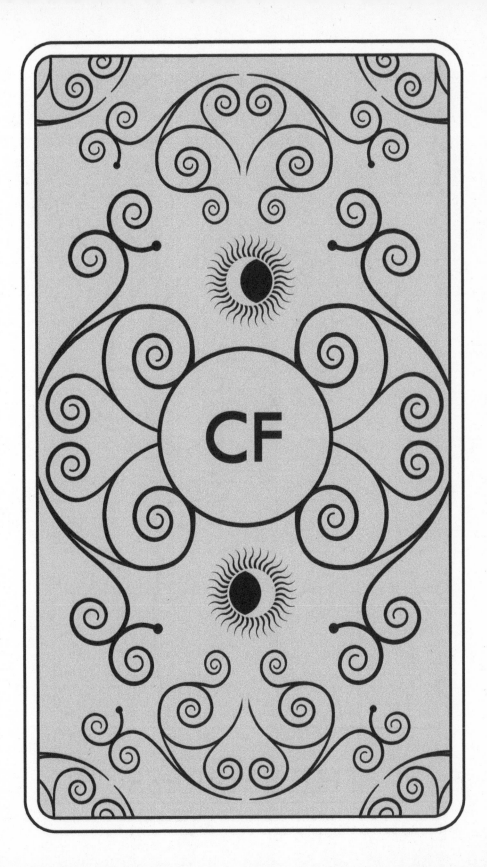

THE EMPRESS

Lucian kissed Jaxon leisurely, even knowing what was outside somewhere waiting for them. When he lifted his head, he smiled down at her. "What did you bring home with you this time, little troublemaker?"

"I hurried to get here to meet Sandu's lifemate. I never get to meet other women. You keep me locked up like some prisoner." She turned her laughing gaze on Adalasia. "Beware of these sexy, charming ancients. They con you into loving them beyond distraction, and then you find yourself in a gilded cage." She gestured at the beautiful mansion.

Lucian's sharp teeth bit her shoulder, and she yipped and then laughed. "Go hunt. All of you. No doubt the master vampire and his pawns took the bait. The poor helpless female traveling home all alone. Sheesh. He should have known when the wolves didn't attack that I was under guard. He'll get a surprise with so many hunters. Sandu, introduce us, please."

Sandu had never met Jaxon, but she knew him, apparently, through Lucian's mind, something that easily happened between lifemates. He gave her a small courtly, respectful bow. "Adalasia, this is Jaxon, Lucian's lifemate." *Adalasia is not fully Carpathian.* He sent that to her through Lucian. "We have only begun our journey together." Adalasia gave him a suspicious look. More and more, he feared their connection was growing stronger, and keeping things from her was going to be difficult.

A shadow crossed Jaxon's face, but she held out both hands to Adalasia. "Welcome to our home. Are you hungry? Or thirsty? We have the guest room prepared."

Sandu knew they would wave a hand and put a room together swiftly over the ground where he would sleep.

"There's so much to see, I'm not tired at all," Adalasia denied. "Your home is so incredibly beautiful. Do the wolves really travel with you?"

Sandu could see that his woman was going to be kept occupied by Lucian's lifemate. He reached out to Lucian. *Are they safe while we hunt?*

The undead cannot come into my home. It is sealed against them. My woman would call to me if they got close, as would my wolves. We are free to pursue the vampire and his pawns.

Sandu thought it strange that a master vampire would make the mistake of traveling into Lucian's home territory. He might mask that he resided in the area, but word got out, and there was the wolf pack. They were dangerous and a large one. They didn't wander over miles as most wolves did. They stayed close to the large estate.

A trap for you? Drawing you out, Lucian?

Perhaps. It could be. I have given that idea some thought, but if it is so, he chose the wrong time. With five ancients to hunt with me, I hardly think a master vampire is going to win this game.

Sandu had to agree, the familiar predator settling over him easily, naturally. At once, his emotions were gone and all color dimmed. He cloaked his presence, as did Nicu, Benedek, Petru and Siv as they drifted out the front door when Lucian stood in the center of it, allowing the light to silhouette him there. If the master vampire had left his spies to tell him when Lucian began tracking him, Lucian wanted those spies to be very aware of him.

Lucian stepped through and closed the heavy door with a wave of his hands and wove the safeguards. The five ancients added their unseen weave to Lucian's to ensure the entire house was surrounded above, below and on every side to keep all evil out while they hunted.

Jaxon reminded Adalasia of a beautiful little fairy princess. Adalasia was tall and had curves. Lots of them. She'd never minded that she wasn't the fashionable, slender model seen on magazine covers. Her life was dedicated from the time she was born to a purpose. She'd been taught that. Raised to believe it. She didn't think too much about her looks until moments like this one, and then just for a brief minute.

"Don't," Jaxon said softly.

Adalasia wasn't going to pretend she didn't understand. "I know I'm being silly. It's just that Sandu is such a beautiful man. He could have anyone. I don't really understand why he's attracted to me." She didn't. She knew the legend in her family, but it didn't make sense that the man was as gorgeous as Sandu. She had believed . . . now she didn't. Or at least she no longer trusted in that fairytale.

"He can't actually have anyone else," Jaxon said. "He can only see you. He can only want you. He's only attracted to you. And when I say 'attracted,' I mean passionately attracted. It's intense. All the time. Never goes away. He won't stray and he won't look at other women. It would be impossible for him to do that. You're his lifemate. You hold the other half of his soul. Did he speak the ritual binding words to you?"

Jaxon sank into the chair opposite Adalasia's and waved her hand to rid the library of all the others. An antique table edged in gold appeared beside Adalasia's chair. On it were a bottle of water and a glass of juice. "The juice always helped me in the beginning. Try that and see if you can get it down."

"Yes, he did," Adalasia admitted, a touch of bitterness in her voice. She couldn't help it, even though she didn't want to discuss her business with a complete stranger. In a way, even that felt like a betrayal of Sandu, when she didn't owe him anything. Not when they weren't partners.

Jaxon's eyebrow shot up, and then she sighed. "He didn't have your consent, did he?"

Adalasia shook her head. "No, he most certainly did not. He took my blood, too, without my consent."

"Did you feel the binding when he said the words to you?"

She nodded. "I know we're connected." She heard the hesitation. Knew Jaxon heard it as well. "He keeps saying things that I don't under-stand. And he's not telling me things I'm very aware he doesn't want me to know right now. He doesn't have one bit of remorse for binding us together. Or for taking my blood. He did something else, didn't he?"

She kept her gaze steady on Jaxon's face. On her eyes. On her expression. She was adept at reading people. She had to be in her profession. She was always careful when reading tarot cards for people. They always said they wanted an honest reading, but there were times when honesty wasn't what anyone was really prepared for. She couldn't tell a mother her child wasn't going to live through a devastating illness, not when the parents had come to her desperate to hear differently. She did her best to prepare them, but she wouldn't come out and read the absolute grim reality.

There were so many instances when her intuition told her to walk softly. She always listened to that. She also watched for telltale signs the body gave. Right now, Jaxon was in the position Adalasia found herself in often—debating how much truth to give her.

Adalasia lifted her chin. "I'm tough, Jaxon. I might get shocked, but I'm tough."

"That isn't the question. I was tough," Jaxon confessed. "Beyond tough. I still went down for a brief time."

Her stomach knotted all over again. She pressed her hand there. Tight. What could possibly be so bad?

Do you have need of me? There are plenty of hunters. I like to keep my hand in, but it is not necessary. I will return to you, ewal emninumam. You have only to use our connection at any time, and I will come to you.

When Sandu poured into her mind like that, she welcomed him. She had realized how alone she felt even with Jaxon in the room. He gave her warmth and made her feel safe in an unfamiliar situation. She hadn't realized until that moment how much the sharing of one's mind could make one feel so close.

I'm fine. Getting to know Jaxon, she reassured him.

"Sandu explained to me that he is not a vampire but rather a Carpathian. He said he survives on blood but doesn't kill when taking blood." She needed confirmation. She didn't know why. Had she grown so mistrustful of Sandu simply because he'd bound them together without her consent?

Adalasia rubbed her temples, frowning. It was more than that. He was keeping something extremely important from her. She knew he was, but she was just as guilty. She couldn't exactly condemn him when she was doing the same thing.

"If one kills while taking blood, they would be giving up their soul and choosing to become vampire," Jaxon said.

Jaxon wasn't exactly volunteering information. Adalasia didn't blame her. She wouldn't want to be in her shoes, maybe accidentally saying something that would send Adalasia running from her lifemate. Jaxon could see she wasn't as enamored with him as she should be—or at least she was still at a crossroads.

"I know you came here for answers, Adalasia," Jaxon finally said. "But I have to ask you this. Do you have the absolute resolve to go forward no matter how difficult and terrifying the journey is? No matter where your path takes you?"

Adalasia's heart went crazy, accelerating like a runaway train. She pressed her palm to her chest and took several deep breaths to calm herself. To slow her breathing. Sandu would notice if she kept it up, and she didn't want him returning or monitoring the conversation.

"When I read the cards, they indicated more than once that my path, if I chose to take it with Sandu, would be extremely difficult and terrifying." The admission came out a little strangled. Her hands were trembling so much she wanted to sit on them.

She looked around the library and took comfort from the old leather-bound books. She liked older things. She'd always been surrounded by antiques growing up. She knew them, their ages, their value, often their origins. Standing, she moved over to the bookshelves to the oldest-looking books kept behind glass. There were gloves sitting in a small jeweled case so fingers never touched those pages if one wanted to open the books.

"Yes, Jaxon, I'm resolved. I'm afraid of the truth, just as some of those coming to me for readings are afraid to hear what the cards say, but in my case, I prefer the truth. It might take me some time to fully get to a place of acceptance, but I will get there. I know that I stepped on the path willingly and began the journey with him. I have no intention of backing out. I was born for this, and I was trained from the time I was a child to be at his side when we get to the end."

Adalasia turned to face Jaxon. "So, if you wouldn't mind, please tell me what it is that Sandu isn't telling me." She knew it wasn't fair to ask the other woman, but it wasn't fair that she didn't know.

Jaxon was silent for a long while. She sighed. "There are some things best to ask your lifemate. He can't lie to you, Adalasia. He can try to side-step answering you if you allow it, but he can't lie to you. In the world I now live in, I have to abide by the rules. We can't interfere in a relationship between lifemates. He bound you to him; that makes you his lifemate."

Adalasia wasn't going to put her on the spot any further. It wouldn't be fair. She nodded. "Do you know much about vampires?"

"I was born human just as you were," Jaxon said. "I was a cop with knowledge of serial killers but not vampires. And yes, such evil creatures do exist. No doubt, your lifemate would prefer you never meet one. I prefer to never meet one, yet I have, all too often. They can only be killed by extracting their heart and incinerating it. Believe me, it isn't easy. Their blood is like acid. No matter what you do to them, they rise again and again unless the heart is incinerated. They're hideous creatures."

Adalasia wasn't shocked in the least. That was another thing her unique deck of tarot cards had prepared her for. She knew there were monsters in the world. Not human monsters. She had never encountered one, but she knew there was more than one kind. She did know that Sandu had battled the undead for centuries. He'd told her he had, and she believed him. Having Jaxon confirm it only made his confession all the more real.

"I was taught to believe in demons," Adalasia admitted. She turned back to look at the titles behind the glass case. The tomes were very old, and she was drawn to antiques, to anything old. "I trained from the time I was a child to fight them. Just in case. I also prepared just in case the stranger came. It was predicated with each birth of a daughter that he might come. If he didn't by a certain age, I was to find a husband, a man of a certain bloodline, and we would produce a child—a daughter. She would be given the same legacy."

"That's fascinating," Jaxon said. "Absolutely fascinating. The soul had to have been passed from mother to daughter at conception. Did you know? Were you always aware you were the keeper of his soul?" There was curiosity in Jaxon's voice. "It would be such a heavy burden to carry."

It was Adalasia's turn to hesitate. Her family's legacy was a secret, one she guarded carefully. Her fingers ached to stroke the cards in the pouch kept on her body at all times. They gave her comfort and courage. "I knew we were soulmates. He carried a piece of me with him, and I carried a piece of him with me. I don't know if that makes any sense. I thought, when I heard him so clearly, it was because of that. Our souls reaching for one another."

She felt silly saying that aloud to anyone. No one talked about souls. Hearts—yes. Souls weren't something anyone could define. Not even her. She *felt* the weight of Sandu's soul often. It wasn't a burden. It was a gift. That was how she would have described it. She was fierce about protecting that gift. She had never said a word to anyone—not even her mother—about the strange feeling of having something so valuable and immense in her that she knew belonged to someone else.

She'd been a young girl—a teen—when she first became aware of that gift. It was as if she could feel another being far off calling to her. The voice was too faint to be heard, but when she felt alone—and more often than not, she was alone—that gift inside her comforted her. In her family, they didn't encourage friendships. They were always polite and, on the outside, appeared to be outgoing, but they kept to themselves. No child was invited into their home. There were no birthday parties. She was often lonely, but she would wrap herself in that warmth, and the loneliness would be gone.

"Anything of Sandu was never a burden for me. He . . . saved me more than once. I have been in training most of my life, separate from others. That can be very lonely."

Jaxon was so silent that Adalasia faced her again and caught the look of complete understanding. She knew. She had firsthand knowledge of what Adalasia was talking about. Maybe they were more alike than she'd first thought.

Jaxon's fingers stroked her throat. "There was a serial killer in my life for years. He stalked me, believing he was my father. He killed anyone he thought came between the two of us. No one was safe, not even a neighbor who was kind to me. I was afraid to smile at anyone, even a clerk in a grocery store."

"Jaxon," Adalasia whispered. "How terrible."

"No one seemed to be able to stop him. He killed my family and then my foster family. Everyone I cared about. I was terrified for Lucian."

"But Lucian is Carpathian, with so many powers."

"Exactly. And used to being so powerful. He dismisses the ordinary as if it could never harm him when that isn't true. Carpathians are not immortal. They have longevity, but they can be killed under the right circumstances. He took so many chances." Her voice trembled as if she were reliving those days.

It occurred to Adalasia that Sandu would do the same. "Is he still like that?"

"He tries not to be and I remind him. Constantly. I think I'm a nag. There is a society of humans that hunt us. They say they hunt vampires, but they don't care if they kill us or vampires. Some, I think, are legitimate. They've run across vampires who have killed loved ones. They've seen evil and want to destroy it. Others like the power of killing and go on witch hunts, naming enemies without proof. They're dangerous, but often, because they are so powerful, Carpathians don't take them as seriously as they should."

In spite of the fact that Adalasia didn't quite trust Sandu, and she didn't yet know how they were going to work out their differences, she knew they had to work them out. She also didn't want anything happening to him. "Thank you for warning me. I'll see to it that Sandu takes heed of human danger. I know that wherever we go, the Castellos will follow us. They are my enemies. He dismisses them as well because they're human. I know they are more than that. I just don't know what they are yet."

She turned back to the books, almost a compulsion now. "May I look at these? I can barely contain myself. I know how to handle old manuscripts. I promise I will be very careful."

"I can provide the proper temperature and humidity the books need while you look through them. Lucian taught me," Jaxon said.

The glass door swung open. Adalasia found her heart pounding. There were so many books that were worth a fortune. Books that belonged in museums. Books that only scholars would treasure. Her gaze found one that immediately intrigued her. It was leather-bound. The leather was clearly a hide of some sort that had been hand-cured. The interesting thing was, the lettering on the edges was in a language long dead. Long gone. She had been forced to study it from the time she was a child and thought her mother crazy for making her learn it, and yet now, she understood.

Tribal Italian and Rome: Unification or Defeat. She pulled it off the shelf and very carefully opened it. Without a doubt, the tome was written in the long-forgotten language that had been swallowed whole by Latin and other dialects. This was pure Etruscan. One more reason to know she was on the right path. The journey might be frightening and difficult, but how could details like this not be a confirmation that Sandu and she were exactly where they were supposed to be?

Jaxon came close. "Is that helpful to you?"

"It must be. Do you know anything about the tribal Italians?"

Jaxon shook her head. "I'm embarrassed to say, I never thought in terms of Italy having tribes, but of course, they had people there pre-Rome and after."

"Exactly. The history is very diverse. That's why their looks are diverse. If my family insisted that I learn a long-forgotten language that was swallowed up centuries ago, then it's safe to say that's a huge clue to Sandu's past. He must have ties that go back to that tribe of people."

"That's a huge leap, Adalasia."

"I always go with my intuition, and this feels right to me. His family could have been somehow involved with the Etruscan tribe. There were quite a lot of wars going on during that time period. So many tribes fighting for territories. There were migrations from Greece, Syria, Central Asia, Macedonia and Northern Europe. That's why you see blond and blue-eyed Italians. Don't forget the Sabines. There were so many more. The point I'm making is, Lucian said that Carpathians didn't have surnames. That they changed them depending on how long they stayed in one place to blend in and not have anyone become suspicious of them."

Jaxon nodded. "Lucian explained that to me. He actually told me he would re-create our house if I loved it, and bring our wolves, or their descendants, but we would have to move occasionally. He told me we would have to shed one name and take on another through the centuries. It is the only way to ensure we stay alive and our species are not ever found out by humans. That made me a little sad because I love our name. He comes from a very respected lineage within the Carpathians. They still use the name amongst themselves, he said. So I guess it isn't lost. I would want any child we have to bear that name."

Adalasia hadn't considered children with Sandu. They were too new. But his name. She turned it over and over in her mind. "In very ancient days, they didn't take surnames, but as time went on, it became necessary. The practice of taking a surname in Rome began in the more affluent households. Sandu goes by Sandu Berdardi. If he kept that name, or just occasionally went back to it, the name could easily have been shortened from Sandu di Berdardo. A common practice in Rome when first assigning a surname was simply stating the boy's name, "son of," and the father's name. In this case, it would be Sandu, son of Berdardo."

Jaxon lifted an eyebrow. "You seem very well versed in the history of Italy."

"I was homeschooled. I am sadly lacking in some things other children are very well versed in. This I was drilled in over and over. Fortunately, I found it fascinating."

"So that would make his father's name Berdardo," Jaxon said. "Maybe one of the Carpathians would recognize that name."

"That's definitely my hope," Adalasia said.

"Lucian's brother Gabriel traveled extensively, and he knows a lot of Carpathians. He's in France. I have this very strong feeling you should go see him. He would welcome you. Francesca, his lifemate, has amazing quilts she weaves strong safeguards into. You might have need of one."

Once more, Jaxon's fingers went to her throat. "You could use all the help and guidance you can get. Perhaps you might seek them out, Adalasia."

France. The thought settled over her. She knew Sandu was with her. The destination felt right to him as well. *Do you recognize the name Berdardo?*

I am sorry, Sivamet, I do not recognize this name. I will return shortly, but I am about to go into battle and must break contact while I engage with the undead.

I would like to stay with you. She wanted to witness a vampire from a safe distance. More, she needed to know he was safe at all times.

Sandu groaned. *I do not want any of them to know you exist.*

Her heart nearly stopped at his admission. Then it began to pound. She could tell he didn't want her with him. *Any of them? As in more than one? Sandu. There are more than one of those evil creatures you told me about?*

Breathe for me, ewal emninumam, there is more than one hunter chasing the master vampire. You cannot be with me. If you gave yourself away . . .

I wouldn't.

I will be injured. When battling a vampire, a hunter is always injured. You must go. He withdrew from her mind.

Very carefully, Adalasia returned the book to its place behind the glass. Her lifemate wasn't going to dismiss her quite so easily. She would obey his instructions to stay silent and not give herself away no matter what, and she would creep into his mind without his knowledge. She knew he was an ancient, and because he was going into battle, his senses would be heightened, but he wouldn't be looking for his lifemate, with the lowest of energies to drift into his mind so silently and small, settling into the tiniest groove where no one would ever find her, least of all Sandu.

It was Abascus Baros who spotted the woman moving alone toward the large sprawling mansion nearly hidden in the shadows of the mountains. Not one of his pathetic, fawning pawns had seen her. Not his servants, the two vampires that were inching closer to becoming master vampires, or the ones serving just below them, four of them he could usually rely on for bringing exquisite gifts—men, women and children for him to feast on.

He was sated, having dined well on the inhabitants of a farmhouse several miles down from where she was. He would have kept going, flying over the forest, but there was something intriguing about the way the night hid her from him. He circled back around, soundless, dropping just a little lower, and then finally taking the shape of an owl to settle onto the branch of a tree in order to watch her. The tree shuddered beneath him, branches shivering, the needles withering. He hissed his impatience and waved one wing to stop the process. Nature had a way of finding him repugnant. He didn't mind.

His servants called out to him, and he waved them to silence, annoyed that they would dare interrupt him. This woman had totally captured his attention, something very hard to do. He didn't want to take his gaze from her, because even if he blinked, she seemed to disappear. He was aware, at times, of shadows slinking in the trees around her. She didn't seem aware of them—or of any danger. She just walked at a steady pace toward that mansion, right up the drive.

He should swoop down and grab her. Call out. He could stop any human with his voice. He opened his mouth to demand she halt, but only the squawk of the owl came out. He hadn't made such an amateur mistake in over eight hundred years. He used the owl's capability to rotate 270 degrees to ensure none of his followers had observed his error.

A few owls sat in the other trees. None dared to share the one he had settled in. They knew to stop the shivering of the branches, but the lesser pawns, still unable to control their impulses and power, couldn't prevent the sap from boiling out of the cracks like black blood. The sight was mesmerizing. He could barely pull his gaze away.

Wind softly shifted the branches, blowing through the needles, creating a strange tune that echoed through the mind of the owl. A clicking of branches. A rhythm. He used such a beat to hypnotize his enemies into inaction while he gained control of them, growing near much like a wolf as it locked in on its prey. The strange noise was very attractive to the owl, to all of them, and they turned their heads this way and that, looking for the source of the sound.

Abascus pulled back abruptly, forcing his mind away from the owl's. He was the driving force, not the bird. He was in total control. In command. He searched the ground once more for his prey. She was at the thick door already, looking small and enticing. Something about her drew him like a magnet. She turned and looked out at the night, at the shadowy shapes slinking in and out of the trees, then into the surrounding forest, even up at the trees where the owls waited. She looked with unseeing eyes, and deep within the owl's body, Abascus gave an evil smile of pure satisfaction. Humans were never aware, even when they were stalked.

Once more, as she turned, placing her hand on the doorknob, the master vampire sent out an order to stop her in her tracks. The mansion was enormous, and he didn't want to have to search for a window or door that was open. Nor did he want to have to resort to trickery to be invited in.

Again, when his voice should have commanded her, nothing emerged but the call of the owl. This time, the others had to have heard. The woman went into her home without a backward glance, leaving him sitting in the owl's body, his temper rising. He took to the air, flying through the forest with all the skill of the owl but the speed of the vampire. He needed the outlet of feeling the air under his wings while he decided if delaying his journey was worth going back to seek answers.

He decided to take one spin around the mansion in an effort to understand why the woman drew him to her. He turned back, slowing his speed, and led his followers back in the direction of the estate. It was a large one for the remoteness of the area. As he approached the house itself, an uneasy feeling came over him. Dread. An oppressive trepidation that came close to actual fear.

Abascus Baros did not feel fear. He instilled terror in humans, vampires and Carpathians alike. Even the most skilled Carpathian hunters avoided him. He would *not* be intimidated. He couldn't afford to show he was in the least affected by whatever oppressive waves this structure was giving off—and he recognized now that the house was safeguarded. A Carpathian, then. The woman belonged to a Carpathian. A lifemate. He had been so close to acquiring a Carpathian lifemate.

He shifted from the shape of the owl to that of a man, the one he used to be. Tall and imposing, quite stocky. Black hair and a neatly trimmed beard and mustache. He clothed himself in a suit. He liked the finer things and made certain his clothes were always of the best quality. He expected his followers to have the same. They were not allowed to ever look disheveled. When they joined him, they learned very quickly to keep up appearances. It was only in battle that he allowed them to appear as they truly were.

He stood at the iron gates of the house, the closest he could get. Clearly, the Carpathian had protected his home with a weave above and below, as well as around all sides of it. Abascus was not going to bother trying to unravel the safeguards. He would set a trap for the Carpathian. Few vampires would ever venture this way. There wasn't enough prey to make it worthwhile. The Carpathian wouldn't have much in the way of experience in hunting vampires.

With a low bow, he turned and made his way into the forest, deliberately allowing a trail to be left behind for the Carpathian to find should he venture out. Abascus could afford a day or two delay in his travels in order to give his lazier followers a chance to learn battle skills. They certainly could use more experience, and he would get the ultimate prize— a Carpathian woman.

The last thing Sandu wanted was for Adalasia to stay connected to him while he hunted the undead. He couldn't afford for her to see him the way he really was. He appeared civilized to the outside world, but he wasn't. He wouldn't ever be again. He had gone well beyond his time to live and he knew it. All of those who had chosen to lock themselves behind the thick walls of the monastery had known it.

They were secreted there for a reason. They had kept their code of honor. They stayed true to their lifemate, but each of them had gone beyond the time most Carpathian hunters had ever been expected to survive. Souls could be blackened. They could be tattered. They could have holes. A lifemate repaired that damage if she could be found in time. Every male was born knowing that truth.

Those Carpathian hunters living too long went beyond the whispers of temptation. They found absolute silence. They found the rage of the kill. The scarring of the soul. The scarring that couldn't be taken away. The thicker that scar, the worse the berserker's rage when battling. Sandu knew he wasn't alone, because anyone first entering the monastery had been asked the question of the scars versus tattering on the soul.

Strangely, Sandu didn't actually *feel* when he was in battle. The emotion was there, though. He recognized it; he just couldn't feel it. Glacier cold—volcano hot. He ripped and tore without hesitation—with a craving for violence that far exceeded anything that should have been. He didn't even recognize that it was a craving or a compulsion, but Sandu knew it had to be.

Sandu couldn't ever allow Adalasia to see that part of him. She feared demons, and he had tied her to one. She was courageous. She didn't back down and she was determined. She also, so far, was polite and hadn't tried to go beyond the very forefront of his mind. They spoke to each other. He felt her fill those lonely cracks and spaces, but she never tried to push beyond the barriers that would lead to the memories of his hunting the undead. It was a good thing, because he hid those memories behind strong shields. If she found them and questioned him, he would have to tell her the truth—that he wouldn't share those battles with her.

Lucian was leading the master vampire and his little army into the position he wanted him. There were eleven vampires. Three were going to be extremely skilled. Four more were question marks and not to be taken lightly. Four were pawns the master would throw at Lucian to test his skills. Sandu doubted if they had much in the way of battle experience. They were newly turned, which meant, as hunters, they had been skilled, but they didn't yet have control over their voracious appetites. That made them very vulnerable on the battlefield.

Lucian was the bait. He appeared a younger, much more naïve Carpathian, tentatively following the trail of the master vampire. Sandu recognized the master to be Abascus Baros. He'd run across him a time or two but hadn't bothered with him because other hunters had been after him. He was a little surprised to see the two others with him. He had heard rumors many centuries earlier that both Ambrus Halmi and Barnat Kardos had chosen to give up their souls to become undead. That they followed Abascus when they had to be so close to becoming master vampires themselves was another surprise. Most skilled vampires didn't serve another. They had egos. Huge egos.

The three very skilled vampires thought they were in for a show. They had spread out, all three choosing to blend into the gray of the boulders making up the backdrop for the waterfall as it poured in a long steady stream down a rocky ravine, winding through the rocks and trees to the small creek that flowed to the river.

Trees rose in all directions, surrounding the falls. The four vampires, servants to the exalted three, had taken their positions, secreting themselves in the trees. One in a trunk beside the waterfall. One high in the branches. A third had shifted into the form of a mountain lion and lay stretched out on top of a fallen log, blending into his surroundings. The fourth had chosen to keep the body of a bird of prey, the owl. He was perched in the branches of a tall tree, his beady eyes on the lone Carpathian male as he slowly unraveled the trail of the master vampire.

Sandu and his four brethren each chose a target. They drifted with the wind. He was no longer in the body of a bat but had assumed the shape of nothing more than the mist, moving like fingers of fog through the trees. He went right on past the waterfall, circling behind Abascus. Benedek drifted behind Barnat, while Petru had chosen to pit his skills against Ambrus. Those three vampires were the most skilled and experienced.

Siv and Nicu each had to take two of the guardians, who would try to protect their master with everything they were. Depending on the ages of the undead and how many hunters they had battled and defeated, if they had fought together before, all of that would determine how difficult it would be to defeat them. Lucian would have to kill all four of the pawns. The ancient, legendary Carpathian continued forward, winding in and out of the trees, appearing almost to stumble as he leaned down to examine a bruised leaf on a bush.

The four pawns leapt out of hiding, surrounding Lucian, so eager to fall on him and drink his rich Carpathian blood, they hadn't managed to keep their true forms from showing. Already, time was telling on their skin, some of it sloughing off to reveal the maggots underneath and the white skulls. Tufts of hair on their heads looked bizarre, and noses were simply holes on flat bones.

Lucian straightened to his full height. "Gentlemen. I see you have come seeking the justice of our people." His voice was low. Velvet soft. Unmistakable in its power.

Abascus caught his breath audibly. "Lucian. Lucian Daratrazanoff." He nearly fell off the boulder he was seated on, looking for a way to escape. He stood up very slowly, trying not to draw the eye of the legendary hunter. When he turned, his pasty skin paled even more. "Sandu," he whispered. "Sandu Berdardi."

Sandu gave a small, courtly bow. "I have not had the pleasure of an actual introduction, although I know you by reputation, Abascus."

Abascus quickly glanced, with satisfaction, both right and left. His lesser vampires had not let him down. Both rose with grim smiles to face the ancient hunter as well. They took their cue from Abascus, acting civil, when neither would prefer to face such a skilled hunter.

"I fear you chose a bad night to pit your inexperienced pawns against Lucian. He has several visitors." Sandu waved his hand. "My friend Benedek. He wishes to try his ancient techniques against one of your best. And Petru. You must have heard of him. He has been around for centuries. His fighting skills are legendary. Petru will be more than happy to engage with your good friend." He nodded toward Ambrus.

Sandu didn't wait. The scent of the battle was on him. A thousand years. Two. Time no longer mattered. Only this. There was only this in his world, the destruction of pure evil. The power moved through his veins. The inching of glacier ice. The ice burned white-hot. So hot it turned blue, like the densest glacier. That blue turned to a flickering flame. The flame smoldered in his eyes, glowed there in the dark, going blue to red, then fiery red. That same flame moved in his veins, slow, like that sluggish burn of magma in a volcano. He welcomed that burn, felt that fire spreading.

Abascus was a master vampire, and as such, he would not be easy to defeat. Sandu was close, and even as he nodded toward Ambrus, he stepped right into Abascus and drove his fist into the master vampire's chest as the burn inside his veins turned into a fiery explosion. Black blood coated his fist and forearm. Acid burned skin away as his fingers stretched, reaching, his nails lengthening into sharp talons, digging for the wizened, blackened heart.

Abascus screamed and slammed his forehead hard against Sandu's head—only at the last moment, Sandu changed the composition of his forehead so that when Abascus struck, he hit pure steel. Black blood erupted from Abascus's head, pouring over his eyes, and with it, tiny white writhing parasites burst out of his skull.

That red fiery hell in Sandu demanded he keep smashing that steel block into Abascus's forehead, obliterating all flesh until it was all white jagged bones and leeching brains, volumes of black acid and those tiny writhing parasites. All the while, Sandu continued digging deep until his nails found the heart and grasped it. He began to extract it from the body.

Abascus contorted, desperate to shift, but Sandu would not release the heart, not even when the vampire slammed his own fist into the hunter's chest in order to try to get to his heart. Sandu was prepared for just such a move. He had fought master vampires for centuries. Once this close, there were only so many moves one could make. The fist came up against that same composition of steel, smashing all the bones in the hand.

With his free hand, Sandu's nails lengthened, and he dug into Abascus's neck and throat with razor-sharp talons, slicing through flesh to get at arteries. Acid poured from the master vampire along with the wiggling parasites. Sandu shoved his hand through the throat to the back of the neck, reaching for the spinal cord as he closed his other fist around that blackened, wizened heart.

In desperation, Abascus shifted his legs to that of a large cat, using long claws to rake at Sandu's thighs and groin. Sandu continued to withdraw the heart, feeling the first rake down his left thigh but turning his body to keep the vampire from scoring his groin. In truth, he was caught up in the red haze of battle, beyond all feeling, by the need to rend and tear the despicable evil creature in front of him, intent on inflicting the most damage possible as he took the heart of the undead. The claws tore at his thighs in desperation, but Sandu changed the composition of his body to break the nails on the talons. He had been at this too many centuries not to know every trick the vampire knew. Now he had the heart out of the body.

Lightning cracked across the dark sky. Abascus took a step back on the boulder, his face contorting into a mask of fury and terror. Sandu brought one foot up and kicked him square in the chest, driving him backward over the falls. As he did, he tossed the blackened heart into the air and with one hand directed the lightning bolt straight at it. The white-hot spear hit the blackened organ, reducing it to ash instantly and then arcing down the rocks straight to the body of the master vampire, where he sat in a daze staring up at Sandu in confusion. The flash of light consumed him instantly, leaving nothing but ash behind. That slowly disappeared from the rocks, washed away by the water pounding down from above.

Still shaking with the adrenaline of battle, Sandu immediately bathed his arms in the light in order to rid his body of the acid before turning to aid his brethren. Flashes of lightning lit up the night sky. He could see his brethren didn't need any help whatsoever. It didn't surprise him. They had all been at this a very long time.

As he turned his attention to his wounds, he felt a small shadow in his mind retreat. His very disobedient lifemate. Adalasia.

THE EMPEROR

S andu had thought to heal his wounds and hunt for blood to replace what he'd lost, but he had to rethink this night. Assess Adalasia's reaction. She was his lifemate, and as such, it would be difficult, if not impossible, for her not to need to heal him when she saw the extent of his wounds. She might be repelled by his actions in battle, but she wouldn't be able to resist the necessity to care for him—even to give him blood. That would work in his favor.

Sandu looked into his mind as he approached the house, seeing that small, shivering woman in the tiny crevice of his mind. She had wanted to see how to kill a vampire in case she needed to aid him in battle. She had been trained to fight demons. He caught glimpses of her battle technique with various weapons. She was intrigued, wondering if any of the systems she'd been taught would aid her in destroying the undead.

She followed his every move, horrified at his love of the battle, at his need to destroy the undead in the brutal way he had. He hadn't felt the emotions, but *she* had. He had feared that would happen if she ever saw him in battle. Sandu could try to assume a mantle of civility. He could even hide his predatory nature under the guise of feigned humor quite a bit of the time, but there was no disguising what he was when he went into battle.

Adalasia had been taught from the time she was a child to recognize a demon from the underworld by the fierce glow of their red eyes. By the casual way they killed. She would see that he killed without feeling, at least on the surface. Beneath it . . . he knew where he couldn't see, she could. There she would feel the joy of battle, the need of his to destroy, uncaring what happened to him in the process. He was her lifemate. He belonged to her. That was an ultimate sin, and he was committing another by manipulating her into giving him her blood.

Sandu wanted to feel remorse for what he was about to do, but his every instinct drove him. Compelled him. He was ancient, and she was his to protect in the way of their people. They had enemies. Too many. His enemies. Hers. They had to be prepared for the worst possible scenario. *Both* had to be prepared.

She stood in the hallway alone, trying to look brave when he materialized in front of her. He hadn't taken the time to clean up from the battlefield, wanting to look his worst, knowing she wasn't certain about him and their relationship, but the ties between them would compel her to take care of him.

Adalasia's blue eyes darkened to pure cobalt as they moved over him, taking in the blood dripping from his neck and shoulder, his chest, and lastly, his thighs and legs. He heard her anguished gasp, and then one small, trembling hand crept to her throat defensively. "Sandu." She whispered his name.

"I came to you as quickly as possible," he said. "Lucian told me they prepared a suite for us to use. It's on this floor at the back of the house."

He held out his hand. She hesitated but then slipped her hand in his. He could feel her trembling as he walked her down the wide hallway to the heavy oak door. She kept casting anxious glances to the blood on his neck and legs.

"Sandu? I didn't do as you asked me. I stayed in your mind when you went into battle." She made the confession in a low voice. "I'm sorry. I just felt it was very necessary to learn how to fight one of these horrible creatures. I was hoping I already had some of the skills. Jaxon did tell me the heart had to be incinerated. Sticking a hand into their chest and dragging their heart out looked extremely difficult." Her entire body shuddered.

She still wasn't looking at him, nor did she approach the more intimate mind connection. He brought her hand to his mouth, inhaling her scent. Taking her into his lungs. After the foul stench of the undead, the fragrance of his woman was intoxicating.

"It was Abascus's bad luck that Lucian had so many of the brethren visiting him this evening. Jaxon had already dulled his senses. He wasn't thinking clearly, staying when just the presence of the wolves should have been a warning to him. The wolves didn't attack Jaxon on her way home. The safeguards on the house should have warned him. When he couldn't call out to Jaxon, her power was more than it should have been against a master vampire, even for a Carpathian woman, but he paid no heed. That is the ego of a vampire." He gave her that insight.

He reached around her and opened the door in human fashion rather than simply waving his hand and willing it open. Adalasia moved ahead of him into the room and then turned to face him. He stepped inside and closed the door, taking the opportunity to lean against the thick oak while her gaze slid anxiously over him. He heard her breath catch in her throat.

"Where else are you hurt?"

"It is of no consequence." He waved her concern away. "When one battles a master vampire, you know you are going to get injuries. I wanted to ensure you were safe before I sought blood and healed myself."

Her long lashes fluttered. "I wish you would explain things better to me, Sandu." Once more, her hand crept up protectively to her throat. "I want to see where else you're injured. And those injuries are not minor, are they?"

"Lifemates cannot lie to each other, Adalasia. Do not ask me questions you may not want the answers to." He didn't move from where he was draped against the door. Blood continued to run down his neck and legs. Now it was soaking through his shirt. He was going to have to do something about the mess fairly soon.

"I'm asking to see the injuries, and I want to know just how severe they really are. Also, if you need blood."

He indicated with a wave of his hand that she could step closer if she wanted to open his shirt and inspect his body. She tilted her chin at him. His woman. She certainly didn't lack courage. She stepped right into him and, unexpectedly, stroked a finger along his neck, tracing the outside line of where the undead had torn a chunk out of his skin.

Her touch sent little sparks dancing through his bloodstream. He didn't change expression, remaining stoic, but he felt what that touch did, not only to his heart and his blood but to those dangerous little wormlike vermin Abascus had managed to inject into his body. They went crazy, moving away from her light, rushing toward his heart so that he had to slow down his system to protect himself.

Those striking eyes of hers met his gaze as she slowly opened his shirt. He felt her brace before she looked down. Her breath caught. Turned ragged. She lifted anguish-filled eyes to his. She really was far too sensitive where he was concerned.

"You're a mess, Sandu."

"There is no need for you to be alarmed or to feel any pain."

Sandu could hear her heartbeat beginning to accelerate. Drum harder. His own heart followed the lead of hers. He needed blood. He had lost quite a bit. The others had gone hunting, seeking to replace what they'd lost in battle. He had gone to his lifemate.

She moistened her lips, her gaze once more dropping to the signs of battle, the wounds still dripping blood in little rivulets. She placed her palm over the worst one. "How do I stop this? What do I do as your . . ." Her brows went together. She looked up at him for clarification.

"Lifemate," he supplied, keeping his voice low and gentle.

"As your lifemate. Tell me what you need."

He had to keep the triumph tamped down. "You're certain, Adalasia? You don't need to help me. I will weave the safeguards for your protection and then go to one of my brethren for healing and blood. You need more time. Doing this would be a step into our world."

"I don't know what that means."

"I know you don't, *Sivamet*. I haven't had time to explain it to you, and my situation is rather dire right now." He slid his thumb over the curve of her lower lip.

"Then explain it to me *after*. Tell me what to do, Sandu." There was demand in her voice. "I am your lifemate. I'm already in your world. I'm willingly stepping onto the path with you, Sandu. I'm afraid, but that doesn't mean I'm going to run when it gets tough. You just need to communicate with me. I have to know what's expected of me and what to do in situations like this. I find that I need to help you. I not only want to, but I have to." She didn't look away from him, clearly wanting him to see she spoke the truth.

"I will need to take your blood. Once I'm strong again, I can heal these wounds easily. Then I'll hunt."

She nodded. "Just do it, then. Don't wait and lose more blood." She stepped closer to him, sweeping her hair from the side of her neck, still looking up at him.

For the first time, Sandu could see trepidation creeping into her eyes. She was offering her blood freely, but the idea of the giving scared her. He didn't wait. He swept her close to him, tight, so he could feel her body, that beautiful feminine form pressed against him. Her curves fit him perfectly, as if he was born for her—and he was.

Sivamet. My heart. He whispered the endearment into her mind as he bent his head toward her offering. Parts of his hair had escaped the leather ties holding it back and swept against her skin, making her shiver at the contact. His lips found the drumming of her pulse, frantic now, a beacon calling to him.

He kissed that rhythmic beat several times, his lips gentle, a brush of velvet, back and forth. Enticing her to calm down. To accept him. To feel something altogether different besides fear. He felt the flutters of arousal first in her mind.

Hän sívamak. He whispered *beloved* in her mind. Meaning it. She had come to be that to him as well. Occupying another's mind meant learning so much about them. His lifemate was far more than he had ever anticipated.

He used his teeth gently, merely scraping over her pulse, an erotic tease, nothing more. Goose bumps rose on her skin, and a small moan escaped her. Her long feathery lashes fluttered, and he felt the answering clench of her body.

Hän ku vigyáz sívamet és sielamet. Keeper of my heart and soul. He whispered the truth into her mind as his tongue slid over her pulse. He felt the slide of his teeth, and then he bit down, sinking deep, connecting them.

She cried out and threw her head back, angling her neck toward him to give him even greater access. Her breasts moved restlessly against him. Her arms slid up his chest to wrap around him, to hold him to her. *Sandu*, she whispered his name in his mind.

Nothing had prepared him. Not the earlier taking of her blood. Not hearing of lifemates from any who had them. The moment his teeth hooked into her vein and rich blood poured into him, *her* blood, meant for him, designed for him, his world became a different place. He was aware of her as a woman. As feminine. Her curves. Her sex. Her blood was an aphrodisiac, a siren's call beckoning to everything masculine in him.

His body reacted to hers. His heart did. His soul did. Her blood, freely given, rich now with the mixture of her awareness of what he was and that she was his lifemate, was a fireball rushing through his system, drowning him in sensation. She moaned again, the sound sensual, adding to the erotic feeling, settling like a wicked punch in his groin.

Temptation and caution warred for a moment, and then he lifted his head reluctantly, his tongue sweeping across the two little holes that were his marks on her. His claim. He would need more blood, but he had taken enough for an exchange and to heal his wounds.

Sandu caught Adalasia's chin and tipped her face up to his. She lifted her lashes slowly, her eyes slumberous, sexy. His body responded to his temptress in spite of his wounds. He gave her plenty of time to pull away from him, waiting, letting her know his intentions. Her eyes searched his, and then, as his lips descended toward hers, those incredible lashes lowered again, and his mouth was on hers.

Kissing Adalasia was like taking her blood. First the soft sensation of her lips, the heat of her mouth, the velvet of her tongue, then her taste wrapped in fire. He had been unable to identify her specific fragrance and taste until that very moment when she was wrapped in his arms and fire was rushing through his veins. The world spun and the ground moved. Magic. He didn't create it, she did. He could kiss her forever. Taste her forever. That subtle blend of Camelot rose, orange blossom, wild plum and clove. He had her now. That oh-so-subtle trail that she left on his skin and in his mouth was now in his lungs and heart. Imprinted forever on his soul.

He lifted his head, running the pad of his thumb over her lips. "With regret, we've got to stop. I've got to heal these wounds."

Adalasia nodded. "I think that would be best."

He didn't move. He couldn't. He held her to him, her body molding perfectly to his. "I've made quite the mess of your clothes. My blood is all over them. You aren't exactly the fainting type, are you?"

"No. I always thought it might be a good idea. My father had a booming voice, and when he was angry, he would yell very loud. Really, really loud. I used to think it would be a great idea to faint like the characters did in the Sherlock Holmes books I read. I seriously tried it, but nothing happened. Then my mother told me about the corsets they wore. She also told me my father just had a very loud voice, and he was really a grumpy bear, and he made her laugh when he was like that. I realized she would raise one eyebrow and just look at him when he yelled. I copied her, and I got so I liked that much better than trying to make myself faint."

Sandu laughed. "How old were you?"

"Twelve. I practiced the eyebrow thing in the mirror until I got it down." She tilted her head to show him. "You can expect to get that look quite a bit."

"What kinds of things did your father yell about?" Sandu asked. He managed to let her go, knowing he needed to heal the wounds in his body. "Yelling doesn't really accomplish anything. I've never really understood why humans do it."

"He would lose things all the time, and when he did, he yelled at himself. He spoke several languages, and he was very colorful in the way he reprimanded himself. I didn't appreciate how funny it was until my mother told me about the grumpy bear thing."

Sandu sank into the armchair. "This won't take long, Adalasia."

"Tell me what you're doing. How you're healing them."

"Carpathians heal wounds from the inside out. The ones on my thighs look bad, and they bled quite a bit but are not that deep. Abascus tore chunks from my shoulder and neck and managed a couple of times to penetrate the armor in my chest. Those are the worst and deepest wounds. I will have to be meticulous about fixing those."

He took his time, pushing out the parasites that were already replicating and doing their best to do as much damage as possible to his heart and lungs as fast as they could.

Adalasia gasped and leapt back across the room as she saw the loathsome, vile parasites the undead had transferred into Sandu's body in his attempt to kill him. The blood he had pushed through his pores, which was now in puddles on the floor, contained so many of the creatures that she was clearly horrified. She raised her eyes to his.

"He put those in you?"

Sandu waved his hand toward the window, and it opened on his silent command. "It is normal. He didn't have time to push many into my bloodstream. We surprised them, and the battle went our way very quickly. Master vampires are not normally so easily defeated."

She couldn't pull her gaze from the disturbing creatures in the pool of blood on the floor. They looked as if they were devouring the blood and growing fatter and larger as they wiggled and rolled mindlessly.

"Adalasia, you must move back even farther, away from the window. Go all the way to the door on the other side of the room and keep your eyes closed with your hand over your eyes. I have to incinerate them."

She shuddered, still not moving or lifting her gaze to his, as if she were hypnotized by the parasites. "How are you going to do that? We're in the house."

"I can control the lightning sword. You have to move back, *ewal emninumam*, so this can be done immediately. I have to make certain I am clean with another inspection before I feed and return to you."

Her gaze jumped to his. "Lightning sword?"

"You saw us wield the lightning," he reminded her, keeping his voice low and gentle. She was trying to process quite a lot of their world all in one night.

"Yes, in your mind. At a distance. It feels like a dream, Sandu."

She moved then, across the room, down two steps and across the sitting room to the door he had indicated. She wrapped her arms around her middle, heedless of the bloodstains his wounds had left on her clothing. Sandu couldn't bear to see them on her and removed them, but she didn't seem to notice, she kept looking at the vile worms growing fatter on his blood.

Adalasia was very pale, leaning now against the door, looking as though she might run if she had the strength. She wasn't afraid enough of him or his teeth to run. She wasn't afraid enough of being part of his world to run. She wasn't even afraid enough of the undead to run, but the parasites the vampire had in his toxic blood horrified her.

Sandu had no choice but to shield her as he built the storm. It wasn't as if she refused to close her eyes and cover them; it was more that she was so fixated on the bloated parasites that she couldn't look away. Almost as if she were spellbound.

Adalasia. He spoke her name sharply in her mind.

She blinked several times and then looked at him. Relief poured into him.

"Turn around, face the door, close your eyes and cover them now." He was still going to shield her, but it was possible the vampire had set some kind of trap in his parasites. Adalasia hadn't yet been caught in the web, but he wasn't taking chances that it might happen. When she hesitated, he commanded it and put a "push" into the order.

His lifemate obeyed, and he summoned the white-hot spear of lightning to incinerate the parasites and blood. He added his clothes to be burned just to be safe before releasing the spear. Once more, he checked his body, inspecting every organ to ensure he had removed the parasites from his system before he clothed himself and then released his lifemate from his command. To be extra safe, he removed her clothes, incinerated them and replaced them with clean, fresh-scented ones.

Adalasia turned slowly, one eyebrow lifted in a replica of the exact look she had shown him earlier. "You took over my will."

"Yes." He stood up and stretched his body carefully. He was weak. He really needed more blood.

"That wasn't very proper, Sandu, not without asking permission."

"I do not ever need permission to protect my lifemate." He had bound her without her permission, and he had already had one blood exchange and intended to have a second one—for her protection. That was the way of his people. He felt no remorse. He not only had the right; it was his duty to her. He intended to explain that very carefully to her when he explained coming into his world. He knew being part of his world meant something very different to her than it did to him.

Sandu, I am in the foyer. If you have need of blood, I have fed well this night, Siv said, using the path of the brethren.

It was not uncommon for the brethren to hunt for one another. Usually the gatekeeper of the monastery hunted for the others to keep them from having to go out and be tempted.

Thank you, brother. I will be there immediately.

His lifemate was back to giving him her distrustful look. He felt her withdrawal, arms going around her waist, her back to the wall as far from him as she could get.

"I will only be a few minutes, Adalasia. My brother has ensured I do not have to hunt this night for more blood. We will continue this discussion when I return."

Adalasia watched as Sandu simply disappeared. One moment he was sitting in the chair across from her, and the next he was literally gone. She hadn't even blinked. She looked down at the floor. There was no blood on the floor. Not one single drop. Those hideous white wiggling parasites that had repelled her were thankfully gone. The window was once more closed and locked. She looked down at her clothes. Not one drop of blood. Not one. Okay, then.

You do whatever you have to do tonight. I'm going to take a bath. A very long one.

Reading about legends and monsters and seeing journeys and futures in tarot cards was definitely not the same thing as living with them. She needed a little time to process what the hell was going on. Some things didn't seem real, even though she'd witnessed them.

Thank heavens, the water pouring out of the taps was steaming hot. There was even, to her shock, her favorite bath oil sitting right there for her to use. She pulled her hair up on top of her head to keep it from getting wet and stripped off the clothes she'd worn, grateful for the radiant heating on the floor Jaxon and Lucian seemed to have.

She left the lights off and lit the candles she found in the room. Six large ones smelling of her favorite scents. Oranges, roses, lemons and sandalwood. There was a hint of cedar. Everything she found comforting. Sinking down into the hot water made her groan, not realizing how the tension had managed to make her muscles so sore. This was perfection. She laid her head against the little cushion attached to the back of the tub and closed her eyes.

Sandu. At once she thought of him. It was odd when she had wanted him to leave her alone so she could think things through, but now that he wasn't in her mind, she felt bereft. Alone. More alone than she'd ever been. She put her hand up, spreading out her fingers, looking at her fingernails.

She had been lonely for so long, not realizing how alone she felt even when she had her parents, until Sandu had come into her life. Was it because she had been born over and over protecting his soul, as the history in her family indicated? Had she lived lifetimes searching for him? Had she been lonely those lifetimes because she had never found him, even though she married and had a child? She only knew that each time she tried to school her mind to stay focused on processing his abilities— and his flaws—she found herself wanting to reach out to him.

"I'm not a needy person," she murmured, resentful that she wasn't coping the way she thought she should be. She wanted Sandu to see her as someone strong. Someone he could depend on. That was part of the reason she had wanted to take time for herself. She needed to process everything so she could go forward with courage to face what was necessary. She also wanted to be his partner. If he refused to treat her as a partner, how could she trust him with her secrets? He would share what was hers with his brethren and cut her out of the journey.

Sandu believed this was his path alone for some reason. She knew she was fulfilling a family destiny. This was *their* appointed task. She had stated several times it was their journey together—and it was. She couldn't succeed without him. He couldn't succeed without her. If she couldn't convince him, they would fail, and all would be lost.

Sandu had believed, when he felt such an urgency to leave the city of

San Diego and his friends behind, that it was because he no longer could take being around humans without his lifemate to anchor him. He had been conditioned for centuries to believe he would be tempted to turn vampire if he battled and killed too often after so long. She knew it was their close proximity, the pull between them that had him so restless. She woke up feeling it as well, that need to leave, to start her journey. She had laid out her cards, over and over, seeking to find help, seeking to find answers, knowing he would come, fearing his arrival and what he would bring.

She closed her eyes and let the hot water perform magic on her aching muscles, taking the tension from them. The fragrance took the troubles from her mind, allowing them to drift away from her. She would talk to Sandu when he got back. Tell him the truth about why he had been so restless. Confess her own need to leave the city as well. The answers hadn't been there, but her enemies had been. *Their* enemies. She would also ask him to give her more of an explanation of what his world was like and why he was doing things without her consent.

She sat up, her lashes lifting suddenly. *Sandu? Why were the Castellos waiting for you to come before they made their move on me? How did they know you were coming?*

She couldn't hide her alarm. The older Castello had come into her shop and asked for a reading. From the moment he'd stepped inside, she'd felt the sinister energy swamping her. She'd calmly seated him, but made certain she could easily get to any of her weapons and had plenty of room to slide away from the table and fight should it be necessary. She had excellent skills. She'd been training since she was very, very young.

The cards had reacted to his touch when he shuffled them. She'd watched very carefully. The subtle retreat from him, as if their magic sank deep inside, where he couldn't feel it. It hadn't been the same reaction as when Sandu had gone to touch the deck. The cards recognized him immediately. She feared him and they were her deck. They knew and reacted to protect her, but they recognized him and accepted him. The cards tried to reassure her he was part of their circle. Castello had been judged harshly—an enemy. The cards were not going to aid him in any way. They hid what they were, and most likely, when her mother had been murdered, they had hidden from her murderer. Adalasia had found the deck on her mother's body, where she always kept them, but that didn't mean they couldn't hide their presence when they didn't want to be seen.

The moment Castello left the shop, she cleansed her deck. She felt as if he was unclean in some way. She didn't practice dark arts. She knew others who did—or tried to. She stayed far away from them. This man, Castello, he was human, but he was also something more than human, and if that were so, he had something to do with the dark arts. She wanted no part of that.

"Why do you believe the Castellos were waiting for me, *ewal emninumam*?" Sandu emerged out of thin air, leaning casually against the bathroom door, dressed immaculately in a charcoal gray suit. His long blond hair was once again pulled back neatly with cords, securing it at the nape of his neck and down his back.

She rather liked his hair when it was disheveled and wild after a battle, although he was as gorgeous as sin draped on the wall in that suit.

"I'm in the bathtub."

"I do have excellent vision, Adalasia," he assured, amusement lighting his eyes. "Better than most, I'm certain."

She drew up her knees to cover her breasts and wrapped her arms around her legs. She gave him her best glare. "That means I'm naked."

"I'm well aware. You are my lifemate. I have no intention of taking advantage until you're certain you're ready. Just looking, which you don't actually mind."

Now she gave him the eyebrow. "Why would you think that?" His smile melted her heart and did incredible things to her sex. Maybe she did want him to take advantage.

"*Sivamet*. I'm in your mind. You like me to look."

She did. She liked knowing he found her attractive. She pressed her lips together and then moistened them with her tongue. There wasn't much point in denying the truth when he could read her mind.

"Castello came into my shop for a reading. I told you that. I thought he would try to steal the cards, or if he was after me, try to kidnap or kill me, but he did neither. His people had their spot set up straight across from the shop so they could watch everything that went on. Any time a single man came into the shop for a reading or just to look around, they became very alert. Inevitably, one would visit the shop if the stranger was just looking around. If he was there for a reading, they would come in after and look around. I noticed they'd take pictures of him with their cell phones."

"It wasn't me specifically. It was a male. They didn't know who they were looking for," Sandu clarified.

He had a little frown on his face. She moved through his mind just so far. Each time she came near the dark well of his memories, she shied away from them. She didn't want to see those endless centuries of loneliness and battles with demons. Not yet. Not until she had processed her new life. She was going to go to him whole. As unafraid as possible. That little frown of his intrigued her. His hard features were usually so expressionless. She had the ridiculous urge to rub it off with her fingers.

"The minute you arrived, they had to have known it was you they were waiting for."

"You were busy with your reading. I went from shop to shop. I arranged for gifts to be sent to some of my friends. I saw they were too interested in your antiques store for it to be normal, so I kept my eye on them. They were paying attention to me, but I kept moving around to the various shops until you were finished with the reading."

"And you pounced."

He smiled, his eyes warming. When he did that, there was no resisting him. Adalasia rubbed her chin on top of her knees, finding herself smiling back at him. "I need to get out, and I can't just wave my hand the way you do. Would you mind stepping out while I get ready for bed?"

"Picture in your mind what you want to wear to bed. Every detail." He waved his hand toward the water, and it was gone. Her body was instantly dry and warm. "Trust me, *ewal emninumam*. I can give you the exact clothes you prefer."

She did her best to remember every detail without showing embar-rassment over the lacy thong she wore to bed with the nearly transparent camisole. She had a warm robe that was very modest, and ordinarily no one knew what was under that thick robe. She didn't look at him directly when she was suddenly clothed in her skimpy night attire with the thick, warm robe enveloping her.

"You need something on your feet. Something warm."

"The floors have radiant heating." Her hands came up to grip the lapels of the robe tightly at her throat as he moved away from the door to allow her to walk by him. She kept walking all the way past the actual bedroom to the sitting room, where she curled up in a chair facing the fireplace.

Sandu was so silent she didn't hear him behind her, but maybe he floated. They'd discussed floating in the library. It seemed Carpathians had quite a lot of fun skills humans didn't have.

"I have friends who can investigate the Castellos for us," Sandu as-sured her.

"I think they may have something to do with the dark arts, Sandu. There was evil clinging to him. He was more than human." She hesitated and then rubbed her temples. Her gaze flicked to his and then away. "I have something I need to tell you. You might not be very happy with me, and I won't blame you if you get upset."

Just please don't yell at me, even if you think I deserve it.

She wasn't certain she could take it if Sandu turned out to be a man who couldn't be trusted to keep his word. Already, she feared he was de-ceiving her over important things, but if they were going to continue for-ward together, someone was going to have to break the ice between them.

"Adalasia, tell me what you need to say, and do so without fear. You are in my mind. You should be able to see that it is impossible for me to ever harm you."

"Harming isn't the same thing as being angry. I'm just going to say this very fast. When you first left your friends to make the decision to leave the city and we connected, you thought you were restless because you had been around humans too long."

Sandu nodded. He studied her pale face over his steepled fingers. His black eyes unsettled her. There were always those red flames flickering in them, reminding her he was a predator. Right now, the flames smoldered low, but they could leap and roar at the slightest provocation. When he looked at her with such focus, it was so intense, and he never blinked, never moved, just watched her the way a predator might, ready to strike at any moment.

She had seen him fighting like a wild animal out of control—no, totally in control, a killing machine. She had no idea how to trust him now, when she needed him to be that one person in her life she could count on. She hadn't expected an easy journey, but she had deceived herself into thinking she would have a fairytale with him. He would be the prince in her love story. *Their* journey together was supposed to be easy, at least in her fantasy. Everything else around them might be wrong and falling apart, but they would stand together.

"I knew that wasn't the true reason. You were so conditioned to believe it, Sandu, but it was because you needed to leave the city with me. And . . ." She trailed off, lifted her gaze to his and then looked away.

"And . . ." he prompted.

She took a deep breath. "You locked yourself away in that monastery because you feared you were a demon, you feared you would eventually be unable to control what was growing inside you, something more than the undead. A monster you feared could be let loose on the world. Something with too many scars on your soul to be redeemed."

He kept looking at her with those frightening eyes. She touched the tip of her tongue to her suddenly dry lips.

"I had no way of knowing that was your fear because you are very good at hiding things. You have barriers in your mind impossible to get through."

"You do not want to see what is behind them."

She tried to control her heartbeat, curling deeper into the chair. "Maybe I didn't before, but now that I realize you are making decisions without me, I do want to see what you're hiding from me." She kept her gaze fixed on his, regardless of the fact that he was frightening. "If we are to continue forward together, Sandu, we have to find a way to bridge this gap between us and learn to trust each other." She had things to tell him, things to confess, but she couldn't make herself reveal them without first knowing if he was trustworthy.

His expression didn't change. "There is no 'if,' Adalasia. The ritual binding words have been spoken, and our souls have been reunited. We are bound together. You feel it just the same way that I do. You don't have to be Carpathian to feel the pull between lifemates."

He spoke the truth. She put trembling fingers to her neck and stroked over her pounding pulse, uncaring that he saw. "Will you explain to me what a lifemate is and what you're keeping from me and why you're making decisions without me?"

He studied her face for what seemed an eternity. She could hear the wind rattling the window. A branch sawed against the balcony above them. She shivered and drew her robe closer. Sandu waved his hand toward the fireplace, and the flames crackled around the logs.

"Carpathians need blood to survive, as you well know. We sleep beneath the ground. The minerals heal our wounds. If I am wounded, you can use saliva and the earth to pack my wounds, and they would heal much faster and better than using any human form." He spoke matter-of-factly. "We heal using our spirits, shedding our bodies, and heal from the inside out. That was how I was able to push the parasites from my body. I found it interesting that they reacted to your blood."

"Reacted in what way?"

"They were attracted to it, very aware of it, yet they stayed away from it as if repelled—or ordered to do so." His eyes never left her face.

That wasn't what she expected. She frowned, turning that over in her mind. "Why would they do that? Have you seen that reaction before?"

He shook his head slowly. "No."

Adalasia rubbed at her forehead with the heel of her hand. "I thought I was prepared for this journey. And for you. I'm not at all. I feel like I don't understand anything. I'm someone used to knowing what's coming at me and planning my moves carefully. I don't leave things to chance. I had this idea that we would be partners and you would be like me. We'd talk things out and decide what we were going to do before we did it. Now I feel like I'm completely alone in a world I don't understand at all."

She raised her eyes and met his gaze. Those flames were still burning, but they were low smoldering embers. Still, he was so focused on her she didn't feel comforted in the way she thought a lifemate would make her feel, not after the ritual words he'd spoken to bind them together. He watched her with that same predatory stare she'd observed in tigers or leopards when she'd gone to a zoo with her mother when she was a child.

"The Carpathian world is complicated, Adalasia, and very old. There are rules that we all must follow, whether we like them or not. We are too dangerous not to follow them."

"Rules such as?" she prompted.

"Binding our lifemate to us," he answered. "When we find our lifemate, we have no choice but to bind her to us. Without her, we either turn vampire, or we suicide." He studied her expression for another long moment. "Why did you try to send me away?"

She pressed the heel of her hand into her forehead again, hating to finish her confession, feeling ashamed. "Costello may look and feel human, but in the close confines of my shop, when he touched the cards, I knew he was something more. There is something evil in him that makes him more than human." She tried to be cautious in what she said. She knew she should tell him. She *had* to tell him.

"What *exactly* does that mean, Adalasia?"

She moistened her lips again and then dared to lift her gaze to his. He didn't seem in the least bit angry. He looked exactly the same. More importantly, he *felt* the same. "I don't know what he is, so I can't tell if I can banish whatever he brings from another realm. I've asked the cards, but it could be that it is too far into the future." She took a breath. Blurted it out. "It's possible he has a demon in him." There. That was the strict truth. She'd told him.

He sat in silence, his black, black gaze drifting over her in that way he had that made her feel as if she belonged to him, whether she wanted it or not. Those red embers were beginning to flare into actual flames.

"That was it, *ewal emninumam*, your big confession that you thought might upset me to the point that I would raise my voice to you?"

"I should have told you right away. It wasn't fair to let you think that you were so close to temptation again. You weren't. You weren't about to lose your honor. You weren't betraying me." Tears burned behind her eyes. "I was betraying you and could have lost you to suicide. I didn't understand what meeting the dawn was."

Sandu was on his feet then, moving in that easy, fluid way he had, all flowing muscle, mesmerizing with a sensual quality that caught at her. She couldn't move, not even when he reached for her, lifting her right out of the chair and carrying her back to the bed, where he sat, cradling her on his lap. Adalasia blinked. His suit jacket was gone, and his shirt was unbuttoned, showing far too much of his thick, heavily muscled chest.

He released the heavy mass of her hair so that it tumbled down her back in long waves. He stroked caresses through the thick strands until goose bumps covered her skin and she felt sensuous, sexier than she'd ever felt in her life. His hand went to the back of her head, fingers continuing to move in the thickness of her hair, massaging her scalp. All the while he murmured soft words to her in his native language.

"There was no betrayal, Adalasia. None." His lips touched the top of her head. "Listen to the sound of my heart." He rocked her gently. Soothingly. His breath was warm against her ear now as he slid her hair to the side of her neck.

She turned her face toward his chest, where his heartbeat beckoned her. There were little dark ruby beads welling up. Small. Like gems. Right over his heart. She felt strange, distant from reality, as if the beating of his heart and the scent of those ruby beads overwhelmed her to the point where she had stepped into a fantasy world.

Adalasia touched her tongue tentatively to one of the drops sliding down his warm chest. The moment she savored him on her tongue, need welled up, sharp and terrible, a hunger so strong, as if she'd been waiting for so long just for this particular taste. She let her lashes fall, let him press her close to him. Let her lips settle over that dark line of addicting droplets. She craved the taste of him. Everything else paled in comparison.

Adalasia slid her arms around him and moved restlessly on his lap. She felt the hard length of him pressed tight against her thigh. Every nerve ending in her body was aware of him. Of the shape of him. Of his hard muscles. Of the width of his shoulders and the thickness of his chest. The way his hips narrowed and how his thighs were columns of muscles. She wanted to explore his body, to taste every inch of his skin. To explore his groin, his heavy erection, every last part of him that would be hers, but she didn't want to stop feeding from him. She hadn't realized how hungry she'd been until that moment.

Very gently he inserted his hand between her mouth and his chest, murmuring something in his native language so low she couldn't quite catch it and closing the line on his skin.

Adalasia licked her lips and lifted her face to his. He caught her chin and kissed her. The moment he did, the world spun away until there was only feeling. Fire. Beauty. Perfection. She leaned into him, giving him everything while he lit up her mind and body with glittering sparks of fire. She could kiss him forever, and when he lifted his mouth from hers, she chased after him, seriously addicted.

He rested his forehead against hers. "We're going to have to stop here, *Sivamet*. I fear I am not a saint."

THE HIEROPHANT

S andu woke Adalasia carefully, keeping her memories of the night before very distant, as if they were more of a dream than a reality. He regretted that it was necessary, but she wouldn't have accepted that they had to advance their relationship so quickly. She was in his mind, yes, but only on the surface. He was in hers. She hid a few things from him, but very little.

Adalasia was extremely intelligent. She was also determined to go her own way, follow the path she was certain she was supposed to be on—with or without him. That wasn't going to happen. Their path was extremely dangerous. That meant he had to protect her at all costs. He couldn't do that during the day when he was in the ground if she was above it. To him, it was that simple, that logical. Adalasia had to come fully into his world. If not immediately, she needed to be ready so if she was ever wounded, he could bring her in fast.

Sandu didn't believe in arguing over important issues such as the life and death of his lifemate. He knew he had to take the time to explain everything to her and get them on the same page as soon as possible. He couldn't blame her for the mounting suspicion. He had sent her to sleep in the bed, but instead of going to ground to heal his wounds, he had carried her to their waiting plane. She was placed in the bed inside the aircraft's bedroom.

Caskets lined the floor, locked in place with bars. Each casket was filled with mineral-rich soil. Once they were in the air heading toward their destination, they entered the caskets, first safeguarding the plane, the room, and lastly, each casket. It was the best they could do in order to protect the pilot and themselves from accidents or enemies.

Waking Adalasia, even with the others out of the room and off the plane, wasn't the best of ideas. He'd hunted already, satisfying his need for blood. The pilot was sleeping. Sandu should have taken her out of the room, where there were no caskets to look at. Instead, those were in plain sight when she sat up, pushing at her long hair, looking drowsy, sexy and way too frightened of him.

Her gaze slid around the room, taking in everything and then settling once more on him. She touched her tongue to her lips. "Are the others still in those caskets? Is that where they sleep? Is that where you slept?"

"No, they aren't in there. And yes, we sleep in them on the plane. It's the safest way to travel and stay with the sun blocked out and the soil around us." He could hear her heartbeat reverberating so loud and fast he feared she would have a heart attack. "Adalasia, slow your heart down."

Her hand came up. "Don't tell me what to do. Not right now. I'm going into the bathroom to get dressed. And no, I don't want you to help me with that. I'll shower and change myself. I need time away from you to process all this." She scrambled off the bed and, without looking at him, disappeared into the small bathroom off the master bedroom.

Sandu shook his head and sauntered out into the larger part of the aircraft. His woman was getting set to rebel in a big way. He couldn't blame her. He would have rebelled as well—done more than rebelled. He needed her to know he would try his best to work things out with her and give her every answer so they could work together from here on out.

He wandered around the plane, knowing when one had lived as he had, it was more than impossible to change what was so deeply ingrained in him. His character traits were set too deep. He was that animal she saw and secretly feared. She tried not to think too much about the demon she saw in him when he battled the master vampire, but it was nearly impossible for her to hide that kind of fear from him.

Sandu sighed. He had known, as did all the ancients that had secreted themselves behind those monastery walls, that their time had long since passed. Most modern women could learn to live with the younger generations, such as the prince. Some of his brethren had gotten lucky in their lifemates. Their matches suited them because of their backgrounds and also the way they were all tied together.

Maybe that was a key component he had yet to explore. Andor's Lorraine shared more than her lifemate bond, and although she was very modern, she seemed to be able to accept the ancient ways. Julija, lifemate to Isai, was mage-born. Dragomir's Emeline was different from many of the more modern women, wishing to give Dragomir whatever he wished for. Ferro and Elisabeta had just come together and were working out their relationship gently and carefully. Elisabeta, like Emeline, tended to be very old-world.

Adalasia's scent filled the small confines of the room, unexpectedly causing Sandu's body to react almost before his brain. He turned slowly to watch her enter. There was both trepidation and determination on her face. Her gaze swept the large room, taking in both exits before settling on him. He had deliberately dressed casually for her, sweeping his long hair back and securing it with leather cords.

"Good evening. We're on the Washington border, up in the mountains. Andre Boroi, one of my brethren, settled here with his lifemate, Teagan. The area is fairly remote. Andre found it difficult to live in the city, although he did try for Teagan's sake. She wanted to live near her grandmother Trixie. They lived in California for a short while, but it was too difficult for him. Teagan was amenable to moving. He is one of the older of our kind." He kept his voice neutral, giving her facts.

Adalasia nodded as if listening to him, but she walked over to the nearest exit and stood in front of it. "I'm not going to meet your friend, Sandu. I've given this a lot of thought. I don't know what went wrong. Your lifemate ritual. My cards. Maybe both of us." She turned and faced him, giving a little shrug of her shoulders. "Something clearly did. I'd like you to ask your pilot, after he rests, of course, to take me back to my home. I can figure out what to do from there. You can continue your journey with your friends."

There was a kind of iron in the sweet dignity of her voice. She didn't want him to convince her otherwise. She believed there was a mistake, a big one, and there was no fixing it. In a matter of where lives were at stake, he didn't blame her for not wanting to move forward, not when one wrong move could cost others their lives.

Sandu indicated one of the more comfortable-looking chairs. "We do need to fix things between us before we involve others in this process. Come sit down, Adalasia."

She tilted her head to one side and then shook it. "You're too dangerous. When you want your way, you don't ask, Sandu. You take. There's no discussion. No explanation. You don't respect the ritual binding words. I went over them very carefully, calling them up so I could see and hear them. They're supposed to mean something, right? Vows between the two of us that are sacred. My happiness? How can I possibly be happy with the crap you're pulling?"

"I give you my word that you are safe from me taking over your mind, Adalasia. In truth, our connection is getting stronger. Last night, I had planned to give the explanations you need and deserve, but there was resistance. You had entered my mind during the battle with the master vampire after I asked you not to. You saw things about me that terrified you. Had that not happened, you would have listened with an open mind."

Adalasia rubbed her palm along the top of one of the high-backed leather chairs bolted to the floor. "That's true. I'm still rather terrified by what I saw in you. You appear so gentle when you're with me, and yet there is something buried deep that comes out when you do battle. It escapes, and once out, I'm not certain you'll always be able to capture it and put it back. If you were to let that loose on the world, Sandu, what then?"

He caught a glimpse of her greatest fear, and it shocked him. He hadn't even, for one moment, considered the possibility. "A demon in hell? Behind the gates you guard? An ancient Carpathian too far gone locked behind the gates no one can control? Do you believe such a thing could possibly exist?" He had to use every ounce of discipline not to take a step toward her. Not to in any way change his tone or frighten her. This was too big. Too explosive. Too dangerous by far.

She bit down hard on her lower lip, so hard two little ruby beads appeared. Her teeth were sharper now. Two blood exchanges would do that, bringing her closer to his world. She nodded her head slowly. "I think it's entirely possible."

"It seems we both have secrets, *ewal emninumam*. I think it is time we both come clean if we are to defeat our enemies and have our happily ever after." He held out his hand to her.

Adalasia stared at his hand for a long time before making up her mind. She nodded and then put her hand in his. He watched his long fingers close around her delicate ones, and he drew her to him. Bending his head, he sipped those ruby droplets from her lips and used his tongue to seal off the tiny pinpricks.

"A lifemate must become part of our world," he said without preamble. "Jaxon was human before she was with Lucian. Teagan, Andre's lifemate, was human. The prince's lifemate was human."

She frowned, her eyebrows drawing together. "*Was* human doesn't sound good to me."

She dropped her hands, twisting her fingers together so tight her knuckles turned white. Sandu wanted to wrap her in his arms and comfort her.

"It will be good, Adalasia," he assured. He used his voice carefully, soothing her.

"What happens if your lifemate remains human?"

"I would choose to grow old, and when you die, I would meet the dawn. At least that is the hope. It is dangerous. Extremely dangerous. You saw me. Or at least had a small glimpse of me in battle. An ancient is difficult to kill. It would take several hunters if I didn't honor my vows and follow you to the next life."

He could see Adalasia was trying hard to process what he was telling her. "I'm a little confused. I thought turning vampire was a choice."

"When one loses one's lifemate, the other goes into what is known as a 'thrall.' Everything is taken from you at once. In that moment, you have to make that split-second decision to follow her. The demon in me is strong. Without the anchor of the two of us building our lives together over a great deal of time, I do not know what could happen. I told you, from the beginning, I worried I was long past my time."

He made the admission, looking her in the eyes, wanting her to believe him, that his soul could be damned for all eternity after all the centuries of his living with honor just by her decision. She was human, and she didn't understand their world or the terrible price the males would pay. The deaths she could cause. The horror he could wreak on the world.

Sandu stood calmly, watching her try to process what he'd told her. Her gaze moved over him a little moodily.

"Why didn't you tell me this from the beginning?"

"I wanted you to have time to get to know me, but we seemed to be thrown into the deep end, moving too fast on a path neither of us quite understands. I do know we have to strengthen our bond before we can go any further."

"You took matters into your own hands, on purpose," she declared.

He steepled his fingers and rested his chin on them, watching her as he nodded. "I did. I knew we didn't have time to argue. Whoever your enemies were and the vampires we would run into were all too real. They were dangerous, and that meant you had to be protected. Our union had to be protected. I had to bring you as close to my world as possible so in the event of you being mortally wounded, or it was necessary for your safety, or you agreed to join with me because you chose me, I could bring you into my world fast."

He didn't feel remorse, so there was none in his voice. Or in his mind. He knew she touched him there, searched for it.

"Okay, just for the moment, let's assume I go along with joining your world, Sandu. How does it work?"

"It takes three blood exchanges. You have had two. On the third one, your body will rid itself of all toxins, essentially 'die' as a human and reshape all organs to become Carpathian."

"I've had two blood exchanges with you," she repeated softly, her gaze steady.

Again, he nodded. "It's there, in your mind. You gave me your blood willingly. You took mine with a partial knowledge. I distanced the experience for you to make it easier, as humans have difficulty overcoming the idea of the exchange of blood."

Adalasia took a deep breath. He was in her mind, and she didn't look into her memories. She was saving that experience for another time.

"You're a very ruthless man, Sandu. You take what you want."

He shook his head. "I do what I know to be right. I'll always do what I know to be right for you. To protect you. Your health and safety will come first before all other things. We are surrounded by danger. I can feel it. I do not know what it is, and that makes me even more apprehensive for you."

He felt her then moving through his mind, a gentle touch but still firm. Adalasia was no fool. She wasn't someone to be deceived with pretty words. She sought the truth of his character. He had wanted her safe. He was determined that whatever enemy she hid from him—and he knew she was hiding something huge—he was going to protect her.

"If I had told you everything, would you have still insisted on two blood exchanges without talking to me first?"

"*Ewal emninumam*, I have no way of knowing what I would have done under those circumstances. I only know that I searched centuries for you. Lifetimes. I held on to my honor, but only barely. When I found you, the miracle was barely to be believed. Even now, looking at you, I can hardly conceive of the truth of it. Do you think I would take the chance of losing you? The slightest chance? I would not. I cannot."

She looked down at her hands, but he was in her mind, and where nothing else seemed to get to her, those words did. He had given her his truth all along, but only this last admission seemed to touch her.

"I began training to fight demons from the time I was a toddler. I didn't attend schools with other children. The stories my mother read to me were from a book handed down from mother to daughter. My father never saw the book. Like the tarot cards, the book doesn't disintegrate with time. That was how I first came to know about the parasites, the ones I saw when you pushed them from your blood."

"You were terrified."

"Not *terrified*." She denied, her lashes lifting, her voice a reprimand. "They freaked me out a little bit, that's all. They were all part of that childhood fairytale, like the original fairytales that weren't so nice."

"Tell me about this book."

"It's a history, really, of our family, the pictures drawn by an ancestor. Most of the book is in picture form rather than text."

"You keep this book with you?"

She nodded. "Always. It wasn't just the cards that told me you were coming. The book did as well. Of course, in the book, you were a lot nicer." She sent him a faint smile.

She wasn't smiling in her mind. She didn't think of him as nice. In the beginning, she had. She had been afraid for him. Afraid those hunting her would harm him. Then, she equated him with those demons she saw in her nightmares. Now, he wasn't only that demon; he was ruthless and dominating, a dictator as well.

"As a lifemate, I seem to be failing everywhere." He gave her a faint smile back.

She touched her lips. "You kiss like sin. Like the very devil. I have to give you points for kissing. And you do have a sweet side when you're not making decisions that you shouldn't without me." She sighed. "I want to be a partner, Sandu. That's what I thought I was signing on for when I began this journey with you. Then, suddenly, I'm out of the loop, you're making decisions and I don't trust you. Why would I tell you anything when I know you're holding very important things back from me?"

"I had to make certain you were safe, Adalasia. I do not expect you to understand a two-thousand-year-old drive, but there is no way I can combat that. I want you as my partner. I have disclosed part of what it entails to become Carpathian. I know the conversion isn't easy. It is painful. You do have to get rid of the toxins before I can put you to sleep for the rest of it. I will shoulder as much of it as I am allowed. I know the brethren are willing to aid in this as well."

She rubbed her chin on the heel of her hand. "As a Carpathian, I would have to have blood to survive?"

He nodded, watching her carefully again. Staying in her mind, studying her reaction. Adalasia seemed to like to compartmentalize. She pushed things to the side in order to take them out and examine them later, which was what she did with that news. She was expecting his answer. It didn't come as a surprise, and she didn't seem particularly upset by it.

"You know it would be difficult for me to initiate that with anyone."

"I would take care of feeding you, but you need to learn just in case I'm wounded severely and you have to care for yourself until I recover."

Her gaze flew to his. "Or you need me to give you blood."

He liked that she'd thought of that. He nodded. "That might be a real possibility. I am a hunter, and I know no other way of life."

"I would have to sleep in the ground." She made it a statement.

He could feel her revulsion of the idea. He'd known all along this was going to be the most difficult hurdle. The moment she saw the caskets, she had retreated significantly in her mind.

"I know that feels nearly impossible, Adalasia. We would take it slow and practice opening and closing the earth. You would have to feel the earth surround you as a blanket would. Until you felt comfortable, I would aid you in sleeping and waking. There are benefits you haven't thought of that you would find amazing." He went to the door of the plane, shifting it so it opened to allow the night breeze in. He needed that cool, fresh air.

"I've thought of them," she countered.

She hadn't said no. That was huge.

"I'd like to take you outside to show you the night." The strip where Zenon Santos had landed the plane was surrounded on three sides with forest. The trees were several yards away, but he could see activity in the branches, small screech owls moving from limb to limb. It was unusual for several to be so close together the way these were. He studied them for a moment, scanning for the undead, but felt no telltale signs of vampires close by. Still, he was uneasy and shifted the door closed again, turning to face her as she spoke.

"I would like to see the night with you, but I need to talk to you about something important. Something I withheld that was important. We started to go into it, and then I got sidetracked. You told me about becoming Carpathian. You need to know about this."

"Then tell me."

"Sandu, we cannot be overheard. We have to place safeguards all around this plane, and we both have to seal it as well."

Sandu didn't laugh at her. He merely inclined his head, suddenly as serious as she was. She felt the difference in him immediately. He treated her opinion with just as much weight as he did the brethren from the monastery. For the first time, she felt like his partner and not a burden that had to be dragged around with him.

They took their time, meticulous in taking care to seal the safeguards, weaving them above and below and around the plane. Both of them used what they felt were right and then wove more together.

"Do you feel safe to tell me aloud, or would you rather talk telepathically, Adalasia?"

She had considered that option. She was getting used to the intimacy of their communication, but truthfully, she wasn't as adept at finding the right words yet. She needed time to think each sentence out and then lay it out for him. If she needed to show him, then she would switch and use images in her head, but she felt it was better to take her time to explain than to have jumbled thoughts.

She also didn't want there to be any misunderstandings. She didn't understand every detail of her family history. To her, growing up, it had been a myth—an outrageous one that kept her apart from other children. She felt like a child out of time with the rest of the world—until she held the tarot cards in her hands.

"I need to choose my words with care, Sandu." She had been standing in the middle aisle of the plane. She looked around a little helplessly, feeling exposed.

"I've gotten rid of our resting places, Adalasia. Come with me into the bedroom. It is much more secluded. I have noticed you like to take your shoes off when you are having difficult conversations." He meant intimate ones. He held out his hand.

She hesitated only for a moment and then let him lead her back into the bedroom. The caskets were nowhere in sight, and he heard her breathe a sigh of relief.

Adalasia sat on the bed, tossing her shoes onto the floor. She was grateful to get rid of her shoes. Sandu also removed his shoes the human way, only when he did it, he kept his eyes on her, even as he bent over to loosen the leather cords of his boots. She found a gravitational pull happening, as if she could get lost in the dark well of his eyes. She wanted to never have to explain what she feared would greatly upset him in spite of his denials.

When Sandu set his boots aside, he sat on the bed, facing her, mirroring her position. Reaching back, he loosened the leather cord holding back his hair. He shook it out, and she found herself mesmerized by the waves of silver running through the darker caramel as it fell around his face and shoulders. She had an unexpected urge to bury her fingers in his hair and find his mouth with hers.

"Adalasia." There was an ache in his voice.

The tone of his voice and the look on his face had an unexpected dark fist of desire forming like a knot low in her stomach. She didn't need that, not when she had to get this out. She had damned him for not sharing, and she was every bit as much to blame for the separation between them.

"I have to tell you this. Fast. I was a child when my mother started training me to fight what she referred to as the Army of Nera. I learned to fight with various weapons, as well as hand-to-hand combat and also spells. Many, many spells. I don't consider myself a witch. I'm not trained that way. I am only trained to defend the tarot cards. And you." Her lashes swept down because she couldn't look at him.

"Against this Army of Nera."

"Yes. I thought it was a crock of shit until Castello showed up. Until my mother was murdered. Until the cards began warning me to be ready for you to come for me and I saw Castello was more than human."

"You keep using that term, *more*. What do you mean by that?"

His voice was so calm. So steady. That kept her steady. On course. She could look at him again. There was no judgment. She should have known. This was the Sandu she'd first met. "I believe he is a member of her army. That would mean he is part demon. He is in the form of a human, but there is a demon inside of him directing his every move. They use animals. Rats. Screech owls."

Sandu's head went up alertly, and he glanced toward the door. "You should have told me this immediately, Adalasia. How can I protect you if you do not disclose everything to me?"

She pushed her forehead into the heel of her hand. "I know I was wrong to withhold anything at all from you. It's just that it all seemed so preposterous, and I was afraid to tell you the truth. You were hiding things from me. I wasn't a partner. Then, when I realized if we didn't work together, neither of us was going to succeed, I almost told you, but I couldn't bring myself to trust you."

"Keep going. Get to the part where you think I would be angry. I am displeased with you holding back information that put you in danger. That does not anger me."

"The story in my family is that a woman, Liona . . ." She watched him closely. He didn't react at all. "Sandu. Do you not recognize that name?"

He shook his head. "Should I?"

She sighed. "I'll just tell you the story I was told. There was a woman, Liona, very sweet, who befriended two sisters, Nera and Tessina Ravasio. They were considered what was called Striga. I know most people think immediately that the Striga were all bad, demons who hunted men and children and turned themselves into birds of prey to feast on them. But there were two factions, and our ancestors were on the side of good, learning to use the elements—air, water, earth and fire—to aid those in need. They learned how to help the sick with plants and herbs. They didn't call up demons or try to use what they knew for personal gain." She paused and looked at him again.

Sandu made no sound. He was very still, and as usual, she couldn't read his expression. His eyes were black, those red flames, just embers, smoldering low, barely there. Waiting. She took a deep breath.

"When the two sisters first met Liona, they had no idea anything was unusual about her. The two sisters had cards they played with, tarot cards. Their mother had painted the cards for them. They both had strong feelings when they saw the cards placed in a certain order, and they would say what they felt. Eventually, they realized the things they saw came true. Liona was intrigued by this. Occasionally, Liona would bring three of her friends along, and the girls would stay up all night with the cards, playing."

Sandu's brows came together. "This is what you were told as a child? As a story?"

She nodded. "I told you there is a book. It is in this book in pictures, but my mother told me the stories as her mother told them to her. I believe Liona was your sister, Sandu. Do you remember anything at all about having a sister?"

He shook his head. "Continue."

Adalasia pressed her hand over the spot where she kept the deck close to her, against her skin. "We have a powerful bloodline, and there were two forces at work in the Striga. They had infiltrated the sisterhood, pretending to be part of that branch, befriending my ancestors and trying to lead them toward the dark arts with promises of immortality and riches. Liona could hear lies, and she cautioned the sisters. Nera chose not to believe her, although she pretended that she did. Tessina did believe her and began watching the women in the order much more carefully."

Adalasia's foot was falling asleep, so she stretched her leg out, careful to keep from kicking him. That required scooting to the other end of the bed. At least that gave her something to rest her back against. She was suddenly feeling raw and very vulnerable. Sandu shackled her ankle with warm fingers and began a slow massage of her foot, bringing the blood back into it.

"Keep going, Adalasia."

"Nera, with the aid of the other two women, the outsiders, set up Liona. They wanted her blood. They claimed she was immortal, and they could use her blood to draw out others like her, and when they had enough, they could open a certain gate and revive a demon beast, one Lilith—the wife of Satan—wanted control of. Tessina found out about their plan and stopped them."

Sandu kept his eyes on hers. "I take it, at that point, a council was called."

She nodded. "My family, your family and the families of the three other women that Liona had introduced my ancestors to. They came from other regions, but they knew women who came from strong, powerful families like mine. It was decided to place four watchers, four guardians, to hold Lilith's Strigas at bay. The Carpathian women would find a like family . . ."

"You mean ones strong in the elements." It was the first time he interrupted her. "Earth. Air. Fire. And water."

She nodded. "The Carpathian women could read the human families and know the traits they sought. Each woman chose a family. My mother painted a deck of tarot cards for each of the other families and included a seventy-ninth card, the card of the goddess. That card represented the Carpathian woman. She mingled her blood with the blood of the ancestor of the family who would help to guard the gate. Your sister coated our goddess card and our book with her blood and Tessina's blood. That's why the cards and book don't disintegrate."

Sandu continued to rub her foot, his touch very gentle but firm. "Is Liona alive?"

"I have no idea. I really don't. I only know that Lilith continues to send her army, led now by Nera, out to try to get the tarot decks. She needs me and you together. She can't just steal the deck. That's why my mother was of no use to them."

There was a long silence. Outside, an owl screeched, the sound an intrusion into their world. The sound ran along her nerve endings, sending tiny pinpricks of unease darting through her body. She looked at Sandu. The red embers still smoldered, as steady as ever. He looked calm and relaxed. His gaze didn't waver. He was aware of the owl, but it didn't bother him. He trusted their safeguards would hold.

"Those parasites, Sandu. I told you, I've seen them before, in the book. I was told of them. To beware of them. It was disgusting and so horrible I could never forget the image."

His eyebrow shot up. "Show me, Adalasia. In your mind."

She shuddered. "The parasites had far-reaching consequences. They came from hell. From the mother demon who wanted to create hardship and chaos. She wanted to make certain families were torn apart. She often would drip parasites into the mouths of pregnant women while they slept, causing them to miscarry in horrible agony. Those pictures are horrendous as well."

"Show me." That was clearly a command.

Adalasia pulled up the memory of the old book her mother had read to her, showing her very graphic pictures of women who seduced men and then, after having their way with them, ripped them open with talons and turned into parasites, crawling inside their bellies, drinking their blood until the parasites were so bloated, they could barely move.

Then she showed him the picture of a gleeful woman standing over a sleeping pregnant woman while her horrified husband, who had clearly just had sex with the demon, shook his head in horror as she dropped parasites into his wife's open mouth. Next came graphic drawings of the results.

This is what your mother read to you when you were a child, Adalasia? There was a touch of horror in his mind.

Did your parents warn you of vampires when you were a child, Sandu? she countered.

His hands soothed the skin of her ankle. *I have no idea, but I suppose they must have.*

"If these parasites were introduced by the Striga as far back as then, they must have given them, or the idea of them, to Xavier, the high mage in the Carpathian Mountains. Was there any mention of that in your books? Or by your mother?"

Adalasia shook her head. "Why, Sandu? What is important about those parasites?"

"Xavier claimed he created them. He had giant vats of them and leaked them into the ground where the Carpathians rested. Our women were unable to get pregnant, or if they did, they couldn't carry. The few babies born were male. This happened slowly, of course, over time. Our people did not realize that Xavier was our enemy. He nearly wiped out our entire species."

She let out her breath slowly. "Let me show you another image." She tried to put as much detail as she remembered. The book was old. It had been handed down, mother to daughter. She had it in her bag, one of the things she always kept with her. She could just show it to him, but she didn't want to. Her mother had drilled it into her that she could only show her daughter. Rather than get out the book, she recalled the picture to her mind. It had been painted, just like the others, by Tessina and

Nera's mother. It depicted a woman with snakes adorning her ankles and wrists and another sliding around her waist, its head up and tongue flicking out toward the man she faced.

The man was no doubt a mage, with his long robe and the walking staff set against a stone. He was reaching for the pail of wiggling worms she was extending toward him. In return, he was giving her, with his other hand, a little girl of about ten. The woman looked gleeful. The child terrified. The mage smug, arrogant even.

"Xavier traded either a Carpathian child or a mage child for those parasites," Sandu said. "Why would she want that particular child? Something had to be special about that little girl for her to bother with Xavier. I suspect that is a demon sent by Lilith."

"You would be right. We need to find out if a child went missing around that same time," Adalasia said.

"This demon that Lilith wants is held behind a gate . . ."

"Four gates. It can escape from any one of them. Any of the four sides. East. West. North. South. All must be guarded. My family guards one gate only. As long as the tarot cards exist and stay out of the hands of Lilith, the gate will hold."

"This demon beast that is behind the gate, what would it accomplish should Lilith manage to release him? Or her? It could be a female beast for all we know." There was speculation in Sandu's voice. "You brought up the possibility that he might be an ancient Carpathian who lived far too long."

"That was pure speculation, Sandu. I have no idea. I only know that I trained to fight any of the Army of Nera, my ancestor who was appointed Lilith's general to recover our tarot deck. Nera can't wield the deck. Should she touch it, it would defend itself or suicide. I don't think any of the demons can put their hands on it safely."

Sandu's eyes turned almost velvet as they drifted over her, stroking her skin the way his hands stroked her ankle. "Ah. Now I see the wisdom of having lifemates. You would do anything to keep me alive, and I would do anything to keep you alive."

She wanted to protest that statement, but he wasn't wrong. She felt those ties, the bindings the ritual words had placed on her. She knew, as much as she'd considered leaving him, it would have been impossible. She wouldn't have been able to. She studied his face, those lines carved so deep. The too-old eyes that could go from savage to sensual in the space of a heartbeat. She wasn't certain she would ever understand him, but she knew instinctively he belonged to her. They were in for a wild ride as they learned about each other.

"That's why they waited for you. That's why I had such a reaction to the idea of you coming anywhere near them," she whispered, trying to ignore the way the stroking of his fingers on her skin made her come alive.

"I know now why those little screech owls made me so uneasy. They can be used to spy on you. Blood draws blood. Your ancestor finds you through her blood."

A cold finger of fear crept down her spine. She hadn't thought of that, but of course, it made sense. No matter where she went, Nera and her army would eventually find her. They might be a few days behind, but they would come after her. And that put Sandu and the others directly in the path of danger at every turn.

THE LOVERS

Andre Boroi was known as "the Ghost" to other Carpathians for a reason. Few ever saw him unless he wanted to be seen. His touch was so light he could kill and be gone before his presence was ever detected in a room. He had four scars on his body, four he had deliberately kept. Only a handful of those he held close to him knew why he had allowed those scars to remain. They were reminders of a human family he knew as a boy, a family he had loved. He had taken their name out of love and respect and given it to his lifemate, Teagan, when she found him nearly dead. She'd saved his life and his soul.

Teagan was a beautiful woman but very small and slender, with black curly hair, gorgeous skin and dark chocolate eyes. She was gracious and sweet, her face very expressive, in complete contrast to her lifemate, who was unreadable, large and intimidating and looked like he was carved from granite.

Their home in the wilds of the Cascade Mountains was quite lovely, and Adalasia told them so. The four ancients quickly excused themselves and left the confines of the structure to patrol outside, leaving the two couples to talk together.

"You said the matter was urgent." Andre was not a man for niceties.

Sandu nodded. "I have no memories of my past, Andre. I have considered that I wiped them myself to keep any hunting me from retaliating against my family. Or perhaps I simply have lived too long, but now I find I have need to know where I come from."

Andre rubbed the bridge of his nose. "In the days when Vlad was prince, there were Carpathians guarding what is now Russia, Italy, Greece and other regions. Only those of us who were sent by the prince to communicate with these families knew them. As you know, telepathic communication cannot reach over endless distances unless it is with life-mates, and then usually it is in dire circumstances."

Adalasia looked up at Sandu. The information didn't sound promising. Sandu slid his thumb gently over the back of her hand in a little caress to reassure her. *My instincts are very strong that we are here for a reason, ewal emninumam. I trust my instincts. Andre will come through for us. He is being cautious because he hasn't yet decided if he can trust us completely with his lifemate. Teagan is his world, just as you are mine. We brought four brethren with us who have no lifemates. They are very dangerous ancient Carpathians. Should they turn, they would be extremely difficult to destroy. He has every right to be cautious.*

Adalasia nodded and visibly relaxed. There was no way Andre's sharp eyes didn't take in her tense body, Sandu's gesture of reassurance and then her body's reaction. Sandu wanted Andre to see that he was every bit as protective of his lifemate as Andre was with Teagan, and yet he did travel with his ancient brethren.

"Adalasia"—Teagan's voice was gentle—"would you care for a cup of tea, water or juice? You really need to stay hydrated. I know that it can be very difficult to keep anything down, but you have to try. I can help you. I've been through this."

Adalasia pressed her free hand to her stomach. "It's just that the thought of eating or drinking anything makes me feel sick."

You need to take control, ekäm, Andre said. He used the path of the brethren in the monastery. Few Carpathians could hear, and certainly none of the undead.

She is afraid.

That is natural. She is entering an unknown world. Her human body must die in order to be reborn as a Carpathian, but she trusts you.

Sandu's thumb continued to slide back and forth along the back of Adalasia's hand. He turned her wrist over so he could feel her pulse. Her heart was beating too fast. She did need to stay hydrated, just as Teagan had suggested. She'd refused anything that evening before their arrival. He didn't like forcing his lifemate any more than he already had. He'd told her they'd be partners, and he wanted to keep his word.

His gaze returned to Andre. The man was meant to be his guide in some way. He was certain of it. Andre held to the old ways, just as Sandu did. They were both traditional. His lifemate, Teagan, had clearly mellowed him somewhat, but Andre would always be an ancient Carpathian: wary, battle-ready, in love with his lifemate and protective of her. She ruled until he felt she might be in danger, and then he would be ruthless in his takeover. There would be no remorse, and Teagan knew him well enough and evidently loved him enough, even though she was a modern woman, to let him be who he was.

Sandu needed Adalasia to love him as fiercely as Teagan loved Andre because, sadly, he was very much like that ancient. He would always be the ancient she feared, with the scars on his soul he couldn't get rid of.

Teagan leaned toward Adalasia. "I know how that is, Adalasia. Any of us can help you get water or juice down to nourish your body. You just have to give consent. Your lifemate is waiting for that. He doesn't like taking from you, but in the end, to keep you safe, you know they have no choice. They can't do anything else."

Adalasia's long lashes fluttered. Lowered. Raised. She flicked him a puzzled glance and then returned to Teagan's face. "Of course there's always another choice."

"Not really," Teagan denied. "They're hardwired a certain way. Carpathian males have no choice but to protect us. You will understand that the more you're in his mind."

Adalasia glanced at Sandu. His fingers tightened around hers. He'd explained that concept to her, but maybe it sounded different coming from a woman who, at one time, had been human.

"So, you're saying if I didn't take care of myself properly, eventually Sandu would be forced to do so because he couldn't stop himself," Adalasia clarified.

Teagan nodded. "Absolutely. It's better to just give in and let him help you drink whatever horrible concoction there is to nourish your body. He'll help you keep it down, and you won't remember drinking it."

Or you could do the third blood exchange and bring her into our world, where she would be safe. I feel very strongly that she would be far safer from this point beneath the ground with you than alone, sleeping aboveground. I have no idea why, but I feel it, Andre said.

The four ancients echoed the assessment. Sandu wanted to bring Adalasia into their world more than anything, but he also wanted Adalasia to come to him fully aware. If she didn't agree, he would have to make the choice for her, and he'd said he would give her time to come to him. Andre's revelation about having such a strong feeling wasn't to be ignored. He felt equally as strongly. He had put that instinctual need down to his ancient Carpathian teachings, but more and more, he was uneasy.

Another murmur of agreement going through the path of communication among the brethren told him he wasn't alone in his worry for her safety. Sandu's nod toward Andre was barely perceptible.

Sandu brought Adalasia's hand to his mouth and spoke very gently against her palm. "I think it best if you have juice, with plenty of vitamins, *ewal emninumam.* Teagan is right about your nutrition."

Adalasia nodded reluctantly. "You'll have to help me get it down. Just the thought of it makes me feel nauseous, Sandu."

Teagan immediately placed a tall glass of what appeared to be a refreshing strawberry-and-orange drink on the table on the other side of Sandu. He infused it with the necessary nutrients before waving his hand to put his lifemate in a receptive state so she was able to drink the liquid and keep it down.

He handed the glass to Teagan as he brought his lifemate out from under his control. Adalasia blinked a few times and looked from him to the empty glass. Teagan waved it away.

"Thank you," Adalasia said simply, "for making me feel accepted and at ease. This is all so frightening to me. I have my own enemies, and now I'm facing Sandu's as well. I appreciate that you've offered your friendship so readily."

"I'm very happy you both came to visit us. We don't get that many visitors," Teagan said. "Still, I need companionship more than he does."

"Csitri." Andre murmured the endearment softly.

She leaned into him. "I'm very happy here. My grandmother and

Fane visit often. My grandmother is so happy with Fane, and it's about time she has her own life. My sisters come to visit with my nieces and nephews. There's Gabrielle and Aleksei—they come sometimes. They live the closest to us, but she is very involved in her work. She's amazing, and I love to help her with her research when she needs it. She's brilliant. But still"—she smiled at Adalasia—"it's nice to have a woman visitor to talk to."

"I would want the occasional visitor," Adalasia said supportively.

"I do love it out here. There's great climbing. As in boulders. I enjoy climbing, although Andre thinks I'm a little crazy, since I can simply float to the top of a boulder, but that isn't as fun to me as figuring out the path to actually climb it."

"You can float to the top of a boulder?"

Teagan laughed. "I could. I don't. I like puzzles, and when I climb the face of a boulder, that's what it is to me—a puzzle. I have to work out how to get up to the top."

"She's my little daredevil," Andre said. "If you only knew half the things this one does to make my life terrifying."

Sandu didn't think he was joking even though Teagan laughed. Her laughter was contagious, and it was impossible not to smile, even under Andre's watchful, piercing blue eyes.

Teagan shook her head. "He fights vampires and doesn't break a sweat, but he says I make his life terrifying because I like to climb boulders even though he knows I can float down to the ground if I fall. Does that even make sense?"

Adalasia looked more at ease than ever, settling back in her chair as if Andre wasn't quite as scary as he had been just minutes earlier. "No, not really. Are there vampires here, too, Andre?"

"I'm afraid they are trying to establish a foothold in as many places as possible. They like the wilds just as we do. We live on the very edge of civilization. Like us, they need blood to survive, so they try to prey on the towns and farms we protect. They have no idea we are in the vicinity. We try to keep a very low profile, so we always have the element of surprise."

"How do you keep those closest to you from suspecting you are Carpathians? You can't possibly be awake during the day, right?" Adalasia glanced at Sandu, her fingernails biting into her palm. "Wouldn't it be better if one of the couple is awake and alert during the day?"

Sandu felt the tiny hopeful note in her mind. She didn't want it there, but he was her lifemate, and it might not be in her voice for everyone to hear, but it was definitely in her mind.

Andre shook his head. "That would cause so many major problems, Adalasia." His voice was as gentle as Sandu had ever heard him.

"You would believe your lifemate was dead to you, and you would not be able to stand it. You would suicide, and he would follow you." Andre stated it as fact—and it was. "You are too far in our world and too far committed to Sandu as your lifemate. He cannot do without you. You cannot do without him. He is not fully anchored, and for long centuries, too long, he has been fighting the temptation to turn into the very vile, evil monster we destroy. Without you, he is still vulnerable—and will be until you are fully in the world with us."

Andre did sound like the mentor now. A wise monk, attempting to guide her along the path by telling her the truth of what could happen to her lifemate and even to her if she wasn't converted.

Adalasia frowned, turning to look at Sandu. *You didn't tell me any of this. Why?*

I did tell you most of it, just not the way he put it to you. I knew you had little choice, and I wanted what little choice you had to be me.

He rubbed their linked hands under his jaw so that the shadow of bristles slid along her knuckles. He knew there was an ache in his mind, and it slid into hers. Her eyes darkened with desire and something else, something very close to affection.

"You are not safe above ground, either, Adalasia," Andre continued. "The undead must sleep in the ground as we must, but they have puppets they send out, ones who eat human flesh. They would seek you. You are in between the two worlds and would attract them. A beacon. Right now, any vampire close would feel you if we were not shielding you from them. The puppets would be sent to acquire you. Sandu and your guardians would be helpless to stop them."

Sandu wasn't so certain that was entirely true. He had practiced, over the centuries, a few tricks while he lay paralyzed beneath the earth.

Adalasia touched her tongue to her lips and then looked from Sandu to Teagan as if for reassurance. "They eat human flesh? Puppets?" Her hand crept to her throat, fingers stroking there delicately.

Teagan turned her head to give Andre a glare. He raised an eyebrow. "What, *Csitri*? Is it not the truth? Better that she knows and both are safe. I believe in the truth."

"You might have been more diplomatic." She turned back to Adalasia. "I'm afraid that is correct. Vampires infect humans and create what we call puppets or ghouls. They do whatever their masters bid them to do. They're like the zombies in movies. Hard to kill, and they seem to have only two desires: to carry out the order the vampire gave them and to eat human flesh. They are truly disgusting."

Adalasia pressed her lips together and shook her head. "And sleeping underground? Do you do that, Teagan? It isn't a choice?"

Sandu tightened his hold on her when he felt Adalasia faltering for the first time. Evidently, she could face vampires and their puppets and taking blood from him, but the thought of sleeping beneath the soil could be the deal breaker.

We talked about this, ewal emninumam, he reminded gently.

I know, but I just can't . . .

Teagan shook her head. "It isn't a choice. It isn't safe to stay above ground. The soil rejuvenates us. It's rich with minerals and other things we need. When there has been a battle and anyone is wounded, the soil aids in healing."

Adalasia sat very still. She suddenly appeared small in the wide chair, with its thick, warm dark gray cushions. Sandu could hear the acceleration of her heart. She didn't pull her hand away from his; instead, she turned her hand so she could thread her fingers through his.

Listen to the sound of my heartbeat, Hän sívamak—beloved. Match your heartbeat to mine. Sandu brought the tips of her fingers to his mouth and bit down gently on them, hard enough to cause a little bite of pain, hoping to distract her.

Her gaze jumped to his. "Sandu talked about it with me. Explained it. Just the thought terrifies me. I can face a lot of things, but if I woke up . . ."

"I was the same way," Teagan confessed instantly.

It is difficult for me to believe she was ever afraid like I am. She feels so confident in herself. In her life.

Of course she feared what she didn't know, beloved, Sandu assured.

"Adalasia"—Andre's voice gentled even more—"do you think we would expect a human woman to become Carpathian and instantly overcome a lifetime of teachings and beliefs? You are Sandu's lifemate. A treasure in our world. Protected by every single one of our people."

There was a slight ripple in Sandu's mind that he kept carefully from Adalasia but allowed Andre to catch. *I have a need to speak with you of several matters, old friend. Matters that make me uneasy.*

Are these matters what prevented you from returning with your lifemate to the compound where Tariq Asenguard resides with so many of our brethren?

Sandu gave the slightest of assents.

Andre stood with his usual grace. "Sandu and I will patrol around the house, Teagan, while you show Adalasia our home. I know how much you like to give visitors the tour. We will return shortly." He gave no chance of a protest, merely dissolving, leaving behind no sign of him, as if he'd never been.

Sandu leaned over to brush a kiss on Adalasia's lips. "If you have need, you have only to reach for me with your mind."

She nodded, and Sandu joined Andre outdoors in the cool of the night. Off in the distance, a wolf howled, and another took up the cry. Sandu smiled and shook his head. "They welcome Nicu. He seems to be known everywhere he goes with the wild ones."

Andre listened for a moment. "Nicu is as wild as they are. It is good they have purpose, guarding your lifemate, Sandu. They need purpose to continue. Tell me what your concern with Tariq is."

"It is not only with Tariq. There was a bond formed between Ferro; Andor; Andor's lifemate, Lorraine; Gary Daratrazanoff and me when it was necessary in order to save Andor's life. Lorraine had to lead Gary to him in the netherworld in order to bring him back. We are bound together, all of us."

Andre turned his piercing eyes on Sandu. "That was a very risky thing to do."

"It still is. Gary is the only one of us now without a lifemate. She has been born and is in the world, we know that much, but she is too young for him to claim at this time, which leaves him without an anchor."

"He is powerful, Sandu. He and Luiz both. No one expected them to survive the claiming of the families. When they were assessed by the ancient warriors and accepted, in order for them to become one of us, they died and were reborn full Carpathian. To do that, every warrior from that family poured their knowledge and skill into them. They poured their darkness in as well. Both lineages are extremely powerful." Andre's voice was low. Cautionary.

Sandu nodded. "We can share Gary's mind at times, Andre. Believe me, I'm well aware he has more knowledge and skill than any of the ancients I've come across. I collected as many skills as I could from him. The others did the same. He allowed it, we didn't just take without his consent. But when Ferro found Elizabeta and claimed her, Gary and Tariq both acted strange. Gary shut down. All of us were uneasy, feeling as if they threatened her life in some vague way."

Andre didn't protest. He wasn't that kind of man. He thought things through before he made any kind of judgment. Finally, he walked toward the forest with slow, measured steps, Sandu beside him. Around them, the trees seemed to be alive with the flutter of wings. Sandu, feeling uneasy, looked up to study the branches moving with the wind. Yellow eyes stared back at him. Little screech owls clung with tiny talons or moved between trees as if seeking shelter from an approaching storm. It was too many owls gathered together in one area for his liking. Screech owls, for the most part, other than mating season, were solitary creatures. They didn't gather in groups.

Spies? For the Army of Nera? Could they have found Adalasia so fast? Blood called to blood. Of course they could have.

"You were in his head, Sandu. Ferro was as well. You cannot tell me you did not get some idea of why Gary might be a threat to a mated pair. He is a healer, and more, he is a second to the prince. He would defend Ferro and Elizabeta with his life. If he had bonded to all of you, Lorraine would hold him to this world. He would have some emotion, distant though it might be, and only for those in that bond, which means it would include Elizabeta when Ferro claimed her. That would make it all the more difficult for him to threaten her. If Elizabeta died, Ferro would die. All who defended and were bonded to him would die, Gary included; and Gary's lifemate, although unclaimed, would be left adrift. What did you see that could have been such a threat Gary would have felt he had no other choice?"

Sandu had few people in the world he trusted for advice. Andre was one of them, particularly since he had found his lifemate. It was also very clear to him that Andre already knew or guessed why Gary and Tariq had been a threat to Ferro and Elizabeta. It didn't surprise him in the least. Gary and Andre had traveled together at one time. Andre rarely traveled with anyone but the triplets, but now it made sense.

"Tariq and Gary were both aware of a group of Carpathians put in place after Vlad's reign. Each held a part of a stone—at least, it appeared to me to be a stone. I didn't ask questions of Elizabeta or Gary. The Malinov brothers were aware of this because their father had been part of this group. As you are aware, the Malinov brothers chose to give up their souls collectively. They had a long-range plan to take down the prince and rule the Carpathian people. Collecting the stones seemed to be part of this plan."

Sandu fell silent for a moment, waiting for a response, but Andre gave none.

"No individual possessing one of the stones knows who the other is. They can decide if the prince should be removed from his duties if they believe he is not performing them to the benefit of the Carpathian people. It was Gary's task to ensure that these five men stay alive and that no one find out their identities in order for our people to remain safe, so anything such as the devastation that occurred when Vlad failed in his duties could ever occur again."

"I imagine the brethren would have fought for Ferro and Elizabeta," Andre said, his tone mild. "Most likely, all of them. Or at least most. Gary and Tariq would know that. You and Ferro had to have known to even consider such a thing, they would have thought the circumstances dire."

Sandu nodded. "That may be true. I could feel Gary distancing himself as much as possible from Elizabeta, even though our bond extended to her once Ferro had claimed her. He tried to reject any emotion, no matter how small of a respite she gave him in order to carry out his task. I knew whatever it was had to have enormous consequences to all of our people, or he wouldn't consider such a terrible thing. In spite of the fact that all of the brethren would have fought for Ferro and Elizabeta, he wouldn't have backed down."

"Did Ferro and Elizabeta return to the Carpathian Mountains with Gary and the others?"

"Yes," Sandu affirmed.

The wind blew in a sudden gust. The wolves howled, the sound challenging, as if they had gotten the scent of prey. They suddenly went silent, and a chill went down Sandu's spine as he heard the flutter of wings again. He looked up at the tree they stood under. Two little screech owls sat in the branches. One was very still, wings folded neatly. The other had just landed, its wings still out, flapping for balance as it clung to a branch. Sandu scanned the owls, looking for the undead, but there were no signs of the vampire in either creature or on the tree itself. Still, he felt an urgent desire to get back to Adalasia.

Andre turned fully to him. "This journey you are on with your lifemate. Does it have anything to do with what you learned through your connection to Gary?"

Sandu considered that carefully before answering. He had been directed to this man for a reason. He wasn't going to answer hastily and not get the guidance he needed. Adalasia's life was at stake. It was one thing to gamble with his own, but he had a woman to protect now.

"I do not know the answer to that question. I do know I had a very strong urge to leave, and once I found Adalasia, I did not want to bring her to Tariq's compound. I had no specific reason why. Adalasia's path is intertwined with mine. Her enemies, she says, are human but *more*. By that, she believes they have called forth demons to aid them."

Andre sighed. "Sandu, Gary had to be certain Elizabeta was not in the compound to locate Tariq's stone. Tariq had to be protected at all costs, as did the others. They guard the Carpathian people. The task may have been abhorrent to him, but he would have had no choice but to carry it out. I know that word was sent to the others to beware and that once it was known that the Malinov brothers had knowledge of the stones and a ruling body, the stones were to be gathered and all power destroyed. They can't fall into the hands of the undead. Mikhail clearly doesn't suffer from the same disease his father did. Nor does he rule by emotion. He does not allow his lifemate to sway his decisions. He has fought hard to bring our people back from the edge of extinction."

Sandu frowned. "That does not mean, in the future, one of his kin wouldn't suffer the same problems his father did."

Andre shrugged. "That is not our present problem. Vampires never banded together or used modern technology as they are at this time. We have to get behind our prince and aid him as best we can. If we are to survive, Sandu, we have to get ahead of our enemies, and they managed to get a foothold on technology while we were trying to survive without lifemates. There are so few. The attack on our people nearly succeeded. Young Josef is one of our greatest treasures, with his knowledge of technology."

Sandu sent Andre a small grin. "I suppose he is. Ferro is quite close to him, which gives me no choice."

"You like the boy."

"Again, I have no choice." Sandu wasn't owning up, but it was impossible not to like Josef, with his spiked hair and sometimes pierced skin. He was as courageous as he was genius.

"You can only follow your instincts, Sandu. If you believe you should go one way, go that way. Danger surrounds both of you. I can't see where it comes from, only that it is there. Your family was one of many that fought the undead for our people in regions far from the help of other Carpathians. I was told your family, and at least three others who also had to battle alone, had other allies but also other enemies every bit as evil as the undead."

Andre turned back toward the house, and Sandu was grateful. He felt even more uneasy that Andre didn't seem to feel the threat that he did in the forest. The screech owls, with their round yellow eyes, continued to stare at them. He felt he was too far from Adalasia. They had kept the front of Andre's home in sight the entire time, and his brethren patrolled, but Sandu found he liked to keep his eyes on his lifemate, especially when he had shielded her from his mind during the conversation with Andre.

"Bring your woman into our world, Sandu, and the two of you get as close as possible. You have to be a unit. That is what I feel above all else. I know your family was one that was far from the Carpathian Mountains and all help from the brethren unless one chanced being in their area. I know danger surrounds both of you and will be coming from every direction. Above, below and both sides. It is good you have the brethren with you."

Andre waved his hand at the door, and it swung open at his command. "I know each pull in the direction you feel or she feels will be the correct one, and you need to follow that instinct. Your intuition will save you. You cannot have an ego or be arrogant simply because you are an ancient. You must listen to your lifemate and the thing she is able to use to guide both of you."

If that was so, Sandu's gut was telling him he needed to stay by her side—that something was wrong. The threat to her was already close.

Andre stopped in the warmth of the living room, with its double fireplace and dark hardwood floor covered in thick rugs. "She has a talent unsurpassed, a gift, but it is more than that. I would speak with her again, Sandu."

"I still feel uneasy, Andre. Strangely, it is not the feeling I get when the undead are near. But I feel as if she is in danger."

"I feel it, too. I think there is an urgency to completing the ritual for both of you," Andre said. "I really need to speak with her again."

Sandu didn't hesitate. The two women had returned to the living room, and both looked up when they entered. *Andre wishes to speak with you, Adalasia, and it is important you give him the truth. He has sight where it is veiled to others.* He didn't know how else to tell her.

Adalasia's gaze jumped to Andre, then back to Sandu. She kept her blue eyes fixed on him as if he gave her the necessary courage.

"Hi, honey," she greeted. When he reached her and had bent to grasp her chin, tilt her head up and brush a kiss on the tip of her nose, she smiled at him, then managed to look at Andre. "Your home is lovely."

"Thank you, Adalasia. The credit goes to Teagan and her grandmother. The two of them spent weeks designing the house and each separate room. I am very pleased with the results." He looked at his lifemate with pride, before switching his full attention back to her. "Would you mind answering a few questions for me? It would help me in giving you both the advice you came for. At least, that is my hope."

"Yes, of course, Andre. I really appreciate that you've opened your home to us and you're willing to help, especially at such short notice. I know it had to be an inconvenience."

Sandu reached for her hand as he sank into the chair beside her. There was no trembling in her voice, but he felt it in her mind.

I cannot share everything about my family with anyone but you, and perhaps those traveling with us.

It is all right, Sivamet. Just tell him what he needs to know. Andre is different. He knows things, and this is why we have been directed here.

"What do you have that guides you on your journey?"

She lifted her chin, her gaze flicking to Sandu. For a moment, he felt her protective barriers rise. She took a deep breath. "I read tarot cards."

There was a small silence. Andre continued to look at her. Adalasia pressed her lips together and then looked again at Sandu.

Tell him the truth.

"They are not just any deck of cards, Andre," Adalasia admitted, her voice a thread of sound. The flames in the fireplace flared so that shadows danced along the wall. She looked at them uneasily. "The deck has been in my family for generations, handed down from mother to daughter."

"The same exact deck?" Andre asked. There was wariness in his voice. Speculation. Beside him, Teagan stirred, but the Carpathian put his hand on her, and she immediately relaxed into him, but the tension in the room increased so that the air seemed to thicken.

"Yes." Adalasia didn't look at Sandu, but he felt her stillness. She gave the barest nod of assent.

"Do you know how they have managed to stay intact without disintegrating with age and use? With your fingers and others' touching them daily? Our ancient books have to be kept under glass and temperature controlled, yet you use those cards and allow others to touch them."

Again, there was a brief silence while Adalasia made up her mind. She moistened her lips. "The cards were sealed with blood," she whispered. "They had a strange reaction to Sandu. He believed it a reaction to power meeting power. I thought it was me being fearful of what the two of us faced together, and they saw my fear. Now I know the tarot cards recognized him specifically and reacted to him."

"I would like to see the cards, Adalasia. Perhaps they would react to me," Andre said. "I am Carpathian. An ancient. It would be an interesting experiment."

Sandu. The protest was almost a wail. Frightened. Almost like a child.

Keep your heartbeat in tune with mine, Adalasia. Sandu rubbed the pad of his thumb along her inner wrist. *Keep in mind that Andre is aiding us.*

What if I should see something in the cards he wouldn't like? Adalasia pressed her lips together as if to keep silent.

Andre might see something we won't like. He wants to help us and intends to. Do you feel he is our enemy?

No, not at all. I just feel . . . out of my depth. Lost.

Then use the cards. When they are in your hands, you have an anchor.

Adalasia straightened her shoulders. Took a breath. She looked out the window into the darkness and then at the dancing shadows on the wall. He saw the moment when she took a leap of faith.

"Sandu, *you* are my anchor." She said it aloud. Sandu could tell she meant it, and his heart did a weird clench in his chest. He found himself smiling at her.

Adalasia smiled back and then pulled her hand free of his so she could reach inside her shirt. Sandu watched carefully. There hadn't been the slightest lump or bulge in her clothing to show that she had anything hidden under that smooth material clinging to her narrow rib cage. Why would that be? Did the deck hide itself on her person? Now that he thought about it, he had never seen evidence of it, yet she carried it on her at all times, and it wasn't small.

The cards fell easily into her palm. Her demeanor changed subtly. She was in charge. She held the tarot cards between her palms for a moment and then offered the deck to Andre. "Shuffle them."

Andre reached for the cards. Sandu watched closely, as did Teagan and Adalasia. The room had gone silent, as if all of them were holding their breath. Andre's long fingers settled around the cards. Grayish white puffs almost like sparks floated around the cards and then settled into them. Andre simply held the cards. For a moment, his eyes were vacant. His body a shell. Once again, the double fireplaces reacted, flames flaring high, casting those ominous dancing shadows. Sandu went on alert.

Carpathians often went outside their bodies to heal others. It seemed as if Andre had done so in order to find the secret of Adalasia's tarot cards. He glanced at Teagan. She was fully Carpathian in that moment. She had always been very small and sweet. Now she was a warrior guarding her lifemate. He had no doubt she was ready for anything that might threaten Andre, and she would fight to the death. She'd been with Andre long enough that he would have taught her many things. A woman who would climb boulders when she could float would learn how to fight the undead, even if she had the Ghost to protect her.

Then Andre was back. His piercing eyes were pure steel as he studied Adalasia. "Carpathian blood was spilled, not on these cards, but they were exposed to what was infused with the blood. So there is no doubt these cards carry the blood of the Berdardi family, although what I feel is subtle but extremely powerful and feminine."

Sandu was grateful that Adalasia had told him. He had felt the reaction of the cards to him, those sparks sinking into his skin, trying to move through him to his bones. It had felt like a million needles, but at the same time, familiar. All too familiar, something he should recognize. Power meeting power. His own blood.

"You are not surprised, Sandu," Andre said.

He felt Adalasia in his mind, holding her breath, trying to keep her faith in him. Beside him, she trembled.

"I held the cards," Sandu said. "I know very little, Andre. What can you tell us?"

"The power comes from your line, Sandu. You have always been extremely laid-back around the rest of the ancients, preferring their talents to shine, but you kept your name. It isn't the original taken in ancient times, but you have carried this one for centuries."

Sandu nodded. "I moved enough and was alone enough that it mattered little."

"Those of us who remember that the Berdardi family guarded alone, unaided by other Carpathians, have always known the power and danger you represent. For these cards to hold this power, and they are not the actual well of power, your line is incredible."

Not the actual well of power? Sandu prompted.

Adalasia didn't reply. She was small in his mind, staying but keeping very still.

Andre handed the deck back to Adalasia with a nod of respect. "That you can wield these cards is a tribute to your courage and prowess."

"Thank you," Adalasia said. She clearly didn't expect that of him. "Have you advice for us?" Very calmly she shuffled the deck and then returned it to the velvet pouch before once more sliding it inside her top, where they completely disappeared again.

"Only that the two of you must be closer than most couples and never falter in your trust in each other. Listen to each other at all times.

Really listen and make decisions together. It is the only way you will get to the end of your journey alive to perform whatever task is meant for you. I wish I could see more for you, but I cannot. Sandu, I cannot stress to you enough the importance of Adalasia being brought wholly into our world. Without that, a full commitment between you is impossible, and that leaves her exposed to too many dangers. More importantly, it leaves an opportunity for your enemies to drive a wedge between you."

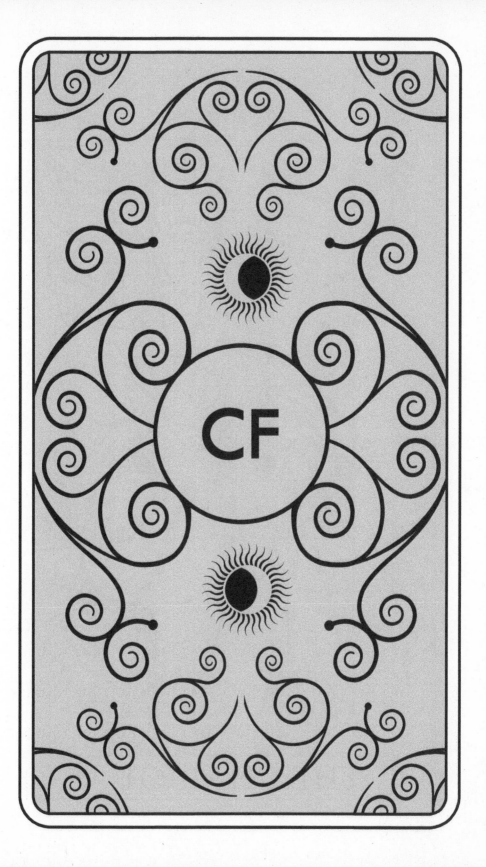

The Boroi guesthouse was hidden right up against the mountain itself, nearly impossible to see the way it was designed, unless you walked right up to it. The entrance looked almost as if one was approaching a set of boulders locked into the side of the mountain, covered in brush and small blades of grass and flowering shrubs. The front could have been a cave entrance.

As they walked through the trees and brush toward the little cottage, in which Andre and Teagan had assured them they would have complete privacy for the rest of the night, Adalasia noted the flutter of wings as very small screech owls moved among the branches. She felt uneasy being in the open, although she hadn't heard the wolves howling in a long while. Sandu glanced up at the trees more than once and then dropped two steps behind her, letting her take the lead to the strange accommodations Andre and Teagan had lent them for the night.

Adalasia wasn't going to show her disappointment. Sandu had made the last cave very nice for her. She just thought since Teagan's home was so lovely, the guesthouse would be as well. Sending them off to a cave didn't seem in keeping with Teagan's idea of entertaining guests, even though the woman was Carpathian now.

The path leading up to that dark entrance in the large gray boulders looked like uneven ground, but when they walked on it, the stones felt smooth, easy to navigate, even in the dark of night. She was very aware of Sandu walking close to her. He had those wide shoulders and that broad, muscular chest, wild hair and eyes that could look so feral when red flames burned in them, like now. When he looked down at her, which he always seemed to be doing, a dark fist of lust knotted low in her stomach. Her sex clenched and her panties were suddenly damp. It seemed as if all she had to do was look into his eyes, and he could do that to her.

When had the physical attraction toward Sandu grown so strong until desire bordered on out of control? She wasn't a woman who had reactions like the ones she was having. The more she was around him, alone with him, in his mind, the more she craved him. She was a little embarrassed that she couldn't control the way her body reacted to the least little brush of his hand or his hip as they walked together.

Then he smiled. Her heart seemed to do a slow roll. She would follow him anywhere. It wasn't just his looks. It was the intimacy they shared with each other. She felt him in her mind, connected to her in a way no one had ever been or would ever be again. He gave off a sense of calm even when everything around them seemed to be sheer chaos. She appreciated that trait in him.

"We're here," Sandu announced.

She had to stop staring at him. She really did. She forced herself to turn her attention to the cave entrance. They had stepped onto the gray and black stones right at the entryway. Adalasia couldn't suppress her cry of delight. It wasn't a cave at all, but a beautiful cottage built into the mountainside.

The front was a little round porch with two comfortable rocking chairs that faced the beauty of the forest. The floor of the tiny verandah was that same gray and black stone, as was the curving railing that surrounded it. The columns leading to the small overhead roof were stone as well, all blending into the mountainside, giving the illusion of being part of the boulders.

"It's like some little fairy house."

Sandu laughed at her expression. "Now you're seeing Carpathian skills at hiding their existence right out in the open."

"It's like magic. I thought it was another cave. Not that I'm complaining about the last cave we were in. You made it very comfortable and beautiful for me." She turned toward him and put her hand on his chest, not wanting him to think she didn't appreciate what he'd done for her.

The moment her palm was over his heart, she was aware of the way her heart tuned itself to his. It was such a strange phenomenon.

Touching his chest with her palm right through his clothing—that might have been a mistake—a *big* mistake. The moment she put her hand on him, the breath left her lungs, and there was no getting air. He felt hot. Scorching. Almost as if he were branding her palm, going through her skin straight to her bones.

She didn't want to make a fool of herself. She was already swinging back and forth, so confused by their strange relationship. She'd wanted the fairytale, and that wasn't anything close to the reality of their situation. Now, she was closer to the reality of the man that would be her life partner. Sandu. Man? Carpathian? Beast? Demon? All of those things? She didn't know, only that he was more real than her fairytale, and she was so desperately attracted to him.

Sandu's hand came up to frame her cheek. His palm was so large he cupped the entire side of her face. His thumb slid along her cheekbone in a little caress that she felt all the way to her toes. "I am so grateful to the universe that you are my lifemate, Adalasia. You are worth every moment of that seemingly endless wait."

The sincerity of his tone, that truth she found in his mind, was heart-stopping. She knew when she looked at him, he would see her heart in her eyes, but she didn't care. They had the intimacy of telepathic communication. It was rather silly to try to hide how she felt about him, nor did she want to.

His arm swept around her waist, and he lifted her like a man would his bride, carrying her across the threshold. He had done the same thing when they entered Andre's home. When they entered Lucian's home. She had her arms linked around his neck. Her small satchel had already been brought to the house, at least she was certain it had been.

Sandu didn't forget details, and the things that mattered to her were in that bag. She wasn't going to leave them behind. He knew that. That was another trait she loved in Sandu. If something was important to her, he remembered. She hadn't wanted to list anything good on the pro side when she mistrusted him, but he did take care of the smallest detail when it came to her.

Right now, as he carried her into the little cottage, she did her best to be wholly alert. Since the two blood exchanges with Sandu, her senses were much more acute than before. She felt the subtle shift of power as he crossed the threshold.

"What is that?"

"Safeguards," Sandu answered. "Every Carpathian weaves them into his homes. If you enter of your own free will, it gives him just that little more edge over you if you're Carpathian. If you're human, it isn't just an edge. He has much more power over you. The safeguards can be woven with all sorts of commands."

She gripped his shoulder hard as he set her feet on the floor. "Sandu, we didn't have to come here. I don't want you to be under Andre's influence."

He laughed softly, his eyes alight with humor. "I came here to consult with him because I have no memories of my past, *ewal emninumam*, and I stayed quiet, giving him the opportunity to speak what came to him. I respect him, just as I do Lucian. That does not mean he is older, has more battle experience or I feel I couldn't defend us in a fight. Andre would never attack us without provocation. He would have to feel as if his lifemate was threatened and we were the ones trying to kill her."

The way he was smiling softened the hard lines of his face. She dared to reach up and trace his mouth with the pad of her finger. "I guess I don't understand Carpathians."

"We use any method we can to protect our lifemate. You are my everything, Adalasia, my entire world, as Teagan is to Andre. I would do anything to protect you. Weaving safeguards into homes is just one way to help ensure we keep out intruders while we sleep the paralyzing sleep of our kind."

Adalasia made herself look around the cottage. It was small but very homey. Warm colors with lighting coming in from above during the day. Because it was night, sconces on the walls were lit with subtly scented candles. Lavender and bergamot—Adalasia identified two of the fragrances, knowing Teagan had thoughtfully put them into the candles to help her with the transition into their world, if she chose to make it.

Her heart stuttered. She knew it was necessary to continue their journey. She'd known once it was explained to her, but the idea was daunting. Terrifying, actually. They had both given up their secrets, although she still had one she had to confess. A big one. She couldn't just blurt it out in front of everyone. It was for Sandu alone, and telling him was a huge leap of faith.

"Before we go into the paralyzing sleep and more exchanging of blood and all of that, Sandu"—she made every effort to keep nerves out of her voice and mind—"I have something important to tell you. I swear it's the last thing standing between us. No one can know but you. Only you." She pressed her lips together and looked up at him, knowing he could hear the pounding of her heart.

His gaze held hers. Those eyes of his, so black. Like two dark holes in the universe, hauling in everything around them. She felt that tremendous pull, like a gravitational vacuum. Then she felt him in her mind, moving gently, searching as if to make certain she was all right, that she could tell him without being afraid.

He took her hand and bypassed the living room, heading unerringly for the bedroom. She knew he hadn't been there before, yet he knew exactly where it was. She frowned up at him. "Do you have some kind of map in your head where every bed is within a hundred-mile radius of you?"

He laughed. "*Sivamet*, I can wave my hand as I did in the cave and create a bed. I do not need a map. Nor do I need a bed." His voice dropped an octave, taking on an even sexier tone than usual. His eyes looked velvet black, a sensual note that seemed to stroke over her skin when his gaze drifted over her body, turning her inside out with need. "To prove that to you, you have only to look into my mind and discover I have worked diligently these last centuries to learn how to please my lifemate."

Her brows drew together in a deep frown. She did *not* want to hear about his sexual exploits.

He laughed again and rubbed the pads of his fingers gently over her eyebrows, proving he was in her mind. "I did not need to have sex with women, nor did my body want to have sex with them. I took in the information. It was very enlightening. Over the centuries, many techniques changed. I am certain all have merit. I wish to try them all and see which you enjoy most."

Adalasia found heat sweeping through her body. It didn't help that the bed was right there, looming large, looking like it took up most of the room. Still, she liked that he felt he could tease her, that he had a sense of humor. That was another trait important in a partner. She had a feeling they were both going to need it.

He bent his head and brushed a kiss to her temple. His hair tickled her neck, but that made her nerve endings spring to life—made her very aware of him.

"Tell me what you need me to know. You feared Andre might find out."

"The cards were able to hide the truth from him when he went seeking," she said. She looked around the room. "Sandu, just like in the plane, we cannot be overheard. I know Andre placed safeguards on this cottage, but we both have to seal it as well."

Sandu didn't laugh at her or point out that Andre was a powerful Carpathian, or that he was and had added his safeguards to Andre's. He merely inclined his head, suddenly as serious as she was. Just like before, she felt the difference in him immediately. He treated her opinion with just as much weight as he did the brethren from the monastery. His consistency meant a lot to her.

Adalasia told him the items she needed, and Sandu didn't hesitate to provide them. She cleansed the cottage first with sage before she began her ritual of safeguarding against Nera's army or any spies she might send or any demons Lilith might send. She had to seal the cottage against the smallest insect. The earth below them, the roof above them, the walls and mountain surrounding them on either side. She wove her guards as tight as she knew how. The rituals had been handed down for centuries from mother to daughter and added to as the pool of knowledge grew. She could only hope what she'd learned was good enough.

When Adalasia had finished, she was surprised that Sandu added his powerful safeguards to her weave as well. She watched him carefully, the graceful movement of his hands an artistry in itself. Everything about Sandu was graceful and flowing. She viewed him as a deadly poet, one of the fallen angels, all too ready to go to battle when necessary. Maybe too eager for the fight but not aware of it, because when he was in battle mode, all emotion was pushed so deep, he had no knowledge he felt it.

She could look at his face forever. An eternity. Those sensual lines carved deep. Those eyes of his, so dark they were black obsidian but burned with fierce red flames that took her breath and caused answering flames to roar deep inside her, like a runaway fire burning out of control.

He suddenly looked directly at her and smiled. The moment he did, her heart stuttered. She wasn't certain how she managed to stay standing when he made her feel as if her knees had gone weak.

"I believe Nera and her spies will have to stay out in the cold this night," he announced. "Tell me what you need to say. Let's be done with secrets between us. We have too many enemies, *minan ewal emninumam.*"

Adalasia sank down onto the bed. She wasn't going to fool herself into thinking she didn't want Sandu with every breath she took. "The card. The goddess card. I told you how important that card is, that it holds the blood of your line."

Sandu nodded.

"The card holds great power, Sandu. Much more than I explained to you. I carry it on my person at all times next to my heart. I told you that. She can ultimately determine life or death." She spoke the last in a whisper, feeling as if she were betraying her family's legacy. Mothers told their daughters what she was giving him. Wives never told their husbands. She counted on the fact that he was the one her family had waited for all those centuries. His soul passed from mother to daughter in the hopes he would continue to live.

Sandu stood by the window, his large frame draped casually against the wall, but suddenly he seemed much more alert. "Adalasia, I think it best if you tell me exactly what you mean by this power the card holds."

"I told you my mother was murdered. She was, but . . ." Adalasia tried not to remember walking into her home and finding her mother's body. The goddess card was exactly where it always was on her mother. Over her heart. "She allowed my mother to die. She could have kept her heart beating, but she didn't. My mother had passed your soul to me when she gave birth to me. If for some reason you aren't the one, Sandu, she will ensure that I will die. The cards will disintegrate. I don't know what will happen at the gate."

There was silence in the cottage. Absolute silence. Then she heard the wind. Branches scraping against the windows, making an eerie sound as if stick figures were trying to enter. She stroked her throat with nervous fingers.

"Is this card capable of stopping your heart, Adalasia?"

There was something in his voice that frightened her. Protectively, she placed her palm over her heart. "Don't think about trying to take her from me. She would fight you, Sandu. She might try to kill you. I don't exactly know what would happen."

"Show her to me."

She had known he would make that demand. It was one of the reasons she hadn't told him about the exact power the card wielded. Sandu was a law unto himself. He seemed every bit as powerful as the goddess card. She was positive Sandu was Liona's brother. Would they recognize each other through their bloodline? Was she wrong? The pull between Adalasia and Sandu was so strong she couldn't imagine that she was wrong.

He didn't repeat his command, but it was a command. He didn't take his gaze from her face, but those red flames began to burn over her.

Adalasia sighed. "No one has ever seen this card but the women in my family, Sandu. This isn't easy for me."

"I am your lifemate, Adalasia," he said gently. "You are my world. If this card is a threat to you in any way, I have to know."

She would only be a threat if Adalasia had chosen unwisely. If she was making a terrible mistake by agreeing to take this last step into Sandu's world. She knew she had entered Andre and Teagan's guesthouse with the intention of at least consummating her physical relationship with Sandu but, more than likely, also agreeing to that last blood exchange. It was a terrifying but, in her opinion, after everything that had been said, a necessary move. She couldn't allow her fears to in any way give Nera and her army the advantage.

"If we've made a mistake, Sandu, this could be disastrous." She had to warn him.

"There is no mistake, *Sivamet*." He placed his hand over his heart.

It was that gesture that gave her the courage to reach under the hem of her shirt and find the card always attached to her skin. Most times it was unseen, always unfelt. Now, surprisingly, it was very prominent, as if the goddess card had been waiting. The moment her fingers secured the card and she withdrew it, she felt the familiar confidence the cards always gave her when she had them in her hands.

She held the card to her for a moment and then out to Sandu. He came to her, and for the first time ever, as he prowled toward her, power crackled in the air around him. There was no doubt that he was fully Carpathian and he ruled supreme. Dominance and control were in every line of his body—in every step he took. Confidence and cool assurance flowed through him. His eyes meeting hers, he reached out for the card.

At once there was a burst of light. Adalasia looked down at the goddess card. The torch in her hand was suddenly lit with bright red-and-orange flames. Silver gleamed off the blade of her knife. The serpent twisted and writhed. The skull's eyes opened to stare at Sandu. The goddess peered at him with her silvery blue eyes, those brilliant blue flames burning in them. Her hair, streaked so much like Sandu's, crackling around her head. The two stared at each other for what seemed an eternity to Adalasia.

Sandu took the card from her, cradling it in his large palm. The pad of his thumb slid over the surface in a reverent, loving caress. "Liona," he whispered, "are you alive?"

The liquid being poured from one chalice to another turned dark red, like blood. The dress seemed to flutter. The two heads facing in the other directions turned toward Sandu to look at him. The roses and vines on the goddess's dress suddenly lit up in vivid color, and then it all began to fade.

Sandu looked down at the card for a long time before he handed it back to Adalasia. "I asked the wrong question and she didn't answer." His eyes met hers over the card.

Adalasia placed the card against her heart. "She answered."

"She did?"

She nodded. "She indicated she was alive. The blood flowing from one chalice to the other. The dress fluttering as if in the wind. Her attention turning directly to you. She recognized you. More, you recognized her." She hadn't expected that. Clearly he hadn't, either.

Sandu sank down onto the bed beside her. "I felt her through our blood connection. It was so strong. I didn't get a lot of memories, only strong ones of her. Of being with her, laughing with her. How could I not remember her? I still don't when I reach for memories of us together as children. There is nothing there. My mind remains blank."

Adalasia heard the frustration in his voice. He hadn't felt that particular emotion before. He'd accepted that he didn't have a past, just like he'd accepted that he would battle the undead until he was eventually killed. Now that he had a memory of his sister, he wanted more.

She reached out to him a little tentatively, rubbing his arm gently. "At least you know she's alive. You know you have a sister. That's more than we knew before we came here, Sandu. We made progress, and it was the best progress. It would have been so terrible to make this journey and, at the end of it, find out Liona was lost to us."

His hand covered hers before she could pull it away. "You are right, *ewal emninumam*, we are learning much on this journey. Those taking this journey with us have bonded with you. Do you feel them?"

Adalasia nodded. More and more she did. They were always in and out of Sandu's mind. Although she had never gone beyond the thick barriers in his mind, she was often catching little pieces of the other four "guardians." She sometimes thought she knew more about them than they knew about themselves.

"If you gave each of them a reading, would you know if they survive and find a lifemate?" Sandu asked.

His thumb moved back and forth on her inner wrist, right over her rapidly beating pulse.

She wanted to be honest with him. "I don't like to do that sort of thing, Sandu. If one of them isn't going to survive, or isn't going to find his lifemate, I don't want to be the one to deliver the bad news. It isn't like I can lie to them or deceive them."

"Nor would they want you to do that."

"Why do you ask?"

"Each has come to me separately and asked if you can verify what was told to them. Someone else has said they each have a lifemate waiting for them. They believe that you can give them the necessary hope to hold out longer against the scarring on their souls in order to find the lifemate promised."

Adalasia rubbed her temples with her free hand. "Let me think about it, Sandu. This has been a very difficult evening to try to take in so much information."

"It isn't the information you need to comprehend, Adalasia," he said gently. "It's your feelings. Whether or not you can fully commit to me. All along, that has been made more difficult because I withheld important issues from you, and you felt you didn't have a partner."

He stroked a caress down the back of her head, fingers lingering in her hair. "Liona approved our relationship. Even I could see that when the roses and vines displayed their vivid colors. She knows you and I belong together." His voice was soft, and she was so susceptible to it.

Rain began to fall in a steady rhythm, sounding musical on the stone roof of the cottage. Sandu's black eyes seemed to darken even more. "Adalasia. *Ewal emninumam.* Come to me all the way. Give yourself into my keeping." His voice was low. Mesmerizing. Seductive.

He was temptation and sin. She knew she wanted him from the first moment she had ever heard the sound of his voice. From the moment she entered his mind and formed such an intimate connection with him. From the moment she saw him, that masculine body that was perfection to her.

Her nod was barely perceptible, but she knew he saw it because those embers smoldering in his eyes suddenly leapt, just for one moment, into red flames. Sparks flew along her nerve endings as she reached slowly for the pearl buttons on the formfitting blouse she wore. Her gaze on his, she slipped each one from the buttonhole and pulled the material from her body. Next, she removed the velvet pouch that lay next to her heart, her palm automatically concealing the seventy-ninth card, sliding it easily into the deck, where it was welcomed. She wrapped the pouch with her blouse and set it on the end table, turning to face him in her simple blue bra and jeans.

It was a huge leap of faith to reveal the last card to Sandu, to let him know she carried it at all times on her person, right next to her heart. Now, she was trying to tell Sandu she was giving him her heart. That he was hers. She trusted him with who she really was. Not the shell she showed to the outside world but the real Adalasia Ravasio.

Pushing down shyness, when she'd never been shy, she reached behind to unhook the bra. She wasn't a small girl. She had curves. She was fit—had to be—but she had curves.

"My woman. So beautiful." He murmured his admiration softly. "I have never seen anyone more beautiful, and inside, the woman you are, even more beautiful, more pleasing to me."

"I'm nervous. I want this. I want you, but I'm nervous. I don't know what to do." She didn't. She wanted him to take over.

He seemed to know what she wanted, because she didn't have to remove her jeans—he did it for her, reaching across the bed, not using Carpathian skills but his own hands to pull down the zipper and slide the denim and her panties from her hips and legs. He tossed them aside and then he was kissing her. The room spun. She caught fire. Tension coiled low, a fist of dark need that grew hotter and tighter. Flames poured down her throat and through her veins. Rushed through her nerve endings and set her on fire. She wanted him until she couldn't breathe without him. Skin to skin. She had to touch him. Feel him against her. He had to feel the way she did. Desperate and hungry for him. Craving him.

His mouth left hers and she felt bereft. But his hands were on her skin, stroking caresses over her breasts, his thumbs moving in time to the rhythm of the rain—at first. He kissed his way to her throat and then her neck. Down to the curve of her breasts. *Dio*, the heat of his mouth as he pulled her right breast deep and stroked with his fingers her left. His tongue did something delicious and sinful. She felt the blood pounding through her sex, hammering in her clit. Her craving grew as his scent enveloped her.

His mouth wandered higher up the curve of her breast over the beat of her heart, lingered there, his lips pressing, kissing there. Her sex clenched. Her fingers fisted in his hair, wanting to keep him there. Her heart called to him. *Sandu*. She moaned his name. Frantic now. In her mind, she found his cock and stroked a caress. She wanted him to feel the same desperation she did.

His teeth sank deep, and the pain sent fiery shock waves straight to her feminine channel. That dark fist of lust wound even tighter. She felt a warm, welcoming slickness increase, the need for him heightened into more as the bite of pain turned to pleasure. She cradled his head, fingers deep in his hair, watching him take her blood. It was the most erotic thing she'd ever seen—or felt. She couldn't stop her hips from moving restlessly, an urgent reminder of her need. One leg slid along his thigh, over and over, trying to find a way to move the immovable. He finally lifted his head, his eyes staring down into hers.

Adalasia's breath caught in her throat. In the depths of all that black were those red flames. She was looking at a pure predator. There was nothing lazy or laid-back about him. His arms were around her, caging her in, his strength enormous. The lines in his rugged face were cut deep. He was fully Carpathian, an ancient who had walked the earth and battled his enemies for centuries. And he was hers.

She wrapped her arm around his neck and pulled his head down to kiss him. One hand slid up his chest. It was bare. Skin to skin. All those muscles. His body was rock hard.

I have waited so long for you. You are my only, Adalasia.

Their tongues tangled in the heat of the moment, a beautiful war. Then he was kissing his way down her body, leaving her breathless, without air. His hair teased her sensitive skin as he moved over her breasts to her belly button and then lower still, holding her thighs apart.

You're my only, too, Sandu. I hoped you would come for me. At the same time, I feared I wouldn't be strong enough to protect you from them. She couldn't say her greatest anxiety, that terrible truth, aloud.

He kissed the inside of her thigh. Gently. Leisurely. As if he had all the time in the world when she was on fire and needed him to hurry. *Ewal emninumam, I believe I am a male Carpathian.*

His tongue licked up the inside of her thigh and stopped just short of where she needed it to be. He pressed several kisses right there and then nipped with his teeth. He sucked gently. She squirmed to try to get him where she truly needed him. He moved to the other leg, ignoring her silent cues.

What does that mean? That you are a male Carpathian?

More kisses and licks up her inner thigh, driving her wild. That fist of tension coiled tighter. Hotter. She wanted to cry with need. His teeth nipped, and he sucked at her skin.

Teagan explained this to you, Hän sívamak.

Before she could reply, his tongue swiped through her folds, and she nearly sobbed his name. *Dio, nothing has ever felt that good. Other than your kisses.* She shared the feeling with him as best she could.

We are just getting started.

She had no idea that he meant exactly what he said. He really had learned skills in those centuries past. His hands and mouth, teeth and tongue built her up slow and then sent her flying, then took her up fast, and she detonated like a rocket. The third time he brought her close, he knelt between her legs and lifted her bottom easily to him.

Wrap your legs around my waist.

You look much bigger than I thought you would look. She tried not to let him see or feel the sudden trepidation. She wanted him with every heartbeat. Every pump of her blood through her veins. He was just a big man.

I was made for you. For your pleasure, Adalasia. You have nothing to worry about. There was no amusement, only love stroking her mind with gentle intimacy. With confidence.

She nodded. Her gaze once again searched his. He was perfection. Hers. *I was made for you, wasn't I?*

She felt him, the broad head of his cock lodged in her entrance, and it felt like a brand. Her body welcomed him. She wanted to impale herself on him, but she'd already learned that patience was rewarded. That building of a slow burn could make the roar so much better. She trusted Sandu to give her everything.

His gaze holding hers captive, he pressed forward, his thick cock invading, stretching her tight sheath, pressing into her until he hit that thin barrier. *Ewal emninumam, you are my heart and soul. Come into my world.*

I would follow you anywhere.

He surged forward, moving into her, past that thin barrier. The bite was far less than his teeth, and the pleasure of his cock filling her, welding them together, binding them, was already making that sensation long forgotten in the new ones he was giving her. He buried himself deep with a long slow stroke, all the way, and held himself there, looking into her eyes. It was intense, beautiful. Heart-stopping.

Tell me you are okay. I am not hurting you.

I want you to move. I need you to move. You haven't hurt me.

He smiled. That smile lit his eyes, and then he shifted positions subtly, just enough that when he began surging into her, over and over, building each thrust harder and faster, she could feel him hitting some spot inside her that felt as if he were lighting a match to dynamite. She was coiling tighter and tighter. Needing more and more. Feeling desperate to fly.

Sandu. She couldn't quite reach what she needed. What she wanted. So close. She was close. He felt so good, she didn't want this to end. It was so perfect. So beautiful. Sharing the same skin. As if they were one body and mind.

Adalasia. Sweet lifemate. His eyes burned into hers so that those red flames leapt. His body moved harder. Deeper. Faster. Feeding the hunger in hers. Driving through her scorching-hot silk as her body suddenly clamped down around his cock like a vise, so hard she swore she could feel his heartbeat, the blood pounding through it like a hammer. She hadn't known it was possible to love so passionately, so intensely. With everything in her. To give another person everything she was.

The powerful waves seemed never-ending, rushing through her body, throwing her into stars, taking him with her so that she felt the hot wash of his seed on the walls of her channel, triggering even more waves. Instead of collapsing over her, Sandu pulled her up, wrapping his arms around her so she was sitting on his lap, his cock still buried deep inside her, where he could feel every aftershock with her.

Adalasia laid her head against his chest, desperate to catch her breath, feeling dizzy with pleasure. How could his cock still be hard? How could her body still want his? She was still trying to just breathe when he was rocking her gently, and with each movement, her sheath clamped down tight around him.

She became aware of his heartbeat under her ear. She turned her head and pressed her lips over that call, her mouth suddenly salivating. For a moment, she actually felt as if two of her teeth were just a little sharper. All she could think of was his taste. Just the thought of that taste made her hips move restlessly on him. Shamelessly, she rubbed her breasts against him and then kissed his chest and used her lips, tongue and teeth to entice him.

Tell me what you wish, Adalasia.

I need the taste of you in my mouth. I want to ride you while I once more taste what is mine. I want to come fully into your world.

You always please me. His hand slipped down, one fingernail lengthening to open a line for her so his blood would entice her.

His palm pressed the back of her head to his chest as her mouth moved over him, seeking those beckoning dark drops. She felt his body in hers. Swelling more. Needing her the way she needed him. This was hers, too. His body. His blood. His mind.

My heart and soul. They are yours, Adalasia. You are their keeper. Come to me, lifemate. All the way. Come to me.

She didn't hesitate. Her tongue licked across that line of dark crimson, and the craving was instantaneous. She would forever need this—

need him. Her mouth settled over that line, and she drew more from him. His groan was sensual. The way his body moved in hers, slow and languorous, building the fire all over again.

Ride me, Adalasia. His hands went to her hips, guiding her. Keeping her movements slow and measured. Once she had the rhythm, one hand slid between their bodies to one breast, where his finger and thumb found her nipple. He began to tug and pinch and roll in time to the way she sucked at the aphrodisiac pouring into her veins and rushing through her body like a fireball.

The overload was too much. She didn't want to ever stop. Once again, it was Sandu who gently stopped her feeding and then captured her mouth with his, pouring fire down her throat. That fireball hit her silken sheath, lighting her up, and she began to rise and fall faster and faster, throwing her head back, riding him like a woman possessed. She clutched his shoulders, digging in with her fingernails while he rose up to meet her. The orgasm swept through her and then him, hard and fast.

They toppled over onto the bed, holding each other and laughing together in a tangle of arms and legs. Adalasia felt whole. Complete. She might be breathing heavily, but she was utterly happy. Satisfied. Feeling sexy. Beautiful. Mostly, she felt loved and protected. Sandu lay beside her, and for the first time, she felt tension in him. Real tension. She turned on her side and regarded him carefully.

"Tell me. What happens now? You're obviously not quite as happy as I am with what we just did." That was upsetting when sex with him was the best thing she'd ever done. She had envisioned a lot of that. Maybe he was disappointed in her. She believed in getting things out in the open.

Immediately his arm curved around her waist, and he brought her up tight against him. "Never think that for a moment, Adalasia. What we have is perfection. To become Carpathian, your human body must, in a sense, die. It is a painful process. I can, hopefully, make it less so, but I am told by many of those who watched their lifemates go through this that it was not easy. I do not want this for you, especially after the beauty of what we just shared."

She always tried to think before she spoke. She'd been warned. It wasn't like this came as a complete surprise. "Can you put me to sleep through it?"

"Unfortunately, not through all of it. There will come a time when I will be able to. At that time, I will open the ground and put us both in it. I'll command you to sleep until I awaken you. You won't accidentally wake underground, Adalasia, I give you my word."

She swallowed hard. "Okay. I do believe you, but just in case, there must be a way to open the ground."

He smiled at her and pushed stray strands of her hair out of her face, tucking it behind her ear. "That's my woman. Very intelligent. You visualize the earth moving away. Always listen for enemies before you emerge, even if it means lying in the soil but with the earth open above you. Use all your senses, Adalasia. They will all be heightened."

She nodded. Her hand found his. "I know you'll be there. I just like to know I can take care of myself in any emergency." She didn't want him to think she thought he would abandon her. She didn't. But sleeping in the ground . . . "I'll need my tarot cards with me. The Carpathian blood on them will allow them to go with me. They have to stay connected to me no matter what. If you put me in the ground, they come with me. And my book. The book is in my bag. Promise me." She was firm about that.

Something moved through her body like a shark with a razor-sharp fin swimming through her intestines. She pressed her hand to her stomach. "Do it now, Sandu. Open the ground where we will be. I have to consecrate it against any demons. Not just safeguard it from the undead. Hurry. There isn't much time."

Sandu immediately floated with her above the bed, waved his hand and opened the earth beside it, making a deep, wide rectangle. The soil was dark, but she could see it was rich with minerals. She took a deep breath and formed her prayer of protection, while Sandu set his safeguards, both weaving their guards east, south, north and west. Above and below.

He didn't remind her that they had already done this; he simply did as she asked. He also went through her bag and removed the book and set it beside her blouse, where the tarot cards were hidden.

Adalasia collapsed onto the floor, avoiding the bed instinctively. Sandu waved his hand to rid the room of it. At once, the combined fragrances of lavender and bergamot permeated the room. She felt it was just in time. There was no way she could make it to the bathroom. The shark had taken shards of glass and a blowtorch to her insides. She began to vomit repeatedly. As fast as she did, Sandu rid the room of all evidence as well as the smell. The pain was excruciating, but she tried to breathe through it, to stay on top of it.

Keep your mind in mine. Stay with me. You aren't protecting me by keeping us apart, Sivamet. Sandu's eyes were black velvet, red flames, both lover and predator.

She nodded, tears streaming down her face, but she cried quietly, her gaze clinging to his. She slid her mind wholly into his. Her body began to convulse before she could take a breath. He breathed for her, for both of them, while the blowtorch burned up her body from the inside out, destroying her internal organs, shredding them with those glass shards.

Through her tears, she could see three bloodred tears tracking down Sandu's face from each one of his eyes. *Don't. This is my choice. You are my choice. You waited endless centuries for me. I can handle a little bit of pain for you. You are worth every single second of this. Breathe for me. For us. Do that soothing thing you do. That comforts me.*

Another massive convulsion took her, this one lifting her body up and slamming her down. Sandu was there to catch her, to float her carefully to the floor. His features had changed. She'd never seen that expression on him. She knew she might never again. He looked at her with pure love. It was there on his face. Raw. Naked. He let himself be that vulnerable to her. And he got her through what could have seemed a lifetime, but with him didn't, before he could put her to sleep.

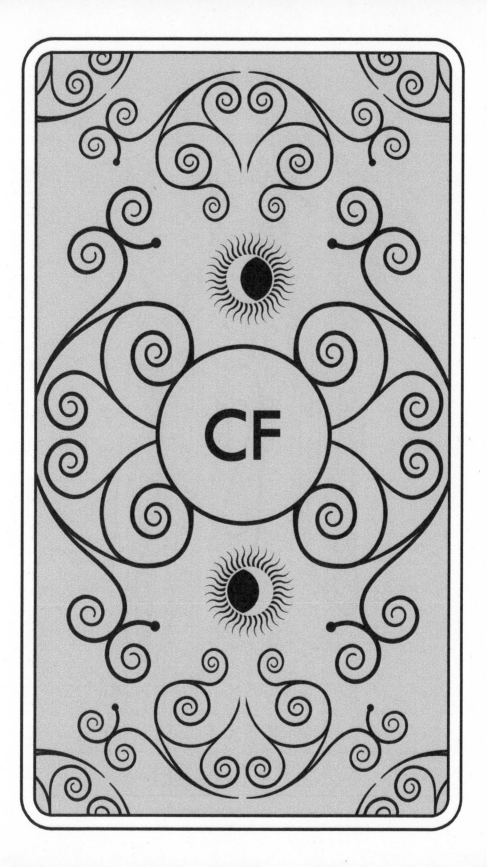

-VIII-

STRENGTH

Adalasia loved most things French. She could honestly say that. She especially loved the language and the accents. Walking beside Sandu at night and listening to the couples laughing and talking to each other made her smile. She couldn't help it. Sandu held her hand or simply walked with her close, his arm around her waist, just like any normal couple in love.

Gabriel and Francesca Daratrazanoff were a striking couple. Gabriel looked exactly like Lucian, his twin. A tall, imposing figure, his black hair was worn long like Sandu's, held at the back of his neck with a tight leather cord, the only concession to his ancient status as a vampire hunter. He looked like he belonged in the city, with the tailored suit that hung so perfectly on his body, emphasizing his wide shoulders and powerful body.

Francesca was tall and slender, with ebony hair that was so glossy it gleamed in the moonlight, tumbling around her face and down her back, framing her feminine curves. Her face was unlined, youthful. She laughed often and looked at Gabriel as if he were the brightest star in the sky. Adalasia had never met anyone that was as restful to be around as Francesca. She had a soothing, compassionate nature.

It had been Francesca's idea to show Sandu and Adalasia some of their favorite places in their beloved city of Paris before they retired for the evening to their home on the outskirts of the city. Wandering along the cobblestone streets, it wasn't difficult to see how Gabriel and Francesca had fallen in love with the beauty and artistry of their chosen home. There was an old-world feel to Montmartre, the quaint streets, the cafés, the style, as if one were stepping back in time and walking through a

Paris of years ago. The view of the city from the top of the hill was so beautiful, Adalasia actually cried.

Francesca was pleased. "I knew you'd get it," she said. "Come see the vineyard. I love the vineyard right here in the middle of the city," Francesca said. "Montmartre is gorgeous and unique anyway, but the vineyard, for me, is such a beautiful addition. The grapes growing on the hillside somehow just shout Paris to me."

Gabriel wrapped his arm possessively around his wife's waist and drew her close to him. "Francesca lived here long before I came into her life. The hospital and shelters are her passions. She takes care of those on the street. That's how she came to find me."

Gabriel ran his lips along his lifemate's high cheekbone and then to the corner of her mouth. His voice had gone as velvet soft as his eyes when he looked at his lifemate. "I woke starving. Disoriented. Afraid I would turn vampire if I took what I needed from anyone but was desperate to feed. I looked old and shaky, covered in a long-hooded cloak, walking the streets of a city I didn't recognize anymore after two hundred years in the ground. Francesca, in her compassion, stopped for me, sensing my distress."

"Did you know he was your lifemate?" Adalasia asked.

Francesca shook her head. "Not at that time. He didn't speak or even really look at me. He was huddled in that cloak. I thought in human terms. I'd lived as a human for so long and was trying to find a way to walk in the sun, to die as a human. I had accepted that my lifemate had chosen another path."

Sandu drew Adalasia to him, her front to his side, tucking her under his shoulder as if she might try to escape him even as they continued their walk through the eight-hundred-year-old vineyards that weren't open to the public. The four of them couldn't be seen. The Carpathians had cloaked their presence so Adalasia and Sandu could enjoy the vineyard and gardens in one of the places they particularly loved. In the night sky, a few small bats wheeled and dipped, chasing the insects hovering above the vines, caught in the silvery rays of the moon. A nightbird sang. Another answered.

"Francesca, there is no other path for a lifemate but to be with his woman," Sandu said.

"Lucian and Gabriel came through my village when I was young, and he looked right at me and turned away. I recognized that he was my lifemate and felt his rejection when he continued on with his brother. Later, I chose to be proud that he was a great hunter of the undead, but at the time, it was hurtful."

"Had I known, Francesca . . ." Gabriel said softly.

"I know," she said. "But I came here so I could live my life the way I wanted to live it, free and unrestricted by the rules of our society." She gave Gabriel a loving smile. "Then along came my lifemate and messed up all my very independent plans."

"You weren't happy to see him," Adalasia guessed. She couldn't help looking at the two of them framed in the silvery moonlight, as if that special spotlight was beaming down on their elegant beauty—and their obvious love for each other.

The night seemed so perfect. She could hear in the distance laughter and the murmur of conversation. Music. Overhead, more little bats had joined the others, feasting on the insects buzzing around the vines.

"No, I had my life all planned out, and he wasn't part of that plan. He did rather quickly change my mind." Francesca smiled up at Gabriel, looking at him as if the stars rose with him.

"I'm not in the least surprised," Adalasia said. She smiled up at Sandu. "They seem to have the art of persuasion down very well."

Francesca laughed. "They certainly do."

"From here, we have another surprise," Gabriel said. "It's located on the banks of the Seine right in the Jardin des Plantes. We can be there in a few minutes."

Sandu swept Adalasia into his arms. "I'll teach you the finer points of flying soon, *ewal emninumam*, and then you'll be able to do this on your own." *I know you like your independence, especially in front of others.*

That's true. She nuzzled his chin with the top of her head, brushing her silky hair against his rougher bristles. *But I do like being in your arms.* She did. She couldn't help it.

Before, she would have felt silly having a man carry her. She was tall and had curves. She was no small, willowy model type. She had firm muscles from years of working out, of practicing fighting arts. Of wielding swords and other instruments of death. Sandu made her feel as if she were as light as a feather.

Flying through the air is still a little scary even though I love it.

I know you do. I can feel the joy in you. Seeing flying through your eyes is a gift, Adalasia.

She didn't know what to say or do when he spoke to her like that, intimacy brushing the walls of her mind like the gentlest stroke of a paintbrush. It made her happy that he was seeing things in a different way, in color and with vivid detail. That made her think of the other Carpathian males, his brethren from the monastery.

Where are the guardian angels?

Sandu couldn't help but laugh. She'd taken to calling his four brethren the guardian angels. They were more like fallen angels, but she had great affection for them already. His lifemate needed a family, and she had quickly claimed one. Sandu and the brethren were her family, and she was attached.

They prefer to remain unseen in this environment. They have remained uneasy since we left Andre's home. Your blood is now fully Carpathian, but you still remain a Ravasio. Your ancestor will be able to track you.

Her arms tightened around his neck, and she laid her ear against his heart. *We knew that we would face danger at every turn, Sandu. When we set out on this path, that warning was always there for us to see, and we accepted it. Andre all but said we would be in terrible danger. I refuse to allow Nera and her army to make me give up one single moment of happiness with you. I hope you won't, either.*

He was grateful to the universe that she had been given to him. *That would be impossible, Adalasia. Every moment with you is one to treasure. But we must always be on guard. The brethren know that and surround us with their protection.*

Even cooler air met them as they dropped down to stand in front of a round platform filled with creatures of the past. Panels were decorated outside with wild animals, as well as what looked like at least twelve scenes from the Jardin des Plantes. Inside panels had a jungle theme, but Adalasia had eyes on the animals.

"What is this?" Adalasia looked up at Sandu, feeling like a child clutching his arm.

Sandu threw his head back and laughed. "It's called a carousel, which you well know. It may have strange animals on it, but it's still a carousel, *Sivamet*."

"A carousel," she echoed, her voice filled with wonder. "I've never ridden on one in my life. I've never even been this close to one. We used to have a tent sometimes where my mother would read tarot cards at fairs when a carnival would come into town, but she wouldn't let me leave the tent. Not ever. She said it was too dangerous."

"You didn't defy her and sneak out?" Gabriel asked. "You seem the type of child to go your own way and ignore authority. We have one of those children. She's grown now, but she gave us, and still gives us, gray hair."

"Gabriel," Francesca chided, but she was laughing.

"It's true, and I can see Adalasia being very much like Skyler." The legendary vampire hunter lifted a black eyebrow at her. "Do you ignore authority figures and just go your own way? Are you going to give your lifemate all kinds of trouble?"

Adalasia couldn't help looking up into Sandu's face. She wanted to trace every sensual line—especially now, when he was smiling down at her, mostly with his eyes. He had a way of melting her heart and setting her stomach into doing some strange loop, like a slow roller coaster might do right before it went off the rails.

"I suppose that might be a fair assessment. Although rebellion didn't start terribly early, and never with my mother. Mostly my father."

"Of course it had to be your father," Gabriel said. "Why is it that little girls are daddy's girls and then they rebel?"

"Perhaps you forget little girls grow up," Francesca ventured. "Just a thought."

Gabriel circled her waist with one arm and pulled her close, pressing a kiss to her temple. "We have a daughter, Skyler, who had been my adorable daddy's girl, until her heart was stolen from me by her lifemate." He sounded grouchy. Like a bear.

Francesca laughed. "You love Dimitri."

"I do *not* love Dimitri. I do, however, love my daughter, and Dimitri takes good care of her. Excellent care. He is a dangerous Carpathian, that one." He sounded very satisfied.

Adalasia got the feeling that Gabriel did like Dimitri, or at least really respected him.

"You gave your consent to their union," Francesca reminded.

"Smartest decision I ever made." Gabriel looked around him. "She was his lifemate. They were going to get together no matter what. I asked them to wait until she was of age. Then, when he disappeared, she went on her own with her two friends to find him, nearly started a war and almost got herself killed. I'll never forget that moment for as long as I live, when I thought we'd lost her."

Francesca leaned into him. "She is alive. Josef and Dimitri saved her life. She's safe, Gabriel, and we are in our beloved Paris with our children and guests. All is well." A soothing calm was in her voice, impossible not to respond to.

Gabriel nodded, one hand smoothing down the long flow of her hair. "Francesca loves this city, and I've grown to love it as well. It's become our home. We protect it and the people in it as fiercely as possible. Even though we are supposed to move every so many years, we want to keep France our home."

Francesca continued to lean into him. "That is our hope." She turned her attention to the carousel. "There is so much to see and do. We brought the children here not long ago, and I thought it might be interesting to you after being in San Diego with Charlotte and Tariq."

"I don't know them," Adalasia said and looked to Sandu.

Sandu slid his arm up her back to wrap around her shoulders. "I didn't take Adalasia to meet Tariq and Charlotte." He gave Adalasia the information she needed. "Charlotte restores old carousels, and Tariq has one of the largest collections in the world. I believe his family enjoyed carving them."

Gabriel nodded. "They did. Tariq has a few of those original horses from when he and his father worked together on them."

"That would be something to see," Adalasia said, turning her gaze back to the unusual carousel. "This is amazing, though, all these interesting animals."

Francesca nodded. "That was the point of the carousel. Its location right in the Jardin des Plantes is perfect. The National Museum of Natural History is close and a great way to continue educating the children on the extinction of species." She looked up at Gabriel. "Our species was—and still is—very close to extinction. We have a special place in our hearts for the subject and try hard to pass that on to the children. We thought this was a fun way to teach them."

"The Dodo *Manege*," Sandu read. *Manege* literally meant "carousel," so it was an apt name, especially since the dodo bird had been extinct for some time. "You want to take a ride, *ewal emninumam*, pick your animal to ride on?"

"The ride is closed," she whispered, looking around.

Gabriel burst out laughing. "What happened to the little rebel? Do you think we're going to get into trouble?"

"You look like bad boys to me. You'll probably break it, and we'll have to pay millions," Adalasia said. "Not to mention, we'll go to jail, and it will be in the news and draw unwanted attention to us."

"There is that, Gabriel," Francesca said, looking very serious. "The children would be mortified. What would their friends say? And those prison clothes, those colors wouldn't suit you at all."

"Vandalism of the Dodo *Manege*." Adalasia shook her head, her blue eyes alive with laughter. "Such a scandal. What would your brother have to say?"

Sandu thought she was beautiful, standing with the moonlight pouring down over her, bathing her in silver while she tipped her head back, teasing the legendary ancients.

"He would tell me I was a lucky man to have two such beautiful women to ride a carousel with on an unexpected clear night in my beloved city."

"I do so love a French accent," Adalasia said sincerely.

Sandu groaned. "Don't fall for Mr. Charming, *Sivamet*. He is every bit as ruthless as his twin. Choose your animal, and you can have your first ride on a carousel. It will be one of many firsts in beautiful, incomparable Paris."

Adalasia pressed her body closer to his while she looked over her choices. Sandu stayed in her mind while she observed each one and read about them. The vulnerable giant panda, the extinct Barbary lion, the critically endangered gorilla, the Sivatherium, which was an interesting mix of a giant giraffe with moose-like antlers, intrigued her. There was an aepyornis, or elephant bird, which looked to her kind of like an ostrich, now extinct. A very cool-looking glyptodon, which was said to be the size of a Volkswagen Beetle, had a hard, armored shell and was a relative to the armadillo.

She stepped onto the platform. Sandu could tell she felt silly to be so excited. It made her feel like a child.

You are giving both of us this first experience. I think the child in us needs it. Pick wisely for us.

Adalasia sent him a genuine, happy smile, and he knew he'd said the right thing to her.

"There is the dodo, of course, the extinct bird. A really nice triceratops, with its three distinctive facial horns and bony crest. I've always loved dinosaurs. There is this giant armored horned turtle, Meiolania, now extinct."

"Those aren't your choice."

"No, this is." She pointed to the one labeled *Thylacine*. "The Tasmanian tiger. I guess I like the look of it, with its stripes and strange body."

Sandu knew that wasn't it. To Adalasia, the animal was lonely. Restless. She read about it, and something in her identified with it. He never wanted her to feel lonely again. She had as a child, watching other children play together, go to school, ride carousels at fairs. He could see those childhood memories playing through her mind as she seated herself on the Tasmanian tiger and flashed him a heart-stopping smile.

Francesca chose the elephant bird, with its blue feathers, looking like an oversized ostrich. Gabriel lifted his wife easily into the saddle and seated himself on the Barbary lion. Sandu had to smile. The two looked an elegant couple even on the carousel of long-lost creatures.

Sandu waved his hand to put a seat on top of the basket the panda was holding so he could watch Adalasia's every expression as the carousel began to play the circus organ music and the animals responded by moving up and down. Adalasia whipped her head around to look at him, her eyes bright, laughter bubbling up, sharing her joy with him through their intimate connection.

Sandu had never thought to experience such a thing. Never. Those long endless nights of gray voids, an abyss of hell really, a bleak nothingness occasionally interrupted by a battle with the undead, there had been no hope left. He had forgotten joy. Laughter. Fun. Maybe he had never known it. Now there was Adalasia with her brightness.

You are very hard to resist when you look at me like that. There was laughter in her voice. She stroked intimacy in his mind, painted those caresses into the recesses where the scars of darkness were deepest.

You are not meant to resist me, ewal emninumam.

The animals rose up and down as the music played. Sandu looked away from his woman to the night sky once more. Bats were heavier in the air than he thought they should be, and his gut tightened. A slow frisson of alarm spread through his body. He was used to feeling the blankness from the undead. This felt different. A watching. A gathering.

Nicu. His brother from the monastery had an affinity with every creature that others didn't. Deliberately, he used the pathway of the brotherhood so all of the guardians could hear. *Reach for the bats. They feel off to me, as if they watch Adalasia. The Striga could be here.*

He didn't want to alarm Gabriel, Francesca or Adalasia yet, or steal their enjoyment of the night. There was no need unless he was certain. He scanned the ground around them. It was time to use all skills against Nera's army. If she was sending bats, rats, dogs, owls—particularly screech owls—as spies, he had to stop thinking in terms of just the un-dead and the society of vampire hunters. They had a newer, particularly deadly enemy, and he had to catch up with the way they attacked.

Insects crawled over the ground hidden by leaves and debris. Beetles and ants coated the ground; little crickets sang and lizards moved stealth-ily. Overhead, bats continued to gather in numbers. Movement close caught Sandu's eye, and he continued staring straight ahead, but he wid-ened his scan. In the distance, a few stray dogs seemed to be foraging for food near some garbage cans.

Bats are shielded. I spotted the dogs, Nicu continued. *They are also shielded. Get Adalasia out of there.*

Sandu didn't hesitate. "Gabriel. We have to go now. The bats are watchers sent by the enemy, as are the dogs down the street. We have to leave right now." He began to build a storm fast, expecting the bats to give chase. He wanted to incinerate them before they could follow them back to Gabriel's home.

Gabriel and Francesca took to the air, two large birds of prey, falling back to aid the brethren in protecting Sandu as he rose with Adalasia. At once, the bats moved, the air darkening with the migration as more joined them. Lightning forked in jagged arcs across the sky. Thunder rumbled and shook the ground hard enough to knock down the dogs, who were baying, giving chase as they did.

Benedek and Petru emerged behind Gabriel and Francesca, two im-posing figures in midair, throwing up nets to block the flight of the bats. Nicu and Siv held the sky nets as the bats were driven in. Lightning burst in overheated, white-hot charges straight into the dense cloud of bats. A burst of blue flames lit the sky, and then a horrible putrid odor spread through the air. Ashes rained to earth. The four men chased after the few remaining bats fleeing, those that had managed to escape the net and had been continuing their pursuit of Sandu and Adalasia. Once they were certain they had managed to destroy every one of Nera's pursuers, they turned their attention to the demons who had taken on the shape of dogs.

The animals raced through the streets, red eyes to the sky, baying, calling to one another as they ran, saliva dripping from their fangs. These weren't the hounds of hell, not even close, but they could do damage if they found their intended victims. The four guardians used their skills honed by years of fighting the undead to send spears of lightning when they had a clear shot without any witnesses close. Each time they struck, the animal was instantly stopped in its tracks, going up in that same blue flame, the putrid odor permeating the air before it was totally incinerated.

Sandu, the ground, Afanasiv warned.

Below them, the ground shook, and a deep schism widened in a long zigzag to expose a wide wall of skulls and bones. The skulls tipped upward, the empty eye sockets burning red to stare up at them as Sandu, with Adalasia in his arms, flew overhead that exposed wall of human remains. Bones shot out of the wall like missiles, aiming straight for them. Arms with hands, bony fingers reaching, while the skulls directed them, bouncing above them, mouths opening and closing obscenely.

Adalasia sat up straighter in Sandu's arms, drawing a small curved athame from one of the many loops in her coat as well as a small vial of salt. She faced outward toward the skulls and bony arms trying to rip her from Sandu. Pointing the athame straight in the air, she drew the boundaries of protection around Sandu and her, although she kept those boundaries very close in order to draw the demons using the bones in close as well.

She felt Sandu hesitate when one of those long-dead hands caught at her dangling ankle and slid off before the bony fingers could close around it. *Don't falter for a moment, Sandu. Keep going no matter what.*

She began to chant softly under her breath as she pulled more items from the loops in her coat. The scent of white sage drifted into the air. She waited until the skulls and their disembodied arms surrounded her on three sides, and she flung the salt in a sweeping arc, following it with a long cut of the athame. The skulls opened their mouths in a silent scream of pain. A blessed athame could cause pain to the demons even when they had no bodies. They fell back with the sound of rattling bones.

They cannot follow us to Gabriel's home. Can you destroy them?

Give me another minute or two. She poured conviction into her voice. She wasn't certain. She'd never been flying through the air before with skulls and bones from the catacombs surrounding her—the demons from hell obviously using them. But they had to be lesser demons. There was no time, and Nera wouldn't have wasted the effort. She pulled a large piece of magnetite from one of the deep pockets in her coat. As she did, she began to chant a prayer softly, holding the mineral rock in her palm facing out toward the skulls and bones. Each time the light from the moon glinted off the stone, the skulls shriveled and dropped back.

At the last moment, she transferred the stone to her other hand, and taking the little vial of liquid she had concealed behind it, she popped off the top with her thumb. Raising her voice, she dispersed the liquid in a wide circle around Sandu so that the contents of the vial scattered like rain on every bone and skull, little tiny droplets landing on them. Smoke rose into the air, long trails of grayish vapor. Wails filled the night. Bones and skulls dropped from the sky, no longer directed by the demons she had banished.

Sandu, can you send them back to the catacombs? They need to find peace again.

Sandu did as she asked, and she watched as the skulls and bones once more returned to the wall and settled back into their original places. He closed the earth, and they continued on their flight to the Daratrazanoff estate.

Gabriel and Francesca were already waiting for their return by the time Sandu reached the safety of their home with Adalasia.

"I am sorry. We nearly brought the enemy to your home."

"We sent the children away when you told us there was every possibility," Gabriel answered. "Come inside. Your brethren seem to have everything under control."

"They will patrol outside your home while we talk," Sandu said.

Gabriel and Francesca's house was old, a mansion surrounded by a high wrought iron fence and a terraced garden with explosions of color from various bushes and flower gardens winding up to the main house.

The mansion rose up like a vision from the past, complete with alcoves and gables, balconies and even a few gargoyles hanging from the eaves. The estate seemed out of place even though it was situated close to an old cemetery and on the very outskirts of Paris.

Inside the house was modern and airy, all Francesca and her soothing ways. The interior felt comfortable and restful, from the colors to the furniture. Each room flowed, one into the other, and the ceilings were high, giving one the feeling of having space. Heavy drapes hung at the banks of windows, which was necessary to block out the sun in case they couldn't escape to the chambers hidden below the basement.

The house looked lived in, everything from the children's rooms to the master bedroom. The family had perfected the art of blending in with the humans around them. Even in the kitchen, there was fresh food in the refrigerator and more stocked in the pantry.

Gabriel and Francesca were known for the many charities they funded. They were very active in their community, particularly in the local hospital, homeless shelters and women's shelters. Unlike most Carpathians, they lived out in the open as if they were human. They would appear to age and then die. Eventually, they would come back as another couple, younger and starting over. The house would be left to one of them, as would the estate. It was easy for Carpathians to amass fortunes over the years. Their children would also do the same thing if they stayed close.

Sandu found it very interesting that Gabriel could live in a city and enjoy it, which he clearly did. Gabriel led them into a room that gave off a soothing warmth after the chase of the demons.

He took a seat on one of the very comfortable-looking sofas that would bring Adalasia close to him. When he drew her down with him, she gave him a smile that he knew was supposed to reassure him. All that did was make him want to carry her off somewhere he could be alone with her, where he knew she would be safe. Where would that be? They had started on this path. They had to stay on it and see it through to the end.

"I have few memories of my past, of my childhood or family," Sandu said. "I believe I erased them deliberately or they were erased for a purpose. Andre told me he believed my family was one that guarded a region other than the one close to those living in the Carpathian Mountains. He indicated Vlad asked a few hunters to carry messages to those families hunting the undead in those far-off regions occasionally. I hope that you might have run across me or members of my family in those early days and might give me some news of them since you and Lucian traveled extensively."

"It is true we did travel far, although we were not used to taking messages. We were hunters. We did come across these families occasionally, but only because we were severely wounded and apart from one another. That would happen if we had to separate to chase after two different master vampires."

Gabriel was silent for some time. "It was a long time ago. There was a family I stumbled across in my travels that guarded what would now be somewhere close to the Russian border. They gave me blood, but in those days, Sandu, there were no surnames. The forest was heavy, especially in that area. I have no idea what became of the family."

"We think Sandu is from an area in Italy," Adalasia said.

"The De La Cruz brothers were in that region before they crossed over to South America," Gabriel said. "Danutdaxton also lives in South America. He is very old. It is possible he would have information for you. I'm sorry I cannot be of more help."

"You have no more information on the family that lived in the Russian area?" Adalasia asked. *Each of the three other women—friends of your sister, according to the history book—had accents from a foreign land, Sandu.*

"Not much. I believe they had a son and daughter, neither of which I met. The father gave me blood, and I was grateful for that. The exchange allowed for me to see glimpses of his home life. I tried not to intrude."

That was very normal. An unmated male, even one as legendary as Gabriel, would have been treated as a potential threat. He was a risk and a very dangerous one, more so than most simply by being the legendary Gabriel. The unknown Carpathian who had given him blood had been courageous to do so.

"Do you remember—again, this would be long ago—a child went missing? A little girl of about ten. She must have been from one of the prominent bloodlines. Dubrinsky. Daratrazanoff. Dragonseeker. Matais. Any of the ancient brethren from the monastery. Perhaps even Danutdaxton's bloodline. Those I cannot remember from my time." Sandu studied Gabriel's face, then looked to Francesca. "Do either of you remember such an occurrence?" Carpathian children were guarded like treasures. They didn't simply just vanish.

"There was such chaos, Sandu," Gabriel said. "But the loss of a child, a female child at that, would have been noted. All Carpathians would have been organized to search for her. I was often out of the country, but I did hear rumors of such a tragedy." He scrubbed his hand over his face and looked to his lifemate. "She was never found."

Francesca shook her head. "No, she wasn't. Her brother had been gone for centuries when she was born, but he had returned when he heard of her birth. She was a beautiful child, intelligent beyond her years. She had a gift already, the sweet sound of her voice could calm a raging beast, some say tame it. I was told she stopped a wolf pack from tearing apart an injured human man, and she was only three. I have no idea if that story is true or not."

Sandu glanced at Adalasia. *Could Lilith have heard of this child's abilities? Did she think the child could get the beast behind the gate to obey her?*

Adalasia frowned. It was clear she had no idea of what Lilith might be contemplating, but Sandu could think of no other reason why Lilith would trade Xavier for that particular child. If she could get raging beasts to listen to her, she might be an asset to Lilith.

How would Lilith have heard of her and her talent? Adalasia asked Sandu.

In Romania, there are reports of the Striga from all kinds of sources and different areas of the country. Perhaps she has spies everywhere.

"You believe this little girl was taken for a purpose," Francesca said softly.

"She must have been," Adalasia said.

She was young. Was it possible, if Lilith was good to her, for the child to grow up feeling as if she owed it to Lilith to protect her? To do anything she asked?

The child would always be Carpathian, and she would grow powerful even if she didn't understand the power she could wield. She would hear lies even from one she might consider her mother, Sandu pointed out.

"What lineage is she from?" he asked Francesca.

It was Gabriel who answered, pulling all information from his life-mate. "Bercovitz. She is Tiberiu Bercovitz's baby sister, Gaia Bercovitz. He never speaks of her. Never utters her name. He holds to the old ways of never talking of the dead, although I believe he still looks to find who took her. He is like an old wolf who will never stop hunting. She was special to him. Important. A sign of hope. He believes if he speaks of her, it might draw attention to those who took her, and they might harm her if she still lives after all this time."

Francesca nodded. "He never believed the story someone started that she just wandered off. She wasn't that type of child. Had she wandered off, she would have found her way home. He believed someone took her and prevented her from calling out for help or coming home on her own. I believe the same way he does, that someone took her."

"If you remember nothing of your past, Sandu, how did you know of this child's disappearance?" Gabriel asked.

Sandu looked at Adalasia, who nodded her head. He would never tell anyone anything without her permission. "We believe she was taken, too. Adalasia's family has a book, a kind of history of her family that an ancestor depicted with little pictures she drew with descriptive journaling. Adalasia was terrified of the parasites that were in my blood when I fought a vampire . . ."

"Not terrified." Sandu's lifemate gave him her best narrow-eyed glare. "Repulsed. Disgusted. Afraid, maybe, a little. *Not* terrified," Adalasia corrected.

Sandu shared a smile of pure male amusement over her head. "I stand corrected. She noticed the parasites and they disgusted her. A little. *Very* little. She showed me an image of them her ancestor had drawn in this book, which was handed from mother to daughter."

Deliberately he sat back in his chair, looking as superior as possible. "Personally, I thought it was inappropriate reading material for children, especially before they went to bed. Adalasia will have to just get used to a male authority figure letting her know that book won't be read to our daughters when they're young, and certainly not before they go to bed." He intentionally poured utter authority into his voice.

"Excuse me while I kick him in the shins really hard." Adalasia smiled sweetly. Sugar dripped from her voice.

Gabriel threw his head back and laughed. Sandu joined him. "She really is your lifemate, Sandu. Perfect for you in every way, isn't she?"

Sandu brought Adalasia's hand to his mouth to kiss her knuckles. "She is perfect for me," he agreed, his voice going soft. He looked at her then. Whenever he did, he went soft inside. That told him he couldn't look at her too often, especially if the enemy might be close.

"Tell us more of this exchange if you can, Adalasia," Francesca said, leaning toward her. "I'm not trying to pry into what is obviously a sensitive family history, but if we're to help you, we need to know who might be able to best give you guidance. While Tiberiu seems the most likely source, I don't think it best until you have more to go on. It just doesn't feel right to me." She looked to her lifemate for guidance.

Gabriel shook his head. "No, Tiberiu is not right yet. You will have to go to him, but not until you have more information. He is not an easy man, as you well know, Sandu. Any mention of his sister must be carefully worded."

"I honestly can't tell you more of the actual exchange between the mage and the old woman, other than I know Lilith wanted the child enough to make some kind of deal with the mage for her. That specific child had gifts she wanted to utilize. I don't understand everything, only that Sandu and I have to figure this all out, and we have to do it together. We're being hunted by an ancestor of mine, which is how she continues to find me."

"A blood trail," Francesca guessed.

"So Sandu tells me, but I did think that if I was fully Carpathian, she wouldn't be able to find me so easily. My blood would be Carpathian blood."

Francesca inclined her head. "That is so. She would have a more difficult time, and she cannot get into your mind. That is blocked to her. You do retain who you are. You will always be Adalasia, which means at your core, your ancestry is still intact. Unlike a male coming into our world—who would literally have to have every single part of him replaced so that only his knowledge is kept intact deliberately—he becomes wholly whatever Carpathian lineage he is taken into. A female isn't changed on such an overall level."

"Why?"

"A male has to have a complete rebirth, his soul split, the ritual binding words imprinted on him to be able to bind his lifemate to him, and his ancestors must judge him and deem him worthy before he is accepted. If he isn't accepted or if he isn't strong enough for the passage, which is extremely difficult, much more so than yours, he will die. It is extremely rare to bring a male into our world for that reason."

Adalasia tapped her finger against Sandu's thigh. Sandu remained a silent presence in her mind, watching her think things over. She was careful about it. Logical. Trying to process the information against what she already knew.

"A child of ten wouldn't provide Lilith with a lot of blood, and she wouldn't make a great sacrifice. It doesn't seem like a good exchange on Lilith's part. She could have asked for a full-grown woman or an infant," she ventured.

Sandu, this has to be about the beast.

"When did Lilith give the parasites to Xavier?" Gabriel asked. "I have to presume the mage to be Xavier."

"I have no idea," Adalasia admitted. "Each of the drawings in the book are little paintings or drawings. No one thought to put in dates until much later, although I know that particular one was painted by Nera and Tessina's mother, but I have no idea of the actual date."

"I wish we could be of more help," Gabriel said. "The best I can offer you is to seek information in South America. Dominic Dragonseeker resides there, and he might be of help. The De La Cruz brothers traveled extensively, particularly Zacarias, the oldest. Danutdaxton is there as well. He will know of many things that may be of aid to you."

Adalasia looked up at Sandu. "That's a very interesting and memorable name."

"Dax, as most who meet him now call him, is a very interesting and memorable Carpathian," Gabriel said. There was the slightest hint of amusement in his voice. "He was locked in a volcano with his greatest enemy for over a hundred years. He became much *more* there in that volcano without blood to sustain him. He will be an experience for you to meet. His lifemate, Riley, was, at one time, human. He guards her with the jealousy of a dragon."

Francesca nudged him when he laughed. "You think you're so funny, Gabriel."

Sandu tightened his fingers around Adalasia's hand. "Gabriel is laughing because Dax carries the heart and soul of a dragon inside him. The Old One resides in him."

Adalasia frowned. "I don't understand. You mean he shifts into a dragon?"

Sandu shook his head. "He found a dragon in the volcano. It was nearly dead, but in the end, it entered Danutdaxton to flee the volcano as it roared to life and the master vampire was escaping."

Her eyes met his. "I think I'm in just a little bit over my head. I can handle demons, but I'm not all that certain about dragons."

-IX-

THE HERMIT

The rain forest was beautiful beyond description. Every tree trunk wept with orchids and vines. Adalasia had never seen colors so vivid. Everything seemed larger than life. The vines hung in thick loops or streamed to the ground like great ropes. It was so much more than that. She hadn't known there were so many shades of green.

Up high in the canopy, crawling up the tree trunks, were plants growing on top of plants. She could see that none of those beautiful, sometimes lacy and sometimes leafy, flora ever had roots in the ground. They grew high in the air, right off the trees, winding their way around the trunks, colonizing over the moss and lichen, the shrubs, flowering plants and vines. It was a different, diverse world and so beautiful, it was breathtaking.

Frogs were as diverse as the plants. She was fascinated by them. The colors, the sizes, the sounds of them. They seemed to be everywhere. The more she looked for them, the more she discovered. Sandu and the others found her highly amusing and kept trying to drag her along toward some destination she knew wouldn't be nearly as beautiful or as captivating as what she was seeing.

"Sandu," Petru said. "The only way you're going to get that woman of yours moving is to throw her over your shoulder caveman style."

Adalasia narrowed her eyes and gave Petru her best glare. She had never expected to grow fond of any of her guardians, but they all shared a bond with Sandu. That meant, since she shared that bond with them now, she also had come to know them somewhat. She was grateful she could lift their tremendous burden from them in a small way occasionally by sharing her emotions with them.

Petru could be mesmerizing with his odd mercury-colored eyes.

Sometimes they would flash an eerie silver or darken to an almost stormy look that was just as scary as the silver one. His hair was that same silvery color as his eyes—platinum, thick and long—tied back like the others, with leather cords. She had been intimidated by him—by all of them in the beginning—although she'd pretended not to be. Now she saw inside them, caught glimpses of who they were, and they were honorable men. They might struggle, as Sandu had, but they had a strict code that had ruled their lives. She counted herself lucky they considered her a little sister.

"I know you aren't suggesting he force his will on me simply because I'm enjoying my first time seeing the rain forest."

"I did not suggest it, *sisarke*, I told him it would be a good idea. Now I am concerned that your hearing is compromised."

She liked that he called her "little sister" in the ancient language. It was a term associated with affection.

"I have to agree," Benedek chimed in. "The night is fading and we have much to do. You are stalling. It is unseemly of you."

Adalasia drew herself up to her full height, which was considerable—unless she was surrounded by giants. It was just her bad luck that the Carpathians were unusually tall and broad-shouldered, making her feel much smaller than she really was.

"I am not stalling. You've seen the rain forest many times and clearly have never taken an opportunity to enjoy the gorgeous sights, but I have never had the chance. Look at those tiny little frogs. They are so cute. And they make the biggest sounds even if they're so tiny. Their feet are almost as big as their entire bodies. So are their eyes. I love them."

Nicu caught her wrist and turned it over so that her hand was palm up. He deposited a little frog right in the middle of her palm. "There you go, take it with you. That way you can stare at it all the way to our resting place."

At the same time, Siv shifted her braid from her left shoulder to her right and placed a frog there. "I thought to give her a gift as well."

Adalasia remained very still. "Afanasiv Belan. Did you just put a frog on me like a ten-year-old schoolboy would do? You're supposed to be two thousand years old. I would have thought you'd outgrown this juvenile behavior. After I put these poor little creatures back where they belong, I'm going to kick your ass. Nicu, take this one right now and put him back in his home. You know better."

Very carefully she extended her hand toward the Carpathian. She used her best teacher voice. It was difficult to keep from laughing. They were acting like schoolchildren, but she liked them teasing her.

Nicu took the little frog with the round golden eyes and put it carefully back on the tree. "At least you didn't jump like a gir— baby."

She nearly forgot the little frog on her shoulder, whirling around to confront him. At the last moment, she put her hand up to keep the little guy from falling, although his sticky feet would have kept him clinging to her. "Nicu Dalca, you were about to say 'girl.' Jump like a girl. Not all girls jump around frogs. And some males do jump around them, just in case you aren't aware of that fact."

She heard a snicker and glared over her shoulder at Sandu, who was looking all too innocent, and she didn't believe that look for a minute. Very gently, she rescued the little frog from her shoulder and placed it on the tree among the vines that were wrapped around and climbing up the trunk.

Sandu held up his hands in surrender. "I'm giving you all the time in the world, *Sivamet*. These four are eager to get to our destination because they want you to read their fate in the cards as you've promised them."

Adalasia narrowed her eyes at him. "I believe you promised them a reading. I hedged. I was very clear about hedging."

"Hedging?" Benedek repeated. "As in evading? Does that more modern word mean you were intending to get out of reading the cards for us?" His very black eyes gave him a feral look. Or he was just plain feral.

"Not exactly. I was concerned, that's all." Adalasia believed in honesty, especially with these men. They were extraordinary and would never be less than honest with her. "The cards can be brutally honest. Removing hope is something I don't want to do, not when all of you mean so much to me. I have no other family. Sandu has explained what happens to the Carpathian male when he has no lifemate and no hope of one."

"It is best to know, *sisarke*," Benedek said. "I would prefer to know while I am still strong enough to make the decision to meet the dawn."

Adalasia knew he meant to suicide. She looked around her at the beauty of her surroundings and detested that they would have to talk of such things. The worst of it was, she knew to these men, it was simply a fact of life, a possibility they had lived with all those centuries, and they accepted it.

Adalasia wanted to shout to the heavens against the unfairness of it. These were good men. They were the best, and she didn't want to be an instrument that in any way contributed to bringing them down.

"Adalasia," Sandu said gently, his hand sliding up to shape his palm around the nape of her neck.

He had to have felt the sadness in her mind. They all did, as much as she tried to hide it from them. She wasn't that adept at keeping her emotions from them, especially when her feelings were intense.

She moved into Sandu without conscious thought. More and more, she was understanding the closeness of lifemates. She knew she would need that to always be in step with him and learn to think with him so that they were as close as possible whenever they confronted Nera's army.

Sandu swept his arm around her and then swept her up, cradling her close. At least she was spared the indignity of being put over his shoulder upside down. The sound of a waterfall was growing louder. She had to admit, she loved waterfalls. The water splashed into a pool below. She could hear it hitting the surface of the water as well as the rocks. It was becoming increasingly easier to identify sounds and smells.

I would not do that to you. There was a hint of laughter in his voice.

She knew he was doing his best to tease her out of her sadness.

"Are you certain you got rid of all the leeches in this cave and the pools inside, Siv?" Petru asked in a low voice. "Last time we used this series of caves, you said you cleared out the leeches, but you did *not*. It isn't a pleasant memory, waking with all those wiggling, bloated creatures trying to attach themselves to suck the life out of me."

Siv gave an overt sigh. "That was over a century ago, even longer. I told you at the time, more of the little fiends must have come during the day. I had no such problem where I chose to sleep in my chamber."

Adalasia clutched Sandu's shoulder and turned her head slightly to make certain she heard every single word. She was not about to sleep under the ground if there were leeches. That was out in a big way. She didn't care if she wouldn't know or if they couldn't suck her blood because it wasn't running through her veins. She began to go through her protection prayers to see if there was anything that would repel leeches.

"I was covered in the vile creatures as well," Benedek said, his voice even lower. "And I was in a different chamber than both of you. They were like a blanket over me. Did you only clear your chamber, Siv?"

"I would not have done such a thing. Perhaps something in your bodies attracted them. A mineral. How would I know why leeches were attracted to your resting spot? Perhaps this cave system is their breeding ground."

"Now that I recall," Petru said, his voice grim, "there were hundreds of gelatinous cocoons with the egg masses inside attached to my body and all surfaces around me and even buried in the soil beneath me. Several of the leeches were curled around one another, still attached. It was a ghastly awakening. At first, I thought the undead had found me."

Adalasia dug her fingers into Sandu's chest. *We are not going into those caves.*

Why are you listening to them? There was a kind of lazy amusement in his voice.

She was silent a moment. *Are you telling me that none of that ever happened? They are making it up for my benefit?*

That is exactly what I am telling you.

She was silent, still clutching his shirt. *Don't let on that you told me, please.*

She got the impression of laughter. She had to turn her head back to see the steady fall of frothy water coming from above them and falling into a pool of inky water below them. Gray-blue boulders half concealed by large lacy ferns lined the edges of the pool and the stream that ran toward the river.

What are you up to, ewal emninumam?

Sandu ducked beneath the waterfall and carried her back into what looked like a very shallow ledge with a wall of rocks behind the water. She couldn't even see the crack in the boulders there, but Sandu waved his hand, and the crack widened.

I'm not certain yet, but I'll let you know.

"I will make absolutely certain to clear out all leeches," Siv promised solemnly. "But I cannot stop leeches from returning to your resting place. You can try to weave your own safeguards against the pesky creatures. They are not the undead, after all. They are part of nature. Normal. I do not think our safeguards work against their invasion. Only if they are working for the vampire."

"I will take the chamber you used," Petru declared, "since they mysteriously did not show up in your soil."

"Unfortunately," Nicu added, "we have returned at the same time of year. It is possible they are breeding again."

Adalasia gave a little shudder that was very visible and hid her face against Sandu's shoulder. Who said she didn't have acting skills? She knew the guardian angels were looking at one another. If they could feel smug, they were.

"I'm going to make us very thin, *Sivamet*," Sandu cautioned. "We'll go through the crack and be on the other side in seconds."

She gripped his shoulder and chest tighter and nodded, already planning out her revenge on the four men following closely. Just before Sandu could step through, Benedek moved in front of him.

"Best to let me lead the way, *ekäm*, just to be certain. There is no evidence of the undead, but we take no chances with either of you."

Whenever he called Sandu "my brother," it melted Adalasia's heart. Still, she was getting them back for trying to scare her with the leeches-in-the-ground story. That was a must. She just had to be very clever about it because they did weave safeguards around their sleeping areas, and they didn't tell others where they were sleeping. She knew they would choose chambers or areas of ground to surround Sandu and her, but she wouldn't know exactly where, so she would have to be very, very cautious in the way she handled the idea already formulating her mind.

Benedek looked like a thin shadow sliding through the crack ahead of them. Then they were slipping through right behind him. Petru followed, then Siv, with Nicu bringing up the rear and closing the crack. All of them turned to weave safeguards.

"Sandu, I have to seal it as well against Nera's army," Adalasia said firmly. "She uses insects and worms, as you well know. I overheard the guardians talking about leeches . . ." She gave another delicate shudder. "Nera can use insects and worms here in these caves if we don't protect ourselves against her demons. Your safeguards hold out against the undead and what they send, but not necessarily all of her spies."

He set her down, and she deliberately looked all around her feet as if looking for leeches before she began to add her weave of protection to the Carpathian safeguard. She was preparing the brethren for her little payback, but she was also serious, and she was thorough, making certain that Nera couldn't penetrate their defenses if she found them.

"Sandu, can you light the way a little better?" she asked as they began moving through the narrow passage toward the deeper spaces away from the waterwall. She kept glancing down nervously at her feet as if she suspected, any minute, that leeches would surge up her feet and legs.

Sandu obliged her, and she caught the guardians giving one another knowing looks. If there was shared amusement, it was through her lifemate. He shared emotions with them when they weren't in her mind so she could lighten their burdens. Let them have their fun. She wanted them to think she believed them.

The passage opened into a series of large chambers, each bursting into startling sparkling light when Benedek waved at the upper walls to install sconces. The moment they lit, the gems embedded in the dirt glittered with shockingly bright colors as if they'd been polished. She wanted to stay and examine each section they passed through, but they kept walking.

Adalasia practiced temperature control. The caves were surprisingly hot. She thought they would be cold so far under the ground, but it was the opposite. Roots had burst through the dirt in many places, looking for all the world like strange, groping, hairy arms. There was that constant sound of dripping water. In some of the chambers they walked through, there were pools of standing water that looked shallow and dirty, others that were deeper. There was mud and there were mostly dry surfaces.

Then the chambers opened up into an entire underground world. Light streamed in from tiny cracks in the rocks, allowing seeds from plants to grow in the rich soil. The cracks were very small but there were many, allowing light to come in from above them and, in some cases, as they continued to walk through the high-ceilinged caves, the sides.

"This is amazing," Adalasia said. "It's crazy that no one is aware it's all down here."

"They will discover it soon enough," Sandu replied. "The grounds above will continue to erode with time, and the cracks will widen. When the water pours through, it chips away at rock. It will take time, but it will happen eventually."

They came to a very large chamber that looked almost like a grassy meadow with a few ferns growing. Sandu waved his hands to help illuminate the space with more sconces. He gave the area more of an indoor feel by spreading a lush carpet and adding chairs and a table.

Adalasia's heart accelerated. The chairs were set in a semicircle around the table. She knew the guardians wanted her to read the cards for them. She'd hoped, as they walked through the chambers, that everyone had just forgotten they wanted readings. Or changed their minds.

As usual, Sandu had paid attention to detail. The chairs were extremely comfortable-looking, but they were antiques. The table was an antique, one that was replicated exactly from the home she'd shared with her mother. The sconces on the wall were very old-fashioned, looking as if they burned candles, and the flickering lights danced on the gem-studded walls.

The brethren stood looking at her expectantly. They were so large. Tall men with broad shoulders and absurdly long hair that didn't belong in this century. Their faces were chiseled and etched with lines, yet they appeared young, with their heavily muscled bodies. They were warriors, and it showed in their stillness and in the fluid, easy way they moved.

They surrounded her. Adalasia thought she'd gotten over being intimidated by them, especially now that she was Carpathian as well, but even drawing herself up to her full height, there were times, like now, when she felt their immense power. Their auras were dark and difficult to read. She shared a bond with them, and yet she couldn't move past the barriers in their minds.

She knew there was that same scarring on their souls that couldn't be removed. They thought of their souls in tatters, dark and beyond saving, with numerous holes, but whatever was left had thick layers of scar tissue built up from battle after battle, kill after kill. Too many, until they were no longer just Carpathian but not the undead. They were . . . predators. Living for battle.

They felt the rush of the fight, the rush of the kill, but didn't realize they did. *She* had experienced it. Sandu hadn't. He didn't wholly realize that the electric energy sizzled through his bloodstream with his adrenaline when he went into battle. That he changed completely into a cunning, animalistic predator eager for the fight.

On some level, all the ancients had to have recognized that they had gone beyond Carpathian hunters; it was why they had elected to enter the monastery—to keep others safe. Now, to find their lifemates, they had once again left those gates of protection and were out in the world seeking. Hunting. Killing the undead. Adding to the burden their souls already carried.

"You're all certain you want to do this?" It took great effort to keep her voice from trembling. She sank into the chair on one side of the table.

Benedek took the chair opposite her as they all nodded. The other guardians took their seats but stayed very close in order to observe.

Adalasia pressed her lips together and looked up at Sandu. He was the only one standing. He stayed right beside her, one hand on her chair. She didn't know if she was looking for courage or if she wanted to strangle him for getting her into this. She knew why these men sought answers. They were courageous, the way they so stoically faced their long lives and the possibility that they might have to end them without ever having the reward of a lifemate.

"*Sisarke,*" Benedek said softly, clearly seeing her apprehension. "Look at me, not your lifemate. I asked for this. If I do not get the answer that I would prefer, there is no blame. There is no right or wrong. It simply is. I was told my lifemate is alive. I was given a direction. The direction became impossible to follow." He looked at his brethren. "Our monastery was protected by the clouds, safeguarded in an illusion, so that any seeking it would become lost. That was what kept happening when we each sought our lifemate using the map given to us by Trixie and Gabrielle, Fane's and Aleksei's lifemates. They may have been wrong and we have no lifemates, but it is better to know than to have false hope. We are too dangerous to be let loose on the world. You know this about us. You see it in Sandu, and we are the same but without anchors."

"Reading these cards is no joke, Benedek. They will tell the strict truth." There was a lump in her throat. She felt raw and hurt inside. "Right now, you do have hope. If it is gone, what then?"

"Each of us has walked this earth alone for a very long time, *sisarke*, even before we went into the monastery and stayed locked behind the gates in the clouds of illusions. When I say a long time, I mean hundreds of years. We had to develop our values and strengths to get through dark times. We are seekers of knowledge. It is constant learning and always the idea of facing the truth, *sisarke*, no matter how difficult, that gets us through with honor. We may walk in darkness, but we turn a bright spotlight inward at all times, looking at who we are, where we are, how close the beast is. While I am strong, Adalasia, I wish to know. If my lifemate is no longer on this earth, then I will choose to meet the dawn while I have the strength to do so. I do not want Sandu or any of my brethren to have to hunt me." His voice was gentle but firm. "I am asking you, Adalasia, as your chosen brother, read the cards for me."

She took a deep breath. Over her heart, the goddess seemed to move with gentle understanding of the overwhelming task she faced. Benedek traveled with her to protect her. She barely knew him, although she sometimes caught glimpses of him in her mind, but she found she had tremendous feelings for him, that of a sibling. He was already family to her. She might not know him, but she knew the heart of him.

She felt the strength of Sandu's hand down the back of her head, his fingers lingering for a moment in her hair, and then on the nape of her neck.

I am with you.

A simple statement, but it meant everything. He knew how difficult she found this reading, as well, and he gave her his support.

There was silence in the cave, other than the dripping of the water and the sound of frogs and cicadas. Somehow, she found those sounds comforting. She drew the pouch from beneath her clothing. The moment the deck was in her hands, she felt the familiar confidence pour into her. The cards felt a part of her. She could almost feel them talking to her.

"You need to shuffle, Benedek, and divide the deck into thirds."

She handed the deck to him, watching closely to see how the cards reacted to his touch. Benedek was powerful, and as with Sandu, she knew he would be recognized as Carpathian. She hadn't been certain which layout she wanted to do for him until that moment.

Benedek took the cards without hesitation. For a moment, there was the smallest struggle, as if power met power, and then sparks in a multitude of colors rose, as if the cards could see past the brutal fighter, the dark aura, to discover the artist in the man. He shuffled and did as she asked.

"Choose one of the thirds and hand them to me."

She went for a simple layout, turning the cards faceup. She could feel the energy running through them. His energy and that of the cards, or the goddess's. The truth. She didn't always know what to call it. She only knew that it was there, guiding her. She saw right away that his lifemate was alive in this century. Not only was she alive, but there had been a distinct reaction, joy throughout the cards at Benedek's arrival.

Adalasia couldn't help smiling. Big. It was there in her mind. In her heart. In her soul. Such a relief. She was so thankful she nearly burst into tears. She looked up at him. "You definitely have a lifemate, Benedek. There is an answer here." She looked over the cards. Although joyful, there were signs of danger. Many signs of danger along the way. He had a journey to take just as Sandu and she were on, and his was twisted and hard to interpret, just as hers was. At least she could tell him he did have a lifemate.

She felt the burst of happiness from the brethren for Benedek in her mind, although there was little expression on their faces. She wasn't certain they even knew they felt any emotion.

"*Sisarke*, you have given me much to think about on this night. I thank you for what you have done." He stood and bowed formally to her before walking away.

The moment Benedek got up from the small table, Sandu was there to help her up. "You need to walk around and stretch, *Sivamet*. These readings wear you out."

"I was very tense. It was frightening to think I might see something I didn't want to in the cards. I have to cleanse them before I read for Petru," she added. "Benedek is powerful, and there can't be a trace of him lingering when I do a reading for Petru."

She was careful to make certain she had cleansed the cards before she sat down once again across from Petru. The idea of reading the cards for Petru was a little easier after Benedek, although she was still tense. She tried not to be. She didn't want to influence the cards, or the goddess card. It was just that, like Benedek, Petru Cioban was a man of honor, and she wanted his lifemate to be alive. She controlled her trembling hands better than her trembling heart, but part of that was her determination to keep the reading as short as possible and just concentrate on whether his lifemate was alive. That was his question.

She watched carefully, as did the others, as she transferred the deck to his hands. Like Benedek, there was no hesitation in Petru. He simply took the cards in his capable, strong hands. The moment the thin material touched his bare skin, there was that flare of life, of recognition, power to power.

Petru's mercury-colored eyes went silver, and his platinum hair crackled the way the cards did. Little jagged streaks of lightning appeared around the cards as if a great storm had suddenly swept in. The storm could be seen in his eyes, but if the white-hot flares snapping at his hands hurt, he didn't drop the cards or indicate in any way he was about to toss them aside. He took charge, shuffling with dexterous fingers while the storm raged around his hands. He didn't falter, not even as the lightning began to recede and finally was gone.

Adalasia hadn't realized she was holding her breath until she let it out, or that she'd pressed her hand over her heart so hard, she was nearly bruising herself. She pressed her lips together, silently sending up a prayer that Petru got his answer in the affirmative.

"Divide the deck into fourths and choose each of the stacks to represent one of the directions. Place them facedown where you want them to be."

He did as she asked. He divided the deck into four and put each stack into positions representing north, south, east and west. Looking at Adalasia with his stormy eyes, he kept one finger on top of each of the stacks.

"This deck is powerful, *sisarke*. It carries a feminine power, wholly Carpathian, and sought to look inside me." There was no accusation, only a statement.

She always relied on her intuition when giving a reading. Petru was an ancient, and there was no way he would let anyone he didn't know see beyond those barriers he had, just as Sandu and the others had them. The goddess had tried to penetrate, but she hadn't succeeded, not even when she'd threatened him. He had remained steadfast.

Adalasia was very familiar with the feeling of the cards. At the moment, they were calming, the aftermath of the storm. Petru didn't lift his fingers until every white spark of energy had ceased, and she realized he was protecting her, as if he thought the deck might burn her in its ferocity. She couldn't help the quick look she sent to Sandu or the way her heart reacted, melting a little at the way his ancient brethren had so quickly bonded with her.

You allow them to share your mind and emotions, Adalasia, Sandu reminded.

These men, her lifemate and his brethren, the ancients, they were guardians, protectors, and they did so automatically, never thinking of themselves. She blinked away the tears burning behind her eyes and forced herself to have a calm mind. She had trained herself to see a pool of water without a single ripple. If a thought came that shouldn't be there, she let it go across that pool, the wave taking it away from her, so she could only see and hear what the cards were telling her.

She nodded at the stacks. "Turn over the top card from each of the stacks." Her mouth was dry. She did her best to try to follow the heartbeat of her lifemate. Steady. Strong. Reliable. *Please, goddess.* Not that the goddess could do anything about his lifemate. She could only provide the answer. It was just that . . .

Petru turned the top cards over with no hesitation. The breath nearly exploded out of Adalasia's lungs. There she was. His lifemate. Alive and well in the century with him. Danger surrounding him. That was not entirely unexpected. Betrayal. A terrible sacrifice.

"There you have it. You don't seem to get off any easier than Benedek or Sandu with your lifemate."

"I have a lifemate," Petru said as he stood. "That is all that matters. The rest can be handled. Thank you, *sisarke*. You have given me much this night."

Adalasia reflected on his simple statement as she cleansed the cards in preparation for her next reading. *That is all that matters.* The ancients reduced everything down to what they believed to be the most important. In the end, Benedek and Petru had lifemates. They had committed to guarding her with Sandu and would stay before setting off on their journey to find their lifemates. She hoped the cards would be more specific now that the question had been answered.

Again, she went back to the table. Sandu was at her back. His touch was light on her shoulders, as if he knew the burden was becoming a little more difficult with each reading. She felt, almost as if by fate, giving the first two lifemates, the other two might suffer a different end.

Afanasiv Belan. Siv. He had lighter hair, like Sandu, with streaks of silver or platinum, and blue-green eyes that could pierce right through to a person's soul. He was, to Adalasia, the most unpredictable of all the brethren, and the most like Sandu.

Like the others, he was hidden behind that solid barrier in his mind, but she felt that same demon lurking close, as she had with Sandu. She knew it was there in the others, that they were all dangerous, but in Siv, as in Sandu, maybe they had just lived that little bit longer or seen just a few more battles. The scarring on their souls was thicker and more wide-spread. He was just . . . feral. She was a little terrified to hand over the deck to him. The goddess seemed to be very exacting when it came to judging anyone asking their question about lifemates.

Siv's eye color had deepened to a kind of turquoise, like the deepest clear sea. Hypnotic. Mesmerizing. Insistent. He wasn't going to let her pass on him. She took a deep cleansing breath and gave in to the knowledge that no matter what, these men faced their fate head-on. Alone. With their heads unbowed.

Adalasia extended the deck of very ancient tarot cards to the man sitting so casually across from her. Without hesitation, Siv wrapped his large, calloused hands around the deck. At once, the cards reacted, power against power, just as they had with the others, only this time, she could see cyclones of water bursting around the deck and between his fingers. The sound of the wind increased so that it roared ferociously through the chamber. The flames in the sconces burst high and then went out.

Afanasiv didn't move. He didn't change expression, but the green swirled darker through the turquoise, a dangerous mix of color that looked as ominous and as turbulent as the cyclones spilling out around his large hands. Adalasia watched the power struggle play out, although it wasn't really much of a struggle. Siv refused to enter into any kind of retaliation, not in the least upping his strength. He simply held the cards loosely while the cyclones leapt and whirled and the wind shrieked through the chamber.

Eventually, the wind began to settle into fierce gusts and then dissipated as if it had never been. Sandu waved his hand toward the sconces to relight them. Siv calmly began to shuffle the cards. Adalasia kept her gaze on the deck, opening her mind so that the right reading would come.

"Divide the deck in half and set one half aside. With the other half, place one card directly in front of you, up high in this position." She indicated where she wanted the card to go. "Then three cards straight across with two cards straight across under that. Each of the two cards is between but below the ones in the row above. Six cards altogether. Yes, like that," she approved. "Set the rest of the deck aside. Now turn them over, starting with the top card."

She waited. Heart pounding. There she was. So beautiful. That card they were all looking for. She pressed her hand over her heart. His lifemate was alive. She waited to see if she was there in the present. His past was one of terrible loneliness and hardship. The card depicting his present—*her* present—was one of the now. This time. This century. His bridge appeared to be more battles, a war of some kind. Swords. His future—it was possible to find her and keep her alive if they believed in each other and surrounded themselves with those they could trust. There was something huge blocking him from reaching that ultimate goal. He had to overcome that in order to achieve what he wanted most.

Afanasiv sat very still looking down at the six cards. "You got all of that from those cards? My lifemate is alive, in this century, I have many more battles to fight and must surround myself with those I trust in order to keep her safe. Also, there is something blocking me from finding her."

Adalasia frowned as she looked the cards over. "Not necessarily blocking you from finding her. Blocking you from achieving what you want most. You not only want to find her; you want to be with her. Or, I don't know, claim her. Form a partnership with her. Whatever your greatest desire is."

Siv sat there a moment longer. "Thank you, *sisarke*. I know this is not easy on you." He stood up and moved away from the table to allow Nicu to take his place.

Adalasia allowed Sandu to help her up. She took her time cleansing the cards. For some reason, she was very reluctant to give Nicu a reading. There was something in him that drew her. A wildness. A freeness. His affinity for animals. She didn't know. Whatever it was, she knew he was just as scarred and as dangerous as his brethren. He was special.

She sat down with him and had him take the cards, not in the least surprised when the struggle manifested itself as wild beasts. The animals escaped the cards, showing razor-sharp teeth and red glowing eyes, but that would in no way deter Nicu. He merely waited calmly, almost soothing the deck, one thumb sliding over the top of it like a stroke he might do in the fur of an animal. Once the cards had settled, he shuffled and laid them out in the pattern Adalasia instructed.

Adalasia frowned down at the cards, trying to read what they were saying to her. It was the first time the meaning was murky. She was certain Nicu's lifemate was alive, but the direction was impossible to see. She was there—and yet she wasn't. That made no sense at all—unless . . .

Nicu began to rise, almost shoving at the little table, nearly sending the cards sliding. Adalasia stopped them with a wave of her hand, not even realizing she'd done it.

"Don't move," she hissed. "This isn't easy. Everything is murky. Don't disturb the cards." She didn't look up at him, keeping her eyes on the cards, afraid if she looked away, she would lose that thread in her mind.

Nicu settled into his chair. "I do not want you to tell me something that is not true. You did not take this long with any of the others, nor did you get that particular look on your face."

Adalasia did look up then. Clearly, Nicu thought the cards told her he had no lifemate. "She's alive, but . . ." She trailed off and looked down at the cards again, her brows going together. She rubbed her hand over her heart, silently asking the goddess card for help in her reading. "I'm going to have you shuffle again and turn over just three cards, Nicu."

Nicu's eyes met hers as he scooped up the cards and shuffled them. He didn't look at them as he divided the deck several times and then chose three cards and laid them faceup on the table in front of Adalasia. The breath left her lungs in a small rush. The devil card again. The chariot. And lovers. She stared down at the cards. Three of the major arcana. What were the odds? The same cards he'd gotten before, only those had been surrounded by other minor cards.

She tried to keep her mind and expression blank. Sandu was adept at reading her and, unfortunately, so were his brethren—now hers. That small wisp of meaning that drifted into her mind was something she didn't want to share. It wasn't strong enough. She wasn't certain—and it wasn't good. She wanted good. She moistened her lips with the tip of her tongue.

"Would you please do it one more time? Shuffle, divide the deck into thirds. Choose one of the thirds, put the other two aside and then fan out the cards facedown on the table from the one you chose." She placed her hand over her heart, over the goddess card, pressing hard, sending up a prayer to anyone who would listen. *Let this be good. Let this be right.* Nicu was such a good man.

The brethren moved closer. Nicu didn't take his eyes from hers. He didn't look at the cards, but he did exactly what she told him to do. He shuffled and he shuffled well. He divided the tarot deck into thirds and set two of the thirds to one side, fanning out the remaining cards facedown on the table.

"Choose three and turn them faceup, Nicu," she instructed quietly. Her heart pounded out of control. She knew the men were predators, hunters, and they couldn't fail to hear. She couldn't stop her reaction. She waited as Nicu chose a card from those in front of him, drew out of the fan and turned it faceup. A second followed. Then a third. The devil. The lovers. The chariot.

"I'm consistent," he said.

She closed her eyes briefly and then looked up at him. "You are," she agreed.

"What does it mean?"

"Your lifemate is alive in this century. You have a journey and will need those you trust to aid you in retrieving her. She is not where she can easily be found." She didn't *know* anything for certain. She could surmise. She could guess. But she didn't know.

Nicu's gray eyes slid over her face. "You do not tell me everything, Adalasia."

"When I do a reading, I try not to put anything of myself into the reading. Speculation or guessing shouldn't be done. I might have intuition, but that isn't the same thing. We can try again another time to get better answers."

"You know for certain she is alive."

Adalasia looked down at the cards. She was exhausted. She wanted to rest. "Yes. She is alive, Nicu. That I can say for certain. I'm really tired, and I still have to make sure Nera's spies can't come in through the ground, walls or ceiling."

She gathered up the cards and returned them to their ancient pouch. She would cleanse them the next rising. Sandu helped her up, and strangely, her legs felt weak, as if she'd run a long race. He wrapped his arm around her waist.

I watched how you sealed the cottage against Nera's spies, ewal emninu-mam. I can do this for you. You are much too tired.

It has to be me.

Sandu caught her chin and tipped her face up to his, his dark eyes searching hers. *You are up to no good.*

She stroked gentle laughter into his mind. *Perhaps.*

The brethren watched her as she sealed the above, below and all four sides against any harm Nera's army or her spies might bring. They didn't notice the little illusion she carefully wove afterward, the one including breeding leeches, as well as egg sacs, and hundreds of leeches rising to attach themselves to the unsuspecting sleeping Carpathian. Since it was an illusion and she was already inside before they set their own safe-guards, they would merely seal her illusion in with them. More than satisfied, she went with her lifemate to find their place of rest for the night.

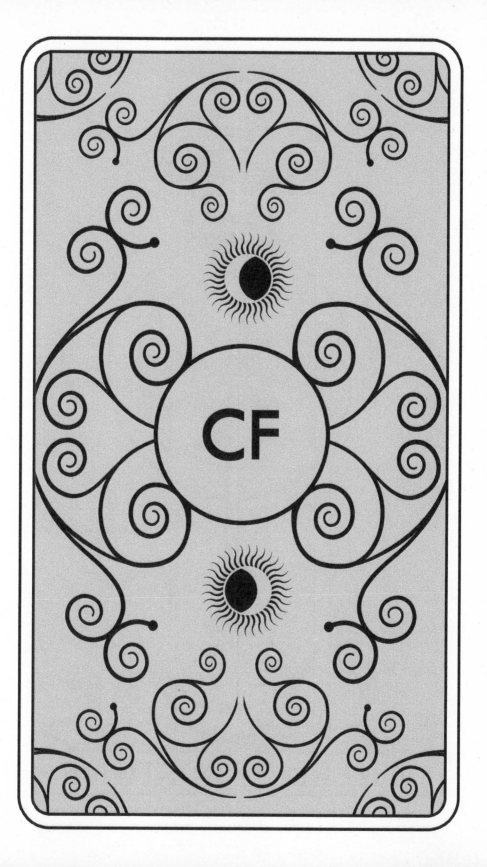

-X-

WHEEL OF FORTUNE

I t was always this first moment, when Sandu became aware that he was not alone as he had been for as long as he could remember. He waved his hand to open the earth but remained very still, feeling the now ever-present ache of desire that rose when he awakened. It was part of him, that craving for her body, that sometimes was just a comfortable longing and other times intense and nearly impossible to ignore.

He allowed his gaze to sweep over her. Adalasia. His. A small smile tugged at his mind. She wouldn't like to admit she enjoyed when he thought so possessively about her, but he did it all the time. He always would. He didn't mind when she thought the same thing about him. She looked so feminine curled next to him. He loved just looking at the shape of her. The long line of her back. Her generous hips and breasts. Her long legs. The way she wrapped them around him when he was moving in her.

The thought of that made his cock thicken more, gave him a pleasant ache. He needed to find blood for them both. It wouldn't be too difficult. This cave system wasn't far from a few of the smaller villages. Just taking a few minutes to savor this first waking, knowing she was with him, that he really had his lifemate after two thousand years of searching.

He had never once looked at a woman in all that time and wanted her. His body hadn't reacted. Not in all the time he'd carefully researched every sexual pleasure known to man in order to be a good lover for his mate. He wanted to bring her the maximum amount of ecstasy one could have with sex, so he had studied meticulously in every country he'd been in. In every century. His body hadn't reacted, but his mind had taken in everything, watching what women seemed to like the best. What made them beg for more. What made them want to please their partners as well.

Now that he had Adalasia, just the thought of doing any of those things he had learned to her had his body reacting. Looking at her had his body reacting. Thinking of her, his cock seemed to grow thick and hard and reactionary. That made him want to smile as well. It seemed a lifemate had much more control over him than he had thought possible. He didn't mind in the least. It made him feel alive. He felt as if every cell in his body had suddenly awakened after a very long slumber.

He touched her hair, that long thick mass she liked to keep in a braid, which he liked to pull out and let loose and free. She gave him a look as if she might protest, but she never did; instead, she laughed. She *laughed*. He loved that about her. That laugh. The sound was so sweet, and it resonated deep inside him.

Sandu was well aware love started in one's mind. It stayed there. Good times, bad times, if you wanted that love to remain alive, you had to keep it forever safe in the mind. He'd been alive too long not to have certain knowledge of that. Still, he was Carpathian and he knew about souls. He lifted Adalasia's much smaller hand and fit it into his palm. She had guarded his soul. She'd been born to guard his soul. She'd been born over and over, and she'd handed his soul to her daughter's keeping when she gave birth to her. He'd never thought how that would work. How the guardian of his soul would have to be born repeatedly. Her soul. His soul.

Had that left her mother an empty shell? She had her body and heart, but she passed their souls to her daughter at birth. That was why she couldn't read the tarot cards the way Adalasia could. Not because she hadn't when she was younger, but because once she gave birth to Adalasia, she'd passed the torch. The cards knew. The goddess card knew. It was heartbreaking.

He knew it wasn't the same for all lifemates, but in this case, when they were tasked to guard the gate of the demon, the women in the family had lived a very difficult life. He hoped the men they chose to go the rest of their life with them had been good to them. Had loved them and been a good companion to them. Surely the cards would have guided them.

There was a gentle stirring in his mind. A flutter, much like butterfly wings. *Sandu? Do you have need of me?*

He could hear the drowsy notes in her voice. She was still tired. The soil was rich and had worked to help nurture her, but she could use a little more time in the ground while he hunted. It was just the fact that she reached out to him, feeling his melancholy when he thought of her continuous rebirth and he hadn't found her fast enough.

Again, he felt that pleasant ache of desire sweep over him, listening to the sound of her voice. There was something about the way she woke so slowly. Not quite awake. Not completely asleep. Drifting. His woman. There was peace. A feeling of being content. He hadn't realized that would come with having a lifemate.

Sleep, ewal emninumam. I will return soon. I go to feed and bring you back what you need. He stroked caresses through her hair once again. All that thick silk.

Emotions were interesting after not feeling for centuries. At first, he had found feelings overwhelming and difficult to control, so he had pushed them aside and buried them deep. Then he had slowly allowed himself to feel, but at a distance. He realized, when he was making the decisions for the two of them—decisions he knew were necessary for his lifemate to be healthy and stay alive—that she was unhappy and no longer trusted him. She was keeping secrets from him. He had expected her to share all her secrets with him while he withheld information from her. Those emotions allowed him to understand her needs a little better. They were necessary in their relationship. Now, he was grateful for them.

He rose slowly, cleaning and clothing himself in the way of his people. He didn't cover their resting place, but he did provide a cloak of soil, rich in minerals, to blanket Adalasia's body. He kept her face free of the soil, so if by chance she should awaken fully, she would not be afraid of being buried alive.

She had practiced over and over opening the earth. That had been her first order of business. She had insisted. More than any other undertaking, she chose to work on that particular task. Sandu knew sleeping in the ground was Adalasia's greatest fear. She was determined to gain control over those fears by ensuring she could get out of the ground herself. Still, for now, she preferred that he always wake first and have the soil removed for her.

He took his time finding a suitable healthy male in the village. The little community was mostly a fishing hamlet, situated just back from the river. It was small, but the people were more modern, with their nets and the many commodities they traded or sold. Two boats came up the Amazon several times a year and brought tourists with them. Those tourists were a much-needed pouring of wealth into the community when they came into the small town to look at their wares.

Sandu was careful when he took blood, making certain not to take too much. He didn't want the donor to be dizzy and perhaps have an accident near the water. The man had a family he provided for with his fishing. His wife made jewelry. His children helped him fish and hunt, and they gathered herbs, roots and plants for food. He was a good man, the kind Sandu preferred to take blood from. It was always a reminder that there was good in the world. Sandu lived too long in the shadows where the undead spread their taint, and he needed the reminder.

As he approached the system of caves, Benedek joined him. "Siv is up to his old tricks. I woke this rising covered in all manner of leeches. They were so heavy, the egg sacs attached to my body, I was unsure I could rise."

Sandu's eyebrow shot up. "Siv did this?"

Petru materialized beside them, his eyes a slash of silver. "That Siv will regret his little prank with the leeches."

"Perhaps the leeches really are in the soil," Sandu ventured. "I left Adalasia alone. I do not wish her to wake with leeches crawling all over her."

"He would not dare have them on her," Benedek said, his voice a threat.

Nicu joined them. "I woke to the weight of leeches this rising," he announced.

"You were not alone," Petru said.

Afanasiv strode out of the trees, his eyes stormy, turbulent like the sea. "I do not appreciate the leeches crawling all over me this rising. Which one of you decided it was payback for a crime I did not commit? There were never leeches in anyone's chamber. We made that up, remember? To put them in my sleeping chamber is a vile transgression, and when I discover who did this thing, one of you will pay."

The four brethren exchanged long looks. They turned their piercing gaze on Sandu. He held up both hands in surrender.

"I did not do this thing." He knew they were adept at hearing lies. He wasn't lying, but it was impossible to keep the amusement from his mind. He wished he could have been an insect on the wall of each of their chambers as they woke to find their bodies covered in the clearly very well-done illusion of leeches in the stages of breeding and attaching their eggs.

The five men exchanged long, puzzled looks again.

"Sandu," Benedek began, then stopped, shaking his head.

"It is not possible," Nicu declared, as if knowing what was in Benedek's mind.

"Do you believe these caves are the breeding grounds for the leeches?" Sandu asked.

"No." Siv was adamant. "And you do not, either, Sandu. You are up to your old tricks."

"I told you, I had nothing to do with the leeches, Siv. I give you my word."

Siv regarded him with suspicion. "What of our little sister? Can you vouch for her? She wove her safeguards into the earth. What is to say she did not also weave in a spell to bring leeches to the surface?"

"Why would she do such a thing?" Sandu asked.

"We may have played a small trick on her," Petru admitted, "while you were carrying her to the caves."

Nicu took up the explanation. "We spoke of leeches. Waking up to the creatures crawling over our bodies and attaching their egg sacs to us."

"Why would you do such a thing?" Sandu asked. He held back his laughter and tried to look as if he smoldered with fury. He was very good at the look. He'd been using it for centuries. Evidently, it must have worked.

Benedek hastened to explain. "We did it to lighten her mood and distract her from having to read the cards for us. We knew she was upset and didn't want to do it."

Sandu deliberately frowned. *Adalasia. Are you awake?*

Yes. I am lying here with Mother Earth's arms surrounding me in warmth. It's a beautiful night. I managed to light the sconces, and the gems in the walls are glittering as if they have been polished. It really is quite lovely in here.

Have you been following the conversation? Sandu persisted, enjoying the intimacy of having her in his mind.

Mm-hmm.

Her laughter was sweet. Tugged at him low, a fist of desire forming into a relentless calling. He savored his ability to feel such a force of nature.

They are becoming suspicious.

Her laughter burst over him. Through him. Leapt from his mind into each of his brethren. Her joy of that moment. Teasing them. So happy she was able to get them back for their little prank on her.

Right under your ancient collective noses, she bragged, her laughter contagious.

There was a moment of silence, as if the rain forest itself had to come to terms with the idea that a newly turned human might actually outwit four ancient Carpathian hunters. They stayed in Sandu's mind, sharing his amusement. Sharing her laughter. Her enjoyment of playing her prank on them, her ability to get them back for their teasing.

Sisarke, Benedek whispered into her mind. *Leeches attached to one's body on rising is quite* . . . He stopped searching for the correct term in her language.

Vile, Nicu supplied.

Disgusting, Petru said simultaneously.

Beyond the foulest of the undead, Siv added.

Her laughter continued. *Surely all of you realized the leeches weren't real.*

Again, there was that collective silence. It was all Sandu could do not

to roar with laughter. He had to turn his head away from the stoic ancients. They were without expression. Their faces refused to show any
kind of shock, but their minds, firmly entrenched in his, reverberated
with disbelief. Amazement. A kind of delight that she was able to actually trick them. All four were bringing up that initial waking, finding the
weight of the leeches attached to them. They'd gotten rid of them quickly
as they hurriedly left the sanctuary of their resting places, none of them
checking to see if the leeches were real or illusion. Petru, Benedek and
Nicu believed Siv had pranked them. Siv believed the others had done
so. None considered the leeches could be illusion.

Sisarke, Siv said, *you do astound me. Why you have been wasted on the
likes of Sandu, I have no idea.*

Sandu didn't bother to take exception. He was just grateful Adalasia
was his lifemate. "I want to spend a little time with her before we seek
Dominic and Solange. I sent word to him we would be coming for a brief
visit. Just to talk. He was amenable."

At once, the four guardians were all business, pulling abruptly away
from their bond with Adalasia.

"The Dragonseeker is careful of his lifemate. Both are lethal, Sandu.
When you have an audience with one, you have an audience with both,
even if you do not see the other," Petru advised. "If he invites us to his
lair, it will not be a home he often uses. It isn't that Dominic necessarily
sits in judgment of others, but he holds strictly to the old ways."

"I have heard that his lifemate was royalty, a Jaguar princess, before
the mages destroyed their species and brought them to extinction,"
Sandu said, mostly for the sake of Adalasia. She might not be able to hear
the entire conversation, but she could hear him. "My understanding is
she can walk in sunlight. If she gives him her blood, doesn't that mean
he can as well? That is not the old way."

Nicu shook his head. "I have visited with Dominic often, and he has
been kind enough to offer his blood when I have been wounded. His
lifemate was somewhere in the trees holding a weapon on me the entire
time, I might add, but even with his blood, I could not take the sun. I
know that Zacarias De La Cruz has often exchanged blood with Domi-

nic, and he has told me he can spend perhaps an hour but uncomfortably. He builds clouds or his skin burns and blisters."

"Is Dominic able to walk in the sun?" Sandu persisted.

"That is the question, isn't it? As we aged, and as we continued to destroy the undead, we became something else. Dragonseeker did not," Nicu said.

"How do you know?" Siv asked.

Nicu shrugged. "I know every beast in the forest, the mountains. They call to me, and something in me answers. Dragonseeker does not have the beast in him. He is the same, calm and steady. He is resolute. Although he is ancient, he is not like we are, and he is very aware of the difference."

Sandu contemplated that information. If Nicu said Dominic Dragonseeker had no scarring on his soul, then it had to be so. Nicu didn't make those kinds of mistakes. "I informed him I was bringing my lifemate. I was very open with him that we were traveling with four of my most trusted brethren and that you were bonded to her and to me. He still issued an invitation. I expect him to watch us carefully. In his place, I would do the same. I still believe that it is worthwhile, since we are so close to him, to seek his advice."

Benedek nodded. "I agree with Sandu. Dominic risks much with his invitation. Even with his warrior woman lifemate backing his play, he knows he could not hope to defeat five ancients in battle. He believes you are in need."

"You consulted with Gabriel and Lucian and also Andre. Dominic could have reached out to them, or they could have reached out to him," Petru said. "With this new technology, everyone seems to be right on top of one another."

Unless you break tablets the way Sandu did. Throwing a tantrum because he did not want to learn modern ways. Siv made certain to include Adalasia in their conversation.

Petru took up the story to give Adalasia a reference point. *Poor young Josef, tasked with teaching ancient minds modern technology. Sandu was first, and he clung to the old ways, insisting he could rip knowledge from young minds.*

You can just take knowledge from anyone? Adalasia asked. *If I wanted to go back to college, I could just take the information I needed from my professor instead of studying?*

Sandu stroked a loving caress through her mind. *Of course you could. You are now fully Carpathian. When you need to know something, you have only to look for the information instead of having to learn to use the tablets young Josef was always pushing on us.*

I can't just take knowledge out of your heads, Adalasia protested, *although I'm not certain I want to see into any of your minds.*

Her laughter was a soft breeze moving through their minds. That was another way she bound them together. That joy of life in her. She gave the brethren a taste of that. It was a small lifeline they could reach for when they needed it.

Nicu agreed with her. *That would be for the best, sisarke, especially if you are peering into Petru's head. You might see only the thick branches of tree roots rather than any real knowledge. Although it is true, he did not smash a tablet the way your lifemate did in a fit of hideous temper.*

My lifemate has a hideous temper? Adalasia asked. *This is news to me. I had no idea.*

Atrocious temper, Afanasiv corrected. *He deceived us as well. We thought him the calmest among us, which was why he was chosen to be the first to learn modern technology from young Josef.*

Atrocious temper? Adalasia echoed.

Sandu felt her laughter. There was no way to tell anyone how she had changed his world just by being in it. Just by the way she interacted with him. With his brethren. He caught glimpses of her still lying where he left her, the soil open so she could look up at the ceiling of the chamber they had slept in. The sconces were lit, and the walls sparkled and glittered. In one corner, she had managed to add a fireplace of stone. The flames burned low, casting dancing lights on the walls along with the candles in the sconces. She was proud of the fireplace. He was proud of her.

The four guardians exchanged solemn looks with one another. *We had no idea, Sandu, of this temper of yours. You have long been considered the calmest among us until you broke what you referred to as the demon's tool,* Benedek said, more for Adalasia's sake than Sandu's.

Young Josef? Adalasia inquired.

Sandu pushed images into Adalasia's head of a young Carpathian male somewhere between twenty and thirty with spiked hair dyed with blue tips. The young man was slender, wiry, with a cocky, defiant grin. *This is Josef. Very intelligent. He was sent to work on the computers in the compound and teach all of us how to use tablets and technology.*

Petru made a small sound of derision. *Sandu was opposed to coming into this century, Adalasia. The vampire has gotten ahead of us with technology. Josef proved his point. Even the prince conceded he should have been paying more attention, which is why the boy was sent to us. We all have to learn.*

He sounded just a little self-righteous. Sandu knew that was on purpose. There would be no inflection in Petru's voice as a rule. He was pouring it on for the sake of making the story fun for Adalasia.

Which is why Sandu broke the tablet in half, I suppose, Siv guessed.

Sandu. You really broke a tablet in half? Now her laughter played down his spine like the touch of fingers. Sandu needed to be in the sleeping chamber with her. He searched her mind to see if there was a particular bed she liked.

Sandu pretended to be unrepentant. There had been extenuating circumstances—a kind of virus at work, but the telling of that would be for another time. This was all in fun. *It was the demon's tool. I couldn't master the keys. My fingers were too big, and the boy talked too fast.*

He waited as did the others. They were rewarded with her laughter spilling into their minds.

That was the problem? Your fingers were too big? Then you just broke the entire tablet in half? Do you have any idea how expensive they are? Poor Josef. I'm keeping all my devices away from you just in case you lose that atrocious temper I didn't know you had.

He tried to sound contrite. *I am certain I will be able to learn much better from you. The boy was difficult. He did not like repeating himself and would grind his teeth together if I asked politely for him to show me a second time how to do something.*

Her amusement continued to feel like fingers stroking caresses down his spine. His belly tightened into dark knots of something very close to lust. He examined that feeling as he did all emotion—stepping back from it to look at it from every angle. The tension coiled tighter and tighter in him, like a fist, a number of them. A dark craving ran through his veins in a slow burn. He tasted her in his mouth. A dark addiction that he knew was his alone, instilled with lifemate ritual. His teeth were sharp against his tongue in anticipation. His cock was full and hard.

I don't know what I can teach you, Sandu, but I am willing to learn from you.

That fist in his belly grew tighter. His cock grew thicker, the girth wider, hot blood pounding through it, along with his heartbeat. There was a sultry tone to her voice. He kept his breathing even only through centuries of discipline.

You are deliberately teasing me. Playing with fire, I believe is the term.

His brethren were speaking to one another, and he really should be paying attention, but his attention was really focused on his lifemate. This time her soft laughter was an invitation. A deliberate caress. Fingers stroking over his chest. Lower, along his belly. He swore he felt the brush of her fingers, so light, along his shaft, dancing over the broad, flared head, cupping the velvet sac and sliding along his balls.

When did you learn to do that?

It is working, then? Her voice sounded a little too innocent. *You can feel what I am doing to you in my mind? I have tried to work out every detail. I memorized you. Your body is so beautiful to me.*

He suppressed a groan. Adalasia was learning how to use her skills as a Carpathian woman, but he hadn't expected her to practice sexual skills. He should have. She was . . . Adalasia. Unafraid. Demanding. Uninhibited. She liked to tease. To play. She knew he did as well.

"There were no signs of the undead when we were in the village," Siv announced, "but that doesn't mean they are not around. We should make certain, Sandu, before we allow Adalasia to move around too freely. Her brightness would be a beacon to a master vampire."

Sandu had to agree. He touched on the chamber where they had slept. The small fire in the fireplace cast shadows around the chambers, adding to the flickering light the candles gave off in the sconces high up on the walls. The entire chamber was shrouded in a dim, dancing light that played through the room.

A bed was in the center of the room, one positioned at a certain height. His woman knelt in front of the fireplace, her long hair tumbling down her back. She was dressed in a covering of red lace that stretched over her generous breasts and tightened around her rib cage and waist to disappear between her legs. The lace did nothing to hide her body from him, and his breath caught in his throat, his blood thundering in his ears.

"We are going to take some time to patrol the forest, Sandu," Benedek said. "We cannot afford to allow her enemies or ours to come near her."

Sandu needed to concentrate on what his brethren said to him, not look at his lifemate waiting so patiently for him. He felt the brushstroke of fingers against his shaft again. Maybe not so patiently. She was practicing in her mind.

I want to get this right, so that when you're here in front of me, I give you the most pleasure. I saw this in your mind, Sandu. I know I can do this right with a little guidance.

Her voice. Sultry. Sexy. This was definitely a lesson in discipline. After a couple of thousand years, he shouldn't be having such problems, but then the heat of her velvet tongue stroked up his shaft, and he nearly jumped out of his skin.

Nicu nodded in agreement with Benedek. "We think it best if you allow us to thoroughly search for signs of the undead. Even with Dominic living here, we know they test him. Also, the occasional jaguar returns to this area hunting Solange. There could be unexpected enemies."

If his enemies came at him right at that moment, Sandu wasn't certain he could defend himself. His focus was on one part of his anatomy and what his woman might do next. His lungs could barely find enough air to breathe.

He cleared his throat. "I will spend time with my lifemate inside the chamber," Sandu said to his brethren, his voice a little huskier than he would have liked.

Her mouth felt hot as she slid it over him, engulfing him, enclosing his cock in a tight, scorching tunnel while her tongue did a little dancing foray over the sensitive broad head and then under it. She released him. *Does that feel good?*

She knew it did. She could feel his shuddering reaction. The way his blood ran hot, as if she lit a match to a stick of dynamite. Before he could answer, she stroked her tongue up his shaft again, over and over, getting him very wet. He had to answer his brethren before he was incapable.

"I will weave safeguards, so if you return, take heed of them. Announce your presence before you attempt to come inside the cave system."

"We will build additional safeguards," Petru added. "One of us will always be close should you have need."

Sandu ordinarily would have considered that his brethren had gotten too old to remember he was in top fighting form, but he didn't want to battle anything. He wanted to spend time with his woman. His lifemate. Adalasia. He inclined his head graciously, thankful he could feel real affection toward his brothers from the monastery.

I am coming in alone, Sivamet. The others will patrol the rain forest to ensure we have no enemies close before we set out to find the Dragonseeker and his woman on tomorrow's rising.

He had this night alone with her. Each time they found themselves alone, they tried to learn as much as possible about each other. Not just what they shared mind to mind, but talking with each other. They needed to find a closeness together. He got that now. The more he allowed himself to feel emotions, the more he understood her need of a partnership and what that would entail. Right at that moment, he cared nothing of learning about partnerships, only about what her mouth could continue to do to his body.

I had hoped you would come alone.

There was that teasing note again, but this time, she once more had her mouth around his cock, and her soft laughter vibrated right through his entire body. Sandu was already through the thin crack and doing his best to protect them by weaving safeguards against any intruder. He had shed his clothes going through the thin fissure leading to the cave system, and now, it seemed she was taking even more liberties, as if she had full access to his body.

He felt her palms cupping his sac, then her fingers stroking and jiggling his balls gently, adding just a little more pressure before backing off while she sucked and moaned around his cock. He took to the air, moving swiftly, needing to get to her, the cooler air feeling good on his overheated body.

Adalasia knelt just as she had appeared in his mind, in front of the fireplace, so the dancing flames could throw their shadows over her face. She had her palms on her knees and her knees were open, allowing him to see that the one tiny piece of scarlet lace was now soaked. Her hair hung in a cloud of dark silk down her back, catching the light from the flames in the fireplace. Her skin looked like satin under the stretch of the red lace.

Sandu. She whispered his name in his mind. A breathless invitation.

He moved to stand in front of her, close, his body already so primed to feel—and see—her mouth on him. Stretched around his girth. *Eyes looking into mine.*

Her long lashes lifted as her hands slid up the twin columns of his inner thighs in a slow burning glide of her palms. Then her fingers were stroking over his straining balls, and the breath left his lungs in a long rush. All the while, he looked down into her dark eyes. She looked adoring. Wanting. Craving him. Her tongue slid over his sac, and while he felt that velvet rasp, a small sound left her throat, a moan of anticipation. Her fingers did a small manipulation, dancing over him as her tongue continued the foray to the base of his shaft and up.

Adalasia never broke eye contact with him. Not when her lips moved up his wide girth and her tongue curled and explored, getting him wetter and wetter. Not when she made a little assault on the V beneath his crown, causing him to nearly lose his mind. Desire deepened the blue in her eyes to that cobalt. Her breasts rose and fell. Her nipples were hard little peaks. The flickering firelight played over her body and caught the gleam of wetness between her legs, telling him that what she was doing to him excited her.

Then her mouth engulfed the broad crown, and he swore he saw stars. He caught the back of her head in his palm without thinking, needing to keep her there. Hold her right where she was. Her lips stretched around his wide girth as she drew another inch of him into that tight, wet heat, sucking, tongue doing some curling dance that threatened his sanity. She made a moaning sound in her throat that vibrated up his shaft and down his spine.

She moved her head back, and his breath hissed out of his lungs. Then she took him a little deeper, her tongue lashing at him, her mouth a tight suction, gripping and milking and then moving back to tease under his crown until he thought his mind might actually unravel. He shared the beauty of what she was making him feel with her. The intensity of the pleasure.

He didn't realize his hand had fisted in her hair, holding her over his cock, while his other hand had strayed to her nipple. He loved the sight of her, the firelight playing over her body. The way she looked so beautiful and so adoringly at him. So wanting to please him. She had no idea how much she pleased him all the time, and this—this gift was beyond his imagining.

Sandu didn't want this to ever be over, but he could feel the more she drew him into the heat of her mouth, the more his body responded, and he wanted to be inside her. He needed that closeness, and so did she.

"That's enough, *ewal emninumam*. I want to be inside you. I need to share your body."

She blinked up at him and reluctantly released his cock. It was that reluctance that made his heart sing. The wetness on his wide girth that was so sensual-looking just added to that joy. He reached down, locking his arm around her waist and lifting Adalasia easily. Turning, he placed her on the end of the bed.

"Hands and knees." His voice didn't even sound like his, almost rough.

She complied readily, and when he placed a hand in between her shoulder blades and applied pressure, she lowered her front to the bed obediently, giving him the access he wanted. He rubbed her cheeks and then pressed the crown of his cock into her heated, slick entrance. She was scorching hot, and he didn't wait, driving forward through her tight folds to bury himself deep. He caught her hips and pulled her into him as he surged forward again and again.

Adalasia.

He breathed her name into her mind, needing her to feel what he was feeling. The physical was beyond description, but it was so much more than that. He wasn't good at expressing emotion, but it was there for her, mixing with the rising tide of carnal lust that just kept growing. Love for her overwhelmed him, could have brought him to his knees. *She* could so easily do that.

He moved in her. That tight silken tunnel, so scorching hot. So perfect. An unknown perfection no amount of research could have prepared him for. Adalasia. A woman who had given him so many new experiences and ideas. When he thought, after the centuries he'd lived, he'd never have much in the way of shocking surprises, Adalasia had given him the best the world had to offer. More, he knew she would continue to do so.

He moved in her, all that heat, her body made for his, so tight, nearly strangling his wide length. Her silken muscles dragged over his cock, the friction sending powerful waves of pleasure rolling through his body, hot blood roaring through his veins and pooling in a wicked mass to expand his erection beyond his comprehension.

She chanted his name softly, a rasping sound when air wasn't quite reaching her lungs, when she wasn't catching her breath. Her body moved back to meet his nearly as aggressively as his moved. She didn't want this to ever end, either, but he could feel that coiling in her, winding tighter and tighter. Strangling him. The friction was nearly unbearable for both of them.

Flames seemed to leap and burn, a firestorm out of control, raging now between them. Without warning, her tight channel clamped down like a vise, a silken fiery fist squeezing, gripping and milking. His cock erupted into jagged bursts of white-hot ropes lashing the walls of her feminine passage, triggering more and more powerful eruptions.

Stars and colors burst behind his eyes, floated around him. Fire raged through his veins and settled in his groin. His legs felt weak, no longer his own. It was all he could do to draw air into his lungs and keep from collapsing over her. She went down onto the mattress, his name on her lips, in her mind, a soft, reverent sound that tore at his heart.

Sandu managed to kiss the small of her back. He wasn't in the least surprised that he was still semihard when he withdrew. Just that act, the sliding of his cock through her tight, slick folds, had the friction sending heat down his spine. He knew when he gave her blood, when he felt her mouth on him, he would want her again—and again. They had this rising before they would meet the Dragonseeker and his lifemate. He wanted to spend as much time with his woman as possible. He had thought . . . talking. Talking seemed overrated.

Adalasia laughed softly, the sound muffled by the mattress. "My Carpathian male is such a man after all."

He lay beside her, tangling his fingers in her hair. She still lay on her belly, her face turned toward him, and he pushed the silken mass aside so he could see her expression. "I am a man, but what does that mean?"

"You're going to be obsessed with sex."

He studied her face. The amusement in her eyes. She was clearly perfectly okay with him being obsessed with sex. He propped himself up on one elbow and rubbed her round buttocks. "I fear you are correct. It may take a few centuries for that to fade—if ever. I have studied so many interesting positions and practices. I wish to try them all with you, now that I know how it feels. There are things I can do to your body to make you feel good. At least, going by the way the women screamed out their pleasure, I would say we should try them. There are things you can do to my body. I am interested in seeing if they are as good as what you did earlier."

"You liked that?"

He nodded.

She smiled. "I am certain I can get much better at it."

He wasn't certain he could survive if she got much better at it.

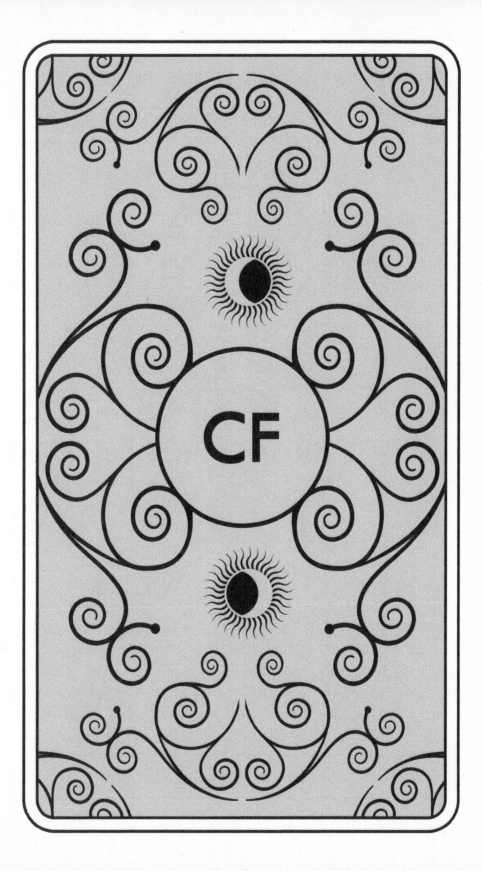

-XI-

JUSTICE

The rain forest wasn't silent in the way one would think under the canopy of trees at night. There was the constant drone or hum of insects, rarely stopping, even in the steady fall of rain. It was hot, very humid, and steam rose from the forest floor even as moisture relentlessly poured down on them from above. The steam was almost as thick as a dense fog that might come in off an ocean, rolling in clouds of unnatural grayish mist.

The overhead canopy from the trees did little to shield them from the rain, the larger leaves acting more like big funnels, gathering water and then pouring it over them if the little group should stop beneath one of the taller kapok trees. Drops of water collected in the vines going up the trunks of trees and in the petals of flowers so that if they brushed against them, they'd get soaked.

Trees lined the swollen banks of the river, hanging over the raging waters, the root systems looking too much like distorted cages, with thick vines shooting out like snakes, eager to grab unsuspecting prey to bring them into those waiting cages. At least, that's what it looked like to Adalasia.

She had to admit the rain forest was beautiful, if she actually looked around at the flowers climbing the tree trunks, but mostly she looked at the insects covering the ground and swarming up the trees. Brightly colored frogs followed them with their eyes. Huge birds of prey seemed to follow their slow progress. Eyes looked at them from everywhere. There seemed an abundance of nocturnal animals and birds with large yellow or red eyes staring at them from the branches of trees. That didn't include the thousands of lizards, or spiders, not to mention the many amphibians that seemed to be all over the trees. Didn't Sandu and his brethren see all the potential spies?

This didn't feel the same as when they had walked in the rain forest to find the hidden cave system just along the river. This was far different. The path took them farther into the interior, although she knew the river wasn't too far in the distance. There was a muggy feel to the air whenever the trail would take them closer to one of the dark ribbons of water that sometimes ran in the shallow reed-choked, mosquito-infested tributaries.

The five Carpathian males walked with absolute confidence along the narrow trail through the darkened forest. The rain didn't bother them in the least. They kept the drops from hitting them. The temperatures of their bodies were always regulated. She had insisted that Sandu not help her. Those were small things she should be able to do for herself, and she wanted to practice. She found herself too busy staring at the sights around her to remember to keep herself cool and not have the rain pouring down on her.

A small sound mixed with the incessant drone of night cicadas and the scurrying of lizards and other creatures under the vegetation on the forest floor caught her attention. She turned her head to look at the two men behind her suspiciously. Benedek and Petru brought up the rear. Siv and Nicu were ahead, with Sandu and Adalasia walking in the center. She knew Nicu was in front because he had such an affinity with wildlife, and he had the most interaction with Dominic and Solange, the couple they were meeting.

"Is there something either of you would like to say?" She challenged. How was it possible to grow so fond of men who seemed to never change expression? And yet she had grown attached to them very quickly, regarding them as the family she no longer had. "I'm fairly certain one of you snickered. It sounded suspiciously like you, Petru." She was wary of them now, certain that after her prank with the leeches, they might try to get her back.

Petru looked straight at her with his strange silvery eyes. His hair color intrigued her. It was as different as his eyes. It wasn't gray, but like his eyes, it was also silvery, almost a platinum.

"*Sisarke*, you wound my heart." He kept walking without breaking stride. There was no change in his facial expression. She still had the impression of amusement through the connection with Sandu. That put her on even more of an alert.

There was happiness in her that she could give some small relief from the unrelenting darkness they were in. It wasn't a lot, but it was enough to keep them going. She knew *sisarke* meant "little sister." She loved that Petru and the others cared enough about her to give her that honor. She regarded them as siblings and was so honored that they viewed her in the same light.

"You look a bit like a drowned rat, your hair hanging in long stringy dripping strands around your face and down your back," Benedek contributed. "Your clothes are soaked. And you're shivering continuously. You will make a wonderful impression on Dominic and his woman. Dominic is a Dragonseeker." As if that said it all.

What is a Dragonseeker, Sandu? I'm clearly supposed to know. They used that term interchangeably, as if it was his surname, and she'd thought it was. Now, she wasn't sure what the others meant.

She realized that as much as they might be teasing her, they were also reprimanding her lifemate for allowing her to be in such a condition.

Dragonseeker is the only lineage in our world that has never had a single member turn vampire in its history.

Adalasia could tell Sandu was having a difficult time not helping her at least regulate her body temperature. She had specifically asked him not to. She didn't really understand why they suddenly went from flying through the forest from their cave system to walking in these miserable conditions, but she was taking every opportunity to learn as many skills as possible—not that she was doing very well.

So the man they were going to see came from a very strong line. *Why do they call them Dragonseeker?*

They are born with a small birthmark, a dragon that will warn them if the undead are near.

She had a small birthmark. Her mother said it was the mark of the warrior, reminding her always to be ready to fight when necessary, to keep the world safe. It wasn't for glory, because no one could ever know. She was a sacrifice, and she had to be okay with that.

You are not a sacrifice, ewal emninumam. You are my beloved lifemate.

She might feel like the drowned rat the others had called her, but Sandu made her warm inside.

What do you know of the Dragonseeker's lifemate?

Solange is Jaguar, royalty in her own right. She is a very tough woman, a warrior through and through. She fought for the women of her species alone for years against impossible odds.

Adalasia thought about that as she rubbed at the wet material of her cotton shirt. She'd chosen the right clothing for walking through the jungle. She'd known what she should wear, but she hadn't been able to stay focused enough to keep herself warm and dry as they moved through that weird steam rising up from the forest floor.

She thought she caught glimpses of a large shadowy cat moving through the branches of the trees above them every now and again. It wasn't even that she caught glimpses. It was more in her mind. As if the creature passed through her mind, more imaginary than real, a transparent shadow she could see through the tree trunks, leaves and vines, but she was aware of its presence as it moved with them.

Do you see that? She shared what she thought she saw with Sandu.

Yes. We are aware of it. Pay it no mind.

Adalasia thought that was a difficult thing to do, but she decided to focus her attention on the two men who had thought to reprimand her lifemate for allowing her to work on her skills.

She concentrated on the large leaves that held the pooling water. As Benedek and Petru walked beneath the trees and automatically protected themselves, she waited until they thought themselves safe.

Trying to be casual, she paused, holding Sandu's arm as she bent to her boot, as if checking it. Using every ounce of focus and concentration, she moved those funnels of water right over the two Carpathian males' heads and dumped them. The water sloshed over them in a cold fall running down their hair and faces.

Sandu, will you help me now? she asked as innocently as possible.

Of course, ewal emninumam.

There was sheer laughter in her mind. She knew Sandu had helped her keep Benedek and Petru from knowing she was sneaking up on them with the water. Siv and Nicu had turned back, hands on hips, observing their two soaked brethren, eyebrows raised, looking sober.

Adalasia stood looking at them also, perfectly dry, her clothes immaculate, her hair in a tight weave up off her neck to give her relief from the unrelenting heat and humidity. Her shirt was long-sleeved, a light tan; pants lightweight, khaki in color; and her boots were made for the jungle.

"Benedek, Petru, have you grown slow as you have aged?" The voice came seemingly out of the trees themselves, as if the jungle had come alive. There was amusement in that rich, mellow tone, a mesmerizing, almost hypnotic quality to the velvet sound.

Adalasia pressed her fingers to her mouth to keep from laughing, turning away from the two men. She noticed Sandu had gone on alert, as had the others. She always found that interesting. They had come to the rain forest specifically to find Dominic and his lifemate, Solange. They had sent word ahead, requesting an audience as they had with the others they had visited. She realized that Sandu had been very formal each time he had made a request to speak with another Carpathian couple. She found that odd.

Why didn't couples welcome visitors, and why were they so wary when they first met with one another? She had so much to learn about the Carpathian way of life. She was always thinking in human terms. Maybe she always would. Would that make her a liability to Sandu?

You are my greatest asset, Sivamet. We can easily navigate two worlds.

Sandu's assurance made her feel as if she were the only woman in his world. She looked up at him, her heart reacting to the absolute conviction and belief in her—in *them*—she saw in his eyes.

If you believe we can, Sandu, then I will believe it.

Dominic Dragonseeker emerged from the trees, striding out of the steamy fog rising from the forest floor. At first, it was difficult to make him out. He appeared almost to be an apparition as he came toward them, a handsome man, like all Carpathian males seemed to be. Formidable. Strong. A force to be reckoned with. He greeted each male in the age-old way of the warrior, clasping their forearms and speaking a greeting in their native language.

Sandu introduced Adalasia to him as his lifemate. "Thank you for seeing us, Dominic, on such short notice."

Dominic's gaze moved over the four brethren guarding them and then came back to rest on their faces. "This is no social call. Are you in trouble, Sandu?"

"I did say we may be bringing trouble to your door, Dominic," Sandu reminded. "It is not the undead on our heels. Another kind of enemy follows us. They use bats, owls, insects and whatever else they can manage to invade as spies to get close to us. Here"—Sandu indicated the trees and forest floor—"there is plenty for them to use."

"How is it they track you?" Dominic was patient, not moving, standing solidly in the exact same position.

Adalasia realized none of her guards had moved from theirs. Sandu hadn't, either. They had surrounded her the moment Dominic had stepped from the rising fog, keeping her in the middle, protected by their superior height, but they weren't protecting her from Dominic. She stretched her senses. She knew it was important to utilize her newly acquired Carpathian senses, all much more acute than her human ones had ever been.

Aside from the peculiar shadow cat in the trees, Dominic hadn't come alone. She should have known. The others knew. Adalasia was annoyed with herself for not paying more attention to the signs the men gave. She had been too busy looking at all the spiders and other potential hazards Nera's army could use in the battle against them. Each visit seemed to escalate the attacks, as if Nera knew they were getting closer to answers that might stop her from being able to open the gate Adalasia was responsible for guarding.

By now, she was positive this was about a concentrated attack on the gate. Her family had been tasked with guarding and keeping it locked for centuries—and they had done so. Now, for an unknown reason, Adalasia's family and her heritage were being tested. She wasn't going to fail. She had been thinking about each of these visits as a way to look into Sandu's past, but now, she thought maybe it was more than that. Just as her childhood had been a preparation to hone her fighting skills, to bring her to this point, was it possible she was supposed to be continuing to learn?

Her tarot cards had always guided her, and yet now that they were on the path of danger, she had jealously locked them away, taking them out to read each evening before they met with a couple. Had she missed the true importance of what the cards were telling her each evening? She could feel heat gathering under her skin, and it wasn't the heat of the rain forest. She had forgotten her training. Her skills. The very gift she'd been given from birth. The cards.

"Adalasia's family has been tasked with a burden handed from mother to daughter. The enemy is from one of their line. Blood calls to blood. We never have much time. They find us very fast. We don't want to put your lifemate in danger, Dominic." There was no mistaking the sincerity in Sandu's voice.

"It appears your lifemate is in danger," Dominic said. "Solange would never forgive me if I allowed a woman to remain in danger if we could aid her simply by having a conversation." A small smile tugged at the corners of his mouth.

That brief action made him appear even more handsome, in spite of his scars, than Adalasia had first thought. One side of his face had scarring, but strangely, those scars only served to make him more appealing.

Sivamet, it would not be a good thing for me to develop a trait as unseemly as jealousy.

Adalasia did her best not to laugh out loud. She wanted to throw her arms around Sandu and kiss him right there in front of everyone, but she could tell he was still protecting her from whoever was in the trees protecting Dominic. She could only assume it was the absent Solange. She wanted to be like Solange—able to disappear and be counted on to have Sandu's back at all times. Dominic didn't look to see if she was there; he *knew* she was. They were partners.

You have no reason to develop such a trait. I observe, that is all. There is no one to compare with you. That is a given. Sandu couldn't fail to read the absolute sincerity in her.

"Our home is not far from here. We will certainly be safe there." Dominic turned and began to walk back into the strange curling fog.

Sandu held out his hand to Adalasia. The farther Dominic got from them, the more he became translucent, as if he were like the cat she saw in her mind rather than in reality. Nicu and Siv were in motion, following the Dragonseeker into the rolling clouds of vapor coming off the forest floor. Sandu urged her to stay in step behind them. She tried to keep her heart in sync with Sandu's, but it was difficult the moment they actually entered the darker fog.

Adalasia felt the difference on her body. She knew what mist felt like when it touched her skin. This wasn't the same at all. When she looked down at her legs, there were tiny pinpricks in her calves and ankles. She moistened her lips and couldn't help tightening her grip on Sandu. So much for being a warrior woman like Solange. She didn't want to look at her body as the steam rose higher and thicker around her.

Ahead of her, Nicu and Siv were nearly transparent. She could see the dark gray fog roiling right through them. It had risen up like a fog-bank, surrounding them, coming through the trees, a shield to hide in or a shimmering veil to transport them from one realm to another. Adalasia wasn't certain which it was, only that the Dragonseeker had created the wall for them to step into, and they were doing so willingly.

Then her body felt as if it were disintegrating slowly, piece by piece. Those little holes widening until, when she looked down, there was nothing left of her. Her breath caught. She nearly called out in fear to Sandu. He must have felt her terror, because his mind moved in hers. Gentle. Steady. He didn't speak to reassure her, and because he didn't, she remained silent as well.

Adalasia had so many questions, but she refrained from asking them. Clearly, Sandu was unfazed by this strange phenomenon. He didn't take it as a threat, and neither did the others. That had to mean they had some kind of protection against it that would extend to her; otherwise, Sandu would never have allowed her to step inside it. Once she reasoned things through, she was able to relax again.

She kept her gaze fixed straight ahead, where Nicu and Siv had been.

Eventually, she caught glimpses of them moving through the trees as the darker gray began to turn a lighter color and thin out. The translucent forms solidified rather quickly, much faster than when they had slowly disappeared into the mist. Neither man turned to see if she and Sandu were behind them, so she knew they were aware of their presence.

Sandu's thumb slid over her inner wrist, right over her pulse. *You did very well. I had no time to warn you what it would be like inside the mass.*

What is it?

It is a ward few know of. Not even insects can penetrate it. Air, earth, water or fire, none of the elements can get through it.

Excitement burst through her. *Do you know how to create such a thing?*

Inside her mind, he nodded. *Those in the monastery shared knowledge. The Dragonseeker was one of the few given some of our secrets. He arrived at our gates with tremendous wounds, and we took him in to heal him. Since it was well known that no Dragonseeker had ever turned, we imparted knowledge to him not given to too many other hunters. His sister, Rhiannon, was taken, her lifemate killed, and Dominic refused to give up looking for her. He is a very tenacious hunter.*

Adalasia looked around the forest. They were still very close to the river, but now moving away from it, going to the interior. Overhead, the tree branches were thicker and connected with one another, forming an arboreal highway. There was an occasional whisper of movement, no more than the passing of something along the leaves, as if a slight breeze had stirred the canopy.

Those parasites you detest so much, Dominic ingested in order to make it appear as if a Dragonseeker had finally turned vampire. There was a plot underway to kill the De La Cruz brothers and then to murder the prince. He infiltrated the ranks of the vampires to get information and destroy them. Enduring the parasites was agony every second, but he did so in order to ensure that the Carpathian people got the necessary information and the master vampires were destroyed.

Adalasia couldn't help but look at the wide shoulders of the Dragonseeker with new respect as he led the way through the forest, that dark gray mat still under their feet as they made their way to his home. She hoped she could have done what he had in order to save the world, but the thought of taking even one of those horrid, vile, wiggling parasites into her mouth was so appalling, she could barely keep from vomiting.

How did he survive?

Solange. She fought at his side. Their story is legendary, told to Carpathian children now. Solange is very quiet and uncomfortable in the presence of others, which is one of the reasons they reside here. Dominic is comfortable anywhere. Solange needs the forest, and he needs her.

The sound of a great body of water had grown louder until it was roaring. Adalasia managed to turn the volume down on her own. Water poured down from above a series of gray boulders. The blue-and-white water spilled in a long fall into an unexpected turquoise pool surrounded by more rocks and large ferns. Trees with orchids winding their way up the trunks and wrapping around lower branches surrounded the pool, standing upright like soldiers guarding a treasure. The sight was breathtaking, even with the dark mist rolling along the ground and moving above the private lagoon.

Dominic didn't give them too long of a time to admire the beauty of the place. He waved his hand and the fall of water parted. They could see the narrow path shimmering into sight from their side of the forest floor. It was designed so only one person at a time could walk along it and enter the grotto behind the falls. Whatever was there was impossible to see. Adalasia tightened her fingers in Sandu's.

This is a really cool place to live if you're going to have a home in the rain forest, Sandu.

It is.

For the first time, she felt his reluctance. The four brethren traveling with them echoed his concerns. The shadow of a cat, for a brief moment, shone on the wall of rock behind the water, the fall shimmering right through the shadow, casting iridescent colors on the gray boulders. Adalasia blinked, and the silhouette was gone, leaving her wondering if it had been an illusion. Dominic walked, without pausing, along that narrow trail, and then he, too, disappeared into the dark, cavernous opening.

Nicu, drop back, Sandu commanded. *We may need you to bring an army of animals to aid us in battle.*

Nicu stepped to the side, and Siv continued forward as if Sandu had not spoken. Adalasia could feel all the brethren connected to him in her mind. Petru moved up to stride behind Siv, covering his back but giving him room to fight should there be need.

Do you really believe Dominic would lead all of you into some kind of trap?

No, but he did not expose his lifemate, even though we revealed you to him. The real Dragonseeker could not be vampire. This does not feel like the undead. I do not believe there is a master vampire capable of deceiving all of us, but it is your life at stake, and none of us are willing to take a chance with you. Being on guard always is our way, Sivamet.

Sandu followed Petru, his hand guiding Adalasia behind him. Around their legs, up to their knees, the same dark mist, as dense as in the forest, tumbled and boiled like a brew in a witch's cauldron. She concentrated on keeping her heart beating in rhythm with Sandu's. Dominic didn't feel evil to her, either. He felt protective. A warrior. She wasn't nearly as concerned as Sandu and the brethren.

It was the mist that intrigued her. The wards in it. If even insects couldn't penetrate it, then Nera and her army of demons couldn't get them. She would have to learn how to add that to their arsenal of protections. More and more, she felt she had been missing the most important point of the guidance her cards had given them. She was happy she'd read the cards and found that the guardians had lifemates alive in the present century. Yes, Sandu and she needed information on Sandu's past to help him find his memories, but this was her journey as well. She was to learn from it, and at each stop, she was being given something extremely important. She couldn't afford not to listen. Not to hear what was being said—or not said.

There was a light spray of cool water that was very real coming off the rocks from above. Sandu passed into the dark cavern, and she was only a few steps behind him, blinking rapidly so her eyes would adjust. She felt Benedek close at her back and knew Nicu was a few paces behind, still bonded in their minds.

Carpathians could see so clearly even in the darkest caves. A few feet inside the narrow opening, the cave suddenly widened into what appeared to be an expansive hallway. The floor beneath their feet was stones of various colors. The walls and ceiling, made of similar stone, curved as if they were the entrance to a magnificent mansion. Sconces of blown glass in soft blues and purples lit the hall. Gold filigree held the glass from the wall, and starbursts shone on the ceilings, beamed from those sconces.

Nicu. Sandu gave him the clearance to enter.

There was a feeling of warm welcome the moment they entered that hallway. This was a home. Adalasia wondered how Dominic and Solange had managed to construct it there in a cave in the rain forest, where Solange felt most comfortable, surrounded by nature. Just the walls and floor were works of art, let alone the sconces and the way they cast stars and galaxies onto the ceiling.

The hallway gave way to a large chamber that clearly was the great room, with high ceilings and gem-covered walls. Diamonds in various colors, as well as sapphires and rubies, sparkled when light played across them. The floor was the same as in the hallway, great flat stones of various shades of gray, highly polished until they gleamed. Even with the exclusivity of the walls, there was nothing cavelike about the room. Adalasia found the artsy style to be rare and lovely. Again, there was a warmth to the room that surprised her.

The furniture was unique, looking like pods inviting one to curl up in. Some were clearly meant for two people, others for a single person. A young woman sat in one of the pods. She had startling emerald eyes the shape of a cat's and thick hair that fell in a long fall to her waist. She was on the thinner side for being Jaguar, and there was no doubt she carried Jaguar blood.

Her gaze jumped to the five Carpathian males. Adalasia couldn't blame her. The ancients were big men, all well over six feet, most six and a half feet tall. They looked imposing with their wide shoulders, their muscles, their warriorlike physiques. She smiled at the woman to try to make up for the fact that none of the men smiled.

In the corner, a young girl had been playing with toys, but she stopped and stepped behind a man, circling his leg with one arm. The child appeared to be around four or five, but Adalasia had little idea of ages on children. The little girl was very small but sturdy. The man facing them looked protective. He had one hand on the little girl's head. Another woman entered the room very quietly behind Nicu and went to stand beside the woman seated in the pod chair.

Dominic smiled at her. "This is my lifemate, Solange." He waved toward the newcomer.

Solange had thick sable-colored hair, very wild, and when she moved, a few golden streaks could be seen. She had very distinctive cat's eyes, amber at times, but green flecks that spread and would turn nearly as emerald as the other young woman's. She was short and curvy, with defined muscles, and looked as if she could handle herself in a fight. Dominic indicated the other young woman. "This is Jasmine. This is Jubal Sanders, and that's Jasmine's daughter, Sandrine."

The little girl stuck her head around Jubal's leg and waved, her little pixie face flashing a smile and then disappearing again.

"I apologize for being so cautious, but we had visitors when your request reached us." He indicated the three in the room. "Your request was worded so carefully, Sandu, and a rumor had also come to us around the same time that an old enemy may be on the way to our part of the world."

Adalasia noted that Jubal once again dropped his hand to the child's head. She had the feeling that he had been the one to bring the news of an old enemy on the way.

"Jasmine is my cousin," Solange said. She looked a fierce warrior in contrast to Jasmine's wholly feminine appearance. Still, her voice was gentle, and when she looked at her cousin, her expression was gentle.

"Please do sit down, everyone. When Dominic told us we were going to have so many visitors, it was quite a shock. Occasionally, my cousin Juliette comes to visit with her lifemate, Riordan. He's a De La Cruz. When that happens, one or more of the other brothers accompanies them, but that's very rare. We usually make the trip to their ranch."

Sandu chose one of the pods that were for two people. The moment

Adalasia sank beside him, the chair seemed to wrap them up, conforming to their bodies. It felt cozy and very nice after the trek through the forest. She rubbed her palm on the arm surrounding her. "This is amazing, Solange. Where did you find it? I've never seen anything like it in my life."

Solange's face lit up. "Actually, it's Jasmine's design. She came up with the idea, and I loved it so much I begged her to let us try it out for her."

"Seriously? You're brilliant, Jasmine," Adalasia said. "This is the most comfortable chair I've ever sat in." She put her head on Sandu's shoulder. "I could live in this chair."

"It is comfortable," Sandu agreed. "I usually pay little attention to such things, but I have to agree with Adalasia."

Color swept into Jasmine's face. "That's kind of you to say. I just came up with the design; Jubal built the furniture. The credit really goes to him."

"Perhaps both of you," Dominic corrected. "They own a furniture company together. It is getting to be quite popular. Solange and I are very proud of them. We knew they'd be successful." He looked very lovingly at Jasmine.

"We can take Sandrine in the other room while you talk," Jubal offered. He held out his hand to the little girl. "It's past her bedtime. We promised her she could stay up to see the company. She doesn't like to miss anything."

Jasmine stood up. "She's very much like Solange."

Jubal held out his hand to Jasmine. There was the slightest hesitation, but Adalasia caught it. Those beautiful emerald eyes lifted to his face, and then she smiled and put her hand in his. Jubal pulled her to his side, as if he hadn't noticed her hesitation at all. "Let's get our girl ready for bed. She wants a bedtime story."

"You have to read to her," Jasmine said. "You do all the voices." She turned back to smile at them. "It was nice to meet everyone."

Jubal nodded toward them but didn't say anything as he escorted the two females from the room.

"This man is related to Joie, Traian Trigovise's lifemate." Sandu indicated Jubal. It was a statement of fact more than a question.

Dominic nodded. "Yes. He is Joie's older brother and has been in our world a long time. He's fought at the side of the Carpathian people against the undead as well as fought with Solange and her family against the Jaguar men and their many attempts to take Solange and her cousins. He knows Danutdaxton and Riley. He saved Riley's life on more than one occasion, along with Gary before Gary's conversion. He is a man much respected in the Carpathian community."

Even the brethren in the monastery heard of Jubal Sanders once we left our sanctuary. He isn't Carpathian; he is human, but he's strong, able to face vampires and every enemy our species must fight.

There is so much to be learned, Sandu. Dominic. Solange. Jubal. Jasmine. All of them are strong in their own way, Adalasia pointed out. She sank farther into the chair and moved against him, her thigh sliding against his.

"How is it we can help you, Sandu?" Dominic asked.

"All memories of my past are gone, Dominic," Sandu said. "I may have wiped them from my mind to ensure my family was safe in the event of my turning, or perhaps it was done before I ever set out on my journeys. I know that you traveled extensively throughout the various mountain ranges and cave systems. Do you have any recollection of my family?"

"Berdardi is a very old name, Sandu. I came across Domizio di Berdardo. It was close to dawn, and he had destroyed many vampires that a master vampire had surrounded himself with. Domizio had crawled toward a cave in an effort to avoid the sun, but he was leaving a blood trail—a very large one. It was evident when I ran across it that this Carpathian hunter was not going to survive his wounds. I followed the blood and found him, almost gone just inside the entrance to a set of caves."

Do you recognize the name? Adalasia asked. She could tell by the way Dominic was studying Sandu's face that he expected him to recognize it, but there was not even the faintest clue of memory on his part. She felt, just for a moment, a hint of his frustration. It welled up and he let it go.

No, Sivamet, I do not.

Sandu shook his head. "I have no memory of such a man, Dominic. Clearly, he must be some relation to me, but if he is, I do not recall who he is."

"He is, or was, your father. He did survive that injury. We spent a few nights together while he was healing. In that time, I learned he had a lifemate, Madolina; a son, Sandu; and a daughter, Liona. I learned most of that information from his mind when I provided blood or went inside his body to heal his wounds. They were quite severe."

Adalasia could feel Sandu struggling to reach back into his memories to find any of those people, but it wasn't as if they were behind a barrier. They were not present. His memories of his past had been wiped away. To Sandu, they were simply people, not family. Although now he knew of Liona; he just couldn't recall memories of her. She slipped her hand in his, wanting to make this easier for him. Sandu was unused to emotion, so he was already reacting how he normally did when feelings threatened to get in his way—he simply turned emotion off.

She didn't like when he turned feelings off; he always felt very far away from her. It was easy for him to do, and he did it often, but it left her feeling as though she was completely alone.

You are never alone, ewal emninumam minan. The way he said "my own sweet goddess" in his language, his voice pouring into her mind like dark, thick honey, filled every perceived emptiness that had ever been in her, warming her. *I am always with you.*

"Domizio had every intention, the moment he was healed, of picking up the trail of the master vampire and his cadre of followers. He was a hunter, and once on the trail, he didn't ever stop. You have a certain reputation, Sandu."

"I believe you are correct, Dominic," Nicu said. "Sandu never stops once he is in pursuit of his prey. They run, but he has never ceased hunting until he destroys them."

"He must have gotten that trait from his family line," Siv said.

Dominic nodded his assent. "Domizio had, without a doubt, a one-track mind when it came to the undead. I suggested that I would con-

tinue the hunt. I had no lifemate or family, and this particular vampire
was quite cunning and had several lesser vampires, but still, ones skilled
in battle. He would hear none of my logic. It was his duty, he proclaimed.
In the end, we hunted together. Domizio had not only strength of body
but strength of will. I see these traits in you, his son."

"Dominic, where were you when you met up with Domizio?" Adalasia asked.

Dominic frowned and rubbed at his eyebrows with the pad of one
finger. "In those days the countries weren't what they are now, Adalasia.
The borders were different. Forests were denser and spread across more
land. One could go for long periods of time without coming across humans, and then there would be farms and villages. Or the bigger cities,
not like we know them today, but big for those times. It was difficult to
define actual countries, especially for a Carpathian. We were like the
animals, moving from one place to the next, without restrictions."

Solange leaned into Dominic, one hand sliding around to the nape
of his neck, her fingers massaging deep. He looked up at her, his expression softening. He reached up and pressed his hand over hers.

"It could have been somewhere close to what now would be Russia.
Domizio had chased the vampire for weeks and was far from what he
considered his territory to guard. The only reason I think this—while we
hunted and eventually caught up with the undead, another Carpathian
hunter had attacked the master vampire. He was a guardian of that territory, and now that I go further into my memory, that hunter called
himself Koshkiny, Alyosha Koshkiny. We joined him in the battle. The
master vampire had surrounded himself with others to do his bidding,
and just as before, when Domizio had taken him on, Alyosha was torn
up by the sheer numbers. We came upon them, and the undead had no
chance against three experienced hunters."

"Russia?" Adalasia said. "I wasn't expecting that."

It is possible one of Liona's friends was from the area that is Russia, she
added to Sandu.

"Danutdaxton had met up with Alyosha a time or two. They may
have been related in some way. I have a strong feeling you should speak

with Dax. He stays in Peru most of the time. He can be . . . charming. If you go, Sandu, never forget, he is a shifter, just as we are, but he is also a dragon, a genuine dragon. He shares his body with the soul and heart of a dragon. It is necessary to always be mindful of that fact. Dax has to be mindful, which is why he prefers to stay as far from civilization as possible. He allows the Old One the freedom to fly as often as he can. In the cities, that would be impossible."

"What of his lifemate?" Adalasia asked.

"Lifemates provide whatever their other half needs," Solange answered.

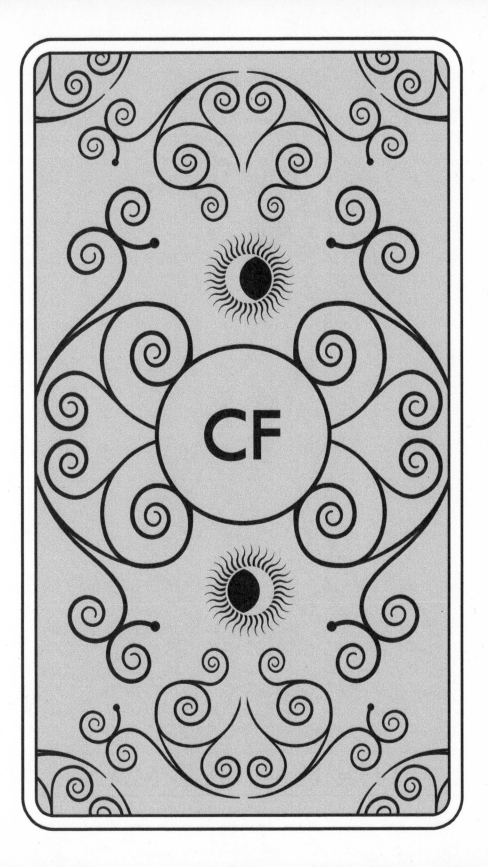

T he animals in the forest are whispering to me in alarm, Dominic," Nicu said as they gathered in the great room on the next rising. "I patrolled to the south of your home. There was no sign of the undead, but every bird, every monkey, even the smallest of them, seemed to be uneasy. When I asked them what kind of creature had passed through, they whispered, *Unsavory. Vile. Traitor.*"

Dominic exchanged a long look with his lifemate and then Jubal Sanders. "Did these animals show you any images of the creatures coming through their territories?"

Nicu shook his head. "I asked, but they only kept to their shelters. I didn't push them but intend to return. I thought it best to warn you first."

"You did not feed yet," Sandu observed.

Nicu shook his head. "I did not waste any time getting back here in case the danger was to Dominic's family. I didn't want to use telepathy because I had no knowledge of what I was dealing with."

Sandu studied Dominic's features even as he brought Adalasia closer to him, sweeping his arm around her shoulders. He had been about to take his leave but would not if there was a threat to Dominic's family.

"We can use the pathway of the brethren," Sandu suggested. "Should this danger be the work of the undead and his pawns, they would not hear. I will reach out to the others. If they have run across any threat, we will have more information."

"I'll go looking," Jubal volunteered. He stood. "I have a feeling—"

"No." Jasmine looked as if she might burst into tears. "No, Jubal, you can't." She looked to Dominic even as her slender fingers wrapped around Jubal's wrist, as if she might be able to physically hold him there.

"You and Sandrine will be safe here, Jasmine." Jubal's voice gentled.

"No one can find you here. Dominic and Solange have safeguards to keep everyone out."

Sandu could have told him Jasmine wasn't worried for her daughter or herself. She didn't want Jubal going out into the rain forest, where something unknown could harm him.

Dominic waved Jubal to his chair. "We do need to gather more information before any of us goes hunting, Jubal. I would appreciate you contacting the others, Sandu. Nicu, you need to feed, especially if you plan to go back out there immediately."

Very casually, without waiting for an answer from Nicu, he lifted his wrist to his mouth and tore a line in the flesh with his teeth so the bright blood bubbled up instantly. Nicu bent his head to the offering.

Brothers, Nicu has encountered strange occurrences among the animals. Sandu sent the images to the three guardians still out. On rising, each had gone his own way to find blood. *Be on the lookout for anything unusual and report back to us. We need to gather as much information as possible. There is an old enemy possibly stalking Dominic's family.*

Benedek was the first to answer. *I took the form of a harpy eagle and flew to the fishing village. I found nothing unusual there, but as I was returning, I caught glimpses of several men moving in the branches of the trees just beyond the ruins. It was unusual to see men in the branches of trees, so I circled back to investigate. They are nowhere to be found.*

Sandu felt a tremor slide through Adalasia's body. She shared his mind, and he hadn't excluded her from the contact. He had included Dominic. Instinctively, he knew the Dragonseeker would not want Jasmine to be privy to their conversation.

Does this mean something to you?

Dominic barely inclined his head. His gaze flicked to Solange. Like Dominic, her expression gave nothing away, but Sandu had the feeling she wanted to gather her cousin very close and hold her.

Unfortunately, yes. There are men who have sought Jasmine for some time. She, like Solange, carries royal Jaguar blood. Jasmine was raped by these men some time ago. Sandrine is . . .

He stopped and glanced at Jubal. The human male was paying close attention to them. Too close. It wasn't possible for him to be on the same pathway. No one but the brethren shared that particular communication route, but although his expression hadn't changed, there was a well of rage rising in the human. It threatened to fill the room. Just when Sandu was certain Jasmine would feel it, Jubal took a deep breath and let out his air in a long sigh.

Mine. Sandrine is mine. My daughter. Jubal made the claim.

So much for their path of communication being private. Dominic didn't look at all surprised. Neither did Solange. Sandu and Nicu exchanged a long look—two battle-scarred warriors uneasy when they discovered something unexplained. Nicu politely closed the wound on Dominic's wrist and moved into a better position to defend Adalasia—and kill Jubal.

Dominic ignored Jubal's declaration, but Solange shot him a look, one that was softer than Sandu had seen her give any male other than Dominic. It was brief, barely there, but she clearly approved of his claiming.

We have always feared these men might return. We knew they had left the country, but before they left, they had declared they would return for Jasmine. Dominic shrugged. *It is time we ensure they are out of her life permanently. They do not get to terrorize her or Sandrine.*

Sandu flashed a small, humorless smile. In that moment, he was all predator. *I suppose it is meant to be that we arrived to be of some assistance to you, Dragonseeker. A small payment for all the times you have aided one of us.*

Jasmine turned to Solange. "They've come for me, haven't they?" Her voice shook, but she didn't cry. "I put all of you in danger by coming here." Her chin went up. "I'm going to leave Sandrine with you, Solange. She'll be so much safer. I can lead them away. They'll follow me. You know they will. I'm fast, and without my daughter, I have a good chance—"

"Over my dead body," Jubal said. "You can forget your plan, Jasmine. Is that what all that practice shifting and running around in the trees has been about?"

Sandu wasn't the best at relationships. In fact, he was really new at the entire relationship thing, but he cleared his throat, hoping to signal Jubal that his tone and his demands weren't the best way to get across his point. It was too late.

Jasmine's emerald cat eyes blazed at Jubal. "I don't think you have any right to tell me what to do, Jubal Sanders."

"Think that all you want, Jasmine. I've had all I'm going to take of this crap. I've given you enough space, but this is sheer lunacy, and it isn't going to happen just so you can prove some sort of feminine-warrior, Jaguar-royalty-in-your-blood crap."

"It's called taking responsibility, Jubal," Jasmine snapped. "What do you mean you've given me enough space? What *exactly* is that supposed to mean?"

Solange threw her hands into the air. "Jasmine. Don't ask him that. He's going to tell you. You're going to get angry. He's going to haul you off and kiss you, or something equally outrageous and pathetic, and we're all going to be waiting around until you two figure it out."

"He is *not*," Jasmine denied.

"Yes, he is," Jubal corrected. "I've been waiting for years for you. *Years*. You aren't going to risk your life when there are six Carpathian ancients, Solange and another Carpathian woman, plus me, ready to take these fools down. No one can possibly mother Sandrine the way you can. You aren't expendable."

"Waiting for me for years?" Jasmine echoed, ignoring the rest.

He sighed. "You're the only one who doesn't know. I've given up on the idea of asking you to marry me. I already talked to Sandrine and Solange. They agree it's a great idea. I asked Dominic for your hand. He said yes. We're doing it. Why do you think we're here? Juliette and Riordan will be here next rising, and we're getting married."

"But . . ." Jasmine looked a little helplessly at Solange, although Sandu could see she was excited. Her breathing had gone a little ragged, and the pupils of her eyes were dilated. "What about your sisters?" She wasn't protesting the idea of being railroaded into marriage at all.

Jubal shrugged. "They'll understand. We'll go visit them when we have the chance. Joie's back in the Carpathian Mountains, but I doubt if

Gabrielle will be coming back any time soon. We might have to make a trip to Washington."

Jasmine didn't seem to object. She did grip his arm again. "Since you all seem to have a plan that you think is so much better than mine, would someone like to tell me what it is?"

Dominic smiled at her. "*Sisarke*, we are going to find the enemy, and we will exterminate them once and for all."

"How many of them are there?"

"Jasmine," Solange cautioned.

"No, I want to know what all of you are facing on my behalf."

"Remember, they would be after Juliette and Solange, as well," Dominic pointed out. "You are not the only one with royal blood running in your veins. There is no guilt here. Whatever these men do, it is on them, not on you or anyone else."

Jasmine nodded. "I do know that, Dominic, it's just so hard after hiding away for the past few years and being so afraid to finally have them be here. I'm actually terrified but glad in a way that it's finally happening."

"Why, exactly, are they after you?" Adalasia asked. "I'm not certain I understand why these men would be so persistent after all these years. It has been years, hasn't it?"

She needs to find a way to talk this out. She really is afraid for everyone. Especially Solange and Jubal. I can see it in her eyes, Sandu. I can feel the fear pouring off her in waves. Look at the way she looks at her cousin.

Sandu couldn't help following Jasmine's gaze. Solange stood very close to Dominic now, a little behind him, so that his imposing figure nearly covered hers, although he was seated and she was standing.

Jasmine moistened her lips. "Yes." Her voice wavered for a moment. Then her head went up as she met her cousin's eyes. "Solange, my sister Juliette and I, and now Sandrine are the last of our bloodline. Even though Solange has been converted, the Jaguar line still runs in her. She is royalty. I can shift, but for a long time, I couldn't maintain my Jaguar side for long. With practice, I've gotten better. Sandrine is very good at shifting. Her jaguar is strong. We don't allow anyone to see her shifting, and these men, those hunting us, if they knew, they would take her, and the moment she was able, they would use her for breeding purposes. That's all they care about. They were part of the downfall of our species, and yet they continue to do the exact same things they did before." There was contempt in her voice. "They don't care about the females of their species. They hunt them, capture them, rape and impregnate them over and over until the woman dies. They don't seem to see that they are responsible for the extinction of the Jaguar people."

"Apparently, the mages had a hand in helping to wipe out our people," Solange said. "From what Dominic and I gathered, Xavier, the high mage, was to rid the world of all Carpathians. He had two brothers. One was to get rid of the Jaguar people and the other the Lycans. They nearly succeeded in all counts. The Lycans and Carpathians nearly went to war. The Jaguar species are all but extinct. The Carpathians are still on the brink. Mikhail, the prince, is slowly turning things around, but it is a slow process, and the tiniest thing might shift the balance against him."

"These men want you, Jasmine, because they think you can provide royal babies?" Adalasia asked.

Jasmine nodded. "I'm the easiest target. Solange would be nearly impossible to capture, let alone hold. I doubt they know she's Dominic's lifemate. She has a certain reputation and most jaguars fear her. It is known that Juliette is with Riordan De La Cruz. If you take on one De La Cruz, you are taking all of them on. No one in their right mind wants to do that. I'm not a fighter, although I've tried to learn how to be one. I'm not the same girl I was when they got their hands on me the first time."

A little shudder went through her body. Her voice trembled slightly at the end of her declaration. Jubal moved his arm around her and pulled her under his shoulder, sliding right into her chair, lifting her onto his lap as if he did it all the time. He nuzzled her neck.

"You're strong, Jasmine. You were then and you are now. You have Sandrine and you've made her strong."

Jubal Sanders looked extremely fit. An outdoorsman. There was nothing soft about him. Nothing. He had the body of a natural athlete, a fighter, a man who could handle himself in any situation. If the rumors were true, he had Jaguar blood in his veins. Judging by the ropes of muscle on his body, Sandu could believe it. There was no doubt that he had psychic abilities and he was telepathic. He'd already proven that. He was well respected and was treated as if he belonged in the Carpathian community.

On his wrist, he wore what appeared to be a bracelet made of solid metal, the color silver. Sandu's gaze strayed often to that bracelet. He noticed Nicu's did as well. Both were certain that was no ordinary decoration on his wrist but a weapon of some kind. He wore boots like the others, and inside his, there were built-in sleeves for knives and a gun. He had other weapons set by the doors, ready to grab as he hurried out. Sandu caught glimpses of them in Jubal's mind when he'd spoken telepathically.

Jasmine smiled up at the man. "You always make me feel strong, Jubal. I love that I can put my designs on paper and you make them come to life. When we first started working together, I had no self-esteem, and you gave it back to me. You gave me confidence in myself again so I could give that to Sandrine."

Jubal shook his head and brushed a kiss on top of her head. "You always had it, honey. Always. You just lost your way for a little while. That was understandable. You focused on your baby. Now you're back to seeing the entire picture again."

Laughter bubbled up. A little pixie giggle that made Sandu want to laugh with her.

"You mean you, Jubal. You're the entire picture again?"

Jubal lifted an eyebrow, looking down into Jasmine's face. "Aren't I?" He looked around the room, then at Solange. "I am, right?" He kept his features deadpan.

Solange, for the first time, actually smiled. More than smiled. She burst into laughter. "I'm certain you are, Jubal," she confirmed.

The tension in the room completely dissipated.

Do you wish for me to track these men, Sandu? Benedek asked.

Sandu caught the impression of the harpy eagle sitting in the branches of a tree, watching the old ruins carefully.

Dominic answered. *We do not want to tip them off that we are on to them if they are still in the vicinity, Benedek. Would you mind keeping watch?*

I am very comfortable sitting here, Benedek responded immediately.

There is a hidden door, Solange said. *It leads inside the temple. If they simply disappeared, most likely they are inside there. It is a large area, and there is plenty of breathable fresh air. When I was a child, we hid there. Eventually, that hiding spot was taken from us, too.*

I will watch, Benedek assured them.

Sandu sent out the call for more information. *Petru? Siv? Anything at all will help us. We are trying to gather as much data as possible to ascertain what we might be facing.*

Afanasiv replied first. *I scanned a large area, looking mainly for the undead as I made my way toward the village beside the river. Several times I found myself uneasy, but there was no clear reason why. I fed and returned to take a closer inspection of the area. That is what I am doing now. The animals and reptiles are not showing alarm unless I approach too closely to the ruins of the old Mayan site.*

Dominic threaded his fingers through Solange's. *What do you mean, Siv? Can you describe the unusual behavior?*

Lizards and frogs have retreated. The baboons and monkeys I generally see with family units in the neighboring trees have deserted the area. They have gone so far as to invade other territories at the risk of war. There has not been all-out fighting, but certainly posturing and verbal threats between the males. The females are cowering but refusing to take their young back to their own territories, and the male isn't forcing them to go. If anything, he's indicating he is willing to fight for new territory.

Sandu felt Adalasia grip his thigh, and he covered the gesture with his larger palm. *You did not bring this enemy to these people, Adalasia,* he assured her.

We don't know that for certain yet. They're guessing. Her hand trembled on his thigh. *I couldn't bear it if I brought harm to Jasmine after all she's been through. You know Nera uses reptiles and animals as spies.*

Dominic, Solange and Jubal looked at her.

Solange sent Adalasia a reassuring look. *I know the feel of rogue Jaguar males when they walk in the forest and disrupt the natural rhythm. While your guardians were talking, I was listening to the background as they sent the images and sounds. Unfortunately, Adalasia, I am all too familiar with those disruptions. As a young child, I was taught to listen for the sound of the rogue Jaguar male. We knew if they came, they brought death and worse.*

We each have enemies, Sandu reminded gently. *They may be different, but we face them with courage. We have no choice if we stand in front of others to keep them safe. In this case, Jasmine and Sandrine or any other woman of Jaguar blood will not be victims of these men if we can stop them.*

Solange nodded at him. *Thank you for standing with us.*

Petru added to the information they were collecting on the intruders. *I did not see these men, but in the village, there was talk of them. They came by boat and they had supplies. The supplies were not all in the way of food. Mostly, they had weapons. The ones that watched them said they didn't recognize all the weapons they carried. I made certain I was not seen so I could follow the ones that had the most information, and I took it from their minds.*

Sandu felt Adalasia wince. She still wasn't on board with the way Carpathians so casually extracted information they needed simply by taking it. They took blood and opened a pathway if they really wanted to delve deeper or if they wanted to monitor the individual from a distance.

We do not have to torture anyone for information, he pointed out.

Adalasia turned her dark eyes on him, and he had to resist grinning at her.

Just wanted to say it was much more civilized.

Now you're just being smug. She kicked him, but very gently.

The images Siv sent filled their minds with containers sitting on the rickety pier. Behind them, giant *Victoria amazonica* were in the shallow water, basically giant green lily pads. Tied to the pier were several crude fishing boats and two modern ones.

The two fishermen from the village sat "guarding" the containers. The two men looked all around them, clearly searching for the men who had come upriver. One stood guard while the other peered into the containers. His eyes went wide and he spoke rapidly to the other. The two hurried away from the pier, clearly afraid of the contents.

There were all kinds of guns and ammunition, but it was the strange weapons Sandu had never seen before that intrigued him the most. *What are those?*

Jubal made a small sound in the back of his throat and then looked at Jasmine. He set her aside and stood up, pacing across the room, putting distance between them.

Some of those are more recent inventions to kill vampires. You point and shoot, and the bullet incinerates the heart. He turned to face the Carpathians, his brows drawing together. *Where the hell would they get these?*

They clearly aren't on the market, Dominic pointed out, as calm and steady as always. *Where did they come from?*

I invented them with Gary. The two of us. We needed weapons for the kids and women when they couldn't go to ground, just in case the undead sent their puppets. These were only in the Carpathian Mountains and . . . Jubal trailed off.

Dominic and Solange continued to look at him. Jubal shook his head and looked away from them as he paced restlessly back and forth across the room.

Sandu caught guilt laced with anger. Jubal Sanders was very angry. Whoever had taken those weapons and given or sold them to those men, he regarded as a traitor. He had an idea of how that particular weapon had gotten into their hands and was worried about others.

Jasmine got up and went to him. "Jubal? What's wrong?"

He didn't stop pacing, nor did he look at her. "Sweetheart, I'm going to go out there and see if I can find these jokers."

"Jubal." Dominic said his name softly. "We just had a talk about responsibility. And self-sacrifice. This is not the time to blame yourself for what others do. You know better. That is a gut reaction."

Jubal shook his head, for the first time not taking advantage of Jasmine's closeness. She wrapped both arms around his waist as if she were holding him to her—and maybe she was. It did stop his pacing, but he didn't put his arms around her. He just stood there in the center of the room, looking torn.

Sandu had no idea who could have betrayed Jubal, but it was someone close to him, someone he cared about, and the cut was deep.

"I suppose you're right, Dominic, but it's difficult not to. These men have the capability to kill you and Solange. To kill all of you." Jubal looked directly at Sandu and then Nicu. "The weapons were to ensure Falcon's children survived when the Carpathian adults were in the ground. Vampires would send their puppets after the children. At times, the children would be attacked during the day, when they had little protection. We were teaching them to fight back, and these weapons were a way for them to survive a puppet assault. We were working with the women as well to use them against a vampire attack."

"Can't vampires compel obedience from humans?" Adalasia asked.

Sandu could see she was trying to get Jubal to get beyond his shock and anger at the betrayal, his need to sacrifice himself in order to make up for the actions of another. He tightened his hold on her hand, pressing her palm deeper into the muscle of his thigh to let her know he appreciated her.

"They can, but our children have learned to counter the compulsion, even the youngest. The weapons have a built-in sound system to help counter any buried compulsion, as well. I've taken every precaution when teaching the kids."

Sandu was certain Jubal didn't realize he referred to the Carpathian children as "ours." He had been in their world for so long he considered himself one of them, yet he also carried Jaguar blood in his veins. Sandu wasn't certain what that would mean for his children with Jasmine, but he did know Jubal Sanders was a good man.

Finally, Jubal looked down at Jasmine. "I've been working with Sandrine, just as a precaution. We play games. That's how I started with Falcon and Sarah's younger children. Sandrine is highly intelligent, and she learns very quickly."

Jasmine smiled up at him. "Of course she does."

Jubal sighed and rubbed his temple as if he had the beginnings of a headache. "I should have told you I was working with her to keep her as safe as possible from the undead and their puppets."

"Honey," Jasmine said softly. "I appreciate that you would even think of it. I should have been. We stay with Juliette and Riordan all the time. Or we come here. We live in the world, where there are vampires. I don't know why I wasn't the one to ask how to protect us against them. I guess I was so busy thinking about rogue jaguars, I didn't consider vampires, and they're an even bigger threat."

Jubal bent over and brushed a kiss on top of her head. "Sandrine is a natural when it comes to learning about any kind of self-defense. She has tremendous reflexes. She's sure-footed in the trees as well."

Solange nodded. "She's very gifted, Jasmine."

There's movement in the forest, Petru reported. *I'm on the trail leading to the ruined temple. Two men are walking toward the ruins through a game path. Both are built stocky, with roped muscles, and are carrying packs around their necks the way jaguars do.*

Sandu and Nicu exchanged a long look with Dominic. If Benedek had been correct and five men had entered the Mayan temple and hadn't come out, where had these two come from?

Petru, how many men arrived in the boat at the fishing village? Nicu asked.

When I saw those on the pier, they were guarding the containers. At no time did I see the original occupants of the boats. The face the fisherman had in his memory was because one approached him and offered money to watch the containers for him.

Petru held the image carefully so that all the brethren could see it. Solange closed her eyes for a moment, clearly identifying the man.

His name is Steve. He was one of the men who raped Jasmine, and he always said he would come back for her. Can you show me the faces of the two men you see on the trail?

I will have to get closer to them. I have taken on the shape of a nightbird, the long-tailed potoo. I do not want to call attention to myself, although the two men do not seem to be nervous at all. They do not appear to be expecting trouble, Petru answered.

Sandu could tell Petru was on the move, the bird flitting from tree to tree, getting closer to the men he wanted to get a good visual for Solange on.

"When I was infiltrating the master vampire's lair in order to determine his plans to assassinate the prince," Dominic said, "there were rogue jaguars and some humans in league with vampires."

"That's how Juliette met Riordan," Jasmine confirmed. "He had been poisoned and kept starved and chained. We had gone into the laboratory to rescue animals, and she found him there."

Petru sent the images of the two men to their minds. Solange studied them. *I know both these men. One is named Brad. The other, Simon. I hunted Brad for some time, but he left the forest, I thought, for good. I honestly am shocked to see Simon with him. He was never a part of the rogues. He stayed away from them when he was younger. He left to go to school. I hadn't heard that he returned.*

"Sandrine is calling, Jasmine," Dominic said. "I think she's ready to take her bath."

"She thinks she's such a big girl," Jasmine said. "She wants to do everything herself now. Jubal, please don't go chasing off into the forest the minute I go take care of Sandrine."

Jubal brushed another kiss on top of her head. "You worry too much, sweetheart. Go take care of our baby."

Sandu noticed he didn't promise her anything at all. The moment she was out of the room, Jubal began to slip weapons into loops inside a jacket he shrugged into. Solange caught up a bow and arrow, and slung it over her shoulder.

Sandu stood as he sent out another call. *Siv? Did you see anything different from where you are?*

Afanasiv had taken up a position of watching the ruins from the opposite side from Petru. With Benedek in the body of a harpy eagle overseeing the ruins, they weren't going to miss much.

Two more men coming toward the temple with packs around their necks.

They're moving at a fast rate of speed. No, there's a third behind them. Lagging back on purpose. He's clearly watching their back trail. This group is a little more cautious than the ones Petru reported.

Any signs of the undead? Dominic asked. He stood and signaled to something unseen in the corner of the room.

Sandu felt rather than saw movement toward the entrance of the room. For a moment, Sandu could see the shadow of a large cat on the wall, and then it was gone, disappearing once more as if it had never been. Solange followed it and then Jubal. No one stopped the human male. He was treated with the same respect as any Carpathian hunter would be treated. Still, Sandu was worried for him. It wasn't as if the man could disappear into mist or shift into a bird and fly. He would have to find a way to keep up with the others as they moved fast through the rain forest to reach the ruins.

"Adalasia . . ."

"I know. You would prefer that I stay here."

"I see no reason for you to come when there are so many of us," Sandu said. "If it is your preference, of course, you should come, but it isn't necessary." He was grateful that she shook her head.

"I'll stay with Jasmine and Sandrine. The last thing I want to do is see these horrid men who performed such atrocities on Jasmine and got away with them for years. Who knows how many other women they raped and possibly murdered?"

Sandu bent his head and brushed a kiss across her upturned mouth. "This shouldn't take long."

She sent him a faint smile and then looked past him to Nicu. "Don't get so smug about being Carpathian that you forget you aren't invincible. They have those weapons, and no doubt, they actually know how to use them. If you get too arrogant, that may be your downfall."

Nicu gave her his expressionless, deadpan look. "We are ancients, Adalasia." As if that said it all.

Sandu knew Nicu was deliberately trying to rattle her, and it was working. She clenched her teeth at him.

"That's *exactly* what I'm talking about. You're getting too big for your britches, and you're going to get your heart incinerated by that nasty weapon Jubal invented."

Nicu looked down at his trousers. "My britches fit just fine, and as my brother's lifemate, it is unseemly for you to be looking too closely."

"Get out," she hissed.

Sandu tipped her chin up and kissed her again, amusement uppermost in his mind.

Nicu and Sandu followed the trail of the others into the night sky. It was easy to see how Jubal traveled so fast. Dominic took him, and Jubal was at ease flying through the air and weaving in and out of trees at a dizzying speed. He didn't seem to be uncomfortable with the height when they settled in one of the taller trees at the outskirts of the ruins.

Are they all inside? Sandu asked Benedek.

Yes. If the original five I saw went in, then the others have joined them. Ten for certain.

Solange leaned her back against Dominic, the very first vulnerable sign she'd shown. *Why would they be recruiting after all this time? There aren't any Jaguar women in the rain forest. All the women are gone. Juliette doesn't live in Peru. There is only Jasmine and me.*

A heartbeat went by. Two. It was Jubal who answered her while Dominic ran his hands gently through her hair.

There is Sandrine. They were told about Sandrine.

Solange froze, her golden skin going pale. *There are few people who know of her existence. Who would betray a child to these vile men, Jubal? And why? What could possibly be their motive?*

Hatred of all things Carpathian and Jaguar. Jubal sounded weary. *Both of my sisters have become Carpathian. Joie is with Traian and Gabrielle is with Aleksei. My mother really detests that they are Carpathian, but above all else, she despises Jaguar with every breath she takes.*

Sandu and his brethren were beginning to understand what Jubal suspected, and if he was right, the betrayal couldn't get any worse. The cut was deep and it was visceral.

That makes no sense. You have Jaguar blood in you.

Yes, I do. Not just any blood. My mother is from a royal line as well. Like you, she was hunted relentlessly, and like Jasmine, she was kidnapped and assaulted. She was held for several years. I thought Rory was my father. He's Gabrielle and Joie's, but he isn't mine. Both of them hid that fact from us. They went to such trouble to hide it. They never told us we had Jaguar blood in us. I think if our mother could have, she would have opened her veins and replaced her blood with someone else's.

There was silence as all of them comprehended what Jubal told Solange.

My father, well, Rory, died last year of an infection. Mom had been acting more and more erratic. She'd always been volatile, but she seemed to be getting worse. Gabrielle is in a very remote area and doesn't see her often. Joie sees her the most, but even that isn't much. Mom would make excuses when I would say I would want to come to see them. When our father was ill with the infection, we all went to be with him. She was different. Very subdued. She didn't leave his side. I believe she had gotten angry and slashed him with her claws. He had evidence of older, deeper wounds that had healed on his body. He never complained. He adored her.

Jubal's sorrow was heavy in his mind.

I'm so sorry, Jubal. I had no idea you were going through so much, Solange said. *I wish you would have shared this with us.*

There wasn't anything anyone could do. After my father died, Mom just seemed to retreat even more. She didn't want to see me. I would drop in on her so she couldn't avoid me, but she clearly didn't want me around. I'd just talk to her about my life, about Jasmine and Sandrine and how much I loved them. I hoped she would want to meet them. That she'd want Sandrine in her life. She never once asked. I did, unfortunately, talk about the weapons the children were learning to use to protect themselves against vampires. I told her far too much in an effort to rally her. I didn't realize how much her resentment toward the Carpathian people had grown.

You believe your mother found these rogue Jaguar men and gave up Sandrine's existence to them? Nicu wanted confirmation. He didn't have a lifemate. He wasn't feeling the bond between Adalasia and the rest of them. He had no sympathy for betrayal. There was only death for such treachery.

She knew the entire story, yes, Jubal said. *All of it. Jasmine's kidnapping, the rapes, the bloodline. She knows they are of royal blood. She told me to stay away from them. I have royal blood from another line, and she said if we were to get together, I would turn into a hideous monster, and any male child I produced would be an abomination on the world.*

Sandu looked down at the Mayan ruins. There was so much hatred and fear in that declaration that a mother would tell her son. She had to be half mad with grief and whatever trauma had happened to her when she was young. Still, that was no excuse to set up that same trauma for another young child. He shook his head, feeling the beast in him rising to counter any compassion he might have had for such a woman.

I am going to bring them out of their little hiding place, Solange said. *We have to get all ten out. Remember, they have those weapons, so be very careful.*

I will go with you, Jubal said. *It will lend more credibility to your walking alone. They know you are with the Dragonseeker.*

Sandu had studied Jasmine carefully. *I will shift into the shape of Jasmine and walk with you.*

There was a small silence. Benedek was the first to speak. *Perhaps to give this scenario even more credibility, Jubal should hold your hand, Sandu.*

This is a good idea, Petru agreed. *Perhaps pull you under his shoulder protectively in the way of lifemates.*

O jelä peje teräd, Sandu replied.

What exactly does that mean? Jubal asked. *It had better not be agreement.*

Sun scorch you, Dominic interpreted, amusement in his voice.

Solange floated down to the forest floor, staying under cover of the trees and waiting while Dominic brought Jubal. Sandu shifted into Jasmine's smaller, curvy form. Her dark, wavy hair cascaded down her back, held by a simple clip at the nape of her neck. Her dark lashes emphasized the vivid green of her eyes. Where before, she'd been thinner, after the birth of her daughter, she had more curves, and her soft, clingy top and light khaki trousers showed her figure and her golden skin to perfection.

Solange was dressed in similar attire, showing off an hourglass figure. She was short, her sable hair braided in a tight weave that hung down her back. She had cat's eyes that glowed green one moment and then would go gold- and amber-colored. She walked with absolute confidence.

"I suppose we're taking Jubal to see the temple," Solange whispered aloud.

Sandu, as always, scanned the entire area around them. They were always looking for the undead. For enemies. For anything or anyone unexpected. There were only the natural animals of the forest that he could feel, but he was still uneasy.

Nicu, there is something else out there watching us. I can feel it. I do not know if Nera's spies have found us after all, or if the rogues have set a trap. Perhaps the undead are here. Sandu spoke on the path of the brethren so that all could hear, but if a vampire was close, he could not detect one. He continued to walk in between Solange and Jubal, finding the faint trail that led to the ruined temple and the crumbling buildings.

All of the Carpathians reached with their senses to scan their surroundings. Sandu hoped someone else would be able to find what he could not. He knew they were being observed. He felt the danger to them, and he was certain it wasn't the rogue jaguars, but he couldn't ascertain where the threat was coming from.

Like you, Sandu, Siv said, *I know something is there, but I can't find it.*

Dominic, what does your cat say? Did you send him out looking? Solange asked.

He says only that we are not alone, that other animals are aware of the rogues and watch for them. He is more interested in prowling around the temple. He can get inside to see what they are doing.

Solange sighed. "Sometimes I think that cat is useless. We can't get near the temple if we're going to lure them out into the open. If we can't get them out, the shadow cat will go in after whoever doesn't come out." She kept her voice low, but as she stepped out of the shelter of the trees, she indicated the houses made of stone, most halfway collapsed, with the rooftops caved in or a wall crumbled.

Jubal walked a few steps away from the women, staring at the stone building Solange had indicated. Jasmine followed him, but stayed to the opposite side of the temple, making it more difficult for anyone inside to see her.

"I should have brought my camera, Solange," Jubal said, his voice carrying clearly. "It takes excellent night shots. Jasmine, you could sketch this for me when we get back. It's beautiful with the way the moon shines on it."

"I think the positioning of the temple had something to do with the moon," Solange said. "I didn't pay that much attention to the history of the place. Did you, Jasmine?"

"Juliette is the historian in the family," Jasmine said. "She loves everything old, including that lifemate of hers." She laughed at her own joke.

Very funny, Sandu, Dominic said.

They are coming out on the opposite side, where you cannot see them, Benedek announced. Still in the body of the harpy eagle, he had a clear view of the men moving covertly out of the secret door built into the steps. *Two carry a weapon that looks like the one Jubal says he invented. One leads; the other has the rear.*

How many? Sandu asked.

Eight. Two remain inside, Benedek reported.

Our shadow cat and I will take the two inside, Dominic said.

Nicu, we will take these men, Sandu said. *You have our backs. This thing in the forest is close. I still feel danger.*

The two men with the weapons were the first that would have to go. They couldn't afford to have any armament that could easily kill a Carpathian.

I will kill the last man in their column, Benedek said. *He is breaking off to circle around and protect them. He is now hunkered down in the stones straight across from where you are standing, Jubal.*

I will take the first man with the other weapon, Siv said. *He has stepped aside to allow the others to move in front of him. He's slipping into the forest and is trying to circle around behind the women.*

That left Sandu, Solange, Petru and Jubal to dispose of the remaining six. *Pick your targets,* Sandu instructed. *When they show themselves, we are not going to talk. We will simply strike at them. There is no reason to hash this out.* He didn't believe in having conversations with the enemy.

The six remaining rogue Jaguar men came out from around the temple. They were built solid, with the roped muscles of their kind. All wore loose clothing they could shed easily if they needed to shift quickly. They knew they had two of their kind covering them with weapons if Solange's partner was anywhere around. They also had two others inside the temple watching.

Weapon secure, Benedek reported.

Weapon secure, Siv said nearly at the same time.

"I hope you remember me, little bitch," Steve greeted Jasmine. "We missed you, didn't we, Brett?" He turned to smirk at the man closest to him.

Jubal sent his weapon spinning from his wrist, the edges of the blades tipped in silver. It moved through the air so fast it was a blur, a silent, deadly projection slicing straight through Steve's neck, cutting off his head so cleanly it stayed on his shoulders as the weapon retreated back to Jubal.

Simultaneously, Sandu, Petru and Solange attacked, Solange going for Brett, using her Carpathian strength and speed, driving straight at him, punching through his chest as she would a vampire. At the same time, she punched through his throat, staring him right in the eyes, letting him know this was retribution for her cousin. She let him drop to the ground and turned toward the next man in her line of vision.

Sandu rushed across the clearing, shedding the illusion of Jasmine's body as he did so, gripping the rogue jaguar's head in his hands before he had the chance to shift, wrenching hard and breaking the neck. He flung the body aside and tried to step around Solange to get to the last two men.

Petru gripped the fourth Jaguar man in his large hands, lifted him over his head and slammed him down over his knee, breaking his back before following him down to the ground to kill him with a finishing chop to his throat.

Two in the temple down, Dominic said.

The two remaining Jaguar men rushed at the ones they thought the most vulnerable—Solange and Jubal, both shifting as they did so. Jubal leapt into the air to meet the large jaguar attacking him. As he did so, he shifted, kicking off his shoes, his clothing ripping. He met the jaguar in midair, the two males roaring challenges.

Solange stood unmoving as the other cat attacked, rushing her, a big male in his prime, bent on taking her down with a killing bite or a swipe of his giant claws. Sandu stepped in front of her, shifting at the last moment so that the cat ran directly into an immovable steel wall so hard, the large animal stopped and shook its head, clearly dazed. Solange killed the shifter with several well-placed arrows.

They turned as another cat leapt from an overhanging branch onto Jubal's back, the weight nearly knocking him off his feet. This was a female, and she tried for a decisive bite to the back of his skull. Jubal's cat was large, fit and had rope after rope of muscles. His spine was flexible, and he spun, nearly bending in half, but at the last second seemed to hesitate. The female gripped him harder, raking with her claws, and once more going for the kill bite, but this time, he reared up fast, dislodging the female, throwing her to the ground.

The male attacked, driving toward Jubal's cat's side in an effort to break his ribs and knock him to the ground. As he did, the female also attacked, this time straight on, leaping for his front leg in an effort to snap the bone in half.

Nicu was there before she could get to Jubal, catching her in his arms and tossing her easily away from the two male cats. She sprang up and attacked Nicu, all teeth and claws. He simply caught her head and jerked hard, breaking her neck.

Solange and Sandu rushed to aid Jubal, but he didn't need their help. He had the other cat down and had already delivered a powerful bite to the back of the skull, killing the other animal. As Jubal shifted, Sandu waved his hand to clothe him. Sorrow pressed so heavily on the man, it weighed on all of them.

"I am sorry," Nicu said.

Jubal walked over to the female lying crumpled just a few feet away, crouching down beside her. Very gently, he buried his fingers in her fur. "She would have killed me, Nicu. Her intent was there for anyone to read. You saved my life. I know I couldn't have killed her." He didn't look up.

Solange put her hand on his shoulder. "She was ill, Jubal. You know she was ill, or she never would have turned to men such as these and conceived of a plan such as this one. This had nothing to do with you. Sacrificing your life to save hers wouldn't have done her any good."

"That had been in my mind."

Sandu could have told him their minds were all linked together. The moment Jubal had been aware the female was his own mother bent on killing him and that he had hesitated and even entertained the idea of allowing her to kill him, they all knew there was no other choice. Nicu had destroyed her to save Jubal's life.

"She was ill," Solange repeated gently. "Let us take care of her in the way of our people. She is royalty and should be treated as such. Then we'll go home to Jasmine and Sandrine while the others dispose of these rogues."

Jubal nodded and gathered the body of his mother in his arms. Dominic was there, wrapping his arm around Solange as they went to the sacred burial ground where the ashes of her mother and aunt were buried. Sandu and the brethren followed them and stood solemnly as Dominic opened the ground and Jubal placed his mother's body in the rich soil. Solange conducted the ritual ceremony, and the body was burned until it was reduced to a fine ash, and the earth was closed over it.

They stood for a long time while the sounds of the rain forest played music for them. Solange put her hand on Jubal's arm. "Let's go home, brother."

Jubal nodded. "Let's walk partway. Just for a little while."

That was what all of them did, allowing the rain forest to bring them all a sense of peace.

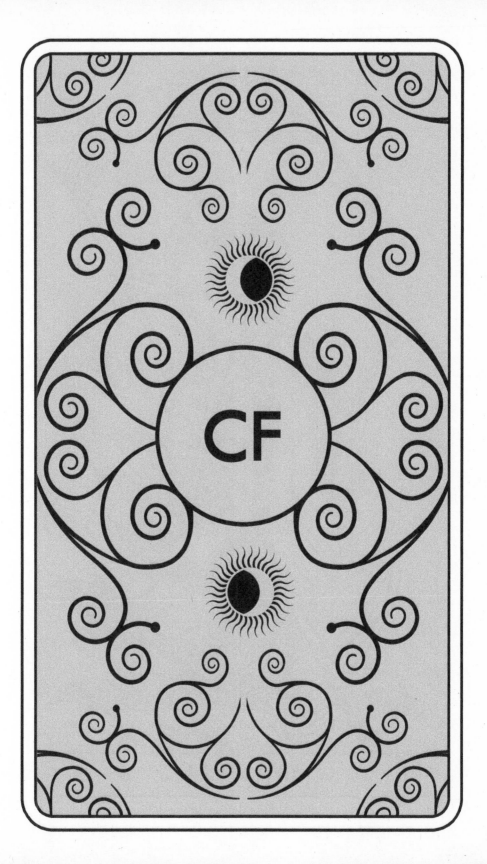

S andu had visited the Brazilian rain forest on many occasions in his travels throughout the centuries. He had never encountered Danutdaxton in Peru. Many centuries earlier, Dax had been in various locations in the Carpathian Mountains, traveling with a Carpathian woman, Arabejila, unclaimed lifemate to a very powerful Carpathian male who had deliberately turned vampire. Mitro Daratrazanoff had led the two on a chase over the continent. He'd been on a terrible killing spree, taunting the hunter and doing his best to kill his lifemate so she couldn't help track him.

Danutdaxton was a renowned hunter, and even as he tracked Mitro, he would destroy any of the undead he crossed. He had always, even as a young boy, long before he had grown in power and skill, made grown Carpathians uneasy. He had a talent that no other Carpathian had ever shown at such an early age and was unsettling to most males. Dax could see the dark shadows growing in the males from the time the boys were young, and he would know instinctively which were going to turn.

He admitted that, at times, he could be wrong. Sometimes honor was equally as strong or stronger in a Carpathian as that darker shadowing. Dax couldn't see that trait, nor could he know when a man would chance upon his lifemate. A lifemate could save a hunter from turning, overcoming the darkest shadowing.

There were many other factors going into what defined a Carpathian hunter. He had to be able to think like his enemy. He had to be experienced in battle. Fast. Have tremendous knowledge of the undead. Each kill brought him closer to the brink of disaster. The whispers of temptation grew louder. The damage to one's soul when it was already dark and only half a soul was tremendous. Dax saw all those things, and no one wanted those sins exposed. It made for a lonely childhood that only worsened as he got older. Everyone avoided him.

Sandu was happy that Danutdaxton had found his lifemate. Dax's life had been extremely difficult hunting a dangerous enemy for so many centuries. He had disappeared for over five hundred years in South America. It was now known he'd been sealed in a volcano with the undead by Arabejila. Somehow, both hunter and hunted had survived—and changed—becoming something different. Dax was tasked with finding Mitro and destroying him once they escaped the volcano, and he had done so, although it hadn't been an easy feat.

The Andes Mountains stretched across the entire length of South America along the western coast. It was the perfect range for a Carpathian like Danutdaxton to call home. He could move from country to country, have several homes in the shelter of the mountain, and find places to set his dragon free. At the same time, if his lady needed the company of humans, he could easily establish a home on the outskirts of a small town, and they could integrate for a time in that area, or visit with any of the Carpathians living in one of the South American countries.

As they had approached the region Danutdaxton had directed them to, they had taken their human forms and walked along the forest trail. This was cloud forest, covered with the mist, a beautiful, unexpected world of explosive color and sound, even at night, different from the Brazilian forest where Solange and Dominic made their home.

"He is watching us," Nicu announced.

"I feel him," Sandu said. "He's been aware of us for some time." Sandu had been careful to keep their approach to Dax's home as open as possible.

Sandu had asked for a meeting, explaining he was traveling with his lifemate and four unmated brethren from the monastery as guards because their journey was dangerous. He added they would meet with Danutdaxton away from his home anywhere, if Dax was willing, as they were certain their enemy was close behind them.

More and more, Sandu had been uneasy. It wasn't the fact that he knew Danutdaxton was aware of their approach. His radar was going off.

He felt the same in the others. Adalasia looked around her, her footsteps slowing, her gaze going to the ground where the carpet of insects moved under their feet. Night creatures were everywhere. Eyes stared at them from branches of trees.

Adalasia, you are going to shift into mist. I will hold the image in your mind if you feel you are unable to do so. No matter what happens, you stay in this form.

I am capable of fighting these creatures, Sandu. And I have practiced holding mist.

We have yet to know what we face. When we know, then you can tell me if you are better suited to fight them than we are.

If we are right and Lilith needs both of us to force me to use the cards, then whatever they do will be directed at our brothers, not you. They might try to wound you to slow us down, but they will try to kill them, she cautioned.

Sandu wasn't certain how Nera and her army had gotten ahead of them, but this didn't feel as though the undead lay in wait for them. If a vampire was anywhere close, Dax would have known and been hunting it. This was his territory, and he was aggressive in his protection of the people in it. The moment a rumor surfaced that sounded anything like a vampire could have been in any of the villages, farms or communities around his territories, Dax took swift action.

Once Adalasia had disappeared into the mist, unable to be detected in the cloud coverage, Sandu sent word to Danutdaxton that their enemy had gotten there ahead of them and laid a trap for them. They would handle it, as they were uncertain of what they were facing. He didn't expect an answer from Dax, and he didn't get one. The ancient Carpathian hadn't seen or heard from him for centuries. He had a lifemate to protect. He wasn't about to risk her for five unknown Carpathians who could easily be the undead trying to draw him out. Sandu would never have answered, either.

The lack of sound came first. Every insect ceased the incessant calling. There was no movement, no rustling of leaves. No fluttering of wings. It felt as if the very earth held its breath. Sandu had faced many horrific things in his life over the centuries, and that ripple of unease that he felt under his feet, as connected as he was to the soil, gave him insight into what was coming his way.

Trees trembled and the ground shivered, as if an earthquake had begun small and grown in strength. Insects burst from the ground, large black beetles with pinching claws, until the forest floor was alive, moving with them. Giant ants crawled up the trees, covering the trunks, building bridges from one limb to another, devouring everything they came across. Spiders jumped at birds and monkeys as they abandoned trees to try to get ahead of the ants.

Far off, the sound of ghostly baying could be heard. Not that of a wolf but of dogs, baying together in unison. The earth shook harder and the trees swayed. Sandu coated his body in hyssop oil as he floated above the forest floor to keep the crawling bugs from reaching him. They were a mere nuisance in comparison to what they would face in a few seconds.

I can get rid of the bugs Nera sent, Adalasia informed him.

Do not give away your presence, even in my mind. We don't know how she got ahead of us. One of these hounds will no doubt try to pull me to Lilith, forcing you to follow. If that happens, I will need you to stop it long enough for the brethren to kill it. Then you can deal with the insects.

He didn't like that much of a prolonged communication with her. They were missing something besides the blood connection, something Nera was able to track Adalasia with. He wasn't taking chances with his lifemate, not in the midst of what could be a true firestorm. She didn't answer, an acknowledgment of his concerns.

He manufactured the necessary arrows, shields and weapons, coating them in the vats of hyssop oil he suspended in the air around him and proceeded forward in the clouds of mist toward the enemy, using the trees as shields although he knew that would never stop what was coming his way.

The eerie sounds grew louder. Sandu lifted his hand to shift the wind slightly so that it would carry the scent of their enemy to them. At once, the sulfuric, foul stench of rotten eggs and burning brimstone told him he had been correct in his guess as to what Nera had chosen to throw at them. He had to give the information to Adalasia just in case.

Hellhounds. Hard to kill. Sometimes they have more than one head. They must be shot in the eye to kill. A throat shot will slow them down but not kill them. You cannot get the saliva or blood on you. Do not let their claws or teeth touch you.

More than using actual words, he let the images flow to her, so it wasn't as if he was actually talking to his lifemate. She would be observing and learning as he and the brethren fought the hellhounds. He knew Adalasia was correct. One would come for him and try to drag him back to the gates of hell with it, while the others would try to kill the guardians. Nera thought she had an advantage here in the cloud forest. He was missing something, and he couldn't afford to miss anything.

Malignant red-and-yellow eyes appeared and disappeared in the thick mist as if giant heads bobbed up and down. Hooves thundered on the ground, and heavy bodies smashed into bushes and tree trunks as the hounds drove forward toward their targets. The scent of burning and smoldering grass added to the noxious smell of the beasts as they rushed forward, but the forest was far too wet to catch fire.

The first one emerged out of the gray mist, an enormous, massive beast, running full out, faster than one would ever conceive, pounding toward Sandu. He was already covered in hyssop oil from his hair to his boots, and as the creature from hell with its gigantic teeth and claws came straight at him, he let loose an arrow straight to its left eye and then another to its right. The hound skidded in the leaves and debris, howling, snapping at the air as black blood ran down its face and jaws, mingling with the thick ropes of saliva that were already streaming to the ground. The hellhound shuddered and his legs gave out. He went down, sides heaving.

At once the beetles began clacking, and they swarmed over the hound, their claws shredding him open, ripping and tearing at his body to spill his insides out onto the forest floor. They crawled inside him, eager to get at the riches there.

Tell the others not to allow the carcasses to touch the ground, Adalasia said.

Sandu was already relaying that message, although the guardians had each found out for themselves, not trusting the beetles' reaction to the fallen hellhounds. Like Sandu, they sensed there was more at work here than the attack on them, as they had felled several of the hellhounds as well.

I can counter what she is doing, Sandu. You have to let me do my job.

Hellhounds came from all directions, coming at the five Carpathian hunters with blurring speed. The beetles, with ravenous appetites, consuming the five carcasses Sandu and the others had first killed before incinerating the dead bodies as quickly as possible in midair, began to keel over, bloated beyond their ability to walk. Sandu couldn't keep an eye on the beetles and the hellhounds at the same time. He had to trust his partner.

Don't touch the ground, he cautioned her. *And don't look into the eyes of these beasts.*

I'm actually well versed in demons, she answered, a little snippy note in her voice.

He wished he had time to appreciate her sassiness, but a particularly large hound was approaching with blurring speed, one with three heads. The heads undulated continuously. It ran at him accompanied by two other hounds on either side, each with two heads that also moved like snakes.

He let loose two arrows fast, hitting two of the eyes on the right and left head of the center hellhound. The two eyes geysered black blood, and then the heads dropped heavily, but the middle one remained malevolently staring at him as the beast thundered toward him. The heads flopped macabrely against the black fur with every step the hellhound took. The two other hounds kept up, rushing with the first one, straight at him.

Danutdaxton emerged out of the cloudy mist, letting two arrows loose at the beast on his left, targeting both heads, hitting one in the eye and the other in the nose as it swung the head toward him. The beast snarled its rage, the red eyes rolling as it looked at the newcomer, but it continued toward Sandu.

Haven't shot a bow in centuries, Dax said and let loose another arrow at the swinging head. He followed it up with two more.

Don't allow the carcass to hit the forest floor, Siv cautioned. *Incinerate it.*

If you leave it in the air, the spiders jump on it, or the ants build a bridge to it. The beetles get it on the floor.

Sandu couldn't take his eyes off the approaching hellhounds to check to see if the spiders and ants were tearing into the carcasses the way the beetles had.

Welcome to our fun, exciting world, Dax, he greeted as he let an arrow fly at the beast to his left. He hit to the side of the eye as the heads swung away from him. He instantly shot several arrows into the hellhound's throat. It staggered and stopped abruptly, shaking both heads repeatedly, giving him time to concentrate his shot on the middle hound.

That hellhound's remaining head was up, the malevolent eyes boring into him. The creature was so close to him, he could feel its foul breath as it snorted and blew noxious air out. Up close, the teeth looked serrated, the canines wicked and sharp. Long strings of thick saliva dripped from its mouth.

Who did you piss off in hell? Dax asked as he released his arrows.

Hellhounds continued to rush them from all sides, as if the pack were endless. Sandu rose swiftly above the threatening hound. It skidded to a halt, the head tipping back, those crimson eyes following him as it tried to spin its bulk around. Sandu shot two arrows into the eyes of the hound from above. Even as he did, he felt the spiders attack, leaping on him, webs casting over him, attempting to pin his arms and legs.

The dying hellhound dropped to the forest floor as he turned his attention to ridding himself of the spiders and webs. The beetles swarmed over the dying hound. Spiders sank fangs into him. The webs tightened around him, trying to drag him to the ground, where the hellhounds waited beneath him, heads up, eyes staring, fangs dripping.

The five carcasses the beetles had devoured were completely gone, and the bloated beetles began to move obscenely, blindly, scooting against one another, thousands of them, melting into one another until they formed themselves into a giant spitting black scorpion with a thick tail that curved over its back. The creature was fast, scuttling toward Dax, going for his legs, rising into the air, reaching toward him, spitting venom to try to blind him as he fired arrows at the hellhounds.

Adalasia emerged from the mist. She was in a long trench coat that swirled around her ankles. It was open, showing the many loops holding weapons that glittered with light and color. She wore light khaki cargo pants with long boots that crunched over the beetles as she walked along the forest floor. The beetles retreated from her rather than rushed to swarm over her. She held a long sword in one hand and a long vial of clear liquid in the other.

For a moment, there was a hush as if even the hellhounds feared his lifemate as she held the sword in front of her. She looked an avenging angel. Then she moved, straight toward the enormous scorpion, rushing at it with the blazing sword. The blade of the sword looked more crystal than steel, and it had a curious light to it, glowing first a soft blue, then green; then, as it approached the scorpion, which swung around in alarm to face her, it changed to a strobing white.

The tail stabbed at Adalasia, and she swung the sword, neatly slicing right through thick segments, dropping parts of it to the ground. She leapt right up onto the back of the scorpion and sliced off its head in one clean, very powerful swing of her arm. Using the back of the scorpion's body, she sprang into the air and touched the tip of the sword to the web encasing Sandu and then dropped to the forest floor in a crouch. The web holding him retreated, as did the spiders, as if in fear of that sword.

"Hear me, demons sent by sister kin to take my lifemate from me."

She plunged the blade of the sword deep into the forest floor. The beetles screamed as if she had pierced each of them with the crystal.

"This ground is lost to you. This shape is lost to you. Each form she sent this night is now locked in this consecrated earth." She scattered drops of the liquid from the vial in four directions and then above her head and onto the ground.

The ants screamed as they seemed to explode in little puffs of smoke all up and down the trunks and branches of trees as well as on the forest floor. Spiders caught flame, the smell foul, and then the ashes floated like so much debris to the forest floor. Thrusting the vial into a loop in her coat, she yanked out a clear shield.

As if on some signal, the hellhounds turned their attention from the

Carpathians to Adalasia, running at her rather than the six men firing arrows at them. The scorpions attacked the Carpathians. There were seven of them due to the fact that the ants and spiders had managed to get to three of the hellhound carcasses as they hung in the air. Adalasia had only killed one of the scorpions, leaving the others to do their mistress's bidding.

Keep the hellhounds off me. Once I get rid of the demons Nera has sent, we can turn the hellhounds back through the gate on her.

Adalasia was already in motion, running toward one of the scorpions attacking Siv. He danced in the air, shooting arrows at the hellhounds while trying to avoid the stabbing tail and spraying venom of the scorpion. As she came up behind it, the creature spun, realizing she was there. The tail swiped at her and then stabbed in an effort to sting her, releasing venom from its thick sac. Her sword lit up as it cut through the segmented tail, and then she was on its back, slicing through the head, dropping it onto the forest floor.

She moved like lightning, leaping from the dead scorpion's body to one dangerously close to Benedek, her sword already in motion. The creature never saw her coming and lost his tail. He swung his head, spraying his venom wide, but she already had the shield up. The sword sliced through his head before he could get another spray of venom off.

Can Danutdaxton incinerate the scorpion carcasses? He has to do it without touching the hellhounds or the living scorpions. The flames would only add to their power.

Adalasia was already moving to get to the two scorpions closing in on Danutdaxton.

Just as she leapt off the dead scorpion's back, a two-headed hellhound broke through the ranks of the others and crashed into the dead arachnid, its mouths yawning wide to show teeth and dripping poisonous salvia. Sandu thrust her away from it, shooting arrows into its eyes from above.

A steady stream of fire burst from Dax's mouth directed at the carcasses already dead on the forest floor, incinerating them instantly. Just the seconds it took to remove the bodies, ensuring Nera couldn't find a way to use them again, was all it took for Dax to be in trouble, with hellhounds and scorpions targeting him, rushing him fast, even as he rose above them.

He was fire, and the demons were attracted to fire. His burnished skin glowed, and little gold and red flecks of glittering ash floated in the air around him. Sandu raced to protect him, actually wading through the bodies of the hellhounds to get to the Carpathian. He was coated in hyssop oil, and he used his arrows, stabbing into eyes as the beasts turned their slavering jaws toward him. He disappeared into mist, only to reappear a half a second later to stab another one in the eye to edge closer to the fire-breathing Carpathian. If he brushed up against the fur, the oil protected him, and the beast howled as if it burned him, veering away, giving Sandu that split second to drive his arrow deep into the creature's eye as he rushed past.

Two scorpions turned toward Adalasia while they attacked Danutdaxton with their stabbing tails. They spit venom at her as she came toward them, daring her to approach closer. She stood just out of their range, studying the pattern they set. One sprayed, releasing a stream of venom, while the other held back, and then they traded. She came in on one at an angle, using the shield to prevent him from getting the venom on her and swinging the sword at the same time. The blade sliced cleanly through the scorpion's neck. Adalasia leapt back and rushed around the writhing body to attack the blindly stabbing tail, removing it before it could hit Dax or anyone else.

The companion scorpion scuttled around quickly to try to face the newer threat, its red eyes staring malevolently at her, spewing venom as the tail lashed wickedly. The hellhounds burst through the trees, coming from all directions, abandoning their attempts to try to get to Sandu or one of the other Carpathians.

Adalasia ignored the hellhounds, slamming her sword into the scabbard at her waist and the shield onto the hook. The demon hounds were the concern of the Carpathians. Her priority was the scorpions. She leapt for the tree branch overhead, caught it, crouching there for one second to once more take up her sword and shield before leaping onto the scorpion's back. She had to time her slice of the blade perfectly. There could be no mistake, or she would pay with her life.

The tail was cut through, the venom sac and stinger flying through the air as she turned to the head and made a quick clean stroke, separating the head from the body. The scorpion's entire frame, as she cut off the head, shuddered violently before crashing to the ground, catapulting her forward. She somersaulted when she hit the ground, still hanging on to her sword and shield, going under the belly of a hellhound. She came up between two hounds. The stench was unbelievable; so foul and toxic, just inhaling it made her feel dizzy and sick.

Get out of there. Over your head. Dissolve now.

Sandu held the mist in her mind, and he all but yanked her into the air and changed her physical form. Her weapons left a trail of colorful light in the cloudy fog, giving her location away to the beasts below. It didn't matter to the Carpathians protecting her. They also had dissolved into mist, thickening the vapor through the trees, suddenly coming back to their physical form to shoot arrows into the hellhounds' eyes and then dissolving again.

I'm ready, Adalasia affirmed. She'd taken in enough fresh air to dispel the rotten stench the hellhounds gave off. *We can't wait too long. I have to get rid of the last three scorpions before Nera can unleash anything else.*

She felt Sandu's reluctance. Not only Sandu's reluctance but that of all the Carpathian males. The concentrated, extremely powerful disapproval was in her mind. The guardians—and Danutdaxton—were not happy with Sandu that he had allowed his lifemate to be in such danger. She hated that for him, that they didn't see how magnificent and courageous he was to go against centuries of tradition and have faith in their partnership when they hadn't been together that long.

She didn't wait; she flooded his mind with overwhelming love, words she couldn't say, but a feeling she could give him, and then she spotted a particularly large and aggressive scorpion tracking the red and gold flecks falling through the clouds. The gigantic demonic creature scuttled through the forest, rounding the trees, forcing the hellhounds to get out of its way, at one point even spraying venom at a hellhound to move it.

This huge scorpion had eight eyes glowing brightly on the surface of its prosoma. She knew, in spite of having so many eyes, most scorpions used their bodies to see, not their eyes, as they had poor eyesight. She couldn't count on that. If this scorpion could see those little gold and red flecks like a beacon, she had to believe those eyes were seeing accurately.

The tail was much thicker than the others were. Each segment as it went up to the stinger, like the others, was larger, but on this scorpion, the segments almost doubled in size. The venom sac was enormous. Even the claws used to pull the massive demon forward could be used as weapons. They looked as if they might be tipped in venom as well.

Keep shooting the hellhounds, but keep his attention centered on Danut-daxton. You have to remember scorpions can jump. He probably can jump very long distances, much more than normal. Sandu, maybe Dax can leave a false trail of those red and gold flecks and just not be anywhere near that scorpion.

The scorpion wasn't silent as he stalked Danutdaxton through the hellhounds. His stinger rubbed along the dorsal surface repeatedly, producing a loud warning, or at least Adalasia thought it was that at first. Most black thick-tailed scorpions warned off intruders by stridulation. The more she listened intently, the more she realized the sound wasn't the same over and over. It changed often, the noises different. That gave her pause. What exactly was the scorpion doing?

All of you, listen to the sounds that scorpion is producing with his stridulations. He's not repeating the same noises as he should be. He's massive. His eyes see where the others don't. I'm hovering over the scorpion to its left, and I can clearly see this one has very poor vision.

She's right, the scorpion is definitely using various sounds, Nicu said.

Adalasia watched the way the hellhounds moved, and the other scorpions repositioned themselves when the red and gold flecks fluttered to earth from above. Suddenly, one of the other scorpions jumped high into the air, stabbing with his stinger, right where Danutdaxton had laid that false trail. She emerged from the fog, the crystal sword slicing through the thick tail of the scorpion. Following it down as it descended to the ground, she cut off its head and was back in the fog before the large scorpion was barely aware she had killed the sixth predatory arachnid. That left two.

The beast rubbed its stinger along its back in a fury of ferocious activity, producing a series of noises. Adalasia watched it carefully: the eyes, the movements, the reactions of the hellhounds and last scorpion. Her breath caught in her lungs.

This was the one directing the battle, reporting back to Nera. A trusted demon resided in that scorpion. Once he was disposed of, the hellhounds would be without a commander. The other scorpion would be easily defeated. She had consecrated the ground. Nera couldn't use it to bring more of her demons through. She shared her belief with the other Carpathians.

Tell me what you need.

Sandu. She could always count on him. Steady. Trusting her. He was close to her. She breathed him in.

Start a heavy assault on the hellhounds, circling around him as fast and as furious as you can possibly make it. We want to confuse him, even if it is just for a few seconds.

She couldn't make a mistake, not with this one. She exchanged the shield for the consecrated vial of water. The demon wouldn't go easily. She would need to make every second of confusion count and add to that time with chaos of her own making.

Sandu suddenly materialized, whirling buckets of hyssop oil in a wide circle so that the contents poured over the hellhounds baying beneath the Carpathians. Baying turned to howls of anguish and roars of rage. The scent of burned fur and flesh permeated the air, and great patches of oozing red skin bubbled up on the relentless hounds. He began firing arrow after arrow into the eyes of the hellhounds, dropping beast after beast to the forest floor.

Carpathians emerged from the fog in various places above the hellhounds scattered throughout the trees in a semicircle around the king of the scorpions, although they didn't deign to notice him. All of the hunters did the same thing, throwing the oil on the hellhounds and following it up with arrows coated in the oil.

The scorpion scuttled toward Sandu and then Danutdaxton. The hellhounds bayed and dropped to the ground, the sheer numbers of dead and dying hounds piling up like a fence around the scorpion so that it hesitated just for a moment, going inward, as if consulting. Adalasia dropped out of the mist, pouring the consecrated water over the eyes even as she sliced with every bit of strength she had through the huge segmented tail. It was as if, halfway through, she ran into a plate of armor.

Sandu! She called to him without hesitation.

He was there, providing the strength she needed, flowing into her without reservation, heedless of the risk to himself. Together they sliced through the thick tail while the scorpion tried to stab at her with its half-sheared stinger. The venom sac leaked, and she had to leap out of the way, slipping over the rocking body toward the ground.

Sandu caught at her to steady her. A hellhound clawed at him, hooking sharp nails into the skin of his back and dragging him off the scorpion. Howling, the hellhound began to run, galloping back through the forest toward the thickest of the fog. Three other hellhounds broke off to join it. Sandu couldn't shift or dissolve, not with the claws hooked into his body. He was dragged relentlessly along the ground.

The hellhounds went into a frenzy, spinning around, rushing after those shepherding Sandu to some unknown destination. There had to be a portal open, one the hellhounds were coming through, one Nera was bent on dragging Sandu back through to bring him to her mistress, Lilith.

Go after him, Adalasia demanded of the guardians. *You can't let that beast take him to the portal or whatever gate is open.*

She felt desperate, needing to get to Sandu before the hellhounds could take him to their ultimate destination. The portal had to be close, the way the hounds were reacting.

The demon scorpion bucked and rolled side to side in a frenzy in an effort to dislodge her. She rode it out, balancing on its back just behind the neck as she'd been taught since she was a child. She swung the sword, desperate to cut through the scorpion's head. She had to get it off, cut all contact between Nera and her army. There it was, that armored plate again. She got the head halfway off, but now it was swinging around, trying to spray venom at her. She dumped the consecrated water right on its head. The demon screamed and shrieked.

Sandu, help me.

In spite of his body bumping over tree limbs and rocks, Sandu, with the hellhound's poisonous claws hooked deep in his flesh, sent his strength to her without hesitation. All of it. Together they sliced through the scorpion's head. She leapt off the scorpion's body as it crumpled to the ground.

Catch the sword. Slam it into the ground. Hurry, Sandu. Coming behind you.

Adalasia knew it was an impossible feat, but she believed in him. She believed in *them*. Crouching, she sent the crystal sword spinning low to the forest floor, directing it with her mind through the mist, around the trees, through the legs of the stampeding hounds and right into Sandu's outstretched hands. His fingers closed around the grip.

We have to stop him right now. He's too close. I can feel the triumph pouring out of the portal. I can feel the danger reaching for him.

She felt Sandu gather his strength. She poured hers into him. The brethren did as well. She swore, within the portal, something or someone else, quite powerful, joined with them to add to their combined strength. Sandu slammed the consecrated sword deep into the earth. The hellhound came to a sudden, abrupt stop, unable to move even a few steps.

Benedek and Siv were on the beasts instantly, shooting arrows into their eyes while Nicu and Petru took on the other hellhounds that had accompanied the one carrying Sandu back to Nera.

Simultaneously, Danutdaxton yanked Adalasia from the ground as the last scorpion attempted to slam his stinger into her.

Adalasia paid no attention to where he took her. She sprinkled more of the consecrated water into the air and allowed it to settle over the forest floor. "I ask Mother Earth to seal the portals against all that would do harm. I call upon all that is good and pure and ask them to stand with your defenders against the demons and all that is foul. Seal earth. Seal air. Seal water. Seal fire. East. West. North. South. Above and below. Let no small fissure be left that evil may creep through. So be it."

The moment she had finished the sealing ceremony, she reached into her coat and pulled another sword free. Her gaze was on the last scorpion. It rattled its thick tail as it tried to follow the false trail Danutdaxton had left in the cloudy mist. She waited until the scorpion turned slightly, the tail stabbing down at an illusion Dax created, then she leapt down, slicing cleanly through the segmented tail. It was so much easier to get through than that of the gigantic scorpion, she nearly put too much strength into the cut. The stinger dropped to the forest floor, and she ran up the back, right over the eight eyes, and took another swing at the head. The body shook and the head ducked. Two hellhounds attacked from either side.

Danutdaxton shot arrows at them, but as he did, a hellhound ran up a fallen tree trunk and used it as a springboard and hit him square in the back, sending him tumbling through the sky. Dax shifted out from under the heavy body, dissolving into mist. The hellhound fell to the ground, landing hard, knocking the breath out of it. It stood up slowly, red eyes filled with rage and madness, locking onto Adalasia instantly.

Sandu felt as if his arms had been jerked out of their sockets, and the claws had ripped flesh and muscles all the way to the bone, but he shut off his ability to feel pain, reversed his energy and strength and yanked the sword from the earth. He rubbed the blade along the backs of his thighs, where the hyssop oil was the thickest, and then, with one swipe of the sharp blade, sliced off the hellhound's front legs with those terrible claws embedded in his back. He couldn't see them, but he felt them, and his strike was true.

The claws were still in his back, deep, leaking poison, the plague, but that was inconsequential at the moment. The hellhound slowly collapsed, black blood spewing in all directions. Sandu rolled out from under it, gripping the sword. Nicu was there, shooting arrows into the eyes of the hound to give Sandu his chance to get away. Sandu dissolved, streaking across the distance like a fallen star, straight to Adalasia.

The sword glittered like a comet as it came straight to his lifemate's

hand. She caught it and spun in a circle, the tips of the two swords pointing outward, then upward toward the sky, then down toward the soil as
she murmured something softly. Sandu was too busy fitting arrows into
a bow and killing the hellhounds as they thundered toward his woman.
There seemed to be less of them. They were slower. Some stopped and
shook their heads in confusion. The brethren finished them off quickly.

Sandu staggered and sat down in the middle of the leaves and rotting
vegetation, away from the dead and dying hellhounds and the bodies of
the scorpions. Adalasia hurried over to him. Benedek and Siv followed her.

"Sandu," she breathed his name.

His skin was already turning gray, the poison in him rapidly replicating. "Adalasia, you can't come near me."

She frowned at him. "I'm your lifemate, Sandu. You need aid."

He coughed, and blood bubbled around his mouth. Under his skin,
she could see bleeding. Siv was already shedding his body against Sandu's
protest. Siv's spirit, his white light, was astonishingly bright. Petru strode
out of the cloudy mist and, without hesitation, shed his body as well,
joining Siv in the fight to save Sandu.

"They will need blood," Benedek said, "Nicu, Danutdaxton and I will
provide that for them." He indicated Dax. "This will be a long battle, and
it is essential to guard their bodies while they attempt to drive the poison
from his body and heal him, Adalasia. When it is necessary, and it will
be, they will have you join with Sandu to hold him to this world."

"Riley, my lifemate, will heal the ground while we work on Sandu,"
Dax added. "She will be another pair of eyes to watch."

Adalasia wanted to remind them that Sandu was *her* lifemate, that
she should be the one to be healing him, but she could tell the situation
was dire. Sandu had risked everything by aiding her, not once but twice.
She had had no choice but to cut all communication between the demon
and Nera. Sandu had saved them all both times. He had known the
poison in the hellhound's claws would move faster through his body
when he had used so much energy, but he trusted his brethren to remove
it, choosing to suffer the agony rather than risk them all.

Danutdaxton began to incinerate the carcasses while he waited to aid the others. Everywhere the hounds had bled, the black acid that was their blood had destroyed every living plant, leaving what appeared to be a barren wasteland behind. Even the trees they had brushed up against had terrible wounds in them.

Adalasia could only breathe deep and wait for the guardians to tell her Sandu was going to survive. He didn't look as if he would, not even with his brethren, powerful ancients, working so hard to save him.

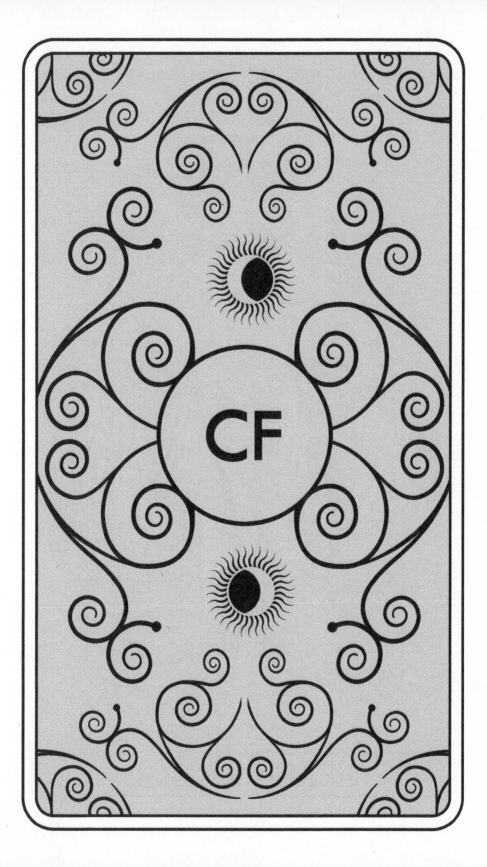

dalasia could barely breathe or even think. She had always been able to think through any problem. She might feel the edges of panic, or even have a panic attack, but in the end, training always won out. But this . . . She was expected to sit back and do nothing while Sandu was dying before her eyes. Anyone with a brain could see the life leaving his body.

Sandu. Don't you leave me. She sent the call to him, terrified of being left alone. She wouldn't be. She would follow him. Go with him. Abandon her duty to her family and take up her duty to her lifemate. The wild thoughts crowded in on one another as she moved closer to the body lying so gray and still on the ground.

"Adalasia, you cannot go near his body yet," Benedek cautioned. "You cannot get infected. Allow Petru and Siv to do their best to heal his body. You have his spirit and soul with you. He would never succumb to death completely."

She tried to hold on to that so she could think clearly. Was he with her? Could she feel him? He was so powerful. Always such a presence. Where was he? Why couldn't she feel him? Sorrow burst through her, but she fought it off. Benedek had no reason to lie to her. Petru and Siv wouldn't be outside of their bodies, attempting to heal Sandu, if he wasn't still alive.

"Tell me what's happening. Step by step, Benedek. I don't know the Carpathian ways, and this is terrifying to me. I don't feel him with me the way I always have. He looks and feels dead to me." She did her best to keep her voice from trembling. She didn't want her guardians to think she wasn't up to whatever task she needed to do to save Sandu. Anything. She would do anything.

Wrapping her arms around her middle, Adalasia couldn't make herself step away from Sandu's body. She felt protective. She even felt protective of the empty shells of Siv's and Petru's bodies. Their spirits had left to enter Sandu, leaving their bodies unprotected. Clearly, they were valiantly fighting for him.

Her heart stuttered. Her breath slowed in her lungs. Her body was suddenly weak. She found herself on the ground beside Siv's body, tears burning in her eyes.

Sandu. Don't you dare leave me.

He was moving farther away from her. She could feel it. He burned. His entire body burned. Why? What was happening to him?

"Benedek? He's in such pain. He's on fire. Burning hot. I have to go to him. He can't survive this, even with the aid of the ancients."

"No." Benedek caught her shoulder in a firm grip.

Nicu suddenly was on the other side of her, also gripping her shoulder, as if they could physically hold her to the earth when Sandu was somewhere else. She felt the guardians in her mind, Nicu and Benedek, taking hold there as well.

"He will need you, but not yet. You cannot go to him yet. It will take you to guide us to him and all of us to bring him back if we are to save him," Benedek said. "You have to trust us, *sisarke*. We are your brothers. We are bound together, all of us. Where Sandu goes, we go. We have sworn to protect you."

Nicu nodded his head. "It is impossible to lie to you, Adalasia. We may tease you, but we cannot deceive you over such a thing as Sandu's death. Trust us to know how to care for him. He has been poisoned with the plague. There are parasites in him. The bacteria have multiplied at an alarming rate and are striking at every organ. It will be a hard fight to remove all of this before we can safely go after his spirit. We know you have his spirit safe. He transferred what he could as quickly as he could to you before he went down. You hold his soul as you did before."

Adalasia knew what Nicu said was true. That was what had alarmed her the most. It felt to her as if Sandu had rejected her in some way, thrusting that part of him she'd guarded so carefully, as she'd been born again and again to keep him safe, back into her keeping. She hadn't thought that he'd once again be asking her to hold him safe. She'd been looking with her human eyes at his dying body, not with Carpathian eyes.

She took a deep breath to calm herself. To find balance. If Sandu was in both worlds, she would find a way to bring him fully back to her. She knew patience. She had to trust in the men he'd surrounded himself with. He'd chosen them for a reason. She looked to Danutdaxton. They had come to him for a reason.

Right at that moment, Dax's lifemate, Riley, was with him. The plants in the rain forest responded instantly to the presence of Riley, a renewal that was incredible to see. She moved through the blackened remains of the forest where the terrible battle had taken place with a grace and soothing calm that Adalasia could see and almost feel that the plant life responded to. She seemed able to coax reluctant growth back just by talking softly as she moved around beneath the scarred trees. Without the bodies of the hellhounds or giant scorpions to tell the supernatural tale of a battle with demons, the rain forest, under Riley's direction, was already returning.

Adalasia rocked herself gently, trying to watch Riley in order to keep her gaze from continually straying to Sandu's lifeless body. Siv's body suddenly jerked and was there, coughing, weak, pale beyond belief. Immediately, Nicu held his wrist to his chosen brother to give him the blood that would aid him after such a fight for Sandu's life. Adalasia bit back her questions. She could see Siv was in bad shape, which meant the fight had been hard.

Benedek shed his body and entered Sandu's. Adalasia was astonished at how fast they could get beyond ego and rid themselves of all things physical to become healing spirit. Danutdaxton moved into position beside Nicu as Petru emerged, every bit as weak and pale as Siv. He was coughing as well, trying to clear his throat. Wheezing even. Dax immediately offered him his wrist.

The moment Siv closed the twin holes in Nicu's wrist, Nicu shed his body and entered Sandu's in order to help fight the poisons in Sandu's body. Everything in Adalasia wanted to go with the two men, to be with them to help her lifemate, but she breathed away the terrible need. She had to rely on their expertise. They were ancients, and they knew what they were doing.

No one was treating this as if it were an easy task. She knew the situation was dire just by their silence and the tension in the air.

"He is in the shadow realm," Siv announced, his voice grim. "But he was pulled into a trap of some kind. We kept him from the gates, but the demon, Nera, had a poisonous brew that took him to the shadow realm, into the Cave of Fire. The fires of hell."

Adalasia frowned. "That makes no sense. Why would Sandu be relegated to hell? I am not even certain he believes in hell. Wouldn't one have to believe in it before they can be sent there? And he's lived an honorable life."

"Not actual hell," Siv countered. He shrugged his broad shoulders. "I do not want to get into a philosophical discussion of what is or isn't, only that I know Sandu was dragged into the shadow realm. He isn't dead. He is partly in that world and was taken to the Cave of Fire. Maybe I should have said the *illusion* of hell."

Danutdaxton crouched in the grass in front of her when Petru had politely closed the laceration on his wrist. "This is no small task, Adalasia, to enter the Cave of Fire, illusion or not."

Petru scrubbed his hand over his face. "You will have to have great resolve if we are to bring him back to us, Adalasia."

"Why would Nera do this? What could she hope to achieve?"

"You are bound to your lifemate," Siv pointed out. "You are willing to follow him into the shadow realm. The moment you enter that realm, they will know. You are fully alive, and every demon will be aware of you. Sandu can move around in that world because he is both alive and dead, and they will not detect him so easily. We cannot know his state of mind. He may be confused and even unaware of what has happened to him. The moment you enter the shadow realm, you will be in tremendous danger."

Adalasia tightened her hold around her stomach. "I have trained from the time I was a mere toddler to fight demons."

Petru shook his head. "We do not want you to have to use those skills, Adalasia. We hope that all of us, bound together, will be enough to drag him out of that realm without a fight. The faster we do it, with the least amount of conflict, the better chance we have of success. This is an elaborate trap that was set."

"How is it that Nera knew I was coming here? She set this before we even got here," Adalasia pointed out. "We hadn't yet met up with Danut-daxton."

There was a long silence while they all tried to puzzle out how Nera had gotten ahead of them. They'd been in France, gone to Brazil and now were in Peru. Nera hadn't been in Brazil, but she had set a trap in Peru.

"We do not know for certain that Nera's spies were not watching in Brazil," Petru pointed out. "Would you have known?"

Adalasia nodded. "I believe I would have. Sandu as well. I felt them in France. We all did, remember?"

"The last time any of you remember the spies of this Nera were close to you was in France," Danutdaxton murmured.

"We were speaking with Gabriel and Francesca," Adalasia said. "We had gone out first to explore the city with them, but then we were attacked and had to make a run for their home."

"No demon could have gotten through the safeguards," Siv said. "We patrolled as well."

"Was my name mentioned?" Danutdaxton asked.

Adalasia nodded slowly. "Yes. It was suggested that you might be able to help us. That was one of the reasons we made the choice to come here. Gabriel felt very strongly that we see and speak with you."

Again, there was silence. Adalasia's gaze strayed to her lifemate. He looked so still. It took great effort not to reach out to him. She bit her lip hard in order to keep from turning inward to try to follow him. The pull was very strong. Her eyes burned again, and she put her head down on her knees to keep from having to look at the three Carpathian males around her. They knew she struggled, but she didn't want them to see any physical evidence of her weakness.

Adalasia groaned, sitting up straight abruptly. "Nera managed to get a spy inside with us. She uses insects, as I've indicated. She could have used one so tiny, it simply attached itself to my clothing and entered the home when I did. The house wasn't sealed against demons until after we were inside," she said. "I sealed it myself after the others did."

She groaned again and rubbed her hand over her face, a little shocked to see there were smears of blood on her fingers when she looked at them. "I actually sealed Nera's spy inside the home with us. For all I know, the darn thing could be in my hair." She gave a little shudder.

"That would be impossible," Siv assured. "You have gone to ground and refreshed yourself. You also seal the earth so it would be trapped. If one has managed to hop aboard again, we now know to cleanse after every battle and encounter." He shrugged. "It is a good lesson. We are always learning."

"Dax, I am so sorry I brought this trouble to you and your lifemate," Adalasia said. "I had no idea Nera had managed to find a way to slip a spy into the house with us when we were having a private conversation."

Danutdaxton gave her a small smile. "Have no worries, Adalasia. Carpathian hunters must always have a small lesson in being a bit humbler every now and again to keep us sharp. This is a good lesson for all of us."

The wind slipped through the forest floor rather than just in the canopy, taking the last smell of smoke and battle away. Riley returned to them, sitting beside her lifemate, giving Adalasia a tentative smile.

"I'm pleased to meet you, although I do wish the circumstances were different. I'll help in any way I can."

"Thank you," Adalasia said.

"Adalasia, I wish to exchange blood with you," Danutdaxton said.

Instantly, Siv and Petru turned their full attention to the dragon man. Petru even moved his body slightly in front of Adalasia.

This is not a good idea. Your lifemate should be consulted, Siv protested. Petru echoed the objection.

Well, he isn't available, is he? Let me hear what he has to say.

"What would an exchange do?" Adalasia asked, trying to ignore her guardians and the way both of them warned her. She didn't understand all of the rules of Carpathian life, but she knew just by bonding with the four ancients, they'd already broken quite a few. What were a few more, especially if it helped her get Sandu back?

"I am dragon. I can bear extraordinary heat. The Old One can take even more. If we exchange blood, you can call on me, and I can follow that path to you. Or, should you be in trouble, I can reach out to you to aid you. The Cave of Fire is very dangerous."

"If she takes the form of a dragon, would that keep her safe?" Siv asked.

"It is merely the form of a dragon, and those in the shadow realm know that. They are already dead. She is not. The fire is real. In the shadow realm, those there are meant to feel all emotion and pain, but they cannot be killed because they are already dead. She can be. Sandu will feel all of it as well as her pain."

"I don't like any of this," Adalasia admitted. "Nera has had time to think up a good plan." Her gaze strayed to Sandu's lifeless body again. "What is taking so long? I didn't think healings took so long."

But she knew why. She knew what they were doing was a nearly impossible feat. They looked so exhausted. Even with Danutdaxton giving his blood and Riley supplying him, she could see and feel they were concerned it was not going to be enough.

Siv suddenly stood. Simultaneously, Dax was on his feet whirling to face away from Adalasia and Riley. Petru rose as well. The three Carpathians placed their bodies between Sandu's, Nicu's and Benedek's bodies, as well as the two women. The wind again moved through the trees, but it didn't carry scent. The forest hadn't gone silent as it should have when there was a disturbance.

"I see you have need of a healer, Danutdaxton." The voice came out of the canopy, but from which direction was impossible to tell. "I offer my services."

Who is this man who can hide himself from all of us? Siv demanded.

As always, Danutdaxton was strictly factual. *He is Luiz De La Cruz. At one time, he was Jaguar, but he was converted, rose, and then when deemed worthy, was taken to the cave of warriors and once again was put in the ground. Zacarias, as head of the family, asked that he be judged worthy to join their bloodline. It is a difficult line, and Luiz was given the choice. He would have led a half life otherwise. He died a second time, and his soul was split in half once he was deemed worthy. This has not been an easy transition for him, any more than it has been for Gary. All of the past warriors of the family poured knowledge and skill into him, but also their despair of not finding a lifemate. He is, however, a tremendous healer.*

Adalasia could feel the two ancients in her mind weighing the risks. "In your opinion, Dax, is he trustworthy?"

"He is a De La Cruz."

As if she should know what that meant. She had heard of the De La Cruz family only because Sandu had mentioned they owned land in several countries in South America. She knew they had human families loyal to them watching over their cattle ranches during the day, but that didn't tell her anything about the men.

De La Cruz is a very respected name, Petru supplied. *They do not go back on their word.*

Adalasia opened her mouth to call to the Carpathian male, but Siv hastily stopped her. *Not you. Do not ask a favor.*

"Please ask him to help," Adalasia pleaded.

"You could be of great assistance," Danutdaxton assured the unseen Carpathian male. "We would be grateful if you tried to heal him."

The air was suddenly charged with energy. With power. It was impossible not to feel it. The tiny hairs on Adalasia's body reacted. She was used to the feel of the ancients and even the difference in Dax with the Old One residing in him, but this new hunter striding with complete confidence out into the opening carried something with him that was unsettling. Too much power perhaps.

He wasn't as tall as the ancients. He was built with roped, dense muscles. He walked in complete silence, so much so that it felt to Adalasia as if the world held its breath as he approached Sandu's body, his

strange eyes going from an amber to a true gold. He had the long hair
the warriors wore, secured at the nape of his neck with a leather cord that
wound around the thickness and length. He didn't walk so much as
prowl, a great jungle cat moving among them.

"Give me the details quickly before I attempt to heal him," Luiz
demanded. His gaze moved over the two women and then settled on
Adalasia. She felt that direct golden gaze like a laser piercing right
through her strongest barrier. "She holds him to her."

"Yes." It was clear Danutdaxton had passed on all information regarding how Sandu had come to have his wounds and what Siv and Petru
had found. "There are two ancients with him now, Nicu Dalca and Benedek Kovac."

Luiz nodded curtly and shed his body without another word, leaving
himself completely vulnerable to attack.

"He isn't too worried one of you will try to kill his physical body,"
Adalasia pointed out.

"As I said, he is a De La Cruz," Dax reiterated. "Should any harm
befall him, his brothers would hunt to the ends of the earth those responsible. I can tell you, Adalasia, we are very lucky to have him chance
upon us."

"I don't believe it was chance," she whispered. She didn't. Things
happened the way they were supposed to. They were meant to meet Dax
and Riley. Luiz De La Cruz was meant to find them. For whatever reason, this was all happening. She had seen terrible danger in the cards.
Each rising she read them, and each rising she could see the dangers
surrounding them, growing worse.

She knew one thing. There was always a balance in the end, between
good and evil. Sometimes it appeared evil was winning. Everything was
relative to the moment. She knew that, but it didn't help when it was
Sandu lying pale and lifeless on the ground.

"Whatever the reason he is here, Luiz is a healer," Danutdaxton assured.

Nicu emerged from Sandu's body, sliding back into his own, looking
for all the world as sick as Sandu, almost a gray color. Like Petru and Siv,

he coughed repeatedly. This time, Adalasia shed her body to become healing light and gently touched his throat to see what was causing the problem. A sticky film coated the inside of his throat.

Adalasia. The reprimand was harsh. Nicu all but threw her out of his body. *You cannot be touched by any of this poison. It will rush to you the moment it feels your presence. Siv, examine her quickly.*

I didn't touch anything. Nothing touched me. It was too late, Siv was already shedding his body and going into hers.

How do you know? The bacteria is microscopic. Remember the insect that was carried into Gabriel and Francesca's home? This is far tinier.

Of course she was aware it would be far tinier. *I don't like that the three of you were coughing. You matter to me, Nicu. You aren't expendable. All of you seem to think it's okay to take these crazy risks. Maybe you're staying in his body too long. I should help, too.*

Absolutely not. That was a mixture of both Petru and Nicu telling her no.

Danutdaxton gave Nicu blood while Siv examined her. She stayed very still. The thick film had to be all through Sandu's body. While he was rushing to save her during the battle, it had spread quickly. He had to have known. Like the other ancients, his life hadn't mattered in those moments, only hers.

"She is fine," Siv said. "We need you whole and uncompromised, Adalasia. I know the waiting is difficult, but it is necessary."

"If Luiz stays to aid us when you go to retrieve Sandu," Dax mused, "there will be more power than this Nera can conceive of for Adalasia and the rest of us to draw on. Luiz has been to the shadow realm twice. The warriors who poured themselves into the vessel to allow a rebirth as a De La Cruz had all passed into the next life. He is familiar with every aspect of it. The Old One can guide you through the Cave of Fire, and if Luiz agrees to aid all of us, we have a much bigger chance of success."

Riley made a small sound of distress. Immediately, Dax turned to her and pulled her beneath the protection of his shoulder. "What is it?"

"You said 'us.' Do you intend to go with them to the shadow realm? If you do, Dax, I will accompany you." Her tone was very firm.

"They will need an anchor in this world, Riley. We are that anchor for them. You, me and the Old One. We cannot travel to the shadow realm, nor would I ever allow you to go."

Riley and Adalasia exchanged a long look before Riley rolled her eyes. Adalasia noted she didn't look too concerned with Dax's dictate.

Benedek emerged next, sliding into his body, coughing, so weak he could barely sit. Adalasia realized that as each of the ancients returned to their bodies and were given blood, either Danutdaxton was healing them as he provided for them, or one of the other ancients healed them. Riley continued to give Dax her blood. Adalasia knew that couldn't continue. They would be far too weak to help her find Sandu in what they referred to as the shadow realm.

"Go, Dax," Nicu said. "I will wait while you and Petru hunt. If Luiz needs blood, I can provide for him."

Petru immediately dissolved into vapor and streamed away from them through the trees.

Danutdaxton leaned down to brush kisses on top of Riley's head. "Let us go," he murmured. Immediately, the two dissolved in the same way Petru had.

Why that surprised Adalasia, she didn't know. She thought Riley would stay with them, but clearly, her lifemate had other ideas. She supposed that made sense. Sandu wouldn't have left her unless all four guardians were with her, not after a battle like the one they'd just gone through.

Her gaze once more strayed to Sandu lying so still in the thick vegetation. A little shudder went through her body at the sight. She didn't like him there on the ground in the open. She would have preferred to be in an enclosed area or at least have the ground open so the rich soil was exposed. Surely the soil with all the minerals would aid in healing Sandu.

She drew up her knees and rubbed her chin on top of them as she studied his long form. Even lying so still, he took up a lot of space. If it wasn't for the graying, now almost a bluish-black, running beneath his skin, she would have expected him to stand up. He was just that powerful.

"I feel so useless just sitting here. He wouldn't be just sitting here if I were the one dying." She raised her sorrowful gaze to Nicu.

"*Sisarke*, I know this is extremely difficult for you." Nicu's voice was gentle. "You are keeping him with us. We are only healing his body. We cannot possibly do what you are doing."

Adalasia frowned. It didn't feel as if she was doing anything at all. "What exactly do you think I'm doing, Nicu?"

"You have his soul."

She rubbed her chin over her drawn-up knees again. "Yes, he sent it back to me. It felt as if he'd rejected me after all the rebirths and lives I led to get to him."

"But you know better."

"I suppose so, intellectually. Rejection still feels very real."

She turned inward, surrounding the half of his soul he'd given back into her keeping with her bright light, warming it, holding it to her a little desperately. There was no warmth emanating from it. No light. It was tiny, as if slowly it was disappearing from her care. She actually saw that small piece shiver, tremble, as if too weak to continue to hold on. Adalasia drew her net of warmth tighter in a circle around his soul.

Don't leave me, Sandu. I can't exist without you. I will follow you. You know that I will. That will leave the gate unguarded after all the centuries our family has held true. I would be the one to lose honor. You have to hold on.

Silence met her alarmed begging. And it was begging. She wasn't too proud to try to convince him of her need of him. She had converted, become Carpathian for him, taken that leap of faith, but somewhere along the line, she had fallen hard for him. He had become her other half.

She became aware of cold. Bitter, icy cold. Whispers. Stings like bees on her skin. No, not her skin, inside her body. Not even her body. Her spirit? His? He was being attacked relentlessly. He was in agony. *Agony.*

"Nicu. That man you thought was a healer, he is harming Sandu. I connected just for a moment, and Sandu is in so much pain. The attack is on his spirit. You have to get him away from Sandu." She stretched her legs out, ready to leap up, but what she planned to do, she had no idea.

"The attack has been going on for some time, Adalasia," Nicu said, his voice soft. "We wanted to spare you the worst. He is long gone from us. You only see what remains of his body. His spirit has traveled down the tree of life and is now in the shadow realm. Luiz is healing his body from the inside out. Driving out the plague. Sandu cannot return to a body with even a small taint in it. We cannot take any chances with either of you."

Adalasia pushed both hands through her slicked-back hair in agitation. "He's suffering."

"Carpathian hunters endure, *sisarke*," Nicu reminded.

She did jump up then, no longer able to contain the restless energy pulsing through her body. There was nowhere to put the sorrow that weighed so heavily in her chest. She did her best to maintain a balance. These men, her guardians, were doing everything they could at the risk of their own lives to save Sandu. She had assured them they had lifemates alive somewhere, and yet they hadn't abandoned Sandu in his worst hour of need. They stood by him in their stoic manner, and they expected the same of her.

Adalasia paced away from the fallen body of Sandu. "What happens when we go to try to retrieve him, Nicu? We can't just leave his body exposed. There are wild animals here."

"All of our bodies would be exposed if we were to make our try from here. We attempted the healing of his body here in order to push out the poisons so we could incinerate all traces of it. We will go to a cave nearby where there is rich soil. It is a place Danutdaxton has told us of that holds many elements for healing. He will guard our bodies for us while we make the trip to the shadow realm."

She frowned. "All of us are living, Nicu. We don't belong there, right? That's my understanding. Won't it make it so much easier for our enemies to find us with so many of us going to this place?"

"You will go with one guide, Adalasia. Most likely me. Perhaps Benedek. The others will be with you in your mind. Together, the power you have will be immense. Should Sandu not recognize you or be able to move on his own, when we join our energy, we can pull him back with us to this realm."

"That's the plan?" She faced him, raising an eyebrow. It sounded far too simple to her.

Nicu nodded. "It is the only one we have."

"What if I can't find him?"

"You will. That will not be the problem. I believe he will be taken to the Cave of Fire."

"He's freezing. Wherever he is, he's alone, sick, disoriented and freezing." Adalasia knew she should be grateful he wasn't in the Cave of Fire already. The fight to save Sandu's body was taking an enormous amount of time. Too much. She didn't want the night to pass. They would all have to go to ground, and Sandu would be lost to them.

"He is a hunter, *sisarke*," Nicu explained. "An ancient. His instincts will be to survive no matter the cost to him, especially if he is aware of you."

Adalasia turned that information over in her mind. "Why wouldn't you want me to reach out to him? That would give him hope. He would know I would come for him."

"He would never consent to you coming for him. The land of the shadow realm is too dangerous. It is reputed to be a place where souls go after death to repent their dark deeds. They are given a chance to see the error of their ways. Most do not want to accept responsibility. Those who turned vampire continually try to find a way back to this realm."

"I could perhaps provide that way?"

"It is possible they would think so. It is possible that you might even be able to," Nicu added. "We discussed the shadow realm at great length when we gathered together in the monastery. It was an intriguing subject. Manolito De La Cruz and two other Carpathian ancients are the only ones I know of personally who managed to come back from that place. All information on that realm came from them."

"Luiz might have more details than we have," Adalasia said.

"Perhaps. He was Jaguar before he was Carpathian. He was turned when he was dying because he was a good man, and he'd saved the women under the De La Cruz protection. When he woke, he would forever live a half life with no lifemate, as he wasn't a true Carpathian male."

"I was given this information."

"But you have to understand it. Jaguars are solitary creatures. He was a Jaguar man, and he went against Brodrick, the ruler who was systematically destroying their species. Luiz tried to tell the other males that they needed to provide for the females and protect them. It didn't make him a popular man. He was shunned by his kind. That made him even more alone. When he rose Carpathian yet not, he was once again on the outside."

"The De La Cruz family don't sound like the kind of people to cast one out because you aren't perfect. They might boss you around, but from all the glimpses I caught in Sandu's mind, that is a very feared but respected family that is tight knit."

Nicu nodded his agreement. He paced away from the body and then looked to the canopy. Adalasia knew he needed blood. She also knew if she were to offer hers, he would refuse.

"You are right about the De La Cruz family, Adalasia," he agreed. "They didn't abandon Luiz, but he knew he was different. Zacarias, the eldest, wanted to ensure that when Luiz rose starving for blood, his true nature would prevail. Although a fierce fighter, he is naturally protective of women and children, which is the Carpathian way."

"That was what they were looking for?"

Nicu shook his head. "Not all. He was also tremendously strong-willed, which would be needed if he was going to become a warrior. When Zacarias saw into Luiz's true soul, he invited him to become a De La Cruz. He explained the risks and all that it would mean to him. You have to remember, very few human males had ever been granted such a gift. I do not remember any others, to be honest.

"In all the centuries you lived, no one converted a human male?" Adalasia was a little shocked.

"There was no reason to do so," Nicu assured unapologetically. "Simultaneously, Gary and Luiz, both humans, were taken to the cave of warriors. There was another taken there as well, Zev. He was both Lycan and Carpathian, mixed blood. We call their kind *Han ku pesak kaikak*, which is 'guardian.' The Tirunul lineage claimed him, but he was also claimed by the extinct line of Dark Blood. They were a powerful line of warriors. Few found lifemates, and it was long thought there was no one carrying that blood in their veins. It was shocking and also very welcome news."

Adalasia paced a distance through the trees and then came back, each time stepping a little closer to Sandu's body. "I thought that if you took them to the cave of warriors and they were judged worthy, they became of that bloodline. They were no longer what they had been before. Their souls were split."

"That was the case for Luiz and Gary. Luiz became a De La Cruz, and Gary a Daratrazanoff. Zev was different in that he was already Dark Blood, a Carpathian. He had a lifemate from the time of his birth. He was unaware of it because he was also Lycan and raised in the Lycan community. It is difficult to understand how the blood works in Lycans and Carpathians."

Luiz was suddenly back in his own body, his skin showing that same grayish tinge. He cleared his throat several times but didn't cough. Nicu instantly became light and energy, entering Luiz to ensure the coating was gone and there was no bacteria or poison clinging to him. When he was certain, he returned to offer the De La Cruz his wrist.

Adalasia noted that Luiz was careful not to take too much from Nicu. Nicu needed to feed as it was. Both men would have to hunt before they could go to find Sandu in the shadow realm.

"His body is clean," Luiz said. "He is far from us." He turned his strange golden eyes fully on Adalasia. "You are going to retrieve him from this place?"

"Absolutely, I am," she said, pouring conviction into her voice. She kept every hint of defiance out of her tone. She was no child to be told what she could or couldn't do by these men. Sandu was *hers*. Her lifemate. She was getting him back from wherever he was.

He nodded. "I will return shortly and I will accompany you." He made it a decree.

He was on his feet and gone so fast, she had only blinked and there was no sign of him. She looked to Nicu. "Is that a good thing?"

Nicu nodded slowly. It was impossible for her to tell if he really thought Luiz escorting her to the shadow realm was really such a good idea, but Benedek returned and Nicu left to go hunting fresh blood.

-XV-

THE DEVIL

S tay close to me," Luiz ordered.

Her escort didn't need to remind her. Adalasia wasn't about to get lost in this strange place. At first glance, it appeared to be the rain forest where they had fought the battle with Nera's demons. The trees rose up above them, but the trunks weren't right. They were twisted and cracked. The branches reached out, limbs not pointing toward the sky but rather each stretched toward the unwary as they walked on the narrowing trail through the dark gray mist.

Her heart began to pound and her mouth went dry. There were vines on the trunks and in the branches, just as there were in the rain forest they'd battled in, but these had a dull green, almost sickening tinge to their leaves. Snakes curled around the woody vines and stared down at them. Lizards and spiders followed their progress, moving on the trunks and in the vegetation on either side of the trail.

"Slow your heart," Luiz commanded.

Adalasia was embarrassed he had to remind her. She might not have been Carpathian long, but she had trained to fight demons. As far as she was concerned, this realm was all about demons, and she needed to pull herself together and have just as cool a head as Luiz did.

She hadn't had any trouble finding a way into the shadow realm. Sandu was her other half. He may have given her back his soul, but she was fully connected to him. They were bound together by the ritual he had imprinted on him before his birth. She had only to reach for him, to let her spirit connect with his, and she was pulled into the shadow realm. She knew instantly they were in the exact spot where he had gone down. She recognized it. She would never forget it. Only now, the trees and landscape were very different from the last time she'd seen it.

Riley had carefully renewed the plant life, but once again, the ground appeared scorched, the dirt and debris rotted and burnt. Where before, there was a vitality to the forest, everything around her appeared dull, the colors not just muted but almost lifeless, as if all the verve had been sucked out of them.

Peering up through the canopy, even the sky looked different, the rolling clouds darker and more ominous. They spun gray masses of threads that looked like sinister webs reaching toward the earth rather than actual rain. Everything looked as if it was a threat.

Lizards and rodents scurried away from them. Frogs on the trees rose up to look at them just as the snakes were doing. Were Nera's spies here as well? It was possible, but she couldn't think about that. She had to concentrate only on finding Sandu and bringing him out of this realm.

She reached for him again. At once, she felt agonizing pain, and she had to break away for a moment to collect herself. "Why would he feel pain when you healed his body?"

"His spirit is no longer in his body. He has no memory of what happened to the shell he was in after he left it. Which way?"

Adalasia took a deep breath and forced calm. Balance. Very slowly, she once more touched Sandu, this time with care. The moment her mind slid against his, she felt his awareness of her. His rejection of her.

You cannot be here.

At least he knew her. The relief was tremendous.

Ewal emninumam, it is too dangerous for you. You are fully alive, a beacon for those evil who would delight in your destruction.

She had a direction on him now. She ignored his warning and indicated to Luiz which path through the forest they should take.

Can you stay where you are, or is it too dangerous for you to stay in one place?

Luiz had picked up their pace. Now that they knew approximately where Sandu was, they wanted to get to him as quickly as possible.

I am surrounded by old "friends," the undead I destroyed who have waited here before moving on to the next life. They were waiting for me. They have been promised a portal to the other world, a way out of the shadow realm, if they take me to the Cave of Fire. They are determined to take me there.

Adalasia relayed the information to Luiz. She knew the guardians were close, very small shadows in her mind, listening to the exchange between Adalasia and Sandu. They didn't give their presence away. Should Sandu be taken and tortured beyond endurance, they wanted the element of surprise in order to gather enough power to bring Luiz, Adalasia and Sandu back.

"He is too weak to fight them. They cannot be killed, already dead, while he is still half alive. You hold his soul in your keeping, and they sense this. Tell him to stall as long as possible."

Sandu, my guide, one of the De La Cruz brothers, asks that you stall as long as possible. He doesn't want you to put up a fight, or at least not one that will take your true strength. If you must be taken to the Cave of Fire, so be it. We have a plan. The Old One has a plan.

Just in case someone could penetrate their shields and actually listen in on their intimate pathway between lifemates, she didn't utter Danutdaxton's name or say "dragon." Sandu didn't answer her, and she bit down hard on her lower lip to keep from calling out his name.

"Can we take to the air? Wouldn't that be faster?" Anxiety colored her voice.

Luiz cast a glance over his shoulder. He was jogging now, his feet barely skimming the ground. She followed his example, not allowing her heart rate to increase or her breathing to change.

"Not yet. They clearly are expecting you to follow him. They will have set traps for you, Adalasia. You are new to the world of Carpathians, but you must look with more than your eyes and the love in your heart if we are to succeed. This is a world of illusion, but those illusions can be deadly."

There was no reprimand in his tone. None in the expression on his face, but she still felt embarrassed. She was forgetting every single thing she'd been taught because she was so focused on Sandu's condition. She was terrified for him. She had the examples all around her of ancient Carpathians going into a battle without emotion. They concentrated on the fight at hand. She'd been taught to put aside ego and pride, to allow her brain to fully function so it could sort through problems at a rapid pace.

"Sandu said the vampires he destroyed were promised a portal, Luiz.

Someone has done that. Nera commands an army of demons for Lilith. Nera could have promised the vampires the chance of going through the portal in return for aiding her."

Several paths meandered off the main one they traveled on. Without thinking, Adalasia tapped him mentally on the left shoulder, indicating for him to take the tiny ribbon of a game trail. It was darker through a grove of trees covered in spiderwebs. She felt the movement of hundreds of the arachnids as they began to stalk the two living Carpathians.

She swept her sword from under her long coat and held it up high as she jogged, the flames running up and down the blade, flickering and pulsing in various colors of red and orange.

"Hear me, evil ones. If even one of you dares to drop down on my companion or me, or if a web is thrown over us, I will set this entire grove on fire. It will burn every single one of you. None will escape."

As a threat, it was very decisive. She *would* set the entire grove ablaze if even one dared to drop on them. She was done with being inactive. She didn't know who the spiders belonged to—this place or Nera—but she didn't care. She kept moving fast, staying right behind Luiz, not changing her breathing in the least.

The spiders followed their progress through the grove, but not one came near them. No net was cast on them to delay them. Just as they emerged from the trees onto the edge of a clearing, birds screamed and dove at them, coming straight at their eyes with razor-sharp beaks and wicked talons. It seemed as though hundreds of raptors flew at them, attempting to drive them back into the trees or claw their eyes out.

Luiz threw up his hands, and the birds slammed into an invisible barrier. Feathers fell like rain. Shrieks filled the air as some fell to the ground, hitting the barrier so hard they broke their necks. He wove a complicated pattern and then indicated for Adalasia to run straight across the clearing to the trees on the other side. She didn't wait, although it was difficult to force her body to take those first few steps out into the open again.

Overhead, the birds went into a frenzy, but she kept running, her gaze locked on the grayish twisted trunk of a kapok tree. She realized as the raptors scraped at an unseen barrier over her head and all around her that Luiz had created a tunnel. She had no idea how long it would last against the violent beating the birds subjected it to, so she ran with Carpathian blurring speed, cognizant of keeping her heart rate the same and her lungs breathing steadily.

She reached the thick grove of trees, took two steps in and halted, Luiz nearly slamming into her. "There is something here." She felt the malevolence.

Behind them, the birds continued their shrieking, but they didn't follow them into the dark forest. They couldn't skirt around the patch of trees, not with the birds flying and darting back and forth, sentries to keep them captive.

Her skin began to crawl. The hair on her body stood up in protest. For the first time, she used the blood bond between the ancient and herself. It had seemed too intimate when she didn't know him. Every instinct told her she needed to face this enemy alone. *Hide yourself. He cannot know you are with me.*

Luiz didn't question her; he simply vanished. Even knowing he was close and the guardians were crouched there in her mind, she continued in the direction Sandu was pulling her in with great trepidation. Luiz's physical presence with his immense power had been a protection she hadn't realized she'd counted so heavily on.

She forced herself to walk at a brisk pace, scanning all around her. The deeper she went into the forest, the more confused she felt, as if her mind were becoming foggy. Things moved in the shadows around her, keeping pace with her. She caught glimpses of shapes slinking around the trees, great hulks of furred creatures. Twice, she saw glowing red eyes when the beasts drew her attention, and once, yellow malevolent eyes stared at her from the branches above her head.

The air was thicker beneath the heavy canopy, and it was much more difficult to breathe with the heat and humidity. Each breath she drew in made her feel as if she were choking on evil. Halting, she ignored the creatures surrounding her. She knew them for what they were: demons hidden in the bodies of forest animals under the command of something far more frightening than a mere wolf.

Whatever malevolent demon she was facing was fogging her mind. The confusion was making it difficult to get a firm lock on where Sandu was. Slowly, she turned in a circle, looking for his direction again. She didn't dare take in deep breaths and draw in the poisonous air.

Once more, she slipped her sword out of the scabbard and held it aloft with both hands. This time, the light glowed bright, throwing the dark shadows into relief. The beasts, looking like a cross between wolves and saber-toothed tigers, rushed away from the light, growling aggressively low in their throats but retreating all the same. Above her head, she heard the flutter of wings, and the yellow eyes disappeared.

"Very nice, my dear. You must put away your childish sword, Adalasia, while we talk."

The voice came out of the trees, seemed to surround her. Sweet. Charming. A hint of male amusement. Not in the least threatened or threatening. Still, goose bumps rose on her skin. That voice was too sweet, too charming. She felt a slight push toward her mind, as if someone were knocking on a door, trying to get in. Adalasia held firmly to her shields, resisting that enticement.

She refused to engage, turning toward the direction she was certain Sandu was in. She didn't reach out to him, certain if she did, Sandu would suffer for it.

"You came all this way to free your lifemate from the shadow world, Adalasia. See? I know you. I know your name. I have been a great admirer of you for some time and had hoped we could visit and get to know each other."

That voice was beguiling. She shook her head mentally in an effort to free her from any ensnarements.

Not vampire, Luiz whispered to her. *Something else.*

She felt the agreement of the others. She didn't want them to speak. She needed to fully concentrate. Whoever this was, he was moving easily with her, just out of her sight. The pull on her was strong to turn away from the path to Sandu.

She tried to create a breeze to give herself a little reprieve from the unrelenting heat. It was oppressive. Her feet felt leaden, although she forced them to move in the direction she was certain was the correct one. No matter how much she tried, she couldn't regulate her body temperature. She closed her eyes for a moment and thought of one of the wonderful pools Sandu had conjured up for her. Right now, it would be so perfect to just wade in and feel the relief of cool water against her hot skin.

When she opened her eyes, she realized she could hear the sound of water in the distance and knew that was what must have put the idea in her head. Her heart jumped at the thought of just bathing her neck and wrists to rid herself of the relentless heat. She forced her heartbeat to settle into a steady rhythm as she hurried as fast as she dared in Sandu's direction.

She smelled the faint scent of sulfur as she rounded the slight bend in the path and found herself looking through the trees toward a little grotto where fresh water spilled from the side of rocks into a beautiful blue pool. After the terrible humidity and heat, the water looked inviting, mesmerizing even.

Adalasia had always loved pools. Any kind of pool, but the more natural, the better. She could stay for hours in a bath. In a hot tub. In natural springs. Her skin felt dirty and salty with sweat, caked with grime. Would it hurt to take a moment to cool off in the refreshing water? It would invigorate her. She would have to detour through the trees away from Sandu, but it didn't look far. It would only take a few minutes.

Adalasia stood for a moment staring at the inviting water shimmering in the distance. She frowned, shaking her head, trying to remember why she was walking in such a dark area when there was sunshine just through the trees. She was so hot. Sweating. She could barely take a breath. She *needed* to feel the cool water on her skin. Nothing else was more important.

Abruptly, she dug her fingernails into her palm so that she felt the bite. What was she thinking? Nothing was more important than her comfort? Nothing? As in Sandu? Her lifemate? He had been suffering in agony, protecting her, shielding her from his pain, and she was worried about being too hot? That didn't make any sense at all.

She turned away from the beckoning water, rubbing her suddenly pounding temples. What was going on? Tiny little needles stabbed at her brain like angry bees. She ignored the sensation and forced her feet to move. To her consternation, the path was no longer there. The vegetation was thick, with moldy leaves covered in a carpet of moving ants.

"I don't need a path," she murmured aloud and continued forward in the direction she knew Sandu to be. When she glanced back at the water, it was no longer there. Had it been an illusion? A temptation? A trick to delay her? She didn't know or care. She had to find Sandu before it was too late for him. There was a sense of urgency beating at her now.

"Why do you persist in thinking he is worthy of you?" the charming, reasonable voice asked her. "Your lifemate woke hungry in this place. Starving for rich, hot blood."

She kept walking, scanning in the way of Carpathians, trying to find the one stalking her. He seemed to be everywhere, surrounding her, circling her. She refused to give in to fear. Of course Sandu would awaken starving for blood. He was Carpathian. Her enemy wasn't telling her anything she didn't already know. She refused to engage with or acknowledge him.

"He was approached by so many willing to serve him," that soft voice continued.

Abruptly, she was at the edge of a clearing, and she could see in the distance beautiful women, most without clothes. They wrapped themselves around a man, stroking him, offering him their bodies, pleading with him to take them.

"Sandu," she whispered his name.

There was no mistaking his tall frame. Those wide shoulders. That long blond hair falling down his back. He was as naked as the women, and one had her hands on his thighs, while another stroked his hard cock, her mouth inches from him. Even as she watched, Sandu bent his head toward a dark-haired woman who swept back her hair to expose her neck while she thrust her breasts at him.

Sandu's teeth bit deep. One hand grasped a breast while the other fisted his engorged cock and thrust it into the waiting mouth. He transferred his hand from his cock to the woman's hair, holding her still while he surged into her mouth over and over, all the while drinking from the dark-haired woman.

"What are you doing?" Adalasia whispered.

The dark-haired woman weakened, and Sandu pushed her aside. She collapsed onto the ground where she lay motionless. Another took her place, sliding up Sandu's body, her hands greedy and grasping. She pleaded with him, trying to pull his head to her breast. He sank his teeth into her as his cock erupted down the throat of the woman kneeling at his feet. The moment she crawled away, another took her place, wrapping herself around him, licking and sucking at his cock, pleading for him to take her. She got on her hands and knees in front of him, deliberately enticing him. When he pushed the second woman to the ground, without even closing the twin holes on her neck, he grasped the hips of the woman on all fours and plunged into her.

Adalasia stared in horror at the scene unfolding before her eyes. Sandu had become a madman, gorging himself on blood and sex. She felt the burn of tears and desperately tried to tell herself he didn't know what he was doing. This wasn't a betrayal. He might not even remember he had a lifemate.

"He indulges himself while you suffer the heat. You risk your life to save him, and he gives in to his real nature. He has always carried the beast in him. You saw it in him when you first looked into him."

She put her hands over her ears in an effort to drown out the voice. She had seen the beast in Sandu.

"He has always been more demon than man. Locking himself away didn't prevent him from wanting these things. Dreaming of them. Why do you think he doesn't share all of himself with you? He doesn't want you to see the cravings he has. The hunger for other women. The way he has acted for centuries, betraying you over and over again."

"Stop," Adalasia whispered, but she didn't know if she was telling the voice to stop or Sandu. He did have a demon in him. She had caught glimpses of the demon when he fought. She felt the rise of it, the need for the kill. The love of the battle. It was an addiction, just like the need for blood and sex.

It was also true that when she merged her mind with Sandu's, there were very strong barricades she couldn't get past. Was this what he had been hiding all along? His need for more than one woman? His dark obsessions?

"Look at him. He thinks nothing of you. He will continue to deceive you. He is an ancient and can hide whatever he wishes from you. You can't trust him. Why did you think that you could? In the beginning, you had concerns, but he used his voice on you, didn't he? He pushed them aside and got from you the things he wished. He will always get what he wishes."

That insidious voice continued to murmur in her ear. To surround her with her own doubts. It was true that she had so many concerns, so many reservations and fears, and yet, in spite of all of them, she had somehow come to the conclusion that she should join forces with him. Why? Her memory seemed hazy. A film over it. She could clearly see her apprehension, feel how strong it was, yet she didn't remember why she changed her mind.

Sandu pushed the woman aside after he finished in her, and he beckoned to others, pointing to the ground so they crawled to him, begging to service him. Someone called out to him, and he looked over his shoulder and laughed. "Join us." She heard that very distinctly. "I like to share."

"He learned many ways to take his pleasure over the centuries," the voice continued.

Adalasia froze as another very handsome Carpathian male strode out of the forest into the clearing. Like Sandu, he caught one of the fawning women by the hair and sank his teeth into her neck. Sandu positioned himself in front of the woman, leaning down to draw her breast into his mouth while his hand went between her legs. The Carpathian lifted his head, laughing, as he caught the woman's hips from behind.

"Have you taught your lifemate these pleasures?"

"Not yet, but she will do as I say. The others surround her, and soon she will want all of us together," Sandu replied and plunged into the woman. He leaned forward and sank his teeth into the side of her neck opposite the one the other man had.

The woman screamed as the Carpathian male behind her entered her, and the two set a fast rhythm. Then he leaned down and once again bit into her neck. It was clear neither had any regard for the woman, only for their own pleasure.

Even with the brutality they showed, more women crawled toward them because the two men demanded it, snapping their fingers and beckoning.

"You gave up who you were. He forced that on you. Took from you without asking and then wasn't in the least remorseful. He thought it his right. What changed in his life? What did he give up for you? Certainly not his way of life. Look at him. This is what he expects of you with the others he introduced into your life."

Adalasia felt sick. Tears tracked down her face, and when she wiped at them, she discovered she was merely smearing blood over her cheeks.

It was true that Sandu's life hadn't changed much. He hadn't given up being Carpathian. He had given her two blood exchanges without her consent. He had bound them together. Converted her. He was the same. She was different. Her entire world was different. She had to learn to take blood, to sleep beneath the ground. Sandu still had everything he had before and more. His emotions. His colors. His friends. *This*. Women. His obsession. His addiction.

Blinking several times to clear her vision, she stared at her lifemate and the ugly, brutal sexual way he and his friend treated the women. At first, all she could see was her own humiliation and insecurities. Her own doubts. These were beautiful women, without a single flaw on their bodies, and yet Sandu and his companion carelessly cast them aside.

She had many flaws. She wasn't nearly as feminine. She never would be. She was raised to be a warrior, a fighter, and she had steel running beneath her curves. Every muscle had been honed into that of a combatant. Sandu would feel every one of those muscles beneath her skin.

She didn't dare take a deep breath, not when there was the distinct smell of sulfur in the air, reminding her this rain forest wasn't the same as the one she had come from.

"Leave him here to his women and his madness. He isn't worth it.

You know that. Don't be made a fool of, Adalasia. He cares nothing for you, only his own pleasures. He seeks to force your obedience as he does with these women. You see he cares nothing for them, either."

She hadn't come to this place to pass judgment on Sandu, or to even decide what was behind those barricades in his mind. Why had she come? She fought with the weird disorientation she felt, as if her brain couldn't retrieve the information. She refused to give up. She kept looking for it everywhere. To return him home. There was her answer. She had come to bring her lifemate home.

She kept blinking, trying to see through a strange ripple that occurred when she cleared her mind even for a moment. Her vision blurred with the ripple, but she kept the sight of Sandu and his companion in her head, examining it from every angle, trying to shed her own ego in the way Carpathians did before they healed one another.

Sandu's broad back was toward her. She stripped away the women crawling around on the ground. Stripped away the one sandwiched between his companion and him. She looked only at Sandu. At his back. At the oath carved into his skin.

Olen wäkeva kuntankért. Staying strong for our people.

Olen wäkeva pita belső kulymet. Staying strong to keep the demon inside.

Olen wäkeva—félért ku vigyázak. Staying strong for her.

Hängemért. Only her.

She murmured the Carpathian vows aloud over and over until they were a chant. A talisman. Sandu had those vows carved into his skin. He'd told her what they meant. She'd heard the truth in his voice. He couldn't deceive her. Those same vows were carved into the back of the man in the clearing, but this was the shadow realm. The land of illusions. The land of deceit.

"Sandu is my lifemate," she stated. "I will go to him and bring him home with me." She took a step out of the forest into the clearing.

Beneath her feet, the ground shuddered. At once, she heard wailing, the sound rising and falling, coming from every direction. The moment she set foot in the clearing, the women turned their heads toward her and their disguises fell away. They weren't female but vampires, their rotted corpses in various stages of decay. They began to drag themselves toward her, their blackened, jagged teeth set in skinless skulls. Tufts of hair stuck out on some of the skulls, while others were bare.

Sandu wasn't there at all. The illusion of him vanished completely, leaving her to face a mob of vampires bent on reaching her. She could hear them calling out to her. Calling her "fresh blood." "Real blood." She forced her heart to stay calm. She doubted this was another illusion, but she had to face the mob with courage.

"You fool. Look at what he's done. Left you to be torn apart by the undead," the voice hissed, clearly displeased.

"Better dead than dishonored," she stated. "He is my lifemate. I believe in him."

"I will see what you have to say when they fall upon you and tear you to pieces, draining you of every drop of blood you have in your body. You will die in torment, in agony, and your lifemate will witness your torture."

"What happened to your charm?" she asked. "Show yourself. If you're so powerful, why do you cloak yourself in a voice rather than show me who you really are? You are now hiding behind these gullible vampires who believe you will give them a portal to the other realm. You can't do that and you know it. If you could, you would slip your demons through all the time. You're here, in the realm of shadows, where it is easy to deceive, and they are so desperate to escape that they have forgotten, even as they tell their own lies. Are you such a coward, then?"

A terrible snarl greeted her challenge. Then a man materialized between her and the vampires, waving his hand to stop those threatening to consume her. He was dressed in what had been an immaculate suit, but now that she had angered the demon, his true self could be seen through his illusion. His thighs were huge and rounded and appeared to be covered in hair where they had split the seams of his trousers. His fingernails were long and pointed, as were his ears. He stared at her with malevolent eyes.

"You dare to confront me?" A sly, very cruel smile curved his slim lips. He waved his hand to open the ground just to the left of them, where the rocks were piled high in a semblance of a mountain. There was no growth on the mountain, not even stunted trees. The ground looked burned and scarred. "This is what happens to anyone daring to test me."

She felt the blast of heat as he opened the rocks to show her the cave inside, where violent masses of red-orange threads spun and shot flames into the air in all directions. It took great effort to keep her heart rate steady.

Adalasia feigned fear, using her tongue to moisten her lips. "The Cave of Fire," she whispered, pushing awe and what she hoped was terror into her voice. "It's real? Not an illusion? I have heard of this place."

"Your precious lifemate dared to challenge me," the demon said.

She stuck her chin in the air. "By refusing your temptations." She made it a statement. "He refused to betray me, didn't he?"

The demon growled and snarled, his eyes taking on a red glow that reminded her of Sandu and the guardians. There was something demonic about them—those demons resided inside of them. The difference was, they fought to keep their honor no matter what the temptation was. No matter what trial they had to overcome. This demon hadn't, just as the Carpathian hunters who had chosen to become vampires had given up all honor and, in doing so, their souls.

"You forced Sandu into the Cave of Fire merely because he had honor and you did not?" she whispered, deliberately angering him more, all the while pretending she wasn't aware she was doing so. "That's so wrong. Don't you even see how wrong that is?"

The buttons on his shirt popped as his chest expanded in his fury. "You have no right to judge me."

"You look at the vampires with such contempt because they are taken in by your smooth lies. You use your voice on them, and they do your bidding. To you, that makes them less than you, inferior. You preen and strut like a peacock, but in truth, you bow before your mistress and lick her boots, don't you? That makes you on par with the soulless Carpathians, doesn't it?" She taunted him deliberately.

He roared, spittle flying from his mouth, his eyes twin pinpoints of sheer red fury. The ground shook. Even the vampires ceased their relentless wailing.

"How *dare* you." His voice was barely human, barely able to be understood.

"I don't know why you're getting so angry." Adalasia sweetened her tone and widened her eyes as she slid her hand inside her jacket to retrieve the sword of light. The sword found her palm, and she wrapped her fingers around it. The hilt was as familiar to her as breathing, a part of her. Once she touched it, she felt surer, much more confident in who she was, Adalasia Ravasio, guardian of the eastern gate that held back the demon.

"Have I said anything untrue? Don't you answer to your mistress? Don't you have to do her bidding? If you fail her, are you punished? Tortured? I think you fear her. That's why you pretend to have such power, so you can frighten others the way she scares you."

"You think I *pretend* to have power." He pointed a long thin finger tipped with a sharp talon at her.

She felt the ground tremble. The air grew heated. Oppressive. She gathered her strength, determination coiling inside her, waiting to spring.

"You will join your lifemate in the Cave of Fire to feel the agony for eternity until the mistress allows you to serve her." He spat the words at her and gestured toward the rocks. They widened, and a blast of heat belched forth.

He turned to wave her inside as if she were no more than a thin piece of paper. Adalasia could see the spinning web of fire that was the portal to the cave. That was all she needed. Using every ounce of skill she had learned throughout her years of training, she leapt at the demon, driving through his heart and straight up his body to his throat, splitting him open with the light pouring from the sword. In midair, she turned and dove into the fire, slamming the sword back into the scabbard while the flames poured over her and burned the flesh right from her bones.

She opened her mouth to scream and scream, but no sound emerged. Nothing had prepared her for the shock of pure agony washing through her. She looked down at her body, and to her horror, all she could see was ash clinging to her bones. Flames rolled over her continually. There was no way to breathe with the terrible heat. Her lungs refused to work. She was choking, strangling, breathing the flames into her body.

Time went by—she had no idea how long—while she fought the terrible pain, writhing and twisting in an effort to get away from it. There was nowhere to go. Not a moment, not a second of reprieve. She had been condemned to eternity in this agony.

You are Carpathian. The voice was calm. Detached. *You are strong. Lower your body temperature as much as possible so you can breathe. Without breathing, you are in panic and cannot think. There is no aid without breath and rational thinking.*

Adalasia didn't recognize the voice, but she did see the wisdom. She fought her way past the pain enough to turn down her temperature as best she could. Once she found control, and the chaos in her brain stopped the terrible downward spiral, she felt the guardians pour into her, shouldering pain, aiding to bring down her temperature even more in the midst of the flames rolling over her bones.

Find him. You had a path to him. Find your lifemate now. Hurry. The voice was still calm, but there was an urgency to it.

She realized immediately she was not alone in the Cave of Fire. She wasn't the only victim there, but she was being stalked by triumphant evil. *Demons,* she told the guardians. *They are holding him. They know I'm here and are waiting for me.*

You knew they would be there, Nicu's voice whispered. *Hurry, sisarke. We cannot be away this long and far from our physical bodies. You must get to him and follow the plan.*

As his lifemate, Adalasia was forever connected to Sandu. She could find him anywhere. Unerringly, she moved through the terrible flames, doing her best to ignore the way the fire burned through her bones. She refused to look down at her body to see what was happening. That only made things worse.

Adalasia knew she was close to Sandu when a rush of sheer agony drove her to her knees. Malicious laughter echoed all around her as she struggled back up.

Adalasia. Sandu's voice was barely there.

A whisper of unease traveled up her spine. He sounded so far from her even though she could see him now. He was ringed by the malicious, laughing demons, and he looked absolutely ravaged. Destroyed. At the same time, he faced them, standing as straight as possible even as some cracked whips of fire over his burning skin.

She refused to give in to the need to weep for him. She stood every bit as straight as she swept toward the circle of demons taunting and torturing her lifemate. Her eyes were on his.

"At last, Adalasia, you have joined us. Your sword of light will do little good to defeat all of us." A man stepped forward, although he no longer resembled a man. His feet were hooves, and out of his head grew horns. His voice, however, was sweet, compelling, almost magical. A deceiver.

"I didn't come to defeat you. I came to join my lifemate," Adalasia replied, still walking straight toward the circle of demons as if they weren't there. She sounded haughty, like a princess talking to a bothersome flea. Like Sandu, she paid no attention to the flames burning through her bones or the holes the unholy fire made in her insubstantial body.

Sivamet. There was sorrow in Sandu's voice.

We are strong together. If the demons could overhear their intimate path, she still wanted him to know they weren't alone if he wasn't beyond the point of reasoning things out.

"Join him, then," the man snarled, his teeth snapping together, his voice no longer sweet but grating and harsh. He flung his hands out toward Adalasia, lifting her as the demons parted to allow her into the circle.

Adalasia thrust Sandu's soul into him, surrounding him with every bit of strength she had to protect him from any further harm. The guardians called to his spirit with her, pulling him through the ranks of demons, out from the circle. The Old One shielded their spirits from the intense heat as the demons screamed with rage and sent vicious fire bursting over and through them.

The head demon flung himself at Sandu, hooking his talons into him, jerking him back, fury in his red-rimmed eyes.

"You cannot have him," Adalasia said calmly. "He has no body for you to hold."

"We have him trapped. He's too weak."

The guardians and Adalasia kept Sandu surrounded, refusing to allow the demon a way in. It was Luiz's power combining with the ancients that thrust Adalasia and Sandu out of the shadow realm and back into the cave where their bodies waited. Weak, desperate for blood, worn and weary from the long journey, they stayed bonded until they sealed off the portal and ensured Sandu was safe.

-XVI-

THE TOWER

Sandu drifted in an agony of pain. He had often been wounded in battle. More than once in his conflicts with master vampires, he had been nearly eviscerated, had his throat torn, holes put in his chest and chunks of his flesh ripped out by poisonous teeth. Nothing in his long centuries of existence was like this kind of pain. He couldn't distance himself from it. He could only endure.

He knew he was in rich soil, but no matter how hard he tried, he couldn't move. He felt the heartbeat of the earth reverberating through his own body. He could feel the minerals attempting to heal him. His need for blood was overwhelming, yet he didn't have the necessary strength to attempt to draw any creatures to him. There was too much pain if he attempted movement, and the feeling of being trapped should have added to his discomfort, but he couldn't summon the necessary emotions to care.

His heart stuttered when he felt the cool touch of a breeze on his face. He couldn't open his eyes. Even that small movement was too painful. His lungs didn't seem to work correctly. He thought perhaps someone was with him, forcing air in and out of his lungs like some great forge. He wasn't breathing on his own. It was an impossible task.

Stay with me, Sandu. Don't leave me alone.

Sandu heard her voice in his mind. Low. Sweet. Adalasia. He examined that tone from every possible perspective. No demon or vampire could replicate her exact pitch. It was too soft with love. Love. He hadn't thought about such an emotion. In truth, he hadn't known it to exist until the feeling began to creep up on him unawares. For her. His lifemate. Adalasia.

He struggled to answer her. To reassure her. He could hear tears in her voice. His mind and memories felt so fractured, he could barely hold on to what was real and what was illusion. He had been in the shadow realm, in the Cave of Fire, tortured for endless time.

First had come the temptations. He was weak, starved, his every cell crying out for blood. The temptations were horrendous, men and women offering him their adrenaline-laced blood if he would just come with them to the dark side. Women wound themselves around him, whispering lewd promises of giving him their bodies in return for their blood. They begged him to take their blood, to allow them to give him that service—for a price.

The whispers and temptations seemed to go on for months. Years. All the while the flames burned his skin and the demons tortured him, flaying the skin from his body with their fire whips. He was already sick and wounded from the fight with multiple vampires. The undead had set upon him the moment he was pulled into the shadow realm. There was no way to kill what was already dead. They tore his already weak body apart and dragged him gleefully to the Cave of Fire, where the demons waited for him.

He refused to betray his lifemate for any reason. They tortured him endlessly, relentlessly, promised him everything and anything if he would open the gate. Eventually, they wanted him to summon his lifemate, promising they both could leave the Cave of Fire if he would persuade her to open the gates.

Sandu knew he was becoming more and more confused, but his duty to Adalasia was never in question. That was the one thing he was resolute about. He would not yield. He would not betray her. She guarded the gate, reborn over and over, waiting for him, her lifemate, to arrive, and he would not jeopardize or cheapen what she had suffered over the centuries to hold back what was behind those gates. He had no idea how long he'd been there, but he feared she would come for him—and she had.

Knowing the demons had their hands on Adalasia was worse than any physical agony they could put him through. Watching them torture her, flaying the skin from her with their fire whips, hearing her screams and pleas, was worse than anything he could have imagined. He was a Carpathian male, an ancient, sworn to protect her, sworn to see to her health. He loved her with every fiber of his being, and yet he couldn't save her.

He felt movement, a sweet voice calling to him to waken, drawing him from his slumber toward the surface—and excruciating pain. He didn't want to answer the call, but it was Adalasia. How could he abandon her?

The roaring in his ears was too loud to hear anything, but he knew she was there with him. Her scent reached him. Surrounded him. Drove out the odious smell of sulfur and brimstone.

You should not have come, Sivamet, he whispered into her mind. *Tet vigyázam.* He told her he loved her because she needed to know.

They were both going to suffer the fires of damnation. There was no way to end it for either of them. He knew, even if they gave the demons what was asked of them, there would be more asked. Always more. He could hear a chant, the words far off, spoken in the ancient language of his kind.

He smelled blood. Tasted it as someone pressed closed to his lips. He tried to turn his head away. He would not betray her. Adalasia. Sweet goddess. His lifemate. He was so tired, and the pain ripped at his insides, scraping him raw. His mind felt fragmented, sanity elusive. He couldn't quite hold on to any real thought.

I know you're weary, Sandu, but you have to take the blood offered to you. Your brethren surround you now. You are no longer in the Cave of Fire. You are here in the healing grounds with me. With all of us.

Was she real? Was she telling him the truth? The shadow realm was a place of illusion and lies. A blowtorch burned through his insides. Fire took off his skin. Parasites ate his flesh and crawled relentlessly through his organs. Acid blood of the vampire was forced into him so that his veins burned every moment of his existence.

Sandu, beloved, come back to me. Feel me with you. Take what is freely given to you.

It was a leap of faith. That voice. The feeling of Adalasia moving in his mind, filling all those fragmented places so that for a few moments he felt whole. His spirit moved against hers. Recognized her. Trusted her.

Sandu allowed the wrist to be pressed to his mouth. At once, he tasted rich Carpathian blood—ancient, powerful, healing. The blood was unlike anything he had ever experienced, not even with the oldest of the ancients. It hit like a fireball, rushing through his veins, so that acid and blowtorches receded before it. Parasites and bacteria exited as quickly as possible through his pores, unable to survive should that powerful blood touch them.

He tried to be polite and thoughtful. He didn't want to be greedy or succumb to the demon prowling so close to the surface inside him, but it was nearly impossible to force himself to stop feeding when he was starving. He shouldn't have worried so much; the ancient feeding him stopped him easily. Sandu was weak, and somehow, the two were connected.

He could hear the Carpathian healing chant all the while he fed and then Adalasia's soft voice urging him to go back to sleep, promising to be with him, to guard him, to never leave him. He felt his brethren close. The ancient who had given him blood, which moved through his body, a powerful healing light, searching out every burn, every ragged tear, each horrendous wound, attempting to lessen the damage done to his body.

Sleep, Sandu, Adalasia said softly. *I will call to you when next you need blood and another healing session.*

Sandu found it ironic that his lifemate was the one taking care of him when he was an ancient, sworn to protect and care for her. Nevertheless, he allowed himself to succumb to the need for healing sleep and soil, trusting his lifemate to watch over him.

Adalasia stared down at Sandu's beloved face there in the moonlight. She had opened the soil herself to allow the silver of the moon to coax him back to the living. His handsome face was still ravaged by the cruelty of the demons in the Cave of Fire. Lines of suffering were carved deep, but along with that were the lash marks where fire had raced up the side of his face from his jaw to the edge of his temple. With a gentle finger, she traced each of the three scars embedded so deep in his skin.

The demons had flayed the skin from his chest and back with their vicious whips. The evidence was everywhere, making her want to weep. She wouldn't. She had seen him when they first got him back to his body. The body had looked normal until his spirit had reunited with it. Every bit of torture inflicted on him there in the shadow realm, in the Cave of Fire, was suddenly manifested on and in his body. The brethren and Luiz had worked each night to heal him and lessen the terrible evidence of what the demons had done to him.

Two weeks he had slept in the healing soil. She had slept beside him, waking to practice her skills in opening the earth, clothing herself, shifting and taking blood. She was determined to learn as much as she could so that if they were alone, she would be able to come to his aid in a battle, even with the undead.

Each of the evenings, one of the brethren waited beside their resting place for her to awaken. He allowed her to practice taking blood from him. Then he trained her in shifting. That was the biggest lesson all of the guardians wanted her to accomplish. Shifting into mist, into animals and birds, into the smallest reptile. Shifting on the run, as fast as possible.

She learned how exacting each of the guardians were. They wanted her to be faster each time she did anything at all. They insisted she practice over and over until she was exhausted. She felt almost like she did when she was first starting her training in fighting demons.

Luiz taught her how to shed her body and become a healing spirit. She had to cast off all ego, all sense of self, and work only to heal another. She especially liked it when he took her with him to heal Sandu's body. The first few times, she hadn't done well, sobbing at the damage she found, finding herself back in her own body, but Luiz didn't give up on her. He patiently explained how she had to push all emotion aside in order to heal a lifemate's worst wounds. She wanted to be able to save Sandu if he was injured in a battle with the undead, so she kept practicing, determined to learn to overcome her emotions.

The guardians and Luiz insisted they give Sandu blood twice each night. They didn't want her to do it. Luiz and each of the guardians examined his body carefully for parasites or bacteria they may have missed. They were careful with him, rarely waking him, and only to insist he take their blood to help him heal. When he was awake, he always reached for her first, and it was those moments she felt she lived for. To feel him in her mind, even for just a moment, to know he really was alive and back with her.

Adalasia hadn't told the others that each time their minds merged, she saw disturbing images in Sandu's. She didn't have time to examine those images before he was gone again, slipping back into the healing sleep of the Carpathian people. Perhaps, before she woke him fully, she should address her concerns with one of them, but it seemed almost a betrayal. Sandu was vulnerable in his present state. He was an ancient, and he wouldn't want even his brethren to know his mind was fractured. His body, yes, but not his mind. She knew that instinctively.

Sandu moved, awareness coming to him wholly, not in stages, just that abrupt, complete cognizance that the Carpathian hunters seemed to have. He was automatically scanning everything around him, looking into his memories, as well as hers. She felt him move in her mind even as his lashes swept up and she found herself looking into his obsidian-dark eyes.

She stayed silent while he gained knowledge of what had transpired during the time he had been in the healing soil. He looked further back, trying to understand what had happened to him, trying to learn what was real and what might be illusion.

Adalasia waited patiently until his focus was completely on her. She smiled at him. "I missed you."

He reached up and framed the side of her face with his palm. "You came for me."

"Did you think I wouldn't?"

"I did not want you to come anywhere near that place. The demons set a trap for you, using me as bait. I feared you would come because I know how courageous you are."

"It wasn't courage, Sandu," she denied. "It was because if that is where you are, then that is where I will be."

His thumb slid gently, almost reverently, over her lips. "All those centuries I was alone and thought I had gone far past my time. The demon in me is strong, Adalasia, and it always will be. There, in the shadow realm, without you, surrounded by the demons Nera sent, they saw that in me, how strong it was. They sent temptation after temptation to me. I was drained of blood and there was so much pain." He frowned. "I could not get away from it. No matter how I tried to distance myself, I could not. I knew then that I would spend my days in agony, but I would not give them the satisfaction of betraying my lifemate."

"I was tempted as well," Adalasia admitted. "And shown things that were disturbing to me. Women offering themselves to you and you taking them as if it was your right. For one terrible moment, my mind was confused, but then I saw the oath carved into your back, and everything was right again. My mind was clear. I knew what I was seeing had to be an illusion."

Sandu floated from the rich soil, cleaning and clothing himself as he did so. He sat beside Adalasia in the cave. The cave was small, but the soil was healing. The guardians and Adalasia had provided strong safeguards. He could feel them, the tight weaves each of his brethren had added for his safety and that of his lifemate. He had chosen well, the guardians for their journey. He owed them much.

"So many helped me bring you back, Sandu," Adalasia said. "If Dax's dragon hadn't protected my spirit from the heat, I'm not certain I could have withstood that fire. The guardians and Luiz De La Cruz had the necessary strength to pull us back to this realm. You were so weak and, quite frankly, so was I."

Sandu reached for her hand and threaded his fingers through hers. "I recognized the power of the De La Cruz, but not specifically that brother."

"Manolito turned a Jaguar male, and Zacarias took him before the warriors to ask that he join their family. At least, that is what I understood," she replied. "I was focused on you. Everyone was trying to heal your body, to drive out the bacteria. It seemed to be eating your body faster than any of them could keep up. He arrived and immediately offered to help. He is very . . ."

"Powerful," he supplied, and brought the tips of her fingers to his mouth. He studied her face over their joined hands.

"I was going to say 'disturbing,' but I shouldn't when he helped us, and at such a huge risk to himself. He didn't have to, and he didn't ask for anything at all in return. I don't know why I feel so uneasy around him when he did nothing but good for us."

"Just as I have a demon dwelling in me, the De La Cruz family has always had a darkness in them from the time of birth. They have fought valiantly to contain it, but that shadowing has never left the eldest brother, Zacarias, even though he has a lifemate. Luiz, if he was accepted by the warriors, would have all the darkness of their family poured into him through those warriors. You are of the light, Adalasia. You have trouble with the demon in the guardians and in your own lifemate. It is easy to see why you would be uneasy in the presence of Luiz De La Cruz."

He rubbed the back of her hand over his jaw, finding comfort in just touching her. The light from that little sliver of the silver moon shone over his woman, casting a bluish tint into the black of her hair. There was worry in her eyes when she looked at him. He found it in her mind as well, but her face was soft with love. She didn't try to hide that raw emotion from him, and he was grateful. He needed to feel it.

"I caught glimpses of what was behind the gate, Adalasia. At least I think I did. It is so difficult to know what was real in that realm and what was illusion. There was so much pain. Sometimes I could barely see, my vision shimmering gray and black with just the edges able to make out some of what was around me." He kept his voice low, once again looking around the cave, up to the sky and then down to the earth, a little fearful of speaking aloud.

"I sealed us from Nera's spies, above and below," she assured him. "They can't get to us. The guardians, Dax and even the Old One made certain you were safe. Whatever you need to say to me, no one else will hear."

He used the edge of her hand to rub his forehead. Adalasia's touch was every bit as soothing as her voice. "They dragged me to a gate and wanted me to open it. They said if I didn't, you would be tortured for eternity. They showed me you burning in flames, demons lashing the flesh off your bones with fire whips. They tortured you in front of me for what seemed like years. I had no idea of time passing. I knew you guarded the gate just as surely as you had guarded my soul."

He would never get the images of her torture from his mind. Not in a thousand years. Longer even. Lifetime after lifetime, he would have those images branded into his mind. Watching her being tortured was far worse than the agony he'd been subjected to. Carpathians didn't dream in their paralyzed state, yet he had replayed those images several times and had to come close to the surface to assure himself she was there beside him in order to rest easy again.

"I have faced many tests in the long years I have existed, Adalasia, but I did not believe I would be able to pass that one." Again, he fell silent, the vicious torture playing through his mind. His body shuddered.

"You held out," she soothed.

"For you," he said softly. "I repeated my vows to you over and over. They couldn't hear them, but—" He broke off and rubbed his temples. He didn't like telling her, but she was his lifemate. His forced his gaze to meet hers. "I may have gone a little insane in that place, *ewal emninumam*. It is a very real possibility. I think it best if you examine my mind."

Adalasia shifted positions so that she was on her knees in front of him. "I have been in your mind, Sandu. There is no hint of insanity. The things you saw were part reality and part illusion. You are an ancient. You know what the realm of shadows is like even better than I do. I learned from the guardians and Luiz. The demons crept in and took over, promising the vampires waiting there a portal out of the realm to this one if they could capture you or me. That was a lie, a huge deceit, yet the undead believed them. The shadow realm is a place that mixes everyone up."

He knew she was trying to reassure him, but he needed her to understand and even *see* what he was concerned about. "Something else heard my vows, Adalasia. I spoke the ancient tongue. I repeated my oath to stay strong for our people, to stay strong to keep the demon inside, staying strong for her—only her. I became aware, after a time, that I was not the only one repeating those vows. There was another voice, a male voice, speaking in the ancient language. He recited the vows with me."

He rubbed the pad of his thumb back and forth over her knuckles, willing her to believe him. In the ensuing silence, he could hear the sound of water in the distance. Cave crickets talked to one another.

"Do you believe there is another Carpathian male trapped in the Cave of Fire?" Adalasia didn't flinch away from looking at him.

His brows drew together. "I do not know where he was. Only that he could hear me and I could hear him. I caught glimpses of a gate at times beyond the flames. The demons were lined up, watching, waiting, as if the expectation was I would break and something huge was going to happen."

"What did the gate look like, Sandu?" she asked, her gaze never leaving his face.

She believed him. The relief was tremendous. Nearly overwhelming. Sandu scrubbed his free hand over his face, refusing to relinquish his hold on her.

"Look into my memories," he invited. "I want you to see and hear what I did."

"First describe the gate. I don't want to take a chance on imposing what I might think into the visual of your memories."

He wasn't certain what she meant, but he was willing to tell her what he thought he'd seen beyond the towers of flames because Adalasia was so receptive.

"The gate was massive, consisting of two doors. Very thick, they were constructed of ancient wood, and I could see that the two gates would swing naturally outward toward the flames if they opened. There was a mark burned into the gates that sat over the center and was embedded onto both to make it one symbol."

Adalasia nodded her head, and her free hand moved up to cover her heart. She pressed her palm there tight, hard, her eyes on his. "Could you make out the emblem at all?"

Sandu wanted to show her the image. It was difficult to describe. "A woman above a mountain, facing forward, but she is also facing to the east and west as well, as if she is watching everything. One guardian to the east holds a skull. The one to the west holds a flame. She holds a serpent in one hand and a dagger in the other. In front of her is a ceremonial chalice pouring blood into another chalice. I did not get all of this at once, Adalasia. I got this in small glimpses over a long period of time."

"You are describing the goddess card," Adalasia said.

There was no judgment in her voice at all, but he immediately doubted what he had seen—and heard. "It was illusion, then. My memory playing tricks."

"Perhaps, but I don't think it was, Sandu," she denied.

He tightened his fingers around hers. "Why?" He didn't want it to be an illusion. He was so certain, and that certainty made him feel as if he were fragmented, on the verge of insanity. On the other hand, if he hadn't been hallucinating, if it wasn't an illusion, what exactly was trapped behind that gate? He feared he knew, and that might be even worse than being on the verge of insanity.

"The gate. I never once showed you a drawing of the gate. I never described it as having double entries. It is there in the book my mother gave to me, and the gate is exactly as you describe, including the goddess burned deep into the double doors hewn of ancient wood. How would you know that?"

"Look into my memories, *Sivamet*, but do not see what happens to you in my memories, only concentrate on the glimpses I got through the flames of the gates and the voice that rose to chant with mine."

He knew it was going to be difficult for her not to see those illusions of her torture, but he really needed her to merge deeper, to find the gates and hear the voice. Particularly the voice. Was that real? It was a low timbre. A rumble like low thunder in the distance. More beast than human. In fact, when he replayed it in his head, each ancient syllable had been a growling snarl.

Adalasia didn't wait for him to ask again. His lifemate, believing in him, standing with him, Sandu realized how lucky he was. Had he been able, he would have commanded her to remain far from the shadow realm. The ancient in him demanded he keep her safe, not allow her to fight the demons as she'd been trained, but somewhere, he had learned compromise with his new lifemate. He had learned that all the old ways weren't necessarily the best or only ways. His lifemate was extraordinary.

"You're staring at me."

"I like looking at you."

"It's distracting."

A slow smile began somewhere deep. Already, without the answers he needed, she was beginning to work her magic on him. He let go of her hand and reached for her waist, lifting her from where she knelt in front of him to settle her on his lap, facing away from him. He pushed her long thick braid over one shoulder with his chin.

"Now what are you doing?" There was a faint hint of amusement in her voice.

"I cannot distract you if you are facing away from me, *Sivamet*. There can be no staring. You can merge your mind with mine without fear of interference." He turned his head so his teeth could find the little shell of her ear. That sweet little earlobe that called to him.

Adalasia laughed softly. "You're definitely feeling better. Behave while I look and listen." She merged seamlessly with him and moved through his memories without hesitation.

Sandu found he wanted to distract her, but he didn't. He merely slid his arms around her, clasping his hands together beneath the temptation of her breasts.

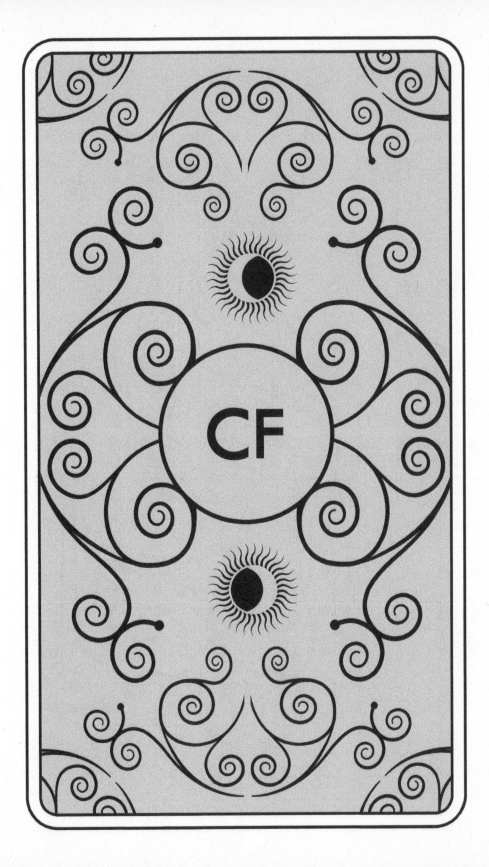

-XVII-

THE STAR

S andu turned his face into Adalasia's neck and inhaled the fragrance that was so unique to her. Wild plum and clove. Orange blossom and rose. The natural perfume of her skin drove out the fragmented pieces of demons clinging to his mind. He ran his lips up and down her neck, savoring the feel of her, the scent of her. All the while, he could feel her merged with him, moving in his mind, searching through his memories.

She leaned her weight back against him as she pulled out of his past. "I saw the gate holding strong, just as you saw it, Sandu. I heard the sound of a male chanting the vows with you in the ancient Carpathian language. You were right, he sounded more beast than man. More demonic than Carpathian."

He pressed his mouth against her pulse. The beat that was steady and rhythmic that called to him. He needed to feel his skin against hers. He had been so close to being the very thing that was trapped behind those gates. A demon beyond all reasoning.

"We don't know that," Adalasia whispered, reading him. "We don't know that he's that far gone."

"I reached out to him, *ewal emninumam*. Once I realized he was an ancient, I tried to connect in the hope that two ancients could break free of the demons. His mind was nothing but red fury, a haze I couldn't break through. I didn't want to be right about him. I told myself it was another demon. Another illusion. He's an ancient Carpathian, Adalasia. For a moment, he even felt familiar to me, as if I knew him. Then all was lost in that red fury. That could have been me. Without you, that most likely would be me."

More than anything, Sandu wanted to be wrong. He shed his cloth-ing. At the same time, he dispensed with her clothes—everything—not wanting a hint of material on either of them. He only wanted her skin next to his. He needed that. Needed to feel every inch of her body. He waited a moment, thinking she might protest, but she only gave a little moan, her body moving subtly against his. An enticement. An invitation. He cupped the soft weight of her breasts in his palms, thumbs sliding over her nipples.

A small shudder of pleasure slipped through her body at his touch. Another moan slipped out, the sound erotic to his ears. Lust mixed with love came crashing together in a potent mix.

"Do you think there is a chance of saving him?" One of her hands reached behind her to shape the nape of his neck. The action moved her full, rounded breasts into his hands.

That soft feminine flesh resting in his palms sent those fingers of desire not only dancing down his spine and along his thighs, but moving through his heart. She comforted him as well as inflamed him.

"No. We cannot save him, Adalasia. What purpose they have for holding him behind those gates, I have no idea, but he cannot be allowed to be unleashed on the world. He is very powerful. Too powerful. There is nothing left of him."

He didn't want to state the truth because it was so close to what he had been before he had found Adalasia. He knew the demon in him had been that strong, that close. Crouching. Threatening to devour him. She had saved him whether she knew it or not. Not just from becoming the undead. That would have been bad enough. Had he not given up his soul, becoming the thing of nightmares few of his kind could destroy would have somehow been worse.

Sandu leaned his head to one side in order to drag his lips up the side of her neck, to scrape his teeth back and forth over her pulse. Tempting himself. Listening to the beat of her heart calling to him. The sound of her blood moving in her veins. The scent of her flooded his senses with a terrible craving, with hunger and desire. Grounding him. Saving him.

"I don't know if even the combined efforts of our greatest hunters could take him down." He made the admission as his teeth lengthened and sank into her.

Her little cry sounded erotic to his ears. Her bottom moved restlessly in his lap, and he parted his thighs to part her legs. Her blood, hot and pure, rushed into him like a thunderbolt, straight to his groin. Lightning strikes jolted him throughout his veins and ran like a ferocious storm through his body. He tugged on her left nipple while he kneaded the firm right mound. The more he tugged and rolled, the more she pushed her bottom against him, rubbing her bare cheeks against the hard steel of his cock.

I need you, päläfertiilam. I need to feel your body surrounding mine. The beauty of her silken fire would take away the sensation of the brutal fire of the whips. *Give yourself to me. Surrender everything to me, Adalasia.*

"I always do, Sandu." Her voice shook. Her body shuddered in anticipation. "Tell me what you would have me do." Her whisper was filled with love. With heavenly sin. With temptation. Such a mixture to lure a man like him.

Deliberately, she moved her body again, a sensual enticement. As she did, she waved her hand gracefully, and candles sprang to life. The flames danced over the walls, igniting a variety of healing scents and giving off a myriad of flickering figures depicting all sorts of erotic positions on the walls of the cavern. There was a pool of shimmering water, steam rising from the surface in the far corner, and the walls were covered in gems so that those figures moved and danced over the reflected light.

Sandu indulged his need of the rich hot blood, savoring the fine taste of her, the way she seemed to explode against his tongue and tease his every sense into a frenzy of want. Fire was good with Adalasia. Those flames licking over his skin didn't hurt, they stroked him in hot caresses, arousing nerve endings and making him feel alive when he thought he was long gone.

Her body was all woman, soft curves and satin skin. He closed the two holes he had made in her skin and lapped at them with his tongue, tilting her head back toward him before kissing his way over her chin to lips, claiming her mouth. Kissing Adalasia was feeling the earth move.

Riding the stars. Knowing he was alive and found in his own sanctuary. He lifted his head for a moment, resting his forehead against her temple.

"Do you have any idea what you really are to me, Adalasia? What you have done for me? First, the endless centuries of gray void. Of nothing. Not even whispers of temptation. Just . . . nothing. I had hunger that would never stop, never be sated no matter how often I fed. It was always there, every waking moment."

Sandu stroked her breasts with his long fingers, tugged and rolled her nipples, clamped down when he bit her shoulder and then licked at the ache. She let out a little gasping moan and rocked her bare cheeks against him, enticing him more. The figures on the wall danced and performed an endless show of a variety of positions, as if they were giving him a visual directory of the Kama Sutra.

"Can you imagine what it was like to feel a demon growing in me? Something worse than the undead. Something evil, something that loved the battle and the killing. A beast that grew to need it."

She turned in his arms, sliding over his straining cock so that he groaned at the sensation of silk against steel. Accelerant pouring over flames. Her belly pressed against his, her thighs straddling his. Her breasts crushed up against his chest, nipples two hot points of fire as she slid her arms around his neck.

"Sandu." Her mouth left a trail of fire from his throat to his jaw. "Not evil. Your demon is not evil. You believe that to be so, but I'm telling you he's not. Nothing about you is evil." She kissed under his jaw and nibbled her way around his neck to lick at his pounding pulse. "You're beautiful the way you are, a fighting machine when you need to be."

Her mouth was distracting him, but he needed to tell her. She had to know what she was to him. "You came for me when I was locked in a place of torture and torment, Adalasia. Where there was no hope. Only pain. Agony. Weakness and temptation. You came for me."

"I wasn't alone, Sandu. I could never have gotten you out of there alone." She whispered it like some terrible confession against his throat.

He heard the ache in her voice. The need and hunger. He also heard the small note of guilt and shame. His gut clenched at the thought she would feel in any way as if she were ashamed because she couldn't get to him by herself.

"What matters to me, Adalasia, is that you came for me. You have that kind of courage, even knowing what you were facing." He whispered the truth to her. As he did, he stood, caging her in his arms so that she was skin to skin with him.

On the floor, where before there had been dirt, Adalasia had fashioned a carpet of fur, thick and sensual under his bare feet. His body moved, hot and aggressive, against hers. He bent her back over the bar of his arm so that her full breasts jutted up toward him and her wild mane of dark hair fell like a silken waterfall toward the floor.

His tongue lapped at those curves, rasped over her erect nipples and then the undersides of her breasts before tracing the way down the deep valley toward her belly. His long mane of blond hair spilled over her, brushing her shoulders and the upper curves of her breasts so that she jumped, her gaze leaping to his.

"*Tet vigyázam,*" he whispered against her belly, transferring his hold to her hips as he went to his knees in front of the woman he worshiped. Telling her he loved her was far easier in his own language. Showing her with his body was even more so.

"Sandu." Her fingers dug into his shoulders as he continued on his journey of exploration, kissing and nipping with his lips and teeth, creating a path from her belly to her mound.

Sandu caught her thighs and widened her stance, looking up at her to see her throat move convulsively, her breath turn ragged and the muscles in her belly ripple with need. He brushed his hand gently, tenderly, from the inside of her knee up to the heat of her weeping entrance, his palm barely there. Just whispering along her skin, following with his lips. Kissing her. Blazing that trail. Creating a line of fire.

She reacted with soft cries and one hand fisting in his hair when she felt his breath on her clit, on her slick entrance. The other hand had fingers digging into his shoulder, her nails little pinpoints of pain that added to the building hunger already raging in his body.

Every time I touch you like this, I feel as if I have been given a miracle.

He switched his attention to her other thigh, not wanting any part of her body to feel neglect.

Sandu. His name was a protest when he took his mouth from her entrance.

He smiled against her inner thigh and continued scraping his teeth up her leg toward his ultimate goal. *You are so impatient, Sivamet. We have all night. I want to take all night.*

I would not live through all night.

He bit down gently on her inner thigh, up high, close to her clit. Catching her hips in his hands, he held her still. She was in continuous motion, unable to stop her restless movement, seeking the heat of his mouth. Her unique fragrance called to him, and he couldn't help circling her clit with his tongue and then lapping at the drops leaking from her sheath. That flavor, all Adalasia and all for him.

The moment his mouth settled over her entrance and his tongue stabbed deep, her fingers tightened in his hair, pulling on his scalp, and she threw back her head with a sensual groan. Her hips rocked into him. He pulled her closer and began to devour her, hearing his own primitive growls. It was as if he'd forgotten the taste of her, that forbidden aphrodisiac that had been created just for him. The more he consumed, the more he needed. The more he took, the hotter the flames inside his body burned for her.

He shaped her left hip with one hand and then brought his fingers to her clit, circling while he drank. He flicked hard, and her entire body shuddered. He licked his way to that hard, straining bud and then settled his mouth over it, switching to use his fingers, burying them inside her. He suckled and then used the edge of his teeth while his fingers plunged deep. Her body clenched hard and rippled with powerful waves while she cried out, nearly sobbing his name.

Sandu took her to the floor, that thick carpet of fur, his much heavier body blanketing hers. His mouth was once again on hers—long, fiery kisses, fiercely possessive. He went from tender to a storm of intensity in a matter of seconds. He turned primitive, almost violent, his hands moving over her, stroking and arousing, his knee pushing her legs apart even as his body held hers trapped there on the unforgiving floor.

Adalasia had never thought to have a wild, out-of-control sexual encounter, one that would take her far beyond her imagination, even push her from her comfort zone, but Sandu was doing just that with his raging storm of fire. His mouth devoured her. Flames poured over and into her. She couldn't catch her breath, but it didn't matter. He had thrust into her mind, invading deep, sharing his mind at the same time.

She felt his urgent desire, a lust building, entwining with intense love. She felt his heightened awareness, the fiery nerve endings sending him deeper into an aggressive, hotter passion. She fisted his hair and hung on as the firestorm raged out of control between them, growing stronger with every fierce kiss and stroke of his hands on her body.

Then his hands were moving again, cupping her breasts, fingers flicking her nipples until she sobbed with need, her mouth open as he bit at her neck and shoulder. His hands found their way along her ribs and then her belly to finally, *finally*, press against the heat of her entrance. She should have been terrified at the strength in his body, in his arms and chest, those hands moving on her. She couldn't move the way he had her pinned, but all that mattered to her was the state of arousal building and coiling, so much pressure, until she thought she might go insane if he didn't fill her.

"Sandu, *please*." She meant to whisper it, but it came out more of a moan. A mewl. Maybe even a sob, but he saw the erotic plea in her mind.

That fuse, already smoldering in him, ignited instantly. His mouth left hers, his eyes wild. Red flames leapt and burned with fierce abandonment against the black backdrop in his eyes as he stared down at her so possessively. His features appeared harsh, cruel even, sensual lines cut deep. His cock was thick, aggressive, the wide crown pressed against her entrance scorching hot. She couldn't stop her hips from moving, trying to impale herself, but his hands were there, holding her still while he looked down at her, that leaping fire moving over her face.

Adalasia felt his claiming. He had never looked or felt more serious.

His gaze holding hers captive, he thrust forward, driving through her tight folds, invading her feminine channel, which seemed far too narrow even though she was slick and welcoming. She felt every hot vein, his girth and length, the pulsing heartbeat and rush of blood. Her walls clamped around him to add to the fiery friction.

His mind was firmly entrenched in her mind. She felt pleasure ripping through his body, a series of violent lightning strikes that sent hot blood pounding through his veins and centering in his cock. She could feel the white-hot heat pushing at the walls of her sheath, her body answering by gripping him tighter. There was an exquisite ecstasy she didn't know if he felt or she did or if they shared it as he surged in and out of her scorching-hot channel. The friction just seemed to increase, and she found herself lifting her hips to meet his, frantic to take him deeper.

The floor had no give in it, so he could leverage his body above hers, using one arm, and pound into her, driving forward so hard it inched her backward over the fur. She didn't care, barely noticed, not with the searing flames consuming her. His insatiable hunger matched her own glorious agony of fire. They were burning up together.

She dug her nails into him, scored down his back, as he rode her mercilessly. She wanted this with him, this perfect torment, harder and faster until she didn't know if it was heaven or hell, only that she didn't want it to ever stop.

Her body seemed to pause for a moment. Take a breath. Then she was exploding, fragmenting into a million pieces, being thrown into some other place where her only anchor was Sandu. She felt her sheath clamp down like a vise on his cock, squeezing like a terrible fist, determined to milk him dry. It went on and on, ripple after powerful ripple, wave after wave. His cock jerked and pulsed hard, rocketing hot semen, coating the walls of her sensitive channel, triggering even more pulse-pounding orgasms.

For a time, there was only the sound of their labored breathing in the cave. Adalasia wasn't certain she was really alive, and it didn't matter if she'd gone out with Sandu inside her. It was the perfect way to go. There was magic in coming together, burning so out of control in a firestorm after nearly losing each other. Adalasia couldn't help but feel a sense of overwhelming love, of power at the fact that she alone could bring this man to such a fever of intensity that his iron discipline was lost.

She nuzzled his chest, uncaring that his weight was heavy and there was no give in the floor of the cave. She could have adjusted that, but she didn't bother. She liked being his. Feeling as if he were surrounding her with his size and the sheer strength of him. She kept her arms around him, holding him to her while he kissed her neck, tracing the path where his teeth had bitten her several times. She wondered if he had left marks behind. She had the feeling he had—and on purpose, too.

"I am heating the water in the pool," he murmured against her neck.

"It's already heated. I prepared in advance." She was certain she'd thought of everything.

"I like very hot water." He waved his hand toward the steaming pool.

Adalasia frowned, flicking her gaze up to his face. He wasn't looking down at her but studying her neck as if it were some kind of artwork. "How hot?"

A faint smile touched his mouth. "Very hot. It will take away any soreness."

"You can remove any soreness several different ways," she pointed out, placing both hands on his chest to remind him to move off of her. "Super-hot water doesn't need to touch my very sensitive skin. I'm not a lobster."

"I have never understood the idea of boiling a lobster," he confessed as he rolled off of her to lie on his back beside her.

"Don't change the subject." Adalasia turned her head to look at him, doing her best to look stern when he looked like sin. She melted every time she looked at him, wanting to give him anything he desired. He probably knew it, too. If he did know it, he didn't make the mistake of smirking.

"You usually prefer to do things the human way."

Of course he would throw that in her face. Did he have to look so gorgeous when he was sitting up, all those muscles rippling and that hair spilling around his face making him look like a fallen angel? Her body should have been sated. They'd had wild, primitive, crazy, feral sex, and yet just looking at him had more erotic images playing through her head, and her sheath pulsed and clenched.

"The human way doesn't include being boiled alive. That is probably more in keeping with the Carpathian way, Sandu." Keeping her hand low by her side, she waved it toward the steaming pool to lower the water temperature by a couple of degrees, just in case. She was fairly certain he had increased the temperature.

Sandu rose smoothly to his feet and reached for her, gathering her up and cradling her to his chest. "You face the Cave of Fire without flinching, but you balk at the thought of a little hot water."

The laughter in his voice and eyes was her undoing. Before she could retort, he was kissing her, robbing her of all ability to think, let alone speak. He could kiss like sin. Perfection. The firestorm was back, the flames licking at her veins, lightning forking through her core so that she could feel pressure building all over again.

Then he was in the pool, wading with her into the center. Steam rose all around them. She could feel the heat seeping into her pores, adding to the feeling of being wrapped in that fiery hunger he could produce so easily in her. He lifted his head slowly, his black eyes still smoldering with those red flames.

"You are truly beautiful, *ewal emninumam*. The way you surrender to me is such a thing of beauty. I can only thank you. I needed to feel you give yourself to me."

Adalasia framed the side of his face with one hand. He could disarm her so easily. Love overwhelmed her every time she looked at him. It was strange how she had gone from distrusting him to loving him more every moment she spent with him.

He lowered her into the pool. At first, the heat didn't register, and then she gasped and would have shot straight toward the ceiling of the cave if he hadn't had his hands firmly around her waist.

"I was thinking loving thoughts, and all along you knew you were going to boil me alive in this hideous water." She tried to climb up his taller frame.

He threw his head back and laughed. The sound caught at her. She actually felt the burn of tears behind her eyes. Sandu rarely laughed like that. Real. Carefree. After the agony he'd suffered, the sound was so beautiful it tugged at her heartstrings and found its way into her soul.

"The water isn't that hot, Adalasia. Already, I can feel your body adjusting, and it is soothing the soreness. I was hard on you."

She wasn't going to admit the water wasn't that hot. "I probably do have skid marks on my back and inside, but who cares? That was . . . awesome. The best. I decided being Carpathian has some really good benefits."

Adalasia ducked her head under the water, and when she surfaced, her lifemate was at the other side of the pool, leaning back, watching her as she swam lazily. He rested his hips against the smooth rocks she'd created to line the pool. She'd been particularly proud of that feature. She'd wanted the rocks very smooth and contoured so they could sit on them either out of the water or just waist deep in it. Sandu rinsed himself off and then sat on the rocks, his thighs apart, his long blond hair drying rapidly with a wave of his hand while he kept his gaze fixed on her.

"Now who doesn't want to come out of the hot water?"

It wasn't the water so much; she liked the way he was watching her. He had a way of focusing so completely on her that made her feel as if there wasn't another woman alive that he would ever notice.

"You know there isn't another woman for me to notice. You are my only. You always will be." Sandu proved he was in her mind. His hand dropped to his semihard cock, fingers wrapping around the girth in a tight fist. "Why don't you swim over this way, little mermaid?"

She raised an eyebrow, the sight of his casual pumping mesmerizing. "Do you have something in mind?"

"I have been thinking about the way your mouth feels when you surround me. I woke with that thought somewhere in the back of my mind, and it suddenly came to the front, and now it is very persistently there. An erotic vison I cannot seem to remove." He looked around him and gestured to the walls where the shadow figures performed. "All of them seemed to be demanding we follow their example."

"I see that." Adalasia smiled at him, a siren's temptation. She had conceived and designed the shadows from the candles and thrown them onto the walls.

Deliberately, her gaze dropped to his hardening cock, and her tongue touched her lips, moistening them so they gleamed wet as she stood and waded slowly toward him. The water came to her waist. Her breasts swayed, little beads dripped from her nipples and more droplets ran down her skin. She stopped to twist her hair, wringing the water out of it before tossing the mass over her shoulder.

"I wouldn't want it to be a hardship on you, Sandu, but who knows what would happen if we didn't do what those little instructors have taken the time to show us we should be doing."

Her hands cupped his heavy sac, fingers brushing his velvety balls. She found the softer cushion she had provided for herself beneath the water so she could kneel comfortably in front of him, her breasts floating on the water as she tipped her head back to look up at him.

"I think I can endure the hardship," he said, his black eyes once again leaping with red flames.

Adalasia laughed softly and did her best to swallow him down.

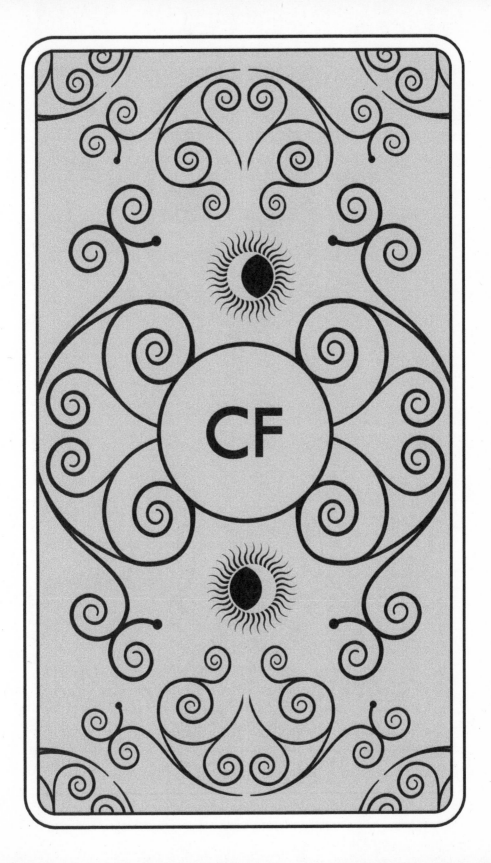

-XVIII-

THE MOON

S andu regarded Danutdaxton and his lifemate, Riley, as they sat outside on the little patio with the rain forest surrounding them. "I had no idea, when I sent the call ahead, what I would be asking of you. I apologize." He was very sincere.

Dax lived his life away from civilization for a reason. The Old One, the dragon sharing his form, would never have tolerated a town, let alone a city. Danutdaxton had been too long in the volcano, and he had become something more than Carpathian. It was possible he couldn't have survived long in a civilized setting even without the dragon in him.

Riley didn't seem to mind. She sat beside her lifemate in one of the many chairs scattered around their side patio. The house was situated in front of the mountainside. The back butted up to the mountain itself, and Sandu was certain there was an entrance leading into the mountain. Dax would have a cave hidden somewhere deep, a place his dragon would be happy and where he and his lifemate could go to ground safely.

This patio was for entertaining guests. It made Sandu wonder who came to visit. Dax wasn't a man to make others comfortable, nor was he comfortable around too many people. Riley, on the other hand, was very good at making her guests feel welcome. She had a soothing quality to her. It wasn't difficult to see that plants grew all around the patio and reached toward her as if she were an integral part of them.

Dax waved off his apology. "This has been good for us. We never want to grow complacent. And it gave the Old One a good workout. He likes to sleep for months on end. Sometimes I think he will choose to leave us. The fact that he was needed was a good thing."

Riley nodded. "He doesn't ever like to admit it when he's very happy, but he was. Protecting you, Adalasia, from the heat of the Cave of Fire meant he was useful, and he needed to feel that way. Having Dax or me tell him we need him isn't the same thing as actually having to be there to help save a life."

"Do you call on him often?" Adalasia asked. "I think it's the coolest thing in the entire world that he exists in you. He might actually be the only dragon left in the world, which is sad. Sad for him and sad for the world."

"Even if we did call on him often," Dax said, "the Old One will only aid someone he deems worthy. He can be very stubborn and arrogant. Bossy, too."

Riley burst out laughing. "You sound like you might be describing yourself."

"Careful, woman. You're going to get your elegant eyebrows singed," Dax warned.

The brethren had opted not to come with Sandu and Adalasia. They preferred to patrol rather than visit. Sandu had no idea where Luiz was. He had simply disappeared without saying a word to any of them. That wasn't unusual for an ancient. They came and went without explanation, but Sandu would have liked the chance to thank him.

Sandu had to admit, it was more than just wanting to thank him. He wanted the chance to size him up. Luiz was now connected to both Sandu and Adalasia through blood. That was a very dangerous connection when Luiz was without a lifemate. He needed to know how much of a threat Luiz De La Cruz was to Adalasia.

"That might be a very useful trait to have, Dax," Sandu said. "Breathing fire at one's unruly lifemate. Adalasia would be without eyebrows most of the time. I cannot believe she went into the shadow realm and then the Cave of Fire. I expressly forbid her to follow me." He didn't need to try too hard to make his voice stern. Every time he thought of his lifemate trapped by the demons, he knew he had to find a way to get the thoughts out of his mind before they overwhelmed him and he became dangerous. The images of her being tortured could bring out the worst in him.

"While it is true I haven't met too many lifemates," Dax said, "their modern ways are enough to make any man pull out his hair."

Riley rolled her eyes. "One has to learn to adapt, Dax. Compromise."

Danutdaxton sent his lifemate an intimate smile. "I have learned many things over the centuries, Riley, and adapting is my specialty."

Sandu pressed his lips together at the implication that had Riley blushing and shaking her head. Dax may look intimidating, but he wasn't to his woman.

"I believe you had some questions for me," Dax said. "We took a detour with the strange battle, but you came for a reason. Hopefully, I can give you aid."

Sandu felt they were closer than ever to their ultimate goal. They just had to find the right path and stay on it. He explained about his memories and what they'd discovered so far of his name. He watched Dax closely. The Carpathian had chased Mitro Daratrazanoff for centuries into lands barely inhabited. It was very possible he had come across Sandu's family in his travels.

Danutdaxton sat quietly for some time, clearly pulling up old memories. Finally, he nodded. "I do recall coming across your family on more than one occasion. I did not see you, but you were spoken of. I traveled with Arabejila, Mitro's lifemate. She opened doors for us that I could never have gotten through. Your family provided us with a safe place for the night as well as good company."

Sandu's heart jumped. At last, someone who had actually been with his family. "I wasn't there?"

Dax shook his head. "No, but your parents spoke of you often, as did your sister. Arabejila was happy to visit with other women. I think your father, Domizio, thought it scandalous for a woman to be traveling alone with a man without his lifemate, but he didn't voice his opinion. Your mother—Madolina, I believe was her name—and your sister, Liona, talked all night with Arabejila."

Adalasia leaned toward Dax. "Do you recall where this was?"

Dax nodded. "They made their home in what now would be considered Italy. They were a very tight-knit family," he added. "I can draw you a map of the area and where I last saw them. That doesn't mean they stayed there. In those days, we were all very nomadic, especially a family like the di Berdardo. Domizio had to cover a tremendous amount of territory, searching for the undead preying on humans. He liked to keep his family close, not just because he wanted to be with them but so he could protect them as well."

That made sense to Sandu. "Did they indicate where I was? Why I left my father to deal with the undead on his own in such a large territory?"

Dax rubbed the pad of his thumb back and forth across his forehead. "Your father didn't say anything to me, but Liona spoke with Arabejila about you. She said she was lonely without you, that the two of you were close. That you and your father hunted together often, and eventually, the two of you spoke in hushed tones, and you left and never returned. Your father refused to tell her or your mother where you went. He said only that it was necessary for you to leave, that all would be revealed someday in the future."

"That's cryptic," Riley said.

"Domizio was said to have precog," Dax said with a shrug of his broad shoulders. "Years later, there was a rumor that he was gone, and with him, Madolina. No one knew what happened to Liona. She disappeared. The family of di Berdardo was no more."

Sandu was quiet for a long time, turning the information given to him over and over in his mind. "Do you know if anyone looked for Liona after my parents moved on to the next life?"

Dax shook his head. "I was traveling fast, hunting Mitro. He was destroying humans and Carpathians alike in his path. Arabejila was growing weary of finding the vicious, brutal kills her lifemate had made. No matter how often I told her she wasn't responsible for what Mitro did, she took that burden on. She believed she should have been able to keep Mitro from turning vampire, that she should have somehow been stronger. When we realized Domizio and Madolina had moved on to the next life, she was certain Mitro had killed him, and Madolina followed him."

"Was that a possibility?"

Dax nodded. "It was, but I have never believed it to be true. Mitro was a braggart. He liked to tell everyone who would listen how he killed and how often. He even would tell hunters he engaged in battle with of the lesser vampires he made into pawns. He would have bragged about killing a hunter such as your father."

"Mitro was that experienced in battle that he always managed to kill his pursuers?"

"He was a master at concealing himself and then running before he was found. He concealed himself in the tiniest of insects or the largest mammal. He did not mind running as long as he was able to live. He hated like no one I ever met before or since," Dax said. "He struck at Arabejila over and over, but although he was undead and he deliberately chose to give up his soul, he could not kill her. He sent others after her so many times I would have to make the choice to save her or chase after him."

Adalasia frowned. "If she died, wouldn't he?"

"He was already vampire. He would not die," Sandu said. "If lifemates are not tied together, the male can rise vampire, or he can follow his lifemate into the next life. Clearly, Mitro would not choose to follow Arabejila."

"Why was it so important to him that she die?" Adalasia persisted, her hand going defensively to her throat. She stroked the pads of her fingers there in the way she often did when she was nervous.

"No matter where Mitro went or how far away he got from us, Arabejila could always find him. She was his lifemate and he couldn't hide from her. When she went on the actual hunt with me when I had him cornered, even his concealment spells didn't work for long. She had a kind of magnet for finding the direction he had taken. Once Mitro realized Arabejila was the one responsible for tracking him, he devised plan after plan to get rid of her."

"That's horrible," Riley said. "I can't imagine how she must have felt."

Danutdaxton nodded, his thumb sliding over Riley's knuckles. Sandu couldn't decide whether that gesture was to soothe Riley or himself.

"It was a terrible time for her and very wearing. By the time we got to the territory the di Berdardo family guarded, Arabejila was very worn and looking forward to the company of the di Berdardo women. Both women had a soothing quality and were easy to be around. They had welcomed her, and I think Arabejila needed to feel as if Carpathian women didn't condemn her for the sins of her lifemate."

Dax studied their faces and then their joined hands. "This is a difficult path you walk, and very dangerous. I am not a seer, but yet I can see clearly that it is very necessary that you go forward with absolute clarity, without hesitation between you or the brethren. You have chosen your brothers wisely, Sandu. I will confess, when I first heard your call and knew you traveled with four ancients without lifemates, I thought you had lost your mind."

"I do rely heavily on my intuition," Sandu admitted. "I knew, without a shadow of a doubt, that Benedek, Nicu, Petru, and Siv had to come with us. I was not altogether certain whether they were to come for our journey to be successful or whether they would discover something along the way that would lead them to their lifemates."

"Perhaps it is both," Adalasia said.

"What is it you hope to find?" Dax asked.

"My past," Sandu said simply. "My sister if possible, or at least what happened to her. I do know she is alive now, where before, I didn't even know that. I have no memories of my family or where I come from. They seem to be deliberately wiped away. I want to know why that is." He threaded his fingers through Adalasia's. "More than anything else, the threat to my lifemate has to be stopped. To do that, we have to know why they keep coming after her."

A slight breeze stirred the warm night air on the patio. The leaves of the surrounding trees fanned them for a few moments, taking the worst of the heat. Sandu realized Adalasia wasn't regulating her body temperature the way she should. She was following the conversation carefully, but she was also caught up in the beauty of the night, looking at it through eyes full of wonder.

Sandu pushed back the need to reprimand her. She needed to take better care of herself. She needed to pay attention to every detail of their existence until the smallest element was automatic. That would save her life one day. He couldn't bring himself to interrupt her enjoyment of the night—not when they'd been through hell. He merged deeper into her mind, needing to share the experience with her. At once, there was a sparkling quality to the sky through the canopy of the trees.

Like thousands of diamonds, she whispered. *You've given me so much, Sandu.*

He shook his head at her statement. He hadn't given her much other than torture and pain. She'd given him laughter and paradise and seeing the world with new eyes. The simplest thing, like looking up at the canopy and seeing the stars, changed the way he viewed things.

That's all you, ewal emninumam. I have no idea what I ever did before you were in my life. Exist. But not live. I do know that much.

Danutdaxton laughed softly. "Sandu, I fear you are completely enthralled with your lifemate. You cannot take your eyes from her."

"I saw her tortured, Dax. I could not get to her, and the demons flayed the skin from her bones. They burned her to ashes over and over. I do not know if I could ever live through that again." Sandu stated the truth. "I think it best if she stays very close to me for a long time to come, perhaps the next thousand years will suffice. If not, she will be used to my continual presence by that time."

Dax's laughter continued. "What do you think of that, Adalasia?"

Before Adalasia could answer, Riley made a little sound of derision. "Dax is the *worst.* He's sounding all modern-day, like we aren't attached at the hip, but I think we're working on that first thousand years of togetherness. Sticking together like glue or something of that nature."

Dax raised an eyebrow. "I am nowhere near as bad as this besotted fool." He made a gesture toward Sandu. "I allow you to go to that shop you like all by yourself."

Adalasia and Riley exchanged a look, and both women burst into derisive laughter. Sandu knew Dax had screwed up by using the word *allow.* That needed to be struck from his vocabulary. And one shop? Was the man crazy?

"It isn't me," Dax said. "The Old One worries incessantly about her. If I don't have my eyes on her every second, he gets crazy and acts like he might do a flyby."

Riley rolled her eyes. "Now you're just plain making up stories."

Dax laughed. "That could be so. I do like to keep you close."

"Since you did travel so much, Dax," Adalasia ventured, "I wonder if you ever heard of the disappearance of a Carpathian child centuries ago. A little girl of about ten. She could talk to animals. No one ever found her, although apparently the search was conducted for months. Years even."

"She supposedly wandered off," Sandu continued. "No one believed she lost her way."

"Why wouldn't they?" Dax asked. "The forests were thick. Very wild. A child easily could have gotten lost. If she was trying to conduct experiments, she could have ended up in the middle of a rock, and no one would be the wiser. If she fell and shattered bones, wild animals could have gotten to her."

"She would have called out to the adults," Sandu pointed out reasonably. "Few spoke of it, but the conclusion most came to was that she was taken."

"Who would take a Carpathian child?" Dax and Riley exchanged a long, measured look.

A ripple of uneasiness went through Sandu. "We believe the child was taken by Xavier, the high mage, in exchange with a demon for the parasites he wanted in order to begin the destruction of our species." Sandu continued to look between Dax and Riley. "Forgive me for prying, but you haven't had problems with conceiving or carrying, have you?"

Again, a look passed between the couple. Riley gave a small nod and Dax sighed. "Riley is expecting our child now. She is quite advanced in her pregnancy for the second time. We are a little apprehensive, as there are three of us to consider. The Old One's soul and spirit resides in me. He's part of me. Twice, he had thought to move on, but in the end, he will not let this child slip away as the others did."

There was a small silence, and then Adalasia leaned forward toward Riley. "Congratulations, you must be so happy to carry a life in you."

Riley's smile was radiant. "I am. We're having a little girl. The Old One is pleased and isn't in the least bit worried, so I haven't been, either, at least not until Sandu told us of the little girl taken by the mage and exchanged for parasites. Is it possible that was what caused my first miscarriage?"

"If you are truly that far along, although you do not look it, and you are not having trouble, then I would say you are free of parasites, but it is easy enough for Dax or the Old One to search."

"We prefer to hide the pregnancy," Dax said. "We have enemies. I wish to learn more of this child taken by the mage in exchange for the parasites."

"That was centuries ago," Sandu said. "I apologize to both of you for bringing up something that is distressing. It is from the past, Riley. No one has so much as whispered of the child's disappearance, that I know of, in centuries."

"Yet now you speak of it," Danutdaxton pointed out. "The child's disappearance is important to you."

Sandu rubbed the bridge of his nose, all the while retaining possession of Adalasia's other hand. He needed the connection—their mind merge as well as the physical connection between them. Having Adalasia's strength with his made for a much clearer path to the thoughts forming in his mind.

"Yes, although I did not realize it at first, not when my lifemate first spoke of the child's disappearance to me, other than I realized that the mage she spoke of had to be Xavier. Over the last few years, we discovered he wasn't nearly as powerful as we thought. He always used someone else's genius, their platform, to build his work on. In this case, the parasites were given to him in exchange for this particular child."

Sandu stopped rubbing the bridge of his nose and began to rub along his jaw. "What was it about this particular child that made her so valuable to the demons? Why would they bother to exchange their parasites for her?"

"Carpathian blood," Dax said, his voice grim. His look to Riley was wholly apologetic. "They wanted her blood. Demons sacrifice children.

We all know that. Carpathian blood has to be more valuable than any species other than perhaps . . ." He broke off, tilting his head as if listening.

Riley hid a smile behind her hand. "The Old One is objecting to Dax's statement."

"I believe the Lycans would object as well," Sandu said, trying not to smile.

"Fine," Danutdaxton conceded. "I stand corrected. Carpathian is among one of the most valuable species whose blood might be something the demons would want from this child."

"Much better," Sandu agreed, "but she was so young, so little. If the demons truly wanted Carpathian blood, it would be better for them if they took a man or grown woman prisoner and used their blood. A child would never be able to give them any kind of volume."

Dax nodded, frowning now. "That is true. But if they wanted a sacrifice, a child would be what they looked for, not an adult. They are evil. You know. You were in the shadow realm, and you experienced this for yourself. We were there with you and saw what they would do."

Sandu tightened his fingers around Adalasia. They might have witnessed part of what the demons did, but they had no idea what a toll they had taken on him. Perhaps Luiz knew, but none of the others.

He nodded his head slowly. "I considered that she might be a sacrifice for them, but I dismissed it. There were other children closer, ones they could have acquired easier without making a bargain with Xavier. He lived far away from them, and he wanted something in return, something precious to them. Demons don't share easily. So I kept coming back to the conclusion that this child had to have something they wanted. That to them, she was special. The more I tried to push the thought of her away, the more she stuck in my head."

Adalasia nodded. "Like a compulsion. I thought of her as well. At first, it seemed often, but now, it's all the time. She is part of our journey. At the time she was taken, she was a little girl with curls all over her head."

"That is very unusual for a Carpathian. Most have very straight hair," Dax said.

"And she had very light hair, not at all black like the majority of Carpathians I've seen," Adalasia continued. "By 'light,' I mean icy blond, almost platinum. That would set her apart."

Danutdaxton's dark eyebrows rose. The lines in his face deepened. "There are only a couple of lineages with hair that color. The Selvaggio and Bercovitz are the two that come to mind. You said she was able to speak to animals at a very young age. The Bercovitz line definitely has that gift. The Bercovitzes lost a little girl, so I would conclude the child taken was that one. Do you believe the demons took this child in order to control animals?"

Sandu nodded slowly. "That is exactly what I have come to believe. This child had a very specific talent and had already proven so at an extremely young age. She'd saved a human from a pack of wolves, was able to keep the wolves from killing the farmer when he was wounded and bleeding, already helpless. She was only eight at the time."

Adalasia arched an eyebrow at him. *I was unaware you even knew what a child was.*

He hadn't realized how tense he was. How guilty he felt. He was a Carpathian male. An ancient, sworn to protect their females.

"Sandu," she said gently aloud, "we came to ask Danutdaxton and Riley for advice."

He was well aware of that. Too aware. Once Sandu spoke of what he believed aloud, he could never take it back, whether it was real or not.

No one hurried him. The breeze moved over him, relieving the humidity there beneath the canopy. He noticed the lack of insects or small reptiles. Even birds were no longer flitting in the branches. There were no owls close. The safeguards woven had been strong. Adalasia had added her own powerful strands to keep Nera's spies away.

"The Bercovitz child would be centuries old if she were alive," Sandu said. "If she still lives, she would be an adult Carpathian woman."

"Raised how?" Riley asked. "Who would have raised her? These demons? What would she have turned out like? How could she possibly know right from wrong? She would be so confused."

Sandu kept his gaze on Adalasia. She stayed very quiet, her eyes on his. She knew he felt guilty; she just didn't understand why. She waited in that way of hers, reserving judgment, letting him figure out how best to tell them what he thought.

He could feel Dax's eyes on him. The man said nothing, either. Even the Old One was waiting, as if he, too, knew Sandu had information important to them.

"She might be confused at first, Riley," Sandu answered. "Carpathian female children have excellent memories. She also holds the light in her, as well as guarding the soul of a male Carpathian. Growing up in whatever environment she was forced into would have been difficult for her, but she would have adapted in order to survive. I believe she survived."

He hesitated again, and when no one spoke, he made the decision to confess. "When the hellhound dragged me through the portal during the battle and Adalasia was pulling at me to bring me back, I could feel the demons trying to surround me, to keep me there. There was unbearable heat and pain. I knew the poison was spreading through my body at a rapid rate. I could hear Adalasia and knew if I could get back, she would seal the portal. Another woman's voice suddenly called out to me in the ancient language. I heard her very distinctly. She said, *Muonìak te kaδa ŋamaŋ mayemet it.*"

"Which means?" Adalasia prompted.

"I command you to leave this place now." Sandu and Danutdaxton interpreted simultaneously.

Adalasia frowned. "If it was this girl—woman now—how would she have learned the Carpathian language? How could she possibly remember it after all those centuries? Do you think the demons speak it?"

Sandu shook his head. "No, I think she speaks this language with another who resides there. The one you guard against, Adalasia. I think the demon you hold back and refuse to allow loose on the world is a Carpathian male, an ancient who has not turned vampire but has gone beyond the point of no return. He is lost. She can communicate with him because she speaks to animals, and he is more beast than man. That is my theory." He had already told Adalasia of his belief that a demon was behind those gates, a demon who had once been a Carpathian hunter.

Again, there was a long silence. Sandu couldn't look at Dax. The women wouldn't condemn him for his actions, but another Carpathian male would. Should. He had left a female Carpathian woman alone in a terrible situation.

Danutdaxton sighed. "Sandu, there was nothing you could do to remove this woman from her fate. She is locked behind a closed portal we cannot open. I do not talk of the gates this Carpathian male lives behind. Any opening between our realm and the demons would cause untold damage on the world. The few demons who do escape cause enough destruction. She had an opportunity when the portal was open to leave, yet she did not. Perhaps this beast behind the gates is her lifemate."

Sandu didn't absolve himself so easily. He pressed Adalasia's palm into his thigh. "I did not get that impression. I know when I recited my oath in the Cave of Fire, he joined with me. He knew the sacred oath. It was clear to me that he still will call upon his oath in an effort to keep darkness at bay. If the Bercovitz child had been his lifemate, he would have recognized that she was."

Adalasia poured into his mind, a gentle loving warmth that filled the tears and rips still present from the ordeal he'd gone through. Once she was there, he didn't want her to leave. She had a way of making him feel whole when he'd been torn apart.

I couldn't find a way to save her—or him.

I looked into your memories, Sandu. I felt her as well. She pushed you from that place and made no effort to follow you. She didn't want to leave. Whatever is holding her there is a powerful force, and it is her choice.

It is my duty to make certain she is all right.

She felt all right, didn't she? When I searched your memories, I didn't feel pain in her. Did you? The male behind the gates was frightening, but she was calm and composed. Purposeful. You cannot take on the world, Sandu. You were close to death. She helped to save your life, and you have to allow her that victory.

Sandu considered what his lifemate was saying. Always, a male protected a female. In this instance, Adalasia and the unknown woman had protected him. He had identified with the beast behind the gate—maybe too much. He wanted a different outcome for him. A way to save him, not keep him there. He wanted the Bercovitz child to be that beast's lifemate, to have been the keeper of his soul. Sandu identified strongly with him, felt he was that feral beast, the demon he knew Adalasia feared.

I feared what I did not know, Sandu. I know you now. I know that beast protects you when you battle the undead. I welcome him because in the end, he will bring you home to me safe.

There was honesty between lifemates. He could hear the honesty in her voice. Feel it in his mind. She had seen him fight the undead. She had seen the demon rise.

Sandu, I love you. You have to feel the way I love you. All of you. Not just pieces of you. You are not divided. That feral beast and the charming, sweet man are one and the same. No person is just one-dimensional. You have many facets to you, and I love all of them. Well . . . your bossy side could tone it down.

That little teasing note stroked over him gently. Playfully. Her palm moved under his hand, fingers pressing deep into his thigh muscle, little points of flame.

"Perhaps you are right, Dax. Adalasia assures me that she searched my memories of the incident and as closely as she was able, inspected the woman's voice and manner. She doesn't believe she was in pain."

"Or under undue duress," Adalasia supplied. "She could have followed Sandu out of the portal, or even used it without aiding him, but she did neither."

Danutdaxton nodded. "I agree with Adalasia on this, Sandu. The Old One does as well, and he rarely bothers to give his opinion. You have to let this go and leave her to her fate."

"I do feel as if I am obligated to inform her brother," Sandu said. "He has searched for news of her for centuries."

Dax sat back in his chair. "That is a difficult decision. It would be wrong to withhold that information, but on the other hand, you have no way of knowing for certain if that child exchanged for the parasites is the Bercovitz girl. It could be giving him false hope. And how would he get to her? He is an ancient and very dark, Sandu. He stays alone for long periods of time. Several of the hunters watch him, and he has the ability to disappear almost before their eyes. He is very skilled in battle. We have no way of knowing what will push him over the edge."

Adalasia sighed. "There are always two paths, aren't there? Both dangerous. I keep thinking we are going to be shown a clear way, but we never are. How terrible not to tell this poor man who has searched for his only sister that she may still live."

"Is she really alive, though?" Riley asked. "In that realm, could she still live?"

"She was alive," Sandu said. "Absolutely she was alive. So was the male Carpathian."

"You are certain he was a Carpathian?" Dax asked.

Sandu nodded slowly. "I would like to say otherwise, but he knew the ancient oath sworn to our people and our lifemates. He recited the oath with me when I needed it most. He even merged his voice with mine to chant. He spoke the ancient tongue. His voice was demonic, like that of a beast at times, but there was no doubt that he was Carpathian." He hesitated and then told the truth. "I felt a brotherhood with him, just as I do for those in the monastery."

"That would be natural," Dax said. "How could you not feel a comradery for a brother after centuries in the monastery chanting those very vows when you were at your lowest point? He must use them as well."

"It grates on me that I had to leave both of them there," Sandu said.

"When you say Adalasia guards these gates this Carpathian demon is behind, what do you mean?" Dax asked.

Sandu glanced at his lifemate. They had come for Danutdaxton's advice, but they hadn't explained the situation fully to him.

You tell him as much as you wish, ewal emninumam. Sandu accepted that this was a journey for the two of them, not just him.

Adalasia didn't hesitate. She told Dax and Riley about her childhood of preparation to fight demons. About her mother passing on Sandu's soul as had her mother before her. About the history of her family and the duty given to them—guarding the eastern gate that held back a demon that could not be set upon the world. Lilith wished to command this demon, and she had armies ready to slip into their realm when she found a portal. The eastern gate was in jeopardy, and Sandu and Adalasia had to find their way to the original source and make the necessary repairs to ensure the demon couldn't escape.

"I had no idea what I was guarding," Adalasia finished. "This has been a huge revelation. A tragedy, really. I hate that he's a Carpathian and can't be saved. I really hate that my family has had a hand in holding him behind that gate for centuries. Maybe if the Carpathian people had known about him, they could have found a way to save him."

Danutdaxton shook his head. "They would have had no choice but to hunt and destroy him. He sounds as if he is very powerful. He would have taken many of our best hunters with him before he died. And that's if he could have been killed. The Old One has taught me many things, Adalasia, and one of the most important is that events unfold as they are meant to. These pieces were put in place long before you were born. You are playing a small part in the drama that is his life, but it has already been unfolding for centuries."

Sandu could see that what Danutdaxton had said gave Adalasia some comfort. He stroked his thumb over the back of her hand.

"You do not know where exactly to go," Dax said.

Sandu shook his head. "My memories are completely gone. I do not remember my family. I now have glimpses of my sister, Liona, but only brief, a very few images. I do not remember much of her. Her laughter. She shared that with me after I lost emotion. I do remember that about her."

"Luiz De La Cruz gave you blood many times, Sandu," Dax said. "He might not be an obvious choice, but he has the De La Cruz warriors in him going back centuries. Long before either of us, I would imagine. If he would answer your call, he might be the one to ask."

"He already has given so much of himself when he prefers to be alone," Sandu said, uncomfortable with the idea.

"Perhaps it is not best for him to be alone all the time," Riley said. "He is so dark that when he comes near, I have a difficult time being close to him. Dax has to stay in my mind."

Is that the same with you, Adalasia? Sandu was alarmed. If Luiz was that close to becoming the undead and he was tied to Adalasia through their blood bond, he could easily find and kill her once he turned.

She gave a slight shake of her head. *There is a difference. I would have a difficult time explaining it to Riley, but you are an ancient. The De La Cruz line holds a troubling dark shadow. They are aware of it and fight to hold honor more than others from the time they are very young. Some have the shadowing more than others. I could see it in the various warriors in Luiz. The more we were together, the more I saw the shadowing. It isn't the undead. It isn't a demon. It is more cunning. An animal, a predator, but still darkness that can overtake them.*

"I will think on what you have said, Danutdaxton. Thank you both for your hospitality," Sandu said formally.

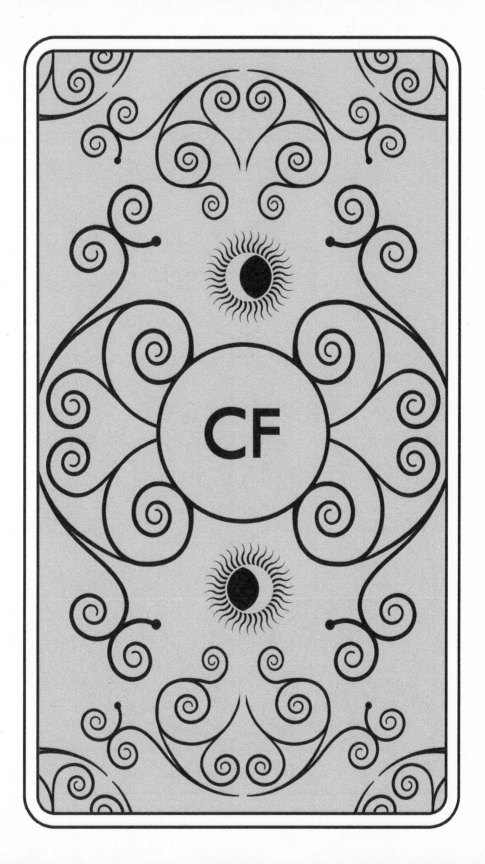

Adalasia put out the call to Luiz De La Cruz two risings later, when the guardians, Sandu and she were a great distance from Danutdaxton's territory. Sandu didn't want Dax to feel as if he might have to help defend them should anything go wrong. They were on the very edge of the rain forest, the Amazon River flowing fast in a wide, powerful stream on one side, with the large kapok trees rising on the other.

They had gone to ground in the rich soil, closer to one another than normal, but they had no real place to hide from enemies. This was not an area any of them were familiar with, so they were extremely wary. They rose the moment the sun set and hunted for blood. It was only luck that led them to some fishermen still dragging their catch into their boats before returning home for the evening.

Sandu thought it wise to stay on the edge of the forest, where they could utilize the animals and alarm systems and yet be close to the river, where there was a ready source of blood if any of them were wounded. The guardians patrolled the immediate area and then expanded their search for any hidden threats to Adalasia while Sandu and Adalasia sealed the air, earth and water against any spies Nera might send.

"Why are the guardians so nervous?" Adalasia asked.

"There were signs of the undead passing through this way not too long ago," Sandu answered. "And Luiz De La Cruz makes even ancients nervous."

Adalasia tapped her fingers against her thigh as she walked along the very narrow animal trail winding in and out of the trees. Luiz made her nervous, but now she felt guilty for feeling that way. He had healed Sandu when he didn't have to. He'd given him blood over and over. He'd gone into the shadow realm with her to guide her, and when she asked him to trust her and not be seen, he had done so without ego, staying in her mind as a shadow rather than walking beside her in the open. That had allowed them to carry out their plan and use his strength to pull Sandu out of the realm and back into the land of the living.

She had been in Luiz's mind more than the ancients had. He hadn't given them access, although he had taken their blood when he had been healing Sandu. Adalasia thought about how many times Luiz had gone selflessly into Sandu's torn and pain-wracked body. How many times he had fearlessly gone after the bacteria and parasites that were doing their best to destroy Sandu and certainly would have tried to kill Luiz, as well.

Luiz might have the De La Cruz shadowing in him very strongly, but he was an honorable Carpathian, and he was equally tough and disciplined. Whatever he had shown to the De La Cruz family that had prompted them to save his life in the first place and then after watching him to make certain they hadn't made a mistake, taking him to the sacred cave of warriors to actually become a De La Cruz, had to have been all about honor, duty and loyalty. That's what the De La Cruz code seemed to be, as far as Adalasia could tell.

"You are walking in circles, *Sivamet*," Sandu pointed out, amusement in his voice.

"I'm thinking," she said. She lifted her lashes to look at him. He was floating in the air in front of her, backpedaling. Showing off, as far as she was concerned, and smirking a little.

"What are you thinking about? We are alone," he said. "The guardians have left us for the time being, and if you have great need of your lifemate . . ." He trailed off, his smirk turning into a smile that held a carnal lust that threatened to keep her knees from working.

She tried a glare. "I've already called to Luiz. Had you been a little faster in your suggestions, we might have had time to actually have some fun this evening."

His eyebrow shot up. "Fun? Is that what you call what is between us? *Fun?*" His gaze dropped to her simple cotton top.

Breathable fabric. Covered everything. Light color to prevent attracting insects and heat. No fragrance. Perfect for being in the rain forest. Suddenly, the material was too tight over the swell of her breasts. Her breasts felt heavy and achy. Her nipples pushed against her bra. Adalasia had the mad desire to take her top off and drag his head to her breasts.

"Stop it, Sandu. We could have company any minute."

"You do not think we can have fun?" he persisted, his voice a dark sin. Sheer temptation.

Adalasia was hot and slick immediately. The little boy shorts with the wicking panel weren't going to be of much use in this situation. He looked so gorgeous and definitely sexy. She put one hand up as a defense.

"Stop right now, you have to stop."

He looked like a feral jungle cat ready to leap on his prey and devour her. "I am not doing anything at all, *ewal emninumam*, just talking to you. Making certain you know how much I appreciate those little garments you like to wear beneath your clothing. I think about taking them off of you often."

It wasn't the words so much as the way he said them, the velvety voice he used, that robbed her of her ability to breathe. Images were crowding in her head. Adalasia standing in just her lacy pale blue bra and matching boy shorts and a pair of boots, surrounded by the trees. Sandu was fully clothed, circling her in the way of a great hunting cat, his glowing eyes feral as he took in every curve.

"Sandu, you have to stop," she whispered to him, a little plea, when she wasn't certain she wanted him to stop. She loved it when he was so playful. She rarely saw this side of him.

In her mind, Sandu circled her a second time and halted in front of her. Leaning close to her, he put his lips against her ear. "Am I the one with these ideas, or is it you?" At the same time, he trailed one hand from her collarbone over the curve of her breast.

She honestly didn't know whose images were in their minds, but she felt his hand on her. Felt his breath in her ear. The air was on her skin, and when she looked down, her bra was in his free hand, and he was shoving it in his pocket. The sight of him doing that, just taking her underwear and casually pushing it inside his clothing, made her so hot, it was ridiculous, but she didn't care. Evidently, he didn't, either.

Sandu reached for her, caught her up in his arms and lifted her. "Wrap your legs around me, Adalasia. I have a need to feel my lifemate surrounding me. Hot and tight the way you do."

She had a need of feeling him filling her, joining them together, and she obeyed him, grateful for the Carpathian ability to rid their bodies of clothes. She settled over his cock, gasping as his wide girth invaded, pushing through her slick folds, and then she was seeing stars, little explosions behind her eyes as he moved in her.

He was strong, and his hips surged over and over. She ground down, riding him while the streaks of fire burst through her veins. Her sheath coiled tighter and tighter around his heavy cock like a silken fist.

"I can't hold back, Sandu," she whispered.

"You do not have to, *Sivamet*." His voice was hoarse. "Fly with me."

She let go, soaring, the waves crashing through her, so formidable, her sheath clamping down on his cock like a vise, feeling the wonder of them together, hot and powerful, exquisite beyond belief. Perfect.

Adalasia rested her head on his shoulder, her arms around him, her heart beating the same rhythm as his. *"Tet vigyázam,"* she whispered, deliberately in the ancient language.

"I love you, too, Adalasia," he whispered back. He lowered her legs to the forest floor with the gentleness only he gave her, cleaning and clothing both of them.

The rain forest suddenly became still, as if for a moment there was a pause in the never-ending life cycle. Adalasia knew it was deliberate, a heralding of Luiz's coming. He moved silently through the trees, using the arboreal highway, his Jaguar form powerful and majestic, a predator at ease in the environment. He leapt from branch to branch, making his way down the trees until he landed smoothly on the forest floor in front of the couple, shifting and clothing himself as he did so.

"Adalasia. Sandu. You called for me."

There was no censure in his voice. No emotion whatsoever. Adalasia

felt Sandu merge tighter with her. The guardians did as well, although
they were mere shadows in the small crevices of her mind. They were
ancients, and yet they didn't seem to realize that if Luiz inspected her
mind, he would know they were there.

"I'm sorry to once again ask for your help," Adalasia said. "We are
searching for memories that have been lost to us. It is vital we recover
them, and it has been suggested that it's possible you would be able, if
you were willing, to look to those warriors in your past for answers for
us. I have no idea what that would entail, so I don't honestly know what
I'm asking of you. If it is too much, Luiz, please say so."

Luiz had startling green eyes that darkened to a forest green or light-
ened to a jade, depending on his mood. Right at that moment as he
studied them, he had jade eyes that seemed to glow like those of a cat.

"If we are to speak of such things, we must go somewhere safe, not
out in the open."

He turned his back on them, something Adalasia could tell not only
Sandu found shocking, but also her guardians. Ancients didn't casually
turn their backs on one another. Luiz took several steps and then shifted
again, settling into the form of a jaguar with ease, taking to the trees.

Are you comfortable in this form? Sandu asked.

Adalasia hadn't tried the form of a cat often, but she had worked
hard on shape-shifting. She quickly shifted, became a female jaguar and
leapt for the lower branches of a tree to pull herself up. *I will be once I have
moved in it a bit.*

Sandu shifted and stayed close behind her. He didn't hold the form
for her, but he did stay in her mind. He needn't have worried. She thought
it was a little silly. Her mind was a bit crowded with the four guardians
and Sandu there.

*Luiz is helping us. Don't get him upset by your mistrust. He saved your
life many times over,* she reminded him.

I am aware, Sandu replied, but he didn't back off.

She noticed that right away. None of the guardians did, either.
Clearly, they regarded Luiz as very dangerous. She knew he was. It wasn't
that she underestimated him in any way. She was careful, but she also felt

that every ancient needed encouragement. The more they bonded with others, the more of a chance they had to share emotions and hold back that moment when they would have to make a choice to seek the dawn or give up their soul. She didn't want that for any of these men.

The powerful male jaguar leading the way had a very broad head and a massive, dense, muscular body. His fur was thick, a golden color with black rosettes. The green eyes were ringed with amber, and there were flecks of gold in the green, but when the male swung his head to check on her, Adalasia could clearly still see mostly green in the jaguar's eyes.

She found it odd that the forest creatures didn't run from him as they might normally from a jaguar. The big cats were predators and hunted for food, yet with Luiz, the birds and even monkeys and baboons didn't react negatively with him around. He was a total predator, with that darkness strong in him, yet the animals seemed to accept him.

The jaguar took them into a particularly dark grove of kapok trees with very wide, thick trunks and heavy branches high off the forest floor. Fungi appeared to grow up the trunks, becoming larger and much more circular, a dull whitish gray that changed color as they traveled deeper into the grove of trees, blending so it was difficult to notice at first.

Thick, sturdy branches reached outward, some curving upward gently, while others simply stretched straight out, and others went skyward and flowed out, providing the canopy from above. Vines and heavy foliage covered the trees, hiding the trunks and strange fungi crawling up the trunks.

Adalasia followed Luiz up a tree, going from branch to branch until the large jaguar switched to one of the rounded fungi pads. She hesitated before she delicately put her paw on the semicircle. Expecting it to be spongy, she found it was solid, giving her confidence to follow, but both she and the cat were curious.

Sandu, this is hard, like wood, not mushroom or fungus. What is it?

I suspect we are about to reach one of Luiz's houses hidden in the trees. This is something I have not seen in many long centuries, although I had heard they could be constructed. We tend to prefer caves so we can safeguard and still have soil to rest in. He is Jaguar and most likely prefers to be high in the trees.

How would he go to ground?

Beneath the tree, perhaps in the root system. I am just guessing, but it would make sense.

The circular pads were wide, like a small verandah, and the male jaguar led the other two upward, going from one to the next until they were at the entrance to a house. The structure was cleverly hidden between two very large trunks and supported on thick branches. She could see that the house was much larger than she expected it to be and very open in design. She could look right inside, as there was no real door to speak of, but more of a fringe of hanging vines covering the entrance.

The male jaguar went through the vines and shifted immediately, stepping back politely to allow Adalasia to enter. This was always the moment she dreaded most. She practiced and practiced, but although she could shift very fast, she couldn't always clothe herself as quickly as she needed to.

Sandu. She detested to admit she wasn't as confident as she had been appearing. *I might need you to help with clothing.*

I appreciate that you would ask me, päläfertiilam. I have found that my new emotions have made it difficult for me to have men looking at you, even when I know they cannot feel as I do. Luiz has been a good friend to us, and I have not been able to treat him as openly as you have, in the event he should succumb to the darkness in him, but I would not want to insult him further by acting unseemly. Thank you.

That was Sandu. Instead of making her feel as if she was inadequate, he made her feel as if she had done him some great service. How could she not love him more with each passing night they spent together? The more she learned of him, the more she respected and admired him.

She shifted and instantly she was dressed. Sandu was meticulous in his memory. He didn't forget the slightest thing, not even the socks she liked to wear. He materialized with her, his body slightly between her and Luiz as he looked around the open room.

There were no real walls, only a low half wall of wood. The floors were polished hardwood, while overhead, the ceilings were high. Branches curved in and out of the open design, high up as part of the structure. A jaguar would have access to the arboreal highway as well as be able to make a quick escape. There were benches woven of sturdy vines set against screens that divided a section of housing that could have been a bed.

Adalasia was surprised to see that Luiz would have a bed in the treehouse, but he had been human for much of his time. Jaguar men lived mostly as humans. There were chairs, also made of vines, as well as a table, indicating that Luiz stayed there occasionally in human form. It was really a beautiful structure and very practical in that, without walls, a breeze could easily blow through the rooms to clear out the heat and humidity.

Adalasia smiled at Luiz. "This is very unique and lovely, Luiz. Thank you for having us." She took the bench seat he indicated. It was surprisingly comfortable.

Sandu stepped close to Luiz and clasped his forearms, greeting him in the way of warriors. *"En jutta félet és ekämet,"* Sandu murmured.

Luiz gripped his forearms with strength. *"Arwa-arvo pile sívadet."*

What did you say to each other?

I told him, "I greet a friend and brother," Sandu said. *And he replied, "May honor light your heart."*

I like that, Adalasia said. *Thank you for calling him brother.*

Sandu sat beside her on the bench made of vines, and Luiz took the chair across from them.

"I didn't get a chance to thank you for aiding me, Luiz. You healed my body and gave me blood and then guided Adalasia into the shadow realm. Without you, we wouldn't have made our way back. I owe you a great debt."

Luiz waved his hand, the gesture dismissive. "I am your brother. Adalasia is a woman, a treasure we cannot afford to lose. Every Carpathian male should be protecting her and you, as her lifemate. If we wish to save our species, we need every woman."

Adalasia rolled her eyes. Luiz meant what he said, but on the other hand, she had shared his mind enough times that she knew he hadn't aided her entirely because he thought she should provide countless babies for the Carpathian males.

"That is true," Sandu agreed. "Adalasia is a seer in the sense that she reads tarot cards. Were you aware of that?"

Luiz's eyes went to that shade of jade that held amber. His cat was looking at her as well as the Carpathian. She felt the impact of both.

"I do know what tarot cards are, but don't know why they would be important."

"She might be able to tell you where in this big world your lifemate exists. When you were born a De La Cruz, at that time, your lifemate was also born into the world. Or at least, your soul was given into the keeping of another. She may not have been born at that precise moment, but she holds the other half of your soul. It isn't easy to find her. It is possible to miss her, even knowing she is born into the same century."

Adalasia twisted her fingers together. Sandu's revelation to Luiz was unexpected. She hadn't offered the man a reading because he was so powerful, and she didn't know if the cards would cooperate, not when he held so much darkness in him. She had felt guilty about it, but then Luiz just disappeared before she had made up her mind or she could ask Sandu's advice.

"That is not why you called me back."

"No, I had to ask you what you may know of my family," Sandu conceded. "But Adalasia's tarot cards are extraordinary. They have great history behind them and have endured for centuries. The blood of my family has kept them intact. We would like to repay you in some small way for your kindness to us."

"While bringing you back to the house, I had time to examine my memories. I had to delve deep to find what you are seeking, Sandu. You do come from an old and very respected line. There were trackers, families that were essentially nomads, those covering wide territories, pursuing vampires who would escape or deliberately leave the countries Vlad had assigned hunters to. Your father, Domizio, was one such nomad, Sandu, an exceptional tracker. He preferred the wildest country, far from civilization and people. He was a trailblazer. He fought on his own against the undead and taught you the skills necessary to do the same from a very early age. It was said he taught his daughter, Liona, as well."

Luiz fell silent again, as if going inside his head to acquire more information. Adalasia felt true excitement for the first time. She glanced at Sandu. *I think this is it, honey. I think he really knows something.*

I'm almost afraid to hope. Did you notice he hasn't said he would allow you to give him a reading? He is afraid to hope, even though he knows he must have a lifemate holding the other half of his soul.

Adalasia had noticed. How could she not? The guardians had taken their time to make up their minds to know. She knew Luiz was doing the same thing. He was giving Sandu what information he could before deciding if he would ask Adalasia to read the cards. In any case, not everyone believed in the reading of tarot cards. They thought the cards were a parlor trick or, worse, some kind of device from the devil. Luiz had been in the human world before he was Carpathian. He might have his own opinions of tarot cards.

"Domizio and Madolina traveled mostly through what would now be Italy for several years. Eventually, Domizio decided to utilize three households, mainly because he liked having his family close to him at all times. There appeared to be some problem, a drawing of the undead toward the eastern end of the country."

"Do you know where they were after I left the family? Where Liona was?"

Adalasia slipped her hand into Sandu's. He had always been calm and very relaxed, as if it didn't matter one way or the other if they found the answers to his past. She knew differently now. He cared what happened to his sister and parents. He didn't like that he had no memories of them.

Again, Luiz was silent for a time. A small breeze fluttered through the open walls, touching Adalasia's face. She couldn't help but look at the De La Cruz brother. He was incredibly charismatic in a very rugged, intense way. There were lines cut deep in his face. His eyes were striking set against his darker skin. He looked remote. More than that. Set apart.

She thought Sandu looked that way. The guardians did. But Luiz took the look to another level altogether. Her heart went out to him.

As if he knew what she was thinking, his gaze shifted and suddenly settled on her face. The stare was piercing. Focused. That of a jungle cat. It should have been uncomfortable, because there was no doubt that Luiz De La Cruz was pure predator, but she felt safe around him. Even with the heavy burden he carried of that terrible shadowing of darkness, he had incredible honor, an iron will.

This was not a man who would succumb easily to the emptiness of centuries of warriors he now carried, as if he'd lived all those lifetimes. He had spent his life standing for women and children against others in his species determined to make them prey. He hadn't changed his fundamental character. Instead, he'd strengthened those traits when he became a De La Cruz. He had taken on their code of honor, adding it to his own.

"Domizio became very secretive after you left, Sandu. He never spoke of you to other hunters other than to talk of your past. He didn't tell anyone where you went or why. There was trouble, a rising of power along the eastern section of the northern Alps. The Dolomites."

Adalasia's heart skipped a beat. There was always the direction of east given to them, but no one had ever included the northern Alps. Or specifically named a mountain range. The eastern section now made sense. They not only had a direction but a mountain range. They were slowly narrowing it down. She hoped Luiz could add just a little bit more.

"Domizio mentioned not only that there was vampire activity in the area, but that he believed there was some kind of portal between this realm and the underworld. He was very uneasy when he spoke of it and mentioned several times to be wary of insects and reptiles. He said owls were used as well. When pressed, he admitted he had no proof. The next time a De La Cruz went through the area, Domizio and Madolina had moved on to the next world, and Liona was missing."

Sandu leaned toward Luiz. "Do you recall where that last location was in the mountains?"

Luiz nodded. "I can give you the coordinates of the cave system." He pushed the images into both Sandu's and Adalasia's minds. He did so casually, as if he weren't giving them a gift beyond compare.

"Thank you, Luiz," Adalasia said. "This is amazing information."

"We owe you a huge debt," Sandu acknowledged. "Have you thought about allowing Adalasia to give you a reading?"

Luiz nodded his head, his gaze once more fixed on Adalasia. Wholly focused. "Yes, I think it would be a good thing, Adalasia, if you believe it is. Do you?"

Her belly knotted. The only reason her heart remained steady was because she was firmly anchored in Sandu and following the rhythm of his. Did she? Why had she hesitated before? The cards had a life of their own, but she believed Luiz was a good and honorable man. If she believed that, she trusted that the cards would see past the shadowing in him and they wouldn't pass a harsh judgment on him.

"I think it would be a good thing, Luiz. The cards hold a great power, and they will react with your power. Follow your instincts. I'll hand them to you, and you shuffle and divide them into three stacks."

She was disciplined, and she believed in herself and her abilities with the cards. She hadn't read Luiz wrong. She slid her hand under her shirt and found the pouch, withdrawing it and opening it to shake the cards into her waiting hands. Luiz had moved a small table made from vines next to the bench and then pulled his chair close. Adalasia reached over the table to hand him the cards.

Before the deck of tarot cards touched his fingers, there was an explosion of lights, of colors, all rain forest greens and silvers. Patterns of the jaguar. Jagged bolts of lightning like violent spears shooting from the cards as if they attempted to pierce Luiz's skin. He didn't flinch or pull back, but calmly took the deck from her, ignoring the wild display of power that only heightened as his strong fingers settled around the cards.

Shadows bounced through the room, playing on the vines hanging from the ceiling overhead. Thunder crashed, and hideous growls merged with snarls to add to the chaos as Luiz calmly shuffled the cards, ignoring the wild display and the sparks flying. Adalasia realized the more he shuffled, the more the deck calmed, became accepting of him, almost as if by feeling him, the cards began to know his true character. Eventually, the display faded away and all noise ceased. She let out the air in her lungs she hadn't realized she'd been holding.

Luiz divided the cards and laid the three stacks in front of her.

"Choose one of the stacks and set the other two aside. Pull three cards from your chosen stack and set the others aside."

Luiz followed her instructions. His gaze flicked to hers. She could see he wanted to question her. Three cards when there were so many. How could she possibly tell him where his lifemate was with three cards? She always went with her intuition. If there was a strong inclination to do a layout with three cards, that was what she went with. She indicated where to place each card and then had him turn them over.

There was his lifemate, and once again, she let her breath out. He needed patience, which she knew he had in abundance. She tapped the card and allowed the pads of her fingers to linger on it while she pressed her palm over her heart and the goddess card, asking for help in locating his lifemate. The cards indicated a short journey for him. She was some-where in his vicinity. Somewhere close to him.

Adalasia looked at Sandu as she realized exactly where Luiz's life-mate was. *I thought when a male Carpathian is born and his soul is split in half, a female child is born right then with his other half.*

Not always. The female can be born, as you were, century after century. Or she can be born a few years later. The soul is waiting for her to keep. The right female has to be matched to the male. There can be no mistakes. It is for eternity.

That makes it harder because the male has to wait longer.

Sometimes, yes. That is why we are born with the ritual binding words.

Adalasia wasn't certain she agreed with the ritual binding words, but she knew she still thought like a human woman, not a Carpathian one.

"You know where my lifemate is." Luiz made it a statement.

Adalasia nodded. "I believe I am correct, Luiz, but I can make mis-takes." She never had. Not once, but she didn't want there to be trouble.

"Where is she?"

She pressed her lips together and cast another quick look at Sandu.

They owed this man so much. He nodded. She took a deep breath. "Riley is pregnant, Luiz. I don't know how far along she is because she didn't say. I know they're hiding the pregnancy as best they can."

"Most Carpathian couples do hide pregnancies now," Sandu said. "It is so much safer."

Luiz's green eyes moved over her face and then over Sandu's. "I can feel your reluctance to tell me, Adalasia. You think Danutdaxton will object to any interference on my part."

She nodded. It was useless to deny it.

"He would never know if I reached out to the infant to confirm."

"The Old One might," Sandu cautioned. "They lost an earlier pregnancy."

Luiz was silent for a moment, his eyes moving over Adalasia. She felt his sorrow, even though she knew he didn't feel it. "My lifemate tried to come into the world once already. The Old One would not know, nor would I care so much. He holds great power, but not in the same way and nowhere near what he would need to discover me should I choose to touch this child to confirm. If she is my lifemate, she is mine to protect."

Adalasia knew he would do so. How could he not? "I don't know why they wouldn't want you to help keep her safe." She turned to Sandu. "Why do Carpathian males object to that?"

Luiz answered. "I carry darkness in me, Adalasia. You're very aware of it. So is Dax. It would be natural for him to worry. There is no need for you to be anxious. I will check out the information you've given me and proceed accordingly." He inclined his head. "Thank you. There is no debt between us."

He stood, shifting as he did so, and just like that, he was gone.

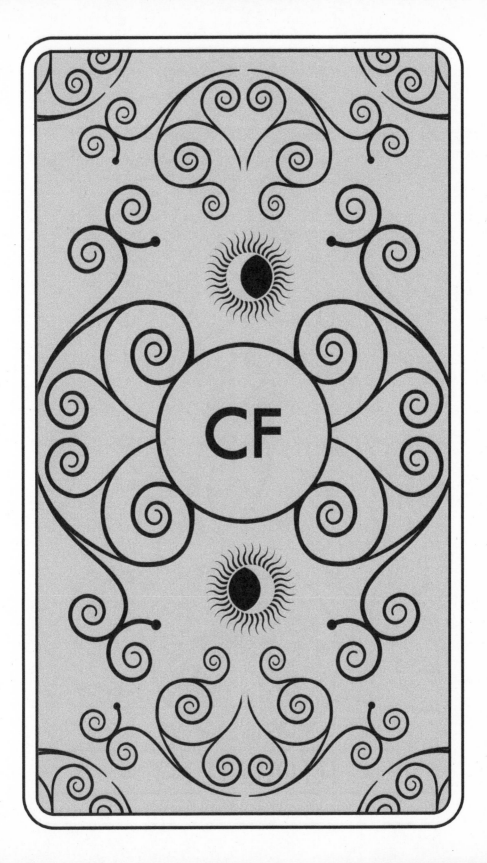

JUDGMENT

The Dolomite Mountains were certainly a different place to travel in now, considering how wild the area had been with so few human inhabitants in comparison to the many who traveled there now. Skiing, hiking, cycling, all of it was advertised to bring in tourists in all seasons to share the beauty of the mountains.

Sandu and Adalasia with the four guardians flew into one of the airports close to Trentino and then rented a private car to drive to Val di Non, where they hoped to start their journey into the mountains. They were feeling their way. Everything was very different, and with so many hotels and people, they had to be very careful to blend in.

The brotherhood of the monastery had put out a call to Tiberiu Bercovitz to meet them in Val di Non if possible. Sandu had thought long and hard before he sent the invitation to the Carpathian, but he knew, had any of his brethren heard possible news of Liona and not told him, he would have challenged them to a fight to the death. Tiberiu deserved to hear what they had learned, and it was up to him whether or not he believed them, or thought it could be his little sister, long lost to the Carpathians.

If Bercovitz wasn't in Val di Non, they wouldn't wait for him. Anxiety was beginning to press on Adalasia. She wasn't saying anything. She hadn't once complained, but he knew she was concerned that somehow she would fail in her responsibility to hold the gate closed. Sandu still was uncertain what they were supposed to do when they reached their destination. He didn't think Adalasia knew either, which added to her anxiety.

Even softening their images, they still drew attention when they reached the farmhouse where they had booked reservations and had hoped to meet up with Tiberiu. The farmhouse had only a few rooms. They managed to rent them all, including one for Tiberiu. They had explained he might not make it, but they would pay for the room just in case. Adalasia was the only woman, and Aria—running the bed-and-breakfast with her husband, Amato Sartori—naturally gravitated toward her.

"Mrs. Berdardi, how lovely to meet you, dear." She looked at the men traveling with her. "You have quite the escort."

"My husband, Sandu, and his brothers, Nicu, Siv, Benedek and Petru. Please call me Adalasia."

Although the brethren were never happy to be in civilized company for long, they could be very charming, and they abided Sandu's silent warning not to let Adalasia down. They gave their hostess their best smiles and even bowed slightly in their old-world way, causing her to blush.

"Please call me Aria. Amato is out with the animals at the moment." She frowned, started to say something and then stopped herself.

Instantly, Sandu felt a shadowing grip him. He glanced uneasily at his brethren. They were every bit as concerned as he was. The owner of the farm was deeply worried, and they were used to seeing, hearing and feeling that particular note. Evil had crept into this couple's world in some manner.

"I'll take you on a quick tour of your rooms and the kitchen area. The farm is, of course, open to you. That's half the fun," Aria added. "Seeing our way of life and the animals. I have breakfast ready early, but it stays in warmers until nine."

"We will be leaving very early," Adalasia said. "We won't be needing breakfast, Aria, so please don't go to the trouble. We tend to travel at night, when we don't run into as many people. Traffic is terrible in the cities during the day, so when we wanted to make good time, we started traveling at night and just got used to it."

Aria frowned, pausing at the door of one of the rooms. "That's not a good idea here, dear. I know you said you were going backpacking and hiking in the mountains. It can be wild country. There are unexplained things here. I don't want to scare you, but it just isn't a good idea to go at night."

Adalasia gestured toward the tall men crowding into the hallway. "I think there's enough of them to handle anything that comes along."

Aria crossed herself as she opened the door and indicated the room. "This is for you and your husband."

"It's lovely," Adalasia said. "I love the quilt. I've always wanted to learn to make them." She rushed over to the bed and ran her hand over the top of the quilt. It clearly was handmade—a work of art.

Aria looked pleased. "I learned from my grandmother."

Sandu took advantage of Adalasia and Aria conversing about quilts and learning to make them. He scanned the woman's memories, looking for anything that would indicate the undead had been near the farmhouse.

The undead or demons, Sandu, Adalasia reminded, never missing a beat as she carried on the conversation with Aria, following her out and down the hall to the brethren's rooms, where Aria was showing off other quilts. *If a portal is close and cracking open or the gate is thinning, demons might be slipping through.*

Sandu and his brothers thought first in terms of the undead. Adalasia thought first in terms of demons. They had to come together and think about both threats all the time. He shared the thought with the guardians as he scanned Aria's memories. There were small problems on the farm at first. Noxious smells unaccounted for. Two of the piglets horribly mutilated a few nights after the noxious smells. Two weeks later, the smells were back. Then it was a cow mutilated a few nights later.

This is no vampire at work. Benedek made his assessment.

No, it is not, Petru agreed.

Continue your conversation, Adalasia, and be cheerful and charismatic, like you can be. Ask her if she likes things like playing with tarot cards for fun. Keep it light. She is very spiritual, Sandu advised.

This isn't my first time with a client.

Adalasia sounded snippy, and Sandu heard the echo of the brethren's amusement at his expense.

"Aria, I love your beautiful silver." Adalasia drifted across the sitting room Aria had taken them to, a room to share in the evening if they desired, with others staying at the farm. There, silver crosses hung above the doors and windows. Adalasia deliberately touched one, tracing the silver lines. It would show Aria she was in no way associated or tainted with the undead if any question came up later.

"Thank you," Aria said.

"I noticed the crosses woven into some of the quilts. I have a quilt made from a friend living in Paris. She wove crosses into mine for me as well. I know it sounds silly, but I had nightmares quite often, and it made me feel protected. Francesca is very talented and spiritual. Her quilts give people comfort. She works with children at the hospital quite a bit to aid them in their recovery, and her special quilts seem to really help them if they have suffered trauma. I imagine yours would do so as well."

Adalasia sounded sincere because she was. She believed Aria had a special gift. Her work with the quilts was not only beautiful, but she wove something of herself into each of them. She wanted her children to be happy and at peace when they slept. She wanted those who stayed at her bed-and-breakfast to be the same. She also wanted them to be safe. There were protections in the quilts. Adalasia felt them each time she touched them. Aria wasn't aware she wove them in, but she had the ability, and she put them there each time she made a quilt.

Aria beamed at her. "I've never had anyone say such nice things to me."

"I assure you, they are very true." Adalasia sat down in one of the comfortable chairs and gave Aria her radiant smile. "Do you ever play around with tarot cards, just for fun? I indulge in reading the cards sometimes and would do so if it would amuse you."

Aria glanced out the window. The sun had already set, and a gray veil covered the landscape, so the trees in the distance looked as if they were cast in a silvery mist, and the valley in between the mountains and farm was a ghostly graveyard of rocks and blades of swaying grasses. She shivered and crossed herself.

"I've never thought, like some of my friends, that tarot cards were the devil's tongue."

Adalasia gasped. "Your friends think that? My family would be horrified. These cards were drawn by my great-grandmother or great-great-grandmother for her daughter to play with and kept in the family. They're an heirloom. We're taught practically from birth to recognize evil in the world and fight against it. I didn't mean to offend you, Aria. I love your home and the quilts so much. I wanted to give you something in return."

"You didn't offend me at all, Adalasia. I would love to get a reading," Aria said firmly and seated herself across from Adalasia.

Adalasia removed the cards deftly from where they were hidden and shook them out into her hands. "What questions would you like answered, if any?"

Sandu doubted if Adalasia realized she had sent a little *push* toward the woman to answer the question as honestly as possible. He had added a subtle weave in as well, needing more specific information from Aria than he was getting.

"There have been strange things taking place on the farm lately, things we can't explain," Aria answered without hesitation. "Amato, my husband, is watchful over our animals. They're our livelihood."

While Aria was preoccupied with her conversation with Adalasia, Sandu and the guardians once more probed her memories, going deeper, looking for more details of events that had taken place on the farm.

The noxious odor had returned a few weeks later after the cow had been mutilated, and this time, her husband had gone outside with his shotgun and dog to keep watch over his livestock. Aria had been terrified for him. She had lit candles and prayed, but Amato had forbidden her to leave the house. They had put strings of garlic at the doorways on the windows, although neither truly believed in the undead. They just weren't certain what they were dealing with.

Two nights later, the dog went crazy, growling and snarling, then charged out of the circle of light toward the barn where the farmer had taken his prize cows. The barn had been illuminated with lights, but then was suddenly plunged into darkness. The dog screamed horribly as Amato chased bravely after it. Aria had rushed to get a second shotgun, her heart pounding, tears running down her face, when she heard the shotgun discharged outside, not once but, after a brief silence, a second time.

When she flung the front door open, prepared to run out to aid him, Amato was there with the dog in his arms. The animal was covered in blood and panting in pain. There were long lacerations on his sides and belly. Amato had wrapped his shirt tightly around the animal in order to save him.

"Hurry, Aria, or we will lose him. He saved the animals tonight. You have to sew him up. There is no time to get him to the village."

When she saw the horrendous wounds, Aria didn't believe there was a chance to save the dog's life, but in the end, the animal had lived. The vet had arrived forty minutes into her meticulous stitching, bringing a blood supply and plenty of antibiotics. He didn't recognize what creature had done the damage to their heroic dog but, like the couple, was determined to save him.

Adalasia wove her spell through the room with her easy smile and contagious laughter. She had Aria shuffle the cards and divide them into three stacks. Aria chose a stack from the three and chose six cards to lay out in the manner Adalasia asked her to, turning the cards over carefully.

"They're so beautiful," Aria exclaimed. "It's strange, but I can almost feel them moving under my fingers." She stroked her finger over the surface of one of the cards, the smile fading from her face. "My burning question is whether these incidents that keep happening will stop before we lose everything and my husband gets hurt or killed."

Adalasia's smile faded as well. Her eyes met Sandu's. *She has great psychic talent, whether she is aware of it or not. She believes in the tarot cards. She is aware I have some talent, or at least that the cards can tell her something.* She glanced down at the cards and then back up at him. *I don't want to do this if I'm going to see her husband or her dead, Sandu.*

We are going to take care of the problem, ewal emninumam. Her husband will live and so will she. Have no fear in giving her a reading, Sandu assured her.

He felt Adalasia take a deep breath. She flashed her million-dollar smile and had Aria turn over the cards one by one. The smile widened.

"I see a very bright future for you and children coming very soon to fill your life with love and laughter." She looked up from the cards. "Grandchildren?"

Aria nodded. "My daughter and her husband have been considering purchasing the property next to ours. Her husband has wanted to get out of the city for a long time. He grew up here and has a good education, but he misses the farm life."

"I believe he will purchase the property quite soon, and those children will be running back and forth." There was joy in Adalasia's voice.

"And my husband?" Aria held her breath, looking over the cards.

"These incidents that are happening will stop immediately." This time Adalasia's voice hitched the tiniest bit, and her gaze flicked to Sandu and the four guardians before coming back to rest on the cards and Aria. She managed another smile, this one not quite so bright or real. "Your husband and you will live a long life together free from these types of attacks."

Aria clearly had more psychic gifts than they gave her credit for. She sat back in her chair and studied their faces, each of them, very carefully. She made the sign of the cross. "You came here to stop them, didn't you?" She whispered the revelation as if she feared to be overheard, even with the silver crosses at each of the entrances. "We are under attack, and you are here to stop them if it is at all possible." Tears filled her eyes. "It is very dangerous work that you do. And thankless."

"Aria."

Adalasia said her name gently when Sandu shifted toward the woman, prepared to erase her memories, if it was even possible. He didn't know. Some people with strong psychic abilities were difficult to control unless he took their blood.

"No, it's true. I never thought to meet one of you. My mother told me about you. Her mother told her. She said if there was ever trouble of this sort, the kind Amato and I have on our farm now, someone would come. There was a story told in our family handed down, really whispered. We don't tell others." She put a shaking hand to her hair. "I don't know that I even believed it to be true until the mutilations started, and then I prayed that it was."

Let her continue, Sandu advised.

Yes, Adalasia agreed. *She needs to talk to someone. She's been holding all of this in.*

That wasn't the same reason Sandu wanted Aria to continue, but he would take whatever he could get.

"The moment I saw the men, I knew. It was the way you carried yourselves. I just knew." Aria ended on a whisper. "I will never tell a living soul other than Amato, and he will never tell anyone. We have been sealed together and we remain as one. This thing you do for us and everyone else will only be told within the family as a folklore tale if you approve. If not, not one word will ever be spoken."

There was honesty in her voice, and Sandu believed her. He was in her mind, as were the guardians. They could see her truth there, as well. Unfortunately, her husband, Amato, wasn't present, but they could easily enough scan his mind as well.

Before Adalasia could answer, Sandu did. "There would have to be safeguards put in place if memories were left behind with you and your husband of our existence and our presence here. You would be tied to us until you pass to the next life, and we would know should you ever betray us. The penalty for betrayal is death."

He allowed her to see the flames flickering low in his black eyes even as he swept his arm around Adalasia to help reassure Aria he wasn't a demon or vampire. "I can erase your memory of us, and there is no need to tie you to us. All will be as it was, without knowledge we were here, and you will just know that the incidents stopped abruptly."

Aria's hand crept to the cross she wore around her neck on a chain of silver. "I usually talk these important decisions over with my husband."

"By all means, that would be a good idea. I believe he is coming in now. The dog is with him," Sandu added.

Adalasia frowned. "The dog is still in pain, Aria. He isn't healed completely."

Aria inclined her head. "We both know that, but Amato doesn't have any other way to warn him. We have to have our livestock in order to run the farm. He keeps Arturo, our dog, with him on a heavy leash. Arturo is a Bergamasco."

Adalasia's eyebrows went up. "That is a wonderful breed, but they don't accept strangers easily, Aria. How in the world did you get him to the point that you could make your home into a bed-and-breakfast?"

Sandu was listening to Amato. He wasn't alone as he entered the house with the dog. The last visitor had arrived. Tiberiu Bercovitz was with Amato, speaking softly with him, well aware that Sandu, Adalasia and the other ancients were in the sitting room with Amato's wife. The dog was aware, as well, and was straining toward the hallway.

Aria laughed at the memories of getting their dog to accept strangers. The breed was invaluable to their farm. It guarded every animal on it, from the smallest to the largest, as well as the children and Aria and Amato, but the dog didn't care for anyone else coming near them.

"We tried to socialize him very early because we wanted him to accept our friends coming, and we'd talked about turning the farm into a bed-and-breakfast. Still, it wasn't easy. He's a good dog and very intelligent. He does make up his own mind. There have been a couple of times he took a dislike to one of our guests and prowled outside their door, growling and carrying on until we had to lock him up so they'd be safe. Amato kept his eye on them, though."

"Probably for the best," Adalasia agreed. "If a dog doesn't like someone, after tolerating every other guest, there could be a good reason."

He probably will come in here and want to tear all of us apart, Sandu told her. *He'll sense the darkness in us.*

Or the demon, Benedek added.

The dog will like me, Nicu said, a smug feeling in all of their minds.

Petru gave some kind of derisive sound, which meant he might just take over the dog and keep it quiet if it decided it didn't like them and launched itself at them.

Adalasia's laughter bubbled up like a gift. *All of you are so ridiculous. Give off waves of friendliness. You're all capable of suppressing the darkness.*

For a dog? Benedek asked.

The others echoed his question, making Sandu want to laugh. Of course Adalasia would think it would be reasonable for five ancient warriors to suppress their true natures in order to keep one farmhouse dog happy.

Yes, Benedek, for a dog, so the very loyal dog will accept you and the couple will, too.

They are human, Petru pointed out. *There is no need for acceptance. We can just take the memories from them.*

Sandu knew Petru had just said the wrong thing to his lifemate. Adalasia gathered up the cards and put them in the pouch. Amato, Tiberiu and the dog, Arturo, came into the room together. Aria stood, turning to greet her husband. Sandu and the guardians stood as well. Adalasia produced a rolled-up magazine and bashed Petru over the back of his head, and just that fast, the magazine was gone.

I'm human, you Neanderthal.

You are Carpathian, Petru corrected. *And if you wish to actually make an impact when you strike one of us, you have to put Carpathian strength in your swing, as I have told you on more than one occasion, not your puny human strength.*

She let her breath out with an ominous hiss. *I didn't want to chance caving your obnoxious skull in. I can't wait until you claim your lifemate, Petru. I'm going to have a long talk with her before she ever accepts your claim.*

I am going to heal the dog, Nicu stated. *I cannot take that he is in pain. I am feeling it through Adalasia.*

Thank you, Nicu, she said, sending Petru another snippy look.

It was all Sandu could do to keep a straight face.

"Amato, these are our guests." Aria went to her husband and quickly made the introductions.

Amato wrapped his arm around her as he acknowledged the five ancients and Adalasia, his too-old eyes resting on each one. There were lines carved deep in his face. He hadn't gotten much sleep over the last few weeks; that much was clear. Like Aria, he seemed to know they were more than ordinary guests.

Arturo, the Bergamasco, was covered in what appeared to be long gray dreadlocks. His eyes were intelligent as they rested on the men and Adalasia. Sandu and the others did as Adalasia asked, keeping their energy low-key and peaceful so as not to agitate him. Nicu connected with him in the way he had with animals, further reassuring him.

Amato introduced Tiberiu to Aria, and then Sandu stepped forward to greet the ancient warrior.

"Arwa-arvo pile sívadet," he murmured as he clasped Tiberiu's forearms in the way of their warriors greeting each other. Facing each other full on made them vulnerable to attack.

May honor light your heart, he interpreted for Adalasia as he introduced her.

"En jutta félet és ekämet," Tiberiu answered him.

I greet a friend and brother. Sandu continued with the interpretations.

One by one, the four guardians also greeted Tiberiu in the same manner, each greeting a little different. All expressing the desire that they hold on to honor.

Aria waited politely until they were finished with their salutations before she put her hand in her husband's. "Amato and I have quite a bit to discuss. We'll leave you to it while we do."

Sandu nodded. "We will be going out in a short time, Aria, so it is best if your talk is a fast one."

She nodded and the two left them alone.

Tiberiu looked around the small room and inhaled with a short breath, as if he couldn't get enough air. "It is long since I have been inside a house such as this. There is unrest here. You summoned me, Sandu, and said the matter was urgent but that you could not wait for me if I was late. I am here."

There was no censure in his voice or curiosity. Neither. Tiberiu Bercovitz was an ancient who went his own way and tolerated few around him. He hunted the undead ruthlessly, with no thought of the damage to his body or soul. There was nothing to hold him to the world, no remaining family and no lifemate.

"We came across information that may pertain to the disappearance of your little sister." Sandu saw no reason to prolong suspense. Tiberiu wasn't the kind of Carpathian male to linger long in one place.

Tiberiu didn't move, remaining as still as a statue. Adalasia was cleansing her tarot cards a small distance from them, with Nicu and Benedek solidly between her body and Tiberiu. He would have noted their protective positions. Petru and Siv were on either side of the room but in good defensible positions, as well.

"Part of what we learned, I will admit, is speculation on our part. Adalasia's family wrote down their history in images, and one depicted a mage, clearly Xavier, exchanging a Carpathian female child of about ten for parasites. He did so with a female demon. The time period was the same as when your young sister disappeared. I was recently dragged through a portal into another realm, and a female thrust me back into this realm."

For the first time, Tiberiu moved, turning toward Adalasia, who stood by the window. "She needs to move away from there. She is a beacon." He didn't speak directly to her. Ancients often didn't address the lifemates of others.

Adalasia didn't wait to be asked or told to move. She did so immediately.

Tiberiu nodded and turned back to Sandu. "Continue, please."

"I was in the shadow realm, in the Cave of Fire, and was chanting my oath of honor. A voice joined me. A male voice. Then I heard a feminine voice. I tried to get her to come with me out of there, but she refused. Adamantly. The male was not her lifemate, but she still refused. She was definitely a Carpathian female. She knew the Carpathian language, I imagine through him."

Tiberiu was silent for a long while. Sandu was uncertain whether he believed, after centuries of not hearing a single whisper of information on his sister, whether or not he could process what Sandu told him. Or dared to believe. Or even cared anymore.

"You go to stop these demons from coming through the portal?"

"Yes."

"It is possible you will encounter this woman again?"

"Yes."

"Then I will accompany you."

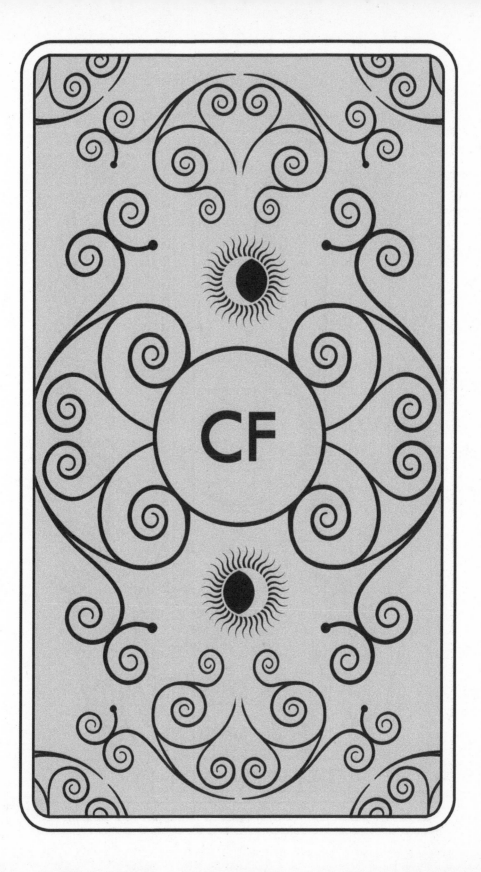

-XXI-

THE WORLD

The wind blew off the mountains in small gusts, as if it were gasping for breath. The smallest traces of sulfur could occasionally be caught and then would be torn away on the next draft. Adalasia felt the guardians and Sandu moving in tight formation around her. Tiberiu seemed to concentrate a certain amount of his attention toward her protection as well. She was much freer than they were to get a feeling for exactly what they were up against. This was no vampire. There was no lair for the undead concealed in the cave system hidden in the mountains.

Sandu's father had discovered something evil making its way into the world. There was something else Domizio had known happened here in these mountains. Something he sacrificed his daughter's future for—and she agreed to it. Adalasia knew Liona agreed because she felt Liona's empowerment every step of the way. She was no shrinking violet, cowed by her father or any other. She had her own power. She made her own choices. In what she had done, she had a choice; her father hadn't made it for her.

The higher they climbed into the shadowy mountains, where the trees disappeared and the boulders began, the more she began to experience flashes of images through the goddess card pressed so tight against her heart. An older woman weeping, her arms around a tall, gorgeous younger woman. The younger woman attempting to console her. It was obvious to Adalasia this was Madolina, Sandu's mother, with Liona in their last moments together. Adalasia wanted to weep with them. She was aware of Sandu sharing her mind and knew he experienced that same intimate vignette with her. That made it even more difficult.

All at once, she felt heat move through her body, like a bright hot sword. The rush of light. Her hair crackled with energy. "We're close to a portal. We have to look for an entrance to the cave. The coordinates given to you by Luiz have to be close to this, Sandu," she announced.

She stopped walking, uncaring what the others did. They had flown through the air until they were in the mountains, and then they set down to cast about for signs of demons or the undead. They studied all rock formations carefully.

Her hands went up, and she began to cast in the four directions, chanting softly to Mother Earth and calling for aid against the epitome of evil. In one of the pockets of her coat, she pulled out several keys that appeared to be forged of different colors on the light spectrum. She ran her fingers lightly over them and looked toward a tall dark gray boulder that was covered in dirt and fungus. It was strangely shaped, almost like a coffin. To the left of it was another boulder, a little squattier but in much the same shape, with a square top rather than the pointed one the right boulder had.

The boulders gave off a low sound, one harsh and abrasive to the ear. The note was much lower than most humans would be able to actually identify. She tuned her hearing to the exact sound, following the notes backward. They weren't just set into the boulders but were *inside* and continued downward. She could tell by the way the sound faded.

Adalasia stepped close to the boulders, and immediately, Sandu swept her back. The guardians inspected the boulders, moving around them carefully, looking at them from above and even from below the ground. She tried not to be impatient, but there was a sense of urgency now that they were close to the end of their journey. She knew this was where Sandu's family had been when Sandu had been sent away. She felt it.

It is true. It is starting to come back to me. This is familiar to me. I remember standing here with my father. It is the first time I have remembered him.

He shared the image with her. His father tall, just like Sandu, light hair, long and wild, held back with a leather cord tied at the nape of his neck. The two stood straight, side by side, looking at the exact same boulders she was looking at. The growth on the rock was a bit different, but she could still recognize the boulders. She knew why Sandu didn't cut his hair. He might wear modern clothes, but he was never going to change his hair, not when he looked so much like his father.

Your father looks like an amazing warrior, just like you, Sandu.

The boulders are not a trap, just have a warning system, Benedek reported.

Sandu answered Adalasia by brushing a caress along the walls of her mind, an intimate gesture between only the two of them. She held on to that as she did her own inspection of the boulders, trying to see what Domizio had when he first realized something was terribly wrong and the threat wasn't coming from the undead.

Her skin continued to prickle with that odd awareness, a white-hot intense heat that refused to allow her hair to stop crackling or settle. Her feet seemed to find a path of their own, gliding just above the ground rather than touching it, skimming the tufts of grass, moving around the boulders and then stopping between them.

She felt the curious pulsing of light from the keys in her palm. The strange and horrible growling notes emitting from the boulders changed slightly, just enough that the difference registered. This was even deeper, pounding now in her pulse, trying to align with her heartbeat. She automatically protected herself, matching her heartbeat with Sandu's.

Do you all hear that change in the beat? Definitely a trap now.

The keys were growing warmer in her hand. She looked down at them. The lights were growing brighter. One, a soft pastel purple, was the brightest. She chose that one, lifting it out in front of her and turning directly toward one of the boulders. The purple light spilled over the boulder, but nothing happened. She tried the other boulder. Same thing. She let her breath out, took a step back until she was directly between the two and the light illuminated both. The keyhole was not on either boulder but in the exact center between them.

Adalasia stepped forward to insert the key into the lock, but Sandu put a warning hand on her arm. "Wait. I remember this as well. This was not my father's safeguard, but he left it because it was so clever. Only he had the keys. How is it that you came by them?"

"These keys have been handed down mother to daughter for centuries," Adalasia said.

"Liona must have given them to your Tessina Ravasio long ago," Sandu said. "This is another memory that I recall. It is hazy and barely there, I warn all of you. Tiberiu, I am sharing on the path of the brotherhood. You have been to the monastery. You did not stay long, but you carry the oath on your back. You will be able to see," Sandu assured.

The vignette Sandu provided for them was shadowy and even grainy, like an older movie that hadn't been cleaned up, nearly impossible for the others to see. He couldn't quite get the imagery to unfold for them.

You are trying too hard to remember, my love, Adalasia whispered on their own path. *Let it come to you. It's almost there. Just breathe. It will come.*

He had to have faith in himself. His father had sent him away from his family without an anchor for a reason. He had to have faith that now that they had found their way, it would come back to him and would make sense.

Sandu kept the connection between them not only mental but physical, his fingers loosely shackling her wrist. She felt him take a deep breath and exhale. The images in his mind cleared.

There was Domizio standing beside Sandu just outside the boulders, both of them looking at another man who stood between them. The man was definitely Carpathian. His back was to them, but his shoulders were wide, his back strong, and his hair was unmistakable. He had very blond hair, streaked with silver, long, to his waist.

The stranger turned and Adalasia tried not to react. None of the Carpathian males reacted. Not a single one. He was the most daunting, scary-looking man she'd ever seen. His facial features were cut from pure stone. Pure beauty, hard lines. At the same time, there was something cunning, like a beast, in every one of those lines carved deep. His mouth held an edge of cruelty, but it was his eyes that seemed to pierce right through time, through centuries, to see them. He had strange blue eyes, but so light they appeared silvery. When he turned his head just slightly, the color deepened so it appeared as if hot blue flames burned in his eyes, just the way the red flames burned in Sandu's.

"Do you recognize him?" Tiberiu asked.

Sandu's breath hissed out of him in a slow exhale. "Yes. He came to us on more than one occasion. Many occasions. He saved our father's life numerous times and hunted with him. He was . . . extraordinary. He also carried darkness in him. A demon that grew with each battle. He was the first ancient I ever encountered that had the oath carved into his back. He forced my father to put it there, over and over, until it stayed."

"Who was he?" Benedek persisted.

"He had many names. Mostly his name was whispered. He was called *Hän ku piwtä*—predator; hunter; tracker. Mostly it was whispered he was a predator, but once set on the trail of the undead, like my father, he never stopped."

"Or like you," Adalasia whispered, her hand going to her throat. She was beginning to put the pieces of the puzzle together, and she wasn't altogether certain she liked the answer. She was in Sandu's mind, and he knew what she was thinking. He caught the impressions before she could hide them. She could tell he didn't like where her mind was going with her conclusions.

"He was often referred to as *Hän ku kaśwa o numamet*—Sky-owner— because there was no one faster in the skies. He moved like lightning. Others called him *Hän ku pesä*—Protector—but most referred to him as *Igazág*—Justice," Sandu said. "If you heard the stories, you would have likely heard that name used."

Petru nodded. "Justice was a legend."

Nicu agreed. "No one could have done the things attributed to him."

"The stories were true," Sandu said. "I witnessed many of his feats. It would be terrifying to have one such as Justice turn vampire or, worse, become fully demon and be let loose on the world. It would not be easy for any to destroy him."

"He is related to you, isn't he, Sandu?" Adalasia whispered aloud. It was terrifying to think that this man was his relative. He was more beast than man.

She felt Sandu go still. She had been afraid of him, distrustful. From the beginning of their relationship, she had held back, and he had pushed and pushed, knowing she was holding back. A part of her knew the demon in him was strong. She had caught glimpses of it, and she had known to be afraid.

"Yes," he admitted, because one never told an untruth to their lifemate, and what was the use? "I do not know how old he was, but he was older than Vlad. He avoided humans other than to feed. He stayed close to Domizio and our family near the end, determined to hold to honor as long as he could, but he believed his time had passed and his lifemate was no longer in the world. Domizio could not provide hope for him."

"He came up with the safeguards for the cave where Domizio took your family?" Petru asked, indicating the purple light in Adalasia's hand.

"Yes. Not the trap of the pounding heart beating. That was placed there by something else. Justice showed my father how to safeguard the cave so the family would be safe. We were seeking a portal where demons were slipping through, and we were certain it was somewhere in this region. Justice was aiding us."

Sandu rubbed his temples and shook his head as the memory faded. "I cannot remember much beyond that at this moment, only that a last safeguard must be removed before you use the key, Adalasia."

Adalasia could feel Sandu watching her closely as she studied the lock and key. She didn't look at him, but she didn't remove herself from his mind, either. They were partners, a team, and they would need each other's strength to get through this. That persistent drumming noise searching to entrap an unwary heart was still there, still beneath them, reaching out to ensnare her the moment she forgot to be on guard.

The brethren moved around the boulders, looking for hidden traps, but they, too, returned to observe her. She was the demon hunter. A Carpathian had set the safeguard, but he had set it against demons, not the undead, she was positive of that. Her hands came up to move in a graceful pattern, the purple light mingling with the lights from the other keys on the ring. She murmured a counterspell to reveal the hidden weave.

"Do you all feel the way my skin keeps getting white-hot and prickly? Justice must have dealt with demons at some time in his life in order to have known to set these guards. These were not set against the undead. These were set to keep demons from getting in or out of this entrance."

She knew this. The weave. The enlightenment spell. Adalasia took down the last of the safeguards and inserted the key into the lock and turned it. Bright light spilled between the boulders, revealing six stepping-stones. Two led to the right. Two to the left. Two straight ahead. Each led to a cave entrance. The cave straight in front of them was wide and open, easy to walk into. The one to the left was much smaller and looked as if they would have to stoop or even crawl to get inside. The one to the right was narrow, with a tall, arched dome.

"The dome," Sandu said. "We were there. Going down that pathway. It is very narrow in places, so only one could go at a time. Justice insisted that he go first. We knew there was much danger. A portal had been opened somehow. We'd been fighting a losing battle for some time, trying to keep humans safe from the demons coming through."

Adalasia could see the images pouring into his mind as he looked at the tall, arched dome that looked a little like a cathedral entryway. She thought that was a tiny bit sacrilegious. How could demons be using such a beautiful archway as a portal to another realm?

"We couldn't stop the attacks on the farms or the animals," Sandu said, rubbing at his temples. "Between the encounters with demons and the undead, we were always wounded and in need of blood. We had no help. My father sent the call out for Justice, even though he knew he shouldn't. He knew Justice was too close to the end. He was asking the impossible of him, and any battle could push him over the edge. He would never have done so, but we were desperate. Too many humans were dying and we could not save them."

Adalasia started into the cave, but Sandu stepped in front of her. "This place is compromised again, *ewal emninumam*. We sealed the portal so they could never use this one to come through, but they have managed to reopen it."

Adalasia shook her head. "It is compromised," she agreed. "But it is not opened. There are places where they have battered it and worn it thin. Demons have slipped through. This is the gate my family, the Ravasio family, was tasked to guard. I know it is. I feel it. The moment I set one foot inside this cave, I knew this was the true path. There should have been guards in place to keep any demons from finding their way out."

The guardians and Tiberiu remained silent, their senses flaring out, scanning continuously, looking for the faintest hint of a threat as they made their way deeper into the cave system. The tunnel turned sharply and descended steeply as the chambers widened, flowing from one room to the next.

Adalasia rubbed at the goose bumps on her arms. It wasn't cold. If anything, it was growing warmer. The prickly sensation was getting worse. The hair on the back of her neck actually hurt, as if each individual hair was sensitive at the root and growing more so with every step. She found herself placing her hand on her sword.

Sandu, I need room.

Simultaneously, the guardians, Tiberiu and Sandu stopped moving. The guardians simply disappeared, as if they'd never been. She knew they'd dissolved into tiny molecules and were still close. She felt them in her mind, but they were moving through the cave, searching for a very real threat. Tiberiu and Sandu kept her between them but distanced themselves from her, giving her the space she needed to fight if need be.

Adalasia pulled the sword from the scabbard, and colors burst from the blade to soar to the ceiling, illuminating the walls and throwing light into every corner. At once, there was a furtive, rustling sound, the scampering of dozens of feet or hands in the dried debris on the cave floor. For just a few moments, red and yellow eyes glinted at them from all around the chamber, and then the creatures managed to hide themselves in crevices in the rock walls.

"Don't get close to the walls," Adalasia cautioned. "You saw the damage to the dog. These are the creatures that eviscerated the cattle and tried to do the same to the dog. This is part of Nera's army. Her soldiers sent to wear us down."

"Yes," Sandu said. "I remember now. They were everywhere. Every farm. Night after night. The senseless destruction. The mutilations."

I will destroy them, but you have to be in the next chamber. Both of you.

All of you. I will follow, and when I do, Sandu, seal this chamber off quickly so none can escape.

Using their common telepathic link, she showed them the tiny white globe that was really a bomb of light. *It will suck all air out of the chamber. You can't use fire against them. They bathe in fire.*

Justice taught us that. We can incinerate them with lightning, Sandu recalled, *but that's useless in these caves.*

Adalasia backed to the entrance of the next chamber, keeping the sword high so the colors bounced off the ceiling and continued to illuminate the walls, making it impossible for any of the creatures to brave the light and attack. *Everyone out?*

Yes, and the other entrance is sealed. Once you step back, I will seal this one, Sandu assured her.

Adalasia didn't wait. She tossed the globe high into the air, right into the center of the room, and stepped quickly back into the next chamber. Sandu slammed a transparent seal in the entrance. They watched as the globe spun, throwing colors throughout the cave. Suddenly, it stopped in midair, the sides opening with audible hissing. Then there was an abrupt stillness, and the chamber was filled with a hundred creatures rushing toward the archways. They looked like strange orange-and-yellow crabs but with legs and arms, their feet and hands claws. Their mouths were filled with double rows of pointed, serrated teeth. They stood approximately a foot high but scuttled across the floor on all fours.

At the entrance, they tore at the invisible seal, desperate to rip it down before their air gave out. The creatures collapsed onto the floor, tearing at their own throats and ribs to try to find a way to breathe. It was a ghastly sight and Adalasia turned away.

"The drumbeat is louder now. Nera knows we're coming."

"Before, we had to fight our way through these next chambers," Sandu's voice was grim as he led the way. "Fortunately, the tunnel is very wide, but it grows very hot. We have to regulate our body temperatures carefully. Do not touch the walls, Adalasia."

"This is where we could use the Old One," Siv said. "His scales would have come in handy."

"A dragon trying to get through these caves would get stuck," Petru pointed out.

"We should cover Adalasia's body in armor," Nicu decided. "Head to toe. Give her a helmet, too. That way, when she fights these things, if they jump on her, they cannot actually bite her or rip her in half."

"That is not a bad idea," Benedek agreed. "Sandu, you are her lifemate. She will be stubborn, because she is always unreasonable, but you have no choice but to protect her. Cover her in scales and armor."

Adalasia continued walking, surrounded by all of them, listening to their ridiculous bantering and registering the way her skin reacted to each of the chambers they passed through as they made their descent. As she walked, she flicked her fingers first toward Nicu, then toward Benedek, maintaining her innocent expression the entire time.

Benedek reacted first, glancing down at his legs, while Nicu started to run his hand over his arm. Both quickly looked at Adalasia and then Sandu.

"Not funny when we are about to be attacked by whatever can get through that portal," Benedek declared.

Sandu shrugged but continued forward. "You are the one who thought scales and armor would be a good idea." Adalasia wanted to kiss him. Telepathically she did just that, and he sent her a little grin of comradery.

Benedek waved his hand to remove the armor, and Nicu did the same. Adalasia's soft laughter bubbled up, dispelling the grim atmosphere in the cavern. She hadn't realized how the very air had carried a feeling of doom, just like that persistent drumbeat tried to ensnare her heart.

Sandu continued along a hallway and made a right-hand turn. At once, Adalasia's skin went white-hot. A thousand needles pricked her skin, warning her. She caught his arm, halting him.

What do you remember of the chamber up ahead? They were all linked, including Tiberiu, and she thought it best that they use the telepathic path rather than speak aloud.

Sandu swept his arm around her, pulling her close to him. The guardians circled them, keeping Adalasia in their center, although they did keep enough of a distance that if they needed to fight, they had room. Tiberiu was on the other side of her, providing an additional guard.

She tried to keep her heart beating in time with Sandu's. It wasn't easy. She knew this was their ultimate goal. They were that close. Whatever they had come to find was just in this next chamber. She had trained her entire life for this moment. Was she strong enough? Good enough? Were Sandu and she close enough?

They attacked us with various demons, a full-on attack. We knew we had to drive them back and seal the portal once and for all. The entire family fought them. Justice was everywhere. Without him, we never would have succeeded. They dragged us past the portal into their realm, but my mother and Liona managed to pull my father back. He was so torn up. So many wounds. They had nearly eviscerated him, tearing him open. I don't know how he lived, how they managed to save him.

Sandu shuddered at the memory of his father's body torn beyond recognition. There was practically no flesh left on him. The demons had left him for dead and turned their attention to Sandu and Justice. The two Carpathians had gone back-to-back, fighting the creatures off, but the demons were already dead, and being in their realm made it nearly impossible to defeat them.

To their horror, Liona returned, fighting her way to them, determined to aid them in getting out of the underworld and closing the portal. The distance to the portal wasn't great, but there were too many demons between them and the way out to fight their way free, as torn up as they both were. The demons had inflicted the same horrendous damage on each of them as they had on Domizio. Now, Liona was trying to get to them. Both saw her go down under the gleeful demons.

Sandu knew the exact moment when Justice sacrificed everything to give Liona, his family and him a chance at life. They both ran to Liona, adrenaline giving them the necessary strength to drag demons from her body and hurl them away from her. Justice yanked her to her feet and thrust her at Sandu.

"Run, Sandu. Take your sister and go. Promise me you will put up strong gates, built to withstand the centuries, place guardians so that I can never be freed. Give me your word of honor. One gate for each corner of the earth. North. South. East. West. Word of honor. Our family does not ever go back on our word. Go now. I will hold them off."

"We can't leave him," Liona cried.

Sandu saw the blue flames consuming the glittering light in Justice's eyes. There was no going back for him. He had let out the beast, fully embraced it in order to give Liona and Sandu, Madolina and Domizio a chance. Sandu fought his way through the line of demons, holding his abdomen together as he ran with one hand so his insides didn't spill onto the ground. Beside him, Liona fought courageously, and he was thankful she'd been taught from the time she was very young to fight the undead.

Fighting demons was different, but she didn't hesitate. They made it through the portal, and it was Justice who slammed the portal closed.

The gates, Sandu. Domizio. Build the gates. Surround me with four gates. Cage me in before it is too late.

There was urgency to Justice's command, and Sandu didn't hesitate. He and his father constructed gates around Justice, giving him room inside, but the gates were thick, made of the best wood available, wood that could not be burned or corrupted over time. They wove safeguards. Then more safeguards.

Both men were in terrible shape. Madolina and Liona didn't even try to move them away from the portal, but worked to try to heal them right there. Madolina lit the chamber with healing candles, packed her lifemate's wounds with soil and her saliva and gave her blood to Domizio while Liona did the same for her brother. They worked fast, the swiftness and silence of their actions betraying the urgency to those seeing the images.

The guardians and Tiberiu exchanged long looks with one another. Justice was alive. An ancient older than Vlad. One so skilled in battle there were few hunters—if any—who would be able to destroy him should he choose to become undead.

This is what my sister was taken to interact with? Tiberiu said after a time.

Sandu inclined his head. *I believe so. She could talk to beasts. Justice is more beast than man. I think she is the only one who can communicate with him, and she refuses to leave him.*

Yet she is not his lifemate, Tiberiu reiterated.

I do not believe she is, Sandu said. *I did not get that impression when he was chanting the sacred oath with me.*

What is the plan? Afanasiv was practical. *The portal is slipping and the gate could be opening. We are here to ensure neither happens.*

I am here to see if my sister still lives, Tiberiu said. *And if she lives, if there is a way to retrieve her from that place.*

Sandu nodded. *I, too, wish to find my sister. She was left to guard this gate. Three other Carpathian women were chosen to guard each of the other gates. Now that I remember who she is and that she exists, I want to find her alive and well. She must feel she's been abandoned.*

Adalasia leaned into Sandu to give him comfort when his past was too close and haunting him.

You didn't abandon her, even if she feels that way, Sandu. We just have to seal the portal for good. I have to make certain the gate is closed and guarded. Any demons on this side of the portal have to be driven back to the underworld or disposed of.

Adalasia gripped her sword. Nera awaited on the other side of the portal. She crowded close to it. Adalasia could feel her now, pushing for her demons to get it open so her army could pour into the realm of the living.

It's best if they think it is only Sandu and I and Tiberiu. They feel him. They know who he is, and they don't want him here. Tiberiu, they will strike at you even before they will at me. They want to acquire both Sandu and me alive. You, they want dead.

I am not so easy to kill, Tiberiu assured her. *They must have Gaia if I present such a threat to them.*

Would she recognize you? Sandu asked. *She was but ten.*

No. I was away and already centuries old when she was born. She saw me once. I returned right after she turned ten but left soon after I visited. I wanted to acknowledge her so she would always know she was wanted. I counted on our mother and father being able to have the time to tell her, Tiberiu said.

That twisted at Adalasia's heart.

Sandu's warmth slid into her mind. *You are always so compassionate, Sivamet.*

Tell me what to expect, Tiberiu ordered.

They will go for your stomach to try to rip you open. Then your eyes to blind you. Then your throat to tear it out, Sandu said. *Just as the demons did when they attacked us in the underworld.*

Adalasia took a breath, trying to keep from breathing in the scent of sulfur that hung heavy in the air. *Only the small ones were able to get through this portal, and they have set an ambush in this next chamber. Even as molecules, stay away from the walls. I don't know what Nera has learned from her spies, but she sent them out not just to learn from us but from others. We have to be careful.*

She raised her sword and, with Sandu, stepped confidently into the next chamber. She recognized the interior from his memories, when Liona and he had made it from the underworld, flinging themselves from the portal onto the floor of the cave. She took the time to study every aspect of the cave, the position of every rock formation. The floor, the ceiling and the walls. She had an excellent memory, and she knew where the portal had been when Sandu had emerged.

They stood back-to-back while she took her time, allowing her gaze to move over the spot where the portal had to be. With the sword gripped in her hands, pointed down toward the floor, she observed the way the shadows played through the cave. The light from the blade of the sword was steady, unmoving, yet the shadows were subtle, restless, a continuous swaying that shimmered a silvery gray and then went dark again. It happened in the blink of an eye, so the first two times, she questioned whether it was real or illusion, that solid arch.

She tried to let her breath out naturally and keep her heart and lungs exactly synchronized with Sandu's. She was grateful that Sandu allowed her to take the lead since she had been trained for this moment. She knew what she was supposed to do. She had gone over and over the scenario in her mind, in her dreams, even her nightmares, thousands of times. As a child, her mother had drilled every move into her head.

He is the epitome of the modern lifemate, Benedek said.

In the human dictionary, we will put his picture beside the word modern, Nicu added, *and immortalize him.*

Petru chimed in. *I will send word to Josef and ensure Sandu is written up in what he calls his advice column: old geezers—lifemates to young, hot party women. Sandu can be used as an example of an ancient who knows how to be hip.*

Hip? Sandu nearly whirled around to face the direction where Petru was drifting close to Adalasia. *Sun scorch you, Petru. Where did you even hear of such a word, and how did you know its meaning?*

Does Josef really have such a column? Afanasiv asked. *That seems to be the most pertinent question.*

It was all Adalasia could do not to burst out laughing, and maybe that was why the guardians were carrying on. She needed to be completely relaxed, and with just that short exchange, she was.

I see the portal. I need to really examine it for places where it could be thinning. Sandu, reach out to Liona and see if she answers you. Tiberiu, see if you can subtly reach out to your sister. They would never have kept her original name. Whatever her given name was, use that, or if there was a special name your family called her, just in case either jogs her memory. It's a long shot, but provided she doesn't betray you to Nera, it will be okay. Don't use the common Carpathian path; she will believe it is a trick. Use your family path.

She felt Sandu's sudden amusement. He shared with her along their private, intimate path: *Tiberiu is very traditional. He is not used to you—or us. You are the one taking charge, not me, and issuing orders. It's a little amusing, that's all.*

She glanced over her shoulder at Sandu. It was difficult not to love him even more when she heard things like that. He was an ancient, and his inclination had to be to take the lead, yet he wasn't. He had faith in her. More than anything else, that gave her the determination to succeed.

One hand rose to the center of her chest, and just barely moving her wrist, she deftly used her fingers to weave a revealing spell. She murmured the accompanying words softly, so softly the sound of water dripping and the persistent drumming noise covered her chant. The portal shimmered in and out of the shadows, but now she could see it in its entirety. An archway, sealed, but there were thin spots. Two of the cracks were tiny breaks just wide enough that the demonic creatures, although a foot high and horribly lethal, were thin enough to scrape through. She could see where they had used their claws to pull themselves through. The claw marks were deep on the portal, as if they had tried to widen the crack for others but were unable to do so.

I've found the breaks and weak spots in the portal. I can close it and seal it, but once I do, nothing will be able to leave that realm from this portal.

Wait. Tiberiu was imperious. *I have reached out to my sister. She has yet to answer me. I feel her, but she will not answer. If you close the portal, I have no hope of recovering her.*

It is possible this woman is not your sister, Tiberiu, Sandu said. *I could be wrong. I could have brought you false hope. It was a guess on my part.*

We have to hurry, Adalasia said. *I feel the demons pushing at the portal. It's bowing in toward us. They're determined to break through, and there is much weakness here.*

Begin to seal it, Adalasia, Sandu ordered. *Tiberiu, tell her the time is now or never. I am reaching out to Liona now. She is not on the other side of the portal. I feel her. But she isn't there.*

Adalasia didn't wait. She hurried to thicken the seals on the portal, pouring in the strongest of the ancient woods and old magic it was originally built with but weaving in webs of more modern material that demons might not understand the composition of: titanium. She added the safeguards against demons taught to her from the time she was a child into every weave. The strongest. She was patient, taking her time.

The demons knew she was working against them, and they struck at her, trying to come up under her, but it was impossible without the portal. The lethal demons clawed at the cracks, doing their best to emerge from the one crack she left open in order to give Tiberiu's sister a way out if she wanted to take it. The demons growled and snarled at her, hissing their hatred, glaring with yellow eyes as they shoved their heads through the opening. The moment they reached for her, Sandu lopped off the arm and incinerated the claw as it scuttered across the floor toward Adalasia.

She continued to work, not allowing anything to stop her from sealing the portal. She was aware of the guardians and Sandu in the background of her mind as they kept her from harm, but every word, every stroke, had to be flawless. She handed the sword to Sandu. The demons and Nera knew she was there. She could use both hands, both arms, as well as her voice, to seal the portal, and she did, making the work easier.

Seal it, Tiberiu ordered softly. *Gaia will not abandon Justice. I cannot persuade her.*

Adalasia felt Tiberiu's heavy sorrow, although she knew he did not. She didn't hesitate but kept working. Sandu worked tirelessly to protect Adalasia while he reached out to his sister on their private family path, calling to her continuously. Over and over. Hoping she was alive. Finally, he fell silent and held the sword aloft, spreading the light through the cave while Adalasia worked to strengthen and seal the portal so that the army of demons couldn't slip through.

There was a gentle movement in the cave, the slightest of breezes, carrying the scent of fresh oranges. *"Ekäm?"* The voice trembled. "Sandu? Have I lost my mind? Is this truly you?"

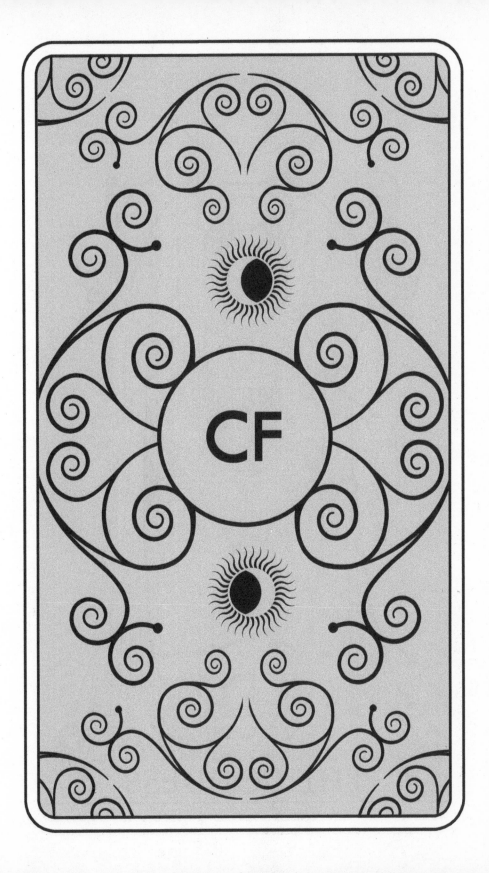

-XXII-

THE GODDESS

S andu spun around, the air leaving his lungs in a long exhale of pure shock. Liona alive. Tall. So beautiful she hurt his eyes. His sister. Every memory of her came rushing back, swamping him, so many crowding together until they were a jumble in his mind.

"Liona." He whispered her name.

Benedek took the sword from him, and Nicu took up guardianship at Adalasia's side while she finished sealing the portal so he could go to his sister. Liona stood just inside the chamber, one hand on the wall to hold herself up, shaking, her skin pale, her blond hair tumbling in a thick wild fall to her waist, her blue eyes enormous.

"Is it really you, Sandu? I had given up all hope. I thought you were long gone from this world." She looked as though she wanted to take a step toward him, but she didn't have the strength.

He wasn't certain he was any steadier. *Adalasia. She is alive.*

Yes, my love.

Joy burst through him at the confirmation. He wasn't hallucinating. The demons weren't playing tricks. Liona was really standing right there in front of him. He crossed the chamber and gathered her to him, pressing her slender frame against his, needing to feel her.

"I could not get to you," he whispered. "Until Adalasia, I could not find you." He pressed kisses on top of her head the way he had when she was a child. He realized his hands shook. "You have guarded the gate all these centuries. So alone, and yet you have lived with honor, Liona." There was pride in his voice, pride welling up. Awe.

"Not entirely alone. I have friends. We support one another." She pulled back, tilting her head to look up at him. "Who is Adalasia?"

Sandu turned to face his lifemate. She staggered, and both Nicu and Benedek reached to steady her. She was very pale but triumphant.

"The portal is sealed and stronger, I think, than before." She flashed a smile at Liona.

"Adalasia, my sister, Liona. Liona, my lifemate, Adalasia, who is in need of blood." He held his free arm out to her while still retaining possession of Liona.

"I am so pleased to meet you, Adalasia," Liona said. "I have always wanted a sister. That you saved my brother and brought him to me makes me love you immediately."

Adalasia pressed her hand tight over heart. "I have waited a very long time to meet you."

Sandu wrapped his arm around her waist. Adalasia was swaying with weariness. Only her iron will was keeping her on her feet. He needed to take her somewhere private to give her blood.

Benedek handed back Adalasia's sword, his gaze on Liona. "You are indeed a warrior. I am Benedek, one of Adalasia's guardians and brethren to Sandu. That is Nicu, Petru, Afanasiv and Tiberiu."

Liona nodded at each of them. Her gaze rested on Tiberiu. "You are the brother of Gaia." She made it a statement.

Tiberiu nodded.

"She is very strong. Without her, there were days I know it would have been difficult, if not impossible, to get through. Would you like to come to my home? It isn't far from here. I had to be able to monitor the portal, the gate and any vampire activity in the area as well."

Sandu's heart dropped. His sister had been left an enormous job once Domizio had passed from their world. The area was still rough and wild, with few hunters visiting. "Liona, did you hunt the undead?"

"Only if I had no choice," she admitted matter-of-factly.

Sandu, Adalasia cautioned as he bristled.

Every ancient had the same reaction. The instant rejection. They wanted to reprimand her, to demand she *never* do such a thing again.

Be careful how you react. I know she is your baby sister, but she has lived centuries on her own. There isn't anything you can do now. She has succeeded in hunting them, in guarding the gate and in holding back demons. She is to be admired, not reprimanded. Adalasia gave all the ancients the advice, not just Sandu.

We will never be modern men, Adalasia, Petru reminded, but he remained silent, allowing Sandu to address his sister.

Oh, how I'm well aware of that, Petru. The lot of you should be in Josef's dictionary under impossible.

What do you mean by that? Benedek demanded. *What does she mean by that, Sandu?*

"Please take us to your home, Liona. Once again, I am in awe of your skills and am grateful that you had Tiberiu's sister as a friend to see you through those dark days when I could not be here for you," Sandu said tactfully.

She means you're hopeless, Sandu added to the brethren, his tone smug. *I might really get written up in Josef's advice column as the epitome of the modern lifemate.*

Adalasia gave the mental equivalent of rolling her eyes. *Let's not get carried away.*

"Sandu," Liona said, "you'll have to let me go long enough for all of us to shift into molecules in order to seep through the tiny vent in the chimney. We may as well leave the chamber sealed. You can follow me home. It is very close."

Sandu dreaded letting go of her. "Funny thing, Liona, I am uncertain if I can actually release you. You might disappear on me again for good."

Liona started to say something, choked and shook her head. "I know what you mean. I feel the same way, but we can't stay in here, not with Adalasia looking like that."

I can supply Adalasia with blood, Nicu offered.

Sandu's progressive attitude went right out the window. He pulled his lifemate up against his body. *That will be unnecessary. Can you wait, Sivamet, until we reach Liona's home?*

He felt Adalasia's silent laughter. *Of course.* But she was pale and leaning most of her weight against him. That was unusual for his woman.

"Lead the way, *sisarke*."

I will hold the image in your head, Adalasia. I am well aware you can do so yourself, but you are exhausted. Shift first and follow Nicu and Benedek out of the chamber. I will be with you. Petru, Siv and Tiberiu will follow us.

He didn't give her a choice. He might have used a soft voice, but there was no denying his was a commanding tone. Adalasia followed, too tired to protest, and she never did just for the sake of asserting her independence anyway.

Liona's home reminded Sandu of the little guesthouse Andre and Teagan had up in the mountains. The entrance was impossible to discover until you were right on top of it, and only when you were there did you actually see it was a cottage. The pathway was made of rocks blending into the surrounding mountain. Natural fauna covered the ground, and bushes climbed the rocks and boulders. Fern laced the pathway of rocks leading to the rectangular verandah with its overhung roof. The roof appeared to be part of the mountainside, a large rock outcropping covered in vines and grass and even wildflowers.

Liona opened the door and stepped inside, looking back at her guests with a little smile. "Please do enter of your own free will."

Sandu was grateful that she remembered to put the onus on each of the ancients to enter of their will, giving her the power if they did so. He held Adalasia back, drawing her into his arms, stepping into the shadows at the very end of the porch. He felt the strong safeguards his sister had woven around her home. She took no chances, ensuring the structure was protected from below the ground as well as above it and from every direction. She certainly remembered her training. She'd had to, spending centuries on her own.

"I'm so happy and grateful that she's alive," Adalasia whispered.

"*Sivamet*, you must feed. You are falling down with weariness." Sandu infused his voice with temptation as he seated himself on the wide railing, pulling her between his thighs and opening his shirt. He cocooned them in the shadowy corner, giving her the privacy she needed. She hadn't been that long in their world, and taking blood was still new to her.

Adalasia turned her face into him, nuzzling the heavy muscles of his chest, her breath warm. His stomach muscles clenched. His cock grew heavy and full. She murmured something he didn't catch, but the way her lips drifted over his skin, her tongue a velvet rasp, felt erotic, far too sensual to be ignored. As much as he wanted to be with his sister, it was impossible not to feel the call between lifemates. Her teeth nipped and scraped back and forth. His blood thundered in his heart. Crashed in his ears. Rushed through his veins. Pounded through his cock. Beckoned her. Called to her.

Sivamet, he whispered. *Tet vigyázam.* Love was overwhelming for her. Swamping him. She gave him so many gifts.

Her teeth sank deep. The pain was exquisite, an erotic bite that quickly turned to pleasure and burned through his body like a brilliant blue flame.

I love you, too, Sandu, more than I can ever tell you.

Even her voice, brushing so intimately in his mind, was deeply sensual. He wrapped his arms around her and allowed himself to enjoy the night. His lifemate. The fact that he could feel the way he did. That he had it all. And now he had his sister back. A part of his family.

Adalasia swept her tongue across the small holes in his skin and then pressed her lips over the spot in a kiss. "She is beautiful, Sandu. And extraordinarily brave. She has fought the undead and guarded the gate for centuries alone. That is . . . magnificent. Unbelievable. I hope she has a lifemate searching for her, one who deserves her. One who will cherish her."

"I would like to make our home here, Adalasia, so she has freedom to do as she wishes," he admitted, tucking strands of her hair behind her ear. "I doubt if she will leave her duty until it is finished, but I would want to stay close, only if you agree."

"I came here knowing that we would most likely be making our home here. I knew the gate was in jeopardy, Sandu. I wasn't certain Liona lived. I thought I would have to guard the gate by myself. Knowing you found your sister is wonderful. I would love to make our home close to her."

Sandu framed her face and bent his head to take her mouth. At once, the fire was there, leaping between them the way he knew it would be. He loved her beyond all imagining.

A soft little giggle played through his mind. *Ekäm, are you going to stay out there all night, or are you going to bring your lifemate in so I can get to know her?*

Sandu lifted his head, sharing that joyous giggle with Adalasia. "I remember that sound. After all this time, I even recognize it." He gave Adalasia an almost boyish grin and held out his hand to her. They entered the house together.

The sitting room wasn't very big, and with six adult Carpathian males, all of them quite large, the space seemed much smaller. Still, it was a welcoming room. Peaceful. It was a mixture of old-world and more modern. The furniture was comfortable, and Liona had acquired several quilts Sandu recognized that Francesca, Gabriel's lifemate, had made. Somehow, his sister had found out about her quilts and sent for them. He touched one of them.

"How did you get this?"

If Francesca had known Liona was alive and where she was, she would have told him.

"I helped a few of the locals over the years. I saw one of the quilts in a house and expressed interest because it clearly held magical properties. A Carpathian had made it. The woman surprised me with one. I was very moved that she cared enough. Over the years, more than once, I've been gifted with a quilt from this extraordinary seamstress."

Adalasia ran her hand lightly over the quilt Sandu had touched. The squares seemed to leap to life, small animals showing themselves in the forest and birds flitting from tree to tree. "Did you ever consider contacting her?"

"No. My duty was to guard the gate. I am a Carpathian woman. My father explained to me that if anyone other than my lifemate or my brother were to discover I was here alone, it could be dangerous. The males would feel it was wrong for me to be without protection and would insist I leave."

The ancients nodded in agreement. "There are very few women, Liona," Afanasiv said. "We have little hope for our males. More and more become undead. At this time, we have under forty couples, and not all bear us children. Fortunately, it was discovered that a few human women with psychic talents, such as Adalasia, are lifemates to us."

Liona gasped. "This cannot be."

"The high mage turned on our people, plotting against us," Sandu explained. "He nearly succeeded in wiping our species out."

"It is possible, then, that my lifemate succumbed to the darkness." There was sadness in her voice. "The others will be unsettled with this news. It has been difficult, at times, to continue with our duty."

"The others?" Petru prompted.

"There are four gates and four of us guarding those gates," Liona said. "Each must be vigilant as the demons try to escape and find a way to get to the guardian of the cards."

"Three other Carpathian women?" Nicu asked. "These women have been alone for centuries? How? How was this possible?"

"We made a commitment to one another," Liona explained. "We sometimes exchanged places so we could at least have a new setting. See new things. Experience new adventures. We spoke often. Gaia was the only one trapped in the same place, but we all made sure to share what we could with her of our world and the changes taking place in it."

"Did all of you hunt the undead?" Nicu asked.

"We hid from them if they were close if we could," Liona said. "But if they killed too many humans in our territory, then we felt as if we had no choice."

Sandu tightened his fingers around Adalasia's in order to keep from blurting out that, of course, she had a choice. He was proud of her, but she had no business fighting vampires. He knew she had been trained by his father to fight vampires, just as his mother had known, but it wasn't an accepted practice. They weren't to hunt them. Only fight them if absolutely necessary, meaning it was life or death.

"We tried to meet up together at first and exchange information on battling the undead. If it was a master vampire, we didn't try to defeat it.

The lesser ones we practiced on until we got pretty good at destroying them. If one of us was injured, the others would come to heal them. The gates and portals were very strong in the first few centuries. It was only later that they began to wear down, and we didn't dare leave our posts."

Sandu brought Adalasia's palm to his mouth and kissed the center of it. "There will be no need of you hunting the vampire now, or guarding the gate. If you wish to go to the Carpathian Mountains or see your friends, you are free to do so, although I would prefer to hold you close to me for a long while."

"Guarding the gate is still my duty, Sandu," Liona said. She sounded very calm, but there was no mistaking the firmness of her conviction.

"I am just saying, I am willing to help you with that duty."

She smiled at him. "I can still scarcely take in that you are here, Sandu. So much time passed. After a time, the years ran together. The other guardians of the gates, like me, knew the portals were wearing thin. We also knew that those holding the cards had to come soon, or one of the gates would fall. The cards have to be renewed every now and then, and it has been centuries.

"Once my blood falls on the card, the repairs to the gate will be made and it will stand. The others like you, Adalasia, have to get here in time. They must seal their portal and renew their deck."

"What of Gaia?" Tiberiu asked. "Is there no chance for her?"

"She believes that Justice has a lifemate and that his lifemate will be able to connect with him. If that were to happen, between the gatekeepers, Gaia and his lifemate, we believe with his strength, we would be able to free him. We are forming a plan just in case that should really happen. The biggest problem would be keeping the demons in that realm while we allow Justice and Gaia to escape. That is a long way away and most likely won't ever really happen. It is something we plan for to keep our minds occupied."

"It seems I must accept her decision," Tiberiu said.

"She will not leave him," Liona reiterated.

"Then I will take my leave," Tiberiu said and bowed in an old-world courtly way. "I have not spent this long in the company of others in a very long time. If you do not mind, I shall return occasionally to ask after Gaia, to ensure she lives and that her decision remains firm."

"I will look forward to your visit," Liona said.

Sandu's gut tightened. An unmated Carpathian male could turn at any time, and Tiberiu was ancient, very close. Liona had given him permission to return alone, and that didn't sit well with Sandu or with any of the ancients.

Sandu stood and went with Tiberiu to the door. He respected the warrior. He'd held out with honor for longer than most Carpathians could ever conceive of doing. Sandu gripped his forearms. *"Arwa-arvod mäne me ködak,"* he said. For Adalasia, he interpreted, *May your honor hold back the dark.*

"Be well, Sandu. Take care of them." Tiberiu was gone, melting away into the night as if he had never been. Sandu stood in the doorway, his heart heavy as the wind slipped through the trees and rustled the leaves.

Come join us, Adalasia whispered into his mind. Stroking caresses. Stroking love. *He will choose honor. He always has, and he will continue to do so.*

Sandu turned his head to look at her. His woman. His lifemate. His gaze slid over his brethren. Good men. The best. How had he managed to find a miracle when they had yet to find theirs? And his sister. She had been so courageous all these long centuries. Waiting for him to come back. Waiting for her lifemate. She'd been alone. Why had he been given this gift, this treasure, and they were not?

Sandu, you are deserving. They will find happiness.

"Adalasia, I must renew the card in order to strengthen the gate," Liona said.

Adalasia slipped her hand inside her shirt to retrieve the final card, the goddess card she guarded fiercely, protectively, even from Sandu in the beginning. He closed the door and returned to the stand behind the two women who meant the world to him.

Liona placed the goddess card on the small table between Adalasia and her and then used the tip of her fingernail to open her wrist. Holding her wrist above the card, she allowed the crimson drops to fall onto the card one by one, until the red rain had saturated the material. Until the image couldn't be seen beneath the coating that was already turning a dark ruby. Liona licked at her wrist to close the wound. They all watched, even the guardians crowding close, fascinated, as the card slowly absorbed the blood and began to clear.

A great roar echoed through the room, a bellow of rage followed by a soothing song as the cards fought the sensation of rebirth.

"The gate is once again strong. It has been repaired," Liona said with satisfaction.

It didn't take long until the goddess stared back at them, wholly clean and looking as if she were brand-new.

Adalasia smiled at Liona as she took out the pouch that held the other cards and slipped the goddess card in with them. "Thank you, Liona."

"I am the one grateful to you. You saved my brother and arrived in time to keep Justice from escaping and the demons from getting free." Liona tipped her head back to look at her brother. "Will you really make your home here?" There was the slightest quaver in her voice.

He dropped his hands on her shoulders. "Yes. Adalasia and I want to stay close to you."

Adalasia is tired and wants to be with her lifemate alone, Adalasia whispered into his mind. Her voice was sultry. Sensual. An invitation.

Sandu dropped a kiss on the top of his sister's head. "We will find a place to go to ground this night, Liona, and meet with you next rising." He looked to the guardians.

"We will stay around until you are settled, Sandu," Benedek said. "Then we will hunt for our lifemates. Adalasia gave us direction, and that is what we needed."

Sandu smiled at his woman. "She is very good at that."

Color crept underneath his woman's skin.

I do not think you need any direction, Sandu.

Not this night, he didn't. He swept her up and took her outside, feeling as if he had everything. He had it all. He was very far from the rooftop where he'd contemplated going back to the monastery or ending everything. He'd been given a miracle, and he wasn't wasting another moment.

CARPATHIAN HEALING CHANTS

To rightly understand Carpathian healing chants, background is required in several areas:

1. The Carpathian view on healing
2. The Lesser Healing Chant of the Carpathians
3. The Great Healing Chant of the Carpathians
4. Carpathian musical aesthetics
5. Lullaby
6. Song to Heal the Earth
7. Carpathian chanting technique

1. THE CARPATHIAN VIEW ON HEALING

The Carpathians are a nomadic people whose geographic origins can be traced at least as far as the Southern Ural Mountains (near the steppes of modern-day Kazakhstan), on the border between Europe and Asia. (For this reason, modern-day linguists call their language "proto-Uralic," without knowing that this is the language of the Carpathians.) Unlike most nomadic peoples, the Carpathians did not wander due to the need to find new grazing lands as the seasons and climate shifted, or to search for better trade. Instead, the Carpathians' movements were driven by a great purpose: to find a land that would have the right earth, a soil with the kind of richness that would greatly enhance their rejuvenative powers.

Over the centuries, they migrated westward (some six thousand years ago), until they at last found their perfect homeland—their *susu*—in the Carpathian Mountains, whose long arc cradled the lush plains of the kingdom of Hungary. (The kingdom of Hungary flourished for over a millennium—making Hungarian the dominant language of the Carpathian Basin—until the kingdom's lands were split among several countries after World War I: Austria, Czechoslovakia, Romania, Yugoslavia and modern Hungary.)

Other peoples from the Southern Urals (who shared the Carpathian language but were not Carpathians) migrated in different directions. Some ended up in Finland, which explains why the modern Hungarian and Finnish languages are among the contemporary descendants of the ancient Carpathian language. Even though they are tied forever to their chosen Carpathian homeland, the Carpathians continue to wander as they search

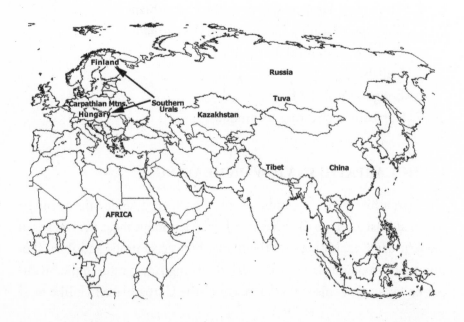

the world for the answers that will enable them to bear and raise their offspring without difficulty.

Because of their geographic origins, the Carpathian views on healing share much with the larger Eurasian shamanistic tradition. Probably the closest modern representative of that tradition is based in Tuva (and is referred to as "Tuvinian Shamanism")—see the map on the previous page.

The Eurasian shamanistic tradition—from the Carpathians to the Siberian shamans—held that illness originated in the human soul, and only later manifested as various physical conditions. Therefore, shamanistic healing, while not neglecting the body, focused on the soul and its healing. The most profound illnesses were understood to be caused by "soul departure," where all or some part of the sick person's soul has wandered away from the body (into the nether realms) or has been captured or possessed by an evil spirit, or both.

The Carpathians belong to this greater Eurasian shamanistic tradition and share its viewpoints. While the Carpathians themselves did not succumb to illness, Carpathian healers understood that the most profound wounds were also accompanied by a similar "soul departure."

Upon reaching the diagnosis of "soul departure," the healer-shaman is then required to make a spiritual journey into the netherworld to recover the soul. The shaman may have to overcome tremendous challenges along the way, particularly fighting the demon or vampire who has possessed his friend's soul.

"Soul departure" doesn't require a person to be unconscious (although that certainly can be the case as well). It was understood that a person could still appear to be conscious, even talk and interact with others, and yet be missing a part of their soul. The experienced healer or shaman would instantly see the problem nonetheless, in subtle signs that others might miss: the person's attention wandering every now and then, a lessening in their enthusiasm about life, chronic depression, a diminishment in the brightness of their "aura" and the like.

2. THE LESSER HEALING CHANT OF THE CARPATHIANS

Kepä Sarna Pus (**The Lesser Healing Chant**) is used for wounds that are merely physical in nature. The Carpathian healer leaves his body and enters the wounded Carpathian's body to heal great mortal wounds from the inside out using pure energy. He proclaims, "I offer freely my life for your life," as he gives his blood to the injured Carpathian. Because the Carpathians are of the earth and bound to the soil, they are healed by the soil of their homeland. Their saliva is also often used for its rejuvenative powers.

It is also very common for the Carpathian chants (both the Lesser and the Great) to be accompanied by the use of healing herbs, aromas from Carpathian candles and crystals. The crystals (when combined with the Carpathians' empathic, psychic connection to the entire universe) are used to gather positive energy from their surroundings, which is then used to accelerate the healing. Caves are sometimes used as the setting for the healing.

The Lesser Healing Chant was used by Vikirnoff Von Shrieder and Colby Jansen to heal Rafael De La Cruz, whose heart had been ripped out by a vampire, as described in *Dark Secret*.

Kepä Sarna Pus (The Lesser Healing Chant)
The same chant is used for all physical wounds. "Sívadaba" (into your heart) would be changed to refer to whatever part of the body is wounded.

Kuńasz, nélkül sívdobbanás, nélkül fesztelen löyly.
You lie as if asleep, without beat of heart, without airy breath.

Ot élidamet andam szabadon élidadért.
I offer freely my life for your life.

O jelä sielam jörem ot ainamet és soŋe ot élidadet.
My spirit of light forgets my body and enters your body.

O jelä sielam pukta kinn minden szelemeket belső.
My spirit of light sends all the dark spirits within fleeing without.

Pajnak o susu hanyet és o nyelv nyálamet sívadaba.

I press the earth of our homeland and the spit of my tongue into your
   heart.

Vii, o verim soɲe o verid andam.

At last, I give you my blood for your blood.

To hear this chant, visit christinefeehan.com/members/.

3. THE GREAT HEALING CHANT OF THE CARPATHIANS

The most well-known—and most dramatic—of the Carpathian healing
chants is *En Sarna Pus* (**The Great Healing Chant**). This chant is reserved
for recovering the wounded or unconscious Carpathian's soul.

Typically a group of men would form a circle around the sick
Carpathian (to "encircle him with our care and compassion") and begin
the chant. The shaman or healer or leader is the prime actor in this
healing ceremony. It is he who will actually make the spiritual journey
into the netherworld, aided by his clanspeople. Their purpose is to ecstatically dance, sing, drum and chant, all the while visualizing (through
the words of the chant) the journey itself—every step of it, over and over
again—to the point where the shaman, in trance, leaves his body and
makes that very journey. (Indeed, the word *ecstasy* is from the Latin *ex
statis*, which literally means "out of the body.")

One advantage that the Carpathian healer has over many other shamans is his telepathic link to his lost brother. Most shamans must wander
in the dark of the nether realms in search of their lost brother. But the
Carpathian healer directly "hears" in his mind the voice of his lost
brother calling to him, and can thus "zero in on" his soul like a homing
beacon. For this reason, Carpathian healing tends to have a higher success rate than most other traditions of this sort.

Something of the geography of the "other world" is useful for us to
examine in order to fully understand the words of the Great Healing
Chant. A reference is made to the "Great Tree" (in Carpathian: *En*

Puwe). Many ancient traditions, including the Carpathian tradition, understood the worlds—the heaven worlds, our world and the nether realms—to be "hung" upon a great pole, or axis, or tree. Here on earth, we are positioned halfway up this tree, on one of its branches. Hence, many ancient texts referred to the material world as "middle earth": midway between heaven and hell. Climbing the tree would lead one to the heaven worlds. Descending the tree to its roots would lead to the nether realms. The shaman was necessarily a master of movement up and down the Great Tree, sometimes moving unaided and sometimes assisted by (or even mounted upon the back of) an animal spirit guide. In various traditions, this Great Tree was known as the *axis mundi* (the "axis of the worlds"), Yggdrasil (in Norse mythology), Mount Meru (the sacred world mountain of Tibetan tradition), etc. The Christian cosmos, with its heaven, purgatory/earth and hell, is also worth comparing. It is even given a similar topography in Dante's *Divine Comedy*: Dante is led on a journey first to hell, at the center of the earth; then upward to Mount Purgatory, which sits on the earth's surface directly opposite Jerusalem; then farther upward to Eden, the earthly paradise, at the summit of Mount Purgatory; and then upward at last to Heaven.

In the shamanistic tradition, it was understood that the small always reflects the large; the personal always reflects the cosmic. A movement in the greater dimensions of the cosmos also coincides with an internal movement. For example, the *axis mundi* of the cosmos corresponds with the spinal column of the individual. Journeys up and down the *axis mundi* often coincided with the movements of natural and spiritual energies (sometimes called *kundalini* or *shakti*) in the spinal column of the shaman or mystic.

En Sarna Pus (The Great Healing Chant)

In this chant, ekä ("brother") would be replaced by "sister," "father," "mother," depending on the person to be healed.

Ot ekäm ainajanak hany, jama.
My brother's body is a lump of earth, close to death.

Me, ot ekäm kuntajanak, pirädak ekäm, gond és irgalom türe.
We, the clan of my brother, encircle him with our care and compassion.

O pus wäkenkek, ot oma śarnank, és ot pus fünk, álnak ekäm ainajanak, pitänak ekäm ainajanak elävä.
Our healing energies, ancient words of magic and healing herbs bless my brother's body, keep it alive.

Ot ekäm sielanak pälä. Ot omboće päläja juta alatt o jüti, kinta, és szelemek lamtijaknak.
But my brother's soul is only half. His other half wanders in the netherworld.

Ot en mekem ŋamaŋ: kulkedak otti ot ekäm omboće päläjanak.
My great deed is this: I travel to find my brother's other half.

Rekatüre, saradak, tappadak, odam, kaŋa o numa waram, és avaa owe o lewl mahoz.
We dance, we chant, we dream ecstatically, to call my spirit bird, and to open the door to the other world.

Ntak o numa waram, és mozdulak; jomadak.
I mount my spirit bird and we begin to move; we are underway.

Piwtädak ot En Puwe tyvinak, ećidak alatt o jüti, kinta, és szelemek lamtijaknak.
Following the trunk of the Great Tree, we fall into the netherworld.

Fázak, fázak nó o śaro.
It is cold, very cold.

Juttadak ot ekäm o akarataban, o sívaban és o sielaban.
My brother and I are linked in mind, heart and soul.

Ot ekäm sielanak kaŋa engem.
My brother's soul calls to me.

Kuledak és piwtädak ot ekäm.
I hear and follow his track.

Saɣedak és tuledak ot ekäm kulyanak.
I encounter the demon who is devouring my brother's soul.

Nenäm ćoro, o kuly torodak.
In anger, I fight the demon.

O kuly pél engem.
He is afraid of me.

Lejkkadak o kaŋka salamaʋal.
I strike his throat with a lightning bolt.

Molodak ot ainaja komakamal.
I break his body with my bare hands.

Toja és molanâ.
He is bent over, and falls apart.

Hän ćaδa.
He runs away.

Manedak ot ekäm sielanak.
I rescue my brother's soul.

Alədak ot ekam sielanak o komamban.
I lift my brother's soul in the hollow of my hand.

Alədam ot ekam numa waramra.
I lift him onto my spirit bird.

Piwtädak ot En Puwe tyvijanak és sayedak jälleen ot elävä ainak majaknak.
Following up the Great Tree, we return to the land of the living.

Ot ekäm elä jälleen.
My brother lives again.

Ot ekäm weńća jälleen.
He is complete again.

To hear this chant, visit christinefeehan.com/members/.

4. CARPATHIAN MUSICAL AESTHETICS

In the sung Carpathian pieces (such as the "Lullaby" and the "Song to Heal the Earth"), you'll hear elements that are shared by many of the musical traditions in the Uralic geographical region, some of which still exist—from Eastern European (Bulgarian, Romanian, Hungarian, Croatian) to Romany ("gypsy"). These elements include:

- the rapid alternation between major and minor modalities, including a sudden switch (called a "Picardy third") from minor to major to end a piece or section (as at the end of the "Lullaby")
- the use of close (tight) harmonies
- the use of *ritardi* (slowing down the pace) and *crescendi* (swelling in volume) for brief periods
- the use of *glissandi* (slides) in the singing tradition
- the use of trills in the singing tradition (as in the final invocation of the "Song to Heal the Earth")—similar to Celtic, a singing tradition more familiar to many of us
- the use of parallel fifths (as in the final invocation of the "Song to Heal the Earth")
- controlled use of dissonance
- "call-and-response" chanting (typical of many of the world's chanting traditions)

- extending the length of a musical line (by adding a couple of bars) to heighten dramatic effect
- and many more

"Lullaby" and "Song to Heal the Earth" illustrate two rather different forms of Carpathian music (a quiet, intimate piece and an energetic ensemble piece)—but whatever the form, Carpathian music is full of feeling.

5. LULLABY

This song is sung by a woman while a child is still in the womb or when the threat of a miscarriage is apparent. The baby can hear the song while inside the mother, and the mother can connect with the child telepathically as well. The lullaby is meant to reassure the child, to encourage the baby to hold on, to stay—to reassure the child that he or she will be protected by love even from inside until birth. The last line literally means that the mother's love will protect her child until the child is born ("rise").

Musically, the Carpathian "Lullaby" is in three-quarter time ("waltz time"), as are a significant portion of the world's various traditional lullabies (perhaps the most famous of which is Brahms's Lullaby). The arrangement for solo voice is the original context: a mother singing to her child, unaccompanied. The arrangement for chorus and violin ensemble illustrates how musical even the simplest Carpathian pieces often are, and how easily they lend themselves to contemporary instrumental or orchestral arrangements. (A wide range of contemporary composers, including Dvořák and Smetana, have taken advantage of a similar discovery, working other traditional Eastern European music into their symphonic poems.)

Odam-Sarna Kondak (Lullaby)

Tumtesz o wäke ku pitasz belső.
Feel the strength you hold inside.

Hiszasz sívadet. Én olenam gæidnod.
Trust your heart. I'll be your guide.

Sas csecsemõm; kuñasz.
Hush, my baby; close your eyes.

Rauho joŋe ted.
Peace will come to you.

Tumtesz o sívdobbanás ku olen lamt3ad belső.
Feel the rhythm deep inside.

Gond-kumpadek ku kim te.
Waves of love that cover you.

Pesänak te, asti o jüti, kidüsz.
Protect, until the night you rise.

To hear this song, visit christinefeehan.com/members/.

6. SONG TO HEAL THE EARTH

This is the earth-healing song that is used by the Carpathian women to heal soil filled with various toxins. The women take a position on four sides and call to the universe to draw on the healing energy with love and respect. The soil of the earth is their resting place, the place where they rejuvenate, and they must make it safe not only for themselves but for their unborn children, as well as their men and living children. This is a beautiful ritual performed by the women together, raising their voices in harmony and calling on the earth's minerals and healing properties to come forth and help them save their children. They literally dance and sing to heal the earth in a ceremony as old as their species. The dance and notes of the song are adjusted according to the toxins felt through the healers' bare feet. The feet are placed in a certain pattern and the hands gracefully weave a healing spell while the dance is performed. They must be especially careful when the soil is prepared for babies. This is a ceremony of love and healing.

Musically, the ritual is divided into several sections:

- **First verse**: A "call-and-response" section, where the chant leader sings the "call" solo, and then some or all of the women sing the "response" in the close harmony style typical of the Carpathian musical tradition. The repeated response—*Ai, Emä Maye*—is an invocation of the source of power for the healing ritual: "Oh, Mother Nature."
- **First chorus**: This section is filled with clapping, dancing, ancient horns and other means used to invoke and heighten the energies upon which the ritual is drawing.
- **Second verse**
- **Second chorus**
- **Closing invocation:** In this closing part, two song leaders, in close harmony, take all the energy gathered by the earlier portions of the song/ritual and focus it entirely on the healing purpose.

What you will be listening to are brief tastes of what would typically be a significantly longer ritual, in which the verse and chorus parts are developed and repeated many times, to be closed by a single rendition of the closing invocation.

Sarna Pusm O Mayet (Song to Heal the Earth)

First verse
Ai, Emä Maye,
Oh, Mother Nature,

Me sívadbin lañaak.
We are your beloved daughters.

Me tappadak, me pusmak o mayet.
We dance to heal the earth.

Me sarnadak, me pusmak o hanyet.
We sing to heal the earth.

Sielanket jutta tedet it,
We join with you now,

Sívank és akaratank és sielank juttanak.
Our hearts and minds and spirits become one.

Second verse
Ai, Emä Maye,
Oh, Mother Nature,

Me sívadbin lañaak.
We are your beloved daughters.

Me andak arwadet emänked és me kaŋank o
We pay homage to our mother and call upon the

Põhi és Lõuna, Ida és Lääs.
North and South, East and West.

Pide és aldyn és myös belső.
Above and below and within as well.

Gondank o mayenak pusm hän ku olen jama.
Our love of the land heals that which is in need.

Juttanak teval it,
We join with you now,

Maγe maγeval.
Earth to earth.

O pirä elidak weńća.
The circle of life is complete.

To hear this chant, visit christinefeehan.com/members/.

7. CARPATHIAN CHANTING TECHNIQUE

As with their healing techniques, the actual "chanting technique" of the Carpathians has much in common with the other shamanistic traditions of the Central Asian steppes. The primary mode of chanting was throat chanting using overtones. Modern examples of this manner of singing can still be found in the Mongolian, Tuvan and Tibetan traditions. You can find an audio example of the Gyuto Tibetan Buddhist monks engaged in throat chanting at christinefeehan.com/carpathian_chanting/.

As with Tuva, note on the map the geographical proximity of Tibet to Kazakhstan and the Southern Urals.

The beginning part of the Tibetan chant emphasizes synchronizing all the voices around a single tone, aimed at healing a particular "chakra" of the body. This is fairly typical of the Gyuto throat-chanting tradition, but it is not a significant part of the Carpathian tradition. Nonetheless, it serves as an interesting contrast.

The part of the Gyuto chanting example that is most similar to the Carpathian style of chanting is the midsection, where the men are chanting the words together with great force. The purpose here is not to generate a "healing tone" that will affect a particular "chakra" but rather to generate as much power as possible for initiating "out-of-body" travel and for fighting the demonic forces that the healer/traveler must face and overcome.

The songs of the Carpathian women (illustrated by their "Lullaby" and their "Song to Heal the Earth") are part of the same ancient musical and healing tradition as the Lesser and Great Healing Chants of the warrior males. You can hear some of the same instruments in both the male warriors' healing chants and the women's "Song to Heal the Earth." Also, they share the common purpose of generating and directing power. However, the women's songs are distinctively feminine in character. One immediately noticeable difference is that while the men speak their words in the manner of a chant, the women sing songs with melodies and harmonies, softening the overall performance. A feminine, nurturing quality is especially evident in the "Lullaby."

THE CARPATHIAN LANGUAGE

Like all human languages, the language of the Carpathians contains the richness and nuance that can only come from a long history of use. At best we can only touch on some of the main features of the language in this brief appendix:

1. The history of the Carpathian language
2. Carpathian grammar and other characteristics of the language
3. Examples of the Carpathian language (including the Ritual Words and the Warriors' Chant)
4. A much-abridged Carpathian dictionary

1. THE HISTORY OF THE CARPATHIAN LANGUAGE

The Carpathian language of today is essentially identical to the Carpathian language of thousands of years ago. A "dead" language like the Latin of two thousand years ago has evolved into a significantly different modern language (Italian) because of countless generations of speakers and great historical fluctuations. In contrast, many of the speakers of Carpathian from thousands of years ago are still alive. Their presence—coupled with the deliberate isolation of the Carpathians from the other major forces of change in the world—has acted (and continues to act) as a stabilizing force that has preserved the integrity of the language over the centuries. Carpathian culture has also acted as a stabilizing force. For instance, the Ritual Words, the various healing chants (see Appendix 1) and other cultural artifacts have been passed down through the centuries with great fidelity.

One small exception should be noted: the splintering of the Carpathians into separate geographic regions has led to some minor dialectization. However, the telepathic link among all Carpathians (as well as each Carpathian's regular return to his or her homeland) has ensured that the differences among dialects are relatively superficial (small numbers of new words, minor differences in pronunciation, etc.), since the deeper internal language of mind-forms has remained the same because of continuous use across space and time.

The Carpathian language was (and still is) the proto-language for the Uralic (or Finno-Ugric) family of languages. Today, the Uralic languages are spoken in northern, eastern and central Europe and in Siberia. More than twenty-three million people in the world speak languages that can trace their ancestry to Carpathian. Magyar or Hungarian (about fourteen million speakers), Finnish (about five million speakers) and Estonian (about one million speakers) are the three major contemporary descendants of this proto-language. The only factor that unites the more than twenty languages in the Uralic family is that their ancestry can be traced back to a common proto-language—Carpathian—that split (starting some six thousand years ago) into the various languages in the Uralic family. In the same way, European languages such as English and French belong to the better-known Indo-European family and also evolved from a common proto-language ancestor (a different one from Carpathian).

The following table provides a sense of some of the similarities in the language family.

Note: The Finnic/Carpathian "k" shows up often as the Hungarian "h." Similarly, the Finnic/Carpathian "p" often corresponds to the Hungarian "f."

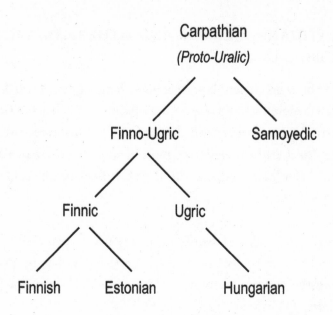

Carpathian (proto-Uralic)	Finnish (Suomi)	Hungarian (Magyar)
elä—live	*elä*—live	*él*—live
elid—life	*elinikä*—life	*élet*—life
pesä—nest	*pesä*—nest	*fészek*—nest
kola—die	*kuole*—die	*hal*—die
pälä—half, side	*pieltä*—tilt, tip to the side	*fél, fele*—fellow human, friend (half; one side of two) *feleség*—wife
and—give	*anta, antaa*—give	*ad*—give
koje—husband, man	*koira*—dog, the male (of animals)	*here*—drone, testicle
wäke—power	*väki*—folks, people, men; force	*val/-vel*—with (instrumental suffix)
	väkevä—powerful, strong	*vele*—with him/her/it
wete—water	*vesi*—water	*víz*—water

2. CARPATHIAN GRAMMAR AND OTHER CHARACTERISTICS OF THE LANGUAGE

Idioms. As both an ancient language and a language of an earth people, Carpathian is more inclined toward use of idioms constructed from concrete, "earthy" terms rather than abstractions. For instance, our modern abstraction "to cherish" is expressed more concretely in Carpathian as "to hold in one's heart"; the "netherworld" is, in Carpathian, "the land of night, fog and ghosts"; etc.

Word order. The order of words in a sentence is determined not by syntactic roles (like subject, verb and object) but rather by pragmatic, discourse-driven factors. Examples: *"Tied vagyok."* ("Yours am I."); *"Sívamet andam."* ("My heart I give you.")

Agglutination. The Carpathian language is agglutinative; that is, longer words are constructed from smaller components. An agglutinating language uses suffixes or prefixes whose meanings are generally unique, and that are concatenated one after another without overlap. In Carpathian, words typically consist of a stem that is followed by one or more suffixes. For example, *sívambam* derives from the stem *"sív"* ("heart"), followed by *"am"* ("my," making it "my heart"), followed by *"bam"* ("in," making it "in my heart"). As you might imagine, agglutination in Carpathian can sometimes produce very long words, or words that are very difficult to pronounce. Vowels often get inserted between suffixes to prevent too many consonants from appearing in a row (which can make a word unpronounceable).

Noun cases. Like all languages, Carpathian has many noun cases; the same noun will be "spelled" differently depending on its role in a sentence. The noun cases include nominative (when the noun is the subject of the sentence), accusative (when the noun is a direct object of the verb), dative (indirect object), genitive (or possessive), instrumental, final, suppressive, inessive, elative, terminative and delative.

We will use the possessive (or genitive) case as an example to illustrate how all noun cases in Carpathian involve adding standard suffixes to the noun stems. Thus, expressing possession in Carpathian—"my lifemate," "your lifemate," "his lifemate," "her lifemate," etc.—involves adding a particular suffix (such as "-am") to the noun stem (*"päläfertiil"*) to produce the possessive (*"päläfertiilam"*—"my lifemate"). Which suffix to use depends on which person ("my," "your," "his," etc.) and whether the noun ends in a consonant or a vowel. The following table shows the suffixes for singular nouns only (not plural), and also shows the similarity to the suffixes used in contemporary Hungarian. (Hungarian is actually a little more complex, in that it also requires "vowel rhyming": which suffix to use also depends on the last vowel in the noun, hence the multiple choices in the table, where Carpathian has only a single choice.)

	Carpathian (proto-Uralic)		Contemporary Hungarian	
person	**noun ends in vowel**	**noun ends in consonant**	**noun ends in vowel**	**noun ends in consonant**
1st singular (my)	-m	-am	-m	-om, -em, -öm
2nd singular (your)	-d	-ad	-d	-od, -ed, -öd
3rd singular (his, her, its)	-ja	-a	-ja/-je	-a, -e
1st plural (our)	-nk	-ank	-nk	-unk, -ünk
2nd plural (your)	-tak	-atak	-tok, -tek, -tök	-otok, -etek, -ötök
3rd plural (their)	-jak	-ak	-juk, -jük	-uk, -ük

Note: As mentioned earlier, vowels often get inserted between the word and its suffix so as to prevent too many consonants from appearing in a row (which would produce unpronounceable words). For example, in the table on the previous page, all nouns that end in a consonant are followed by suffixes beginning with "a."

Verb conjugation. Like its modern descendants (such as Finnish and Hungarian), Carpathian has many verb tenses, far too many to describe here. We will just focus on the conjugation of the present tense. Again, we will place contemporary Hungarian side by side with Carpathian because of the marked similarity between the two.

As with the possessive case for nouns, the conjugation of verbs is done by adding a suffix onto the verb stem:

Person	Carpathian (proto-Uralic)	Contemporary Hungarian
1st singular (I give)	-am (andam), -ak	-ok, -ek, -ök
2nd singular (you give)	-sz (andsz)	-sz
3rd singular (he/she/it gives)	— (and)	—
1st plural (we give)	-ak (andak)	-unk, -ünk
2nd plural (you give)	-tak (andtak)	-tok, -tek, -tök
3rd plural (they give)	-nak (andnak)	-nak, -nek

As with all languages, there are many "irregular verbs" in Carpathian that don't exactly fit this pattern. But the table is still a useful guide for most verbs.

3. EXAMPLES OF THE CARPATHIAN LANGUAGE

Here are some brief examples of conversational Carpathian, used in the Dark books. We include the literal translation in square brackets. It is interestingly different from the most appropriate English translation.

Susu.

I am home.

["home/birthplace." "I am" is understood, as is often the case in Carpathian.]

Möért?

What for?

csitri

little one

["little slip of a thing," "little slip of a girl"]

ainaak enyém

forever mine

ainaak sívamet jutta

forever mine (another form)

["forever to-my-heart connected/fixed"]

sívamet

my love

["of-my-heart," "to-my-heart"]

Tet vigyázam.

I love you.

["you-love-I"]

Sarna Rituaali (**The Ritual Words**) is a longer example, and an example of chanted rather than conversational Carpathian. Note the recurring use of *"andam"* ("I give"), to give the chant musicality and force through repetition.

Sarna Rituaali (**The Ritual Words**)

Te avio päläfertiilam.

You are my lifemate.

Éntölam kuulua, avio päläfertiilam.
I claim you as my lifemate.

Ted kuuluak, kacad, kojed.
I belong to you.

Élidamet andam.
I offer my life for you.

Pesämet andam.
I give you my protection.

Uskolfertiilamet andam.
I give you my allegiance.

Sívamet andam.
I give you my heart.

Sielamet andam.
I give you my soul.

Ainamet andam.
I give you my body.

Sívamet kuuluak kaik että a ted.
I take into my keeping the same that is yours.

Ainaak olenszal sívambin.
Your life will be cherished by me for all my time.

Te élidet ainaak pide minan.
Your life will be placed above my own for all time.

Te avio päläfertiilam.
You are my lifemate.

Ainaak sívamet jutta oleny.
You are bound to me for all eternity.

Ainaak terád vigyázak.
You are always in my care.

To hear these words pronounced (and for more about Carpathian pronunciation altogether), please visit christinefeehan.com/members/.

Sarna Kontakawk (**The Warriors' Chant**) is another, longer example of the Carpathian language. The warriors' council takes place deep beneath the earth in a chamber of crystals with magma far below it, so the steam is natural and the wisdom of their ancestors is clear and focused. This is a sacred place where they bloodswear to their prince and people and affirm their code of honor as warriors and brothers. It is also where battle strategies are born and all dissension is discussed, as well as any concerns the warriors have that they wish to bring to the council and open for discussion.

Sarna Kontakawk (The Warriors' Chant)

Veri isäakank—veri ekäakank.
Blood of our fathers—blood of our brothers.

Veri olen elid.
Blood is life.

Andak veri-elidet Karpatiiakank, és wäke-sarna ku meke arwa-arvo, irgalom, hän ku agba, és wäke kutni, ku manaak verival.
We offer that life to our people with a bloodsworn vow of honor, mercy, integrity and endurance.

Verink sokta; verink kaŋa terád.
Our blood mingles and calls to you.

Akasz énak ku kaŋa és juttasz kuntatak it.
Heed our summons and join with us now.

To hear these words pronounced (and for more about Carpathian pronunciation altogether), please visit christinefeehan.com /members/.

See **Appendix 1** for Carpathian healing chants, including the *Kepä Sarna Pus* (The Lesser Healing Chant), the *En Sarna Pus* (The Great Healing Chant), the *Odam-Sarna Kondak* (Lullaby) and the *Sarna Pusm O Maγet* (Song to Heal the Earth).

4. A MUCH-ABRIDGED CARPATHIAN DICTIONARY

This very-much-abridged Carpathian dictionary contains most of the Carpathian words used in the Dark books. Of course, a full Carpathian dictionary would be as large as the usual dictionary for an entire language (typically more than a hundred thousand words).

Note: The Carpathian nouns and verbs that follow are word **stems**. They generally do not appear in their isolated "stem" form. Instead, they usually appear with suffixes (e.g., *andam—I give*, rather than just the root, *and*).

a—verb negation (*prefix*); not (*adverb*).
aćke—pace, step.
aćke éntölem it—take another step toward me.
agba—to be seemly; to be proper (*verb*). True; seemly; proper (*adj.*).
ai—oh.
aina—body (*noun*).
ainaak—always; forever.
o ainaak jelä peje emnimet ŋamaŋ—sun scorch that woman forever (*Carpathian swear words*).
ainaakä—never.
ainaakfél—old friend.

ak—suffix added after a noun ending in a consonant to make it plural.

aka—to give heed; to hearken; to listen.

aka-arvo—respect (*noun*).

akarat—mind; will (*noun*).

ál—to bless; to attach to.

alatt—through.

aldyn—under; underneath.

alə—to lift; to raise.

alte—to bless; to curse.

amaŋ—this; this one here; that; that one there.

and—to give.

and sielet, arwa-arvomet, és jelämet, kuulua huvémet ku feaj és ködet ainaak—to trade soul, honor and salvation for momentary pleasure and endless damnation.

andasz éntölem irgalomet!—have mercy!

arvo—value; price (*noun*).

arwa—praise (*noun*).

arwa-arvo olen gæidnod, ekäm—honor guide you, my brother (*greeting*).

arwa-arvo olen isäntä, ekäm—honor keep you, my brother (*greeting*).

arwa-arvo pile sívadet—may honor light your heart (*greeting*).

arwa-arvod—honor (*noun*).

arwa-arvod mäne me ködak—may your honor hold back the dark (*greeting*).

aš—no (*exclamation*).

ašša—no (before a noun); not (with a verb that is not in the imperative); not (with an adjective).

aššatotello—disobedient.

asti—until.

avaa—to open.

avio—wedded.

avio päläfertiil—lifemate.

avoi—uncover; show; reveal.

baszú—revenge; vengeance.

belső—within; inside.

bur—good; well.

bur tule ekämet kuntamak—well met brother-kin (*greeting*).

ćaða—to flee; to run; to escape.

čač3—to be born; to grow.

ćoro—to flow; to run like rain.

csecsemō—baby (*noun*).

csitri—little one (*female*).

csitrim—my little one (*female*).

diutal—triumph; victory.

džinõt—brief; short.

eći—to fall.

ej—not (*adverb, suffix*); *nej* when preceding syllable ends in a vowel.

ek—suffix added after a noun ending in a consonant to make it plural.

ekä—brother.

ekäm—my brother.

elä—to live.

eläsz arwa-arvoval—may you live with honor; live nobly (*greeting*).

eläsz jeläbam ainaak—long may you live in the light (*greeting*).

elävä—alive.

elävä ainak majaknak—land of the living.

elid—life.

emä—mother (*noun*).

Emä Maγe—Mother Nature.

emäen—grandmother.

embε—if; when.

embε karmasz—please.

emni—wife; woman.

emni hän ku köd alte—cursed woman.

emni kuŋenak ku aššatotello—disobedient lunatic.

emnim—my wife; my woman.

én—I.

en—great; many; big.

en hän ku pesä—the protector (literally: the great protector).

én jutta félet és ekämet—I greet a friend and brother (*greeting*).

en Karpatii—the prince (literally: the great Carpathian).

én maɣenak—I am of the earth.

én oma maɣeka—I am as old as time (literally: as old as the earth).

En Puwe—The Great Tree. Related to the legends of Yggdrasil, the *axis mundi*, Mount Meru, heaven and hell, etc.

enä—most.

engem—of me.

enkojra—wolf.

és—and.

ete—before; in front of.

että—that.

év—year.

évsatz—century.

fáz—to feel cold or chilly.

fél—fellow; friend.

fél ku kuuluaak sívam belső—beloved.

fél ku vigyázak—dear one.

feldolgaz—prepare.

fertiil—fertile one.

fesztelen—airy.

fü—herbs; grass.

gæidno—road; way.

gond—care; worry; love (*noun*).

hän—he; she; it; one.

hän agba—it is so.

hän ku—prefix: one who; he who; that which.

hän ku agba—truth.

hän ku kaśwa o numamet—sky-owner.

hän ku kuula siela—keeper of his soul.

hän ku kuulua sívamet—keeper of my heart.

hän ku lejkka wäke-sarnat—traitor.

hän ku meke pirämet—defender.

hän ku meke sarnaakmet—mage.

hän ku pesä—protector.

hän ku pesä sieladet—guardian of your soul.

hän ku pesäk kaikak—guardians of all.

hän ku piwtä—predator; hunter; tracker.

hän ku pusm—healer.

hän ku saa kuć3aket—star-reacher.

hän ku tappa—killer; violent person (*noun*). Deadly; violent (*adj.*).

hän ku tuulmahl elidet—vampire (literally: life-stealer).

hän ku vie elidet—vampire (literally: thief of life).

hän ku vigyáz sielamet—keeper of my soul.

hän ku vigyáz sívamet és sielamet—keeper of my heart and soul.

hän sívamak—beloved.

hängem—him; her; it.

hank—they.

hany—clod; lump of earth.

hisz—to believe; to trust.

ho—how.

ida—east.

igazág—justice.

ila—to shine.

inan—mine; my own (*endearment*).

irgalom—compassion; pity; mercy.

isä—father (*noun*).

isäntä—master of the house.

it—now.

jaguár—jaguar.

jaka—to cut; to divide; to separate.

jakam—wound; cut; injury.

jalka—leg.

jälleen—again.

jama—to be sick, infected, wounded or dying; to be near death.

jamatan—fallen; wounded; near death.

jelä—sunlight; day, sun; light.

jelä keje terád—light sear you (*Carpathian swear words*).

o jelä peje emnimet—sun scorch the woman (*Carpathian swear words*).

o jelä peje kaik hänkanak—sun scorch them all (*Carpathian swear words*).

o jelä peje terád—sun scorch you (*Carpathian swear words*).

o jelä peje terád, emni—sun scorch you, woman (*Carpathian swear words*).

o jelä sielamak—light of my soul.

joma—to be underway; to go.

joŋe—to come; to return.

joŋesz arwa-arvoval—return with honor (*greeting*).

joŋesz éntölem, fél ku kuuluaak sívam belsö—come to me, beloved.

jŏrem—to forget; to lose one's way; to make a mistake.

jotka—gap; middle; space.

jotkan—between.

juo—to drink.

juosz és eläsz—drink and live (*greeting*).

juosz és olen ainaak sielamet jutta—drink and become one with me (*greeting*).

juta—to go; to wander.

jüti—night; evening.

jutta—connected; fixed (*adj.*). To connect; to join; to fix; to bind (*verb*).

k—suffix added after a noun ending in a vowel to make it plural.

kać3—gift.

kaca—male lover.

kadi—judge.

kaik—all.

käktä—two; many.

käktäverit—mixed blood (literally: two bloods).

kalma—corpse; death; grave.

kaŋa—to call; to invite; to summon; to request; to beg.

kaŋk—windpipe; Adam's apple; throat.

karma—want.

Karpatii—Carpathian.

karpatii ku köd—liar.

Karpatiikunta—the Carpathian people.

käsi—hand.

kaśwa—to own.

kaδa—to abandon; to leave; to remain.

kaδa wäkeva óv o köd—stand fast against the dark (*greeting*).

kat—house; family (*noun*).

katt3—to move; to penetrate; to proceed.

keje—to cook; to burn; to sear.

kepä—lesser; small; easy; few.

kessa—cat.

kessa ku toro—wildcat.

kessake—little cat.

kidü—to wake up; to arise (*intransitive verb*).

kim—to cover an entire object with some sort of covering.

kinn—out; outdoors; outside; without.

kinta—fog; mist; smoke.

kislány—little girl.

kislány hän ku meke sarnaakmet—little mage.

kislány kuŋenak—little lunatic.

kislány kuŋenak minan—my little lunatic.

köd—fog; mist; darkness; evil (*noun*). Foggy, dark; evil (*adj.*).

köd alte hän—darkness curse it (*Carpathian swear words*).

o köd belső—darkness take it (*Carpathian swear words*).

köd elävä és köd nime kutni nimet—evil lives and has a name.

köd jutasz belső—shadow take you (*Carpathian swear words*).

koj—let; allow; decree; establish; order.

koje—man; husband; drone.

kola—to die.

kolasz arwa-arvoval—may you die with honor (*greeting*).

kolatan—dead; departed.

koma—empty hand; bare hand; palm of the hand; hollow of the hand.

kond—all of a family's or clan's children.

kont—warrior; man.

kont o sívanak—strong heart (literally: heart of the warrior).

kor3—basket; container made of birch bark.

kor3nat—containing; including.

ku—who; which; that; where; which; what.

kuć3—star.

kuć3ak!—stars! (exclamation).

kudeje—descent; generation.

kuja—day; sun.

kule—to hear.

kulke—to go or to travel (on land or water).

kulkesz arwa-arvoval, ekäm—walk with honor, my brother (*greeting*).

kulkesz arwaval, joŋesz arwa arvoval—go with glory, return with honor (*greeting*).

kuly—intestinal worm; tapeworm; demon who possesses and devours souls.

küm—human male.

kumala—to sacrifice; to offer; to pray.

kumpa—wave (*noun*).

kuńa—to lie as if asleep; to close or cover the eyes in a game of hide-and-seek; to die.

kuŋe—moon; month.

kunta—band; clan; tribe; family; people; lineage; line.

kuras—sword; large knife.

kure—bind; tie.

kuš—worker; servant.

kutenken—however.

kutni—to be able to bear, carry, endure, stand or take.

kutnisz ainaak—long may you endure (*greeting*).

kuulua—to belong; to hold.

kužŏ—long.

lääs—west.

lamti (or lamt3)—lowland; meadow; deep; depth.

lamti ból jüti, kinta, ja szelem—the netherworld (literally: the meadow of night, mists and ghosts).

laña—daughter.

lejkka—crack; fissure; split (*noun*). To cut; to hit; to strike forcefully (*verb*).

lewl—spirit (*noun*).

lewl ma—the other world (literally: spirit land). *Lewl ma* includes *lamti ból jüti, kinta, ja szelem*: the netherworld, but also includes the worlds higher up *En Puwe*, the Great Tree.

liha—flesh.

lōuna—south.

löyly—breath; steam (related to *lewl*: spirit).

luwe—bone.

ma—land; forest; world.

magköszun—thank.

mana—to abuse; to curse; to ruin.

mäne—to rescue; to save.

maɣe—land; earth; territory; place; nature.

mboće—other; second (*adj.*).

me—we.

megem—us.

meke—deed; work (*noun*). To do; to make; to work (*verb*).

mić (or mića)—beautiful.

mića emni kuŋenak minan—my beautiful lunatic.

minan—mine; my own (*endearment*).

minden—every; all (*adj.*).

möért?—what for? (*exclamation*).

molanâ—to crumble; to fall apart.

molo—to crush; to break into bits.

moo—why; reason.

mozdul—to begin to move; to enter into movement.

muonì—appoint; order; prescribe; command.

muonìak te avoisz te—I command you to reveal yourself.

musta—memory.

myös—also.

m8—thing; what.

na—close; near.

nä—for.

nâbbŏ—so, then.

ŋamaŋ—this; this one here; that; that one there.

ŋamaŋak—these; these ones here; those; those ones there.

nautish—to enjoy.

nélkül—without.

nenä—anger.

nime—name.

ńiŋ3—worm; maggot.

nó—like; in the same way as; as.

nókunta—kinship.

numa—god; sky; top; upper part; highest (related to the English word *numinous*).

numatorkuld—thunder (literally: sky struggle).

ńůp@l—for; to; toward.

ńůp@l mam—toward my world.

nyál—saliva; spit (related to *nyelv*: tongue).

nyelv—tongue.

o—the (used before a noun beginning with a consonant).

ó—like; in the same way as; as.

odam—to dream; to sleep.

odam-sarna kondak—lullaby (literally: sleep-song of children).

odam wäke emni—mistress of illusions.

olen—to be.

oma—old; ancient; last; previous.

omas—stand.

omboce—other; second (*adj.*).

ŏrem—to forget; to lose one's way; to make a mistake.

ot—the (used before a noun beginning with a vowel).

ot (or t)—past participle (*suffix*).

otti—to look; to see; to find.

óv—to protect against.

owe—door.

päämoro—aim; target.

pajna—to press.

pälä—half; side.

päläfertiil—mate or wife.

päläpälä—side by side.

palj3—more.

palj3 na éntölem—closer.

partiolen—scout (*noun*).

peje—to burn; scorch.

peje!—burn! (*Carpathian swear word*).

peje terád—get burned (*Carpathian swear words*).

pél—to be afraid; to be scared of.

pesä—nest (*literal; noun*); protection (*figurative; noun*).

pesä—nest; stay (*literal*); protect (*figurative*).

pesäd te engemal—you are safe with me.

pesäsz jeläbam ainaak—long may you stay in the light (*greeting*).

pide—above.

pile—to ignite; to light up.

piŋe—little bird.

piŋe sarnanak—little songbird.

pion—soon.

pirä—circle; ring (*noun*). To surround; to enclose (*verb*).

piros—red.

pitä—to keep; to hold; to have; to possess.

pitäam mustaakad sielpesäambam—I hold your memories safe in my soul.

pitäsz baszú, piwtäsz igazáget—no vengeance, only justice.

piwtä—to seek; to follow; to follow the track of game; to hunt; to prey upon.

poår—bit; piece.

põhi—north.

pohoopa—vigorous.

pukta—to drive away; to persecute; to put to flight.

pus—healthy; healing.

pusm—to heal; to be restored to health.

puwe—tree; wood.

rambsolg—slave.

rauho—peace.

reka—ecstasy; trance.

rituaali—ritual.

sa—sinew; tendon; cord.

sa4—to call; to name.

saa—arrive, come; become; get, receive.

saasz hän ku andam szabadon—take what I freely offer.

saγe—to arrive; to come; to reach.

salama—lightning; lightning bolt.

sapar—tail.

sapar bin jalkak—coward (literally: tail between legs).

sapar bin jalkak nélkül mogal—spineless coward.

sarna—words; speech; song; magic incantation (*noun*). To chant; to sing; to celebrate (*verb*).

sarna hän agba—claim.

sarna kontakawk—warriors' chant.

sarna kunta—alliance (literally: single tribe through sacred words).

śaro—frozen snow.

sas—shoosh (*to a child or baby*).

satz—hundred.

siel—soul.

sielad sielamed—soul to soul (literally: your soul to my soul).

sielam—my soul.

sielam pitwä sielad—my soul searches for your soul.

sielam sieladed—my soul to your soul.

sieljelä isäntä—purity of soul triumphs.

sisar—sister.

sisarak sivak—sisters of the heart.

sisarke—little sister.

sív—heart.

sív pide köd—love transcends evil.

sív pide minden köd—love transcends all evil.

sívad olen wäkeva, hän ku piwtä—may your heart stay strong, hunter (*greeting*).

sívam és sielam—my heart and soul.

sívamet—my heart.

sívdobbanás—heartbeat (*literal*); rhythm (*figurative*).

sokta—to mix; to stir around.

sõl—dare, venture.

sõl olen engemal, sarna sívametak—dare to be with me, song of my heart.

soŋe—to enter; to penetrate; to compensate; to replace.

Susiküm—Lycan.

susu—home; birthplace (*noun*). At home (*adv.*).

szabadon—freely.

szelem—ghost.

ször—time; occasion.

t (or ot)—past participle (*suffix*).

taj—to be worth.

taka—behind; beyond.

takka—to hang; to remain stuck.

takkap—obstacle; challenge; difficulty; ordeal; trial.

tappa—to dance; to stamp with the feet; to kill.

tasa—even so; just the same.

te—you.

te kalma, te jama ńiŋ3kval, te apitäsz arwa-arvo—you are nothing but a walking maggot-infected corpse, without honor.

te magköszunam nä ŋamaŋ kać3 taka arvo—thank you for this gift beyond price.

ted—yours.

terád keje—get scorched (*Carpathian swear words*).

tõd—to know.

tõdak pitäsz wäke bekimet mekesz kaiket—I know you have the courage to face anything.

tõdhän—knowledge.

tõdhän lõ kuraset agbapäämoroam—knowledge flies the sword true to its aim.

toja—to bend; to bow; to break.

toro—to fight; to quarrel.

torosz wäkeval—fight fiercely (*greeting*).

totello—obey.

tsak—only.

t'śuva vni—period of time.

tti—to look; to see; to find.

tuhanos—thousand.

tuhanos löylyak türelamak saγe diutalet—a thousand patient breaths bring victory.

tule—to meet; to come.

tuli—fire.

tumte—to feel; to touch; to touch upon.

türe—full; satiated; accomplished.

türelam—patience.

türelam agba kontsalamaval—patience is the warrior's true weapon.

tyvi—stem; base; trunk.

ul3—very; exceedingly; quite.

umuš—wisdom; discernment.

und—past participle (*suffix*).

uskol—faithful.

uskolfertiil—allegiance; loyalty.

usm—to heal; to be restored to health.

vár—to wait.

varolind—dangerous.

veri—blood.

veri ekäakank—blood of our brothers.

veri-elidet—blood-life.

veri isäakank—blood of our fathers.

veri olen piros, ekäm—literally: blood be red, my brother; figuratively: find your lifemate (*greeting*).

veriak ot en Karpatiiak—by the blood of the prince (literally: by the blood of the great Carpathian; *Carpathian swear words*).

veridet peje—may your blood burn (*Carpathian swear words*).

vigyáz—to love; to care for; to take care of.

vii—last; at last; finally.

wäke—power; strength.

wäke beki—strength; courage.

wäke kaδa—steadfastness.

wäke kutni—endurance.

wäke-sarna—vow; curse; blessing (literally: power words).

wäkeva—powerful; strong.

wäkeva csitrim ku pesä—my fierce little protector.

wara—bird; crow.

weńća—complete; whole.

wete—water (*noun*).

Y047140